VIRAGO
MODERN CLASSICS
657

Angela Thirkell (1890–1961) was the eldest daughter of John William Mackail, a Scottish classical scholar and civil servant, and Margaret Burne-Jones. Her relatives included the Pre-Raphaelite artist Edward Burne-Jones, Rudyard Kipling and Stanley Baldwin, and her godfather was J. M. Barrie. She was educated in London and Paris, and began publishing articles and stories in the 1920s. In 1931 she brought out her first book, a memoir entitled *Three Houses*, and in 1933 her comic novel *High Rising* – set in the fictional county of Barsetshire, borrowed from Trollope – met with great success. She went on to write nearly thirty Barsetshire novels, as well as several further works of fiction and non-fiction. She was twice married, and had four children.

By Angela Thirkell

Barsetshire novels

Non-fiction

Three Houses

Collected Stories

Christmas at High Rising

NORTHBRIDGE
RECTORY

Angela Thirkell

virago

VIRAGO

This edition published in Great Britain in 2016 by Virago Press

1 3 5 7 9 10 8 6 4 2

First published in Great Britain in 1941 by Hamish Hamilton Ltd

A CIP catalogue record for this book
is available from the British Library.

ISBN 978-0-349-00742-7

Typeset in Goudy by M Rules
Printed and bound in Great Britain by
Clays Ltd, St Ives plc

Papers used by Virago are from well-managed forests
and other responsible sources.

 MIX
Paper from
responsible sources
FSC FSC® C104740
www.fsc.org

Virago
An imprint of
Little, Brown Book Group
Carmelite House
50 Victoria Embankment
London EC4Y 0DZ

An Hachette UK Company
www.hachette.co.uk

www.virago.co.uk

Contents

Contents

I

Literary Tea-Party

As everyone knows Northbridge High Street there is no need to describe it, so we will proceed to do so. Northbridge, a famous centre for the wool trade of the South in the sixteenth and seventeenth centuries, had gently declined ever since. It had indeed risen for a short period to eminence as a rotten borough, but now for more than a hundred years its calm had been unbroken. The town and its famous High Street are synonymous, for apart from the odious row of council houses on the Plashington Road and the incredibly small gasometer which has never in human memory inflated itself more than six feet from the ground and is tucked away behind the Church School, a building of which, in saying that the date 1874 is carved in Runic letters upon its Gothic gable, we have said quite enough, apart, we may say, from these three modest monstrosities the High Street with its lovely curve is the whole town. At the upper end are the gentry houses, still in many cases inhabited by descendants of the woolstaplers or prosperous graziers who had built them three or four hundred years ago of honey-coloured stone that has weathered to soft greys and browns lightly stained with lichen here and there, the roofs made of thin stone slabs. Just where the street swings round the curve that is known to every tourist, stands the little Town Hall on its twelve stone legs, the little open market place below it. Beyond the Town Hall the houses are newer; late eighteenth and early nineteenth century, flat-fronted, with great sash windows on the ground and first floors, suddenly losing heart on the nursery or servants' bedroom floor with windows so low that even when the lower sash is pushed up and the upper sash pulled down, there is but a chink of air. These have slate roofs. A good many of them have fine plaster ceilings and there are one or two circular staircases whose curve is like a reflection of the High Street and the despair of every architect that tries to copy them, though their designer left no name. Here live the professional classes, doctors, lawyers, bankers, and so forth, most of whom have rooms in Barchester where they carry on the larger part of their business, attending in Northbridge on the first Wednesday in every month, or Tuesday and Friday from eleven to four. And beyond them the street tails off into the picturesque and insanitary cottages of wood and clay, or lath and plaster, white-washed, with thatched roofs, descendants of the original mud huts of Barsetshire under the Kings of Wessex and not much changed in all those years. Bunces and Scatcherds had lived on the same spot and almost in the same house when Barsetshire was half forest and travellers took the higher paths by the downs to avoid wild beasts and the marshy lands by the river; while the cathedral was building;

while wool was sent all over Europe from Barsetshire markets. Each generation had stoutly resisted improvements, and the public feeling which had kept the railway at an extremely inconvenient distance from the town was the same as that which had prophesied woe when the Abbot of Barchester cleared the lower slopes of the downs for sheep runs, and had done its best to frighten away by its own methods, including two very brutal murders for which no one was ever brought to book, the shepherds with new-fangled ways imported by the Abbot from his native Suffolk.

At the end of the High Street is the river. There was a ford hereabouts for as long as history can tell and the antiquity of the original bridge is shown by the fact that the town is called Northbridge and not Northford. It is known to have been burnt in 1066 (locally attributed to the comet), destroyed in the Wars of the Roses (locally attributed, to the joy of antiquaries, to Crooked Dick), and was rebuilt in its present graceful shape about 1816, by a pupil of Rennie. It has six public-houses of which the Mitre is the most important and several sweet shops where you may buy beer by the jug or the bottle. The church stands on a little eminence and behind it is the rectory, an ugly but commodious house whose long garden slopes to the river, while in the town itself are various chapels or conventicles patronized by the lesser tradespeople. Half a mile down the river is Northbridge Manor whose present owner, Mr Robert Keith, of the well-known Barchester firm of solicitors, will not live there till the war is over.

In every war, however unpleasant, there are a certain number of people who with a shriek of joy take possession of a world made for them. Mrs Villars, the Rector's wife, who had come to Northbridge just before the war began, anxious to do her best with the parish work for which her husband's previous career as a schoolmaster had not prepared her, suddenly found herself, rather to her relief, quite o'ercrowed by a number of women who had during what is mistakenly called The Last War driven ambulances, run canteens, been heads of offices, of teams of land girls, of munition welfare, and had been pining in retirement on small incomes ever since. Under their ferocious, yet benignant reign, evacuee children were billeted, clothed and communally fed; visiting parents were provided with canteens; a cottage hospital was staffed and stocked; National Savings were collected; householders were bullied into Digging for Victory in unsuitable soil; other householders were forced to keep chickens which laid with reluctance and sickened and died with fervour of unknown diseases; stirrup-pumps were tested; blackmail in the shape of entertainments to provide comforts for every branch of the services at home and abroad was levied. In fact, as Miss Pemberton said, If the Government had shown the same Team Spirit as Northbridge the war would have been over long ago. This improbable statement put fresh heart into her hearers who, having talked about nothing but Their Work before, now discussed any other such irrelevant subjects as Germany, Vichy, or the United States even less.

Miss Pemberton was one of Northbridge's crowning glories. This eminence she had achieved, involuntarily, by three separate paths. In the first place she was literary, having written a life of Edward IV's queen, Elizabeth Rivers, with great accuracy, an exhausting number of footnotes, and complete dullness, besides several essays on Umbrian

4

Landscape in expensive Quarterlies. In the second place she was unusually short and ugly, habitually dressed in a kind of homespun sackcloth, stout boots and a battered felt hat, and took her walks with a small alpenstock with which it was her practice to poke the dogs of Northbridge off the pavement into the gutter. In the third place, and this was what consolidated her position, she lived with a distinguished philologist who sometimes edited Anthologies.

'Of course,' said Mrs Villars, the Rector's wife, to Lieutenant Holden of the Barsetshire Regiment who had been billeted on her, 'one doesn't like to use the word "live" exactly.'

'Well, people *do* live,' said Mr Holden broad-mindedly.

'What I really mean,' said Mrs Villars, 'is that when Miss Pemberton first came down here she took Punshions, you know that charming little stone cottage that stands back just beyond the Mitre.'

'Why Punshions?' said Mr Holden, an earnest student of the past, wherever he happened to be.

'Gregory would tell you,' said Mrs Villars, who could never remember to call her husband The Rector, 'all about it. There was a small brewery there up to the end of the last century I think, or some people say it is the name of the family who built it. But she had a spare bedroom because Effie Bunce, whose father is the ferryman, comes by the day and won't live in. Old Bunce is rather a tyrant and I believe he beats his daughters sometimes.'

Mr Holden, scenting the trail of old English customs, said he must look up old Bunce and wondered if he ever beat his wife. His mild student's eyes gleamed through his spectacles as he uttered this wish and Mrs Villars felt sorry for him as she said that it was Mrs Bunce who was popularly supposed to beat her husband on Saturday nights, but seeing in Mr Holden's eye that he would shortly require a scold's bridle and a ducking-stool at her hands or her imagination, she hurried on to say,

'Of course Miss Pemberton doesn't write for *money*—'

'It wouldn't be any good if she did,' said Mr Holden, who had been for ten years in a publisher's office before the Army engulfed him, 'she couldn't.'

Mrs Villars had sometimes wondered about that herself, but loyalty to a Northbridge character had bidden her restrain her thoughts, so she went on, determined to say what she had started out to say.

'And having a spare room, she wanted to make a little money,' said Mrs Villars, 'so she used to have Mr Downing for weekends as a paying guest, because he was literary, and gradually he took to living there more and more – of course when I say "living", I don't *mean* anything as indeed you would know if you had seen Miss Pemberton.'

'No, no, of course not,' said Mr Holden.

'It is quite dreadful,' said Mrs Villars, putting down her knitting (which was mittens for her younger son in the Royal Air Force), 'the way some words behave so that you *cannot* use them. "Living" has almost got out of control.'

Mr Holden nearly said, 'So has "sleeping",' but checked himself, for he felt towards his hostess, who was at least fifteen years his senior and had a son who was a Professor in a provincial University as well as the Wing-Commander in the Air Force, a rather sacred respect. There is no accounting for these things.

'Some people won't visit them,' said Mrs Villars, 'but I must say it is partly because Miss Pemberton has been rather snubbing. She doesn't like people to come to the house when Mr Downing is there, in case they ask him to lunch. Gregory,' she said as the Rector came in, 'I was telling Mr Holden about Punshions.'

'A fine piece of restoration,' said Mr Villars, who had a passion for archaeology. 'Barton did it about 1919, just in time. The Council had condemned it, but Lord Pomfret, the late Earl, wouldn't hear of it coming down. Verena, did I give you half a crown to take care of this morning?'

'If you did, it is in my bag,' said Mrs Villars, 'on my writing table. I meant more about Miss Pemberton and Mr Downing and the way they live together – at least I don't exactly mean *live*, but you know what I mean.'

'I have it, I have it!' said the Rector, holding up a half-crown. 'It is Mrs Turner's subscription to the British Legion and I thought I might spend it on stamps if I had it about me.'

'But you could have given another half-crown to the Legion, sir,' said Mr Holden.

'I could,' said the Rector, 'but it is the principle of the thing. So I entrusted it to Verena.'

'As a matter of fact I spent your half-crown at the chemist's,' said Mrs Villars, 'so I don't know whose this is.'

The Rector looked disappointed.

'Well, it is the thought behind the deed that matters,' he said, though not with complete conviction. 'Yes, the matter of Miss Pemberton and Mr Downing living together, not of course that I mean anything by the expression which has fallen so lamentably by the way, has made some difficulties

7

socially. I have preached against judging one's neighbour more than once, but I must say it appears to me incredible that a man of Downing's fastidiousness – we were at College together and I knew him well – can live, can associate let us say, with a woman of such complete absence of charm, though doubtless highly cultivated, of such revolting exterior if the expression is not too strong, as Miss Pemberton.'

Mr Holden said that he had always wanted to see a pig-faced lady, but didn't want a World War to make his wish come true. But that, he added, was just like Providence. He then, as often, wished he had not spoken, for he feared the Rector might be hurt, but Mr Villars confessed that he too had had doubts. He had long wished, though not in any complaining spirit, that there was a little more life in Northbridge. Now that the Rectory was full of officers he sometimes felt, he said, that if Europe was to be plunged into war to gratify his wish, he would have done better to be content with his lot. He then remarked that he had not added Mrs Turner to the list of subscribers to the British Legion and went off to the study.

At the beginning of the war Mr and Mrs Villars, looking at the Rectory with its ten bedrooms not counting the servants' and the large old-fashioned kitchen quarters, felt that their duty was to take in evacuee children. As soon as Mrs Villars mentioned this all the servants gave notice, but even while Mrs Villars was determinedly not taking it, they were asked to have part of the office staff of the Barsetshire Regiment. Workmen were sent down and the big laundry and servants' hall converted into offices, five of the bedrooms were taken over, central heating and fixed basins were installed, and Colonel Passmore with his staff came into residence. Batmen cheered the kitchen and cleaned all boots and shoes impartially till they shone, the servants in a fit of patriotism withdrew their notice, and Mrs Villars found herself at the head of a very large and quite pleasant family. Unless we count Colonel Passmore, who was what he himself described as a leftover from the last war, only one of the officers was a professional soldier, and Mrs Villars more than once felt that she and her husband were back at the boys' preparatory school where he had been Headmaster for some years before coming to Northbridge in the summer of the previous year. Of the officers who had kaleidoscopically come and gone during the past year, Mr Holden was the nicest and the Villarses hoped he would be allowed to stay. He had arrived a month or so before our story begins and three days later the Rector discovered that his new guest was cousin of one of his former assistant masters. Upon this Mr Holden had been made free of Mrs Villars's sitting-room (for the drawing-room had been given up to the officers' use) and it had quickly become his habit to drop in at odd times during the day. In spite of a rather social life in London where the head of his publishing firm, Adrian Coates, believed in cultivating personal contacts with everyone who was an author, possible or impossible, actual or potential, he had felt no more than a very passing fancy for any girl or woman. Now, quite suddenly, he saw in Mrs Villars someone who (as he fondly thought) understood him and whom (he quite blitheringly thought) he could understand. That her husband was so nice and that the couple so obviously got on very well was perhaps disconcerting to his

9

romantic feelings, but although Mrs Villars never raised large eyes brimming with tears to his, or with a tragic gesture bared her arm to the shoulder to show him the livid mark of a man's cruel grip, he managed to feel quite happily sentimental about her. Mrs Villars felt nothing about it at all, looking upon her lodger as a kind of assistant master and being a good deal occupied with her own business, running her large household, and thinking about her sons. But the impulse to give pleasure was always strong in her, so she said to Mr Holden:

'If you are free after tea would you care to walk down to Punshions? I want to ask Miss Pemberton about Effie Bunce who has quite given up coming to the Girl Guides, which is a pity. As it is Wednesday I don't think Mr Downing will be there, so we shall be able to get in. When he is in residence it is rather difficult.'

Mr Holden said he would be delighted, so after tea he and his hostess left the Rectory. There was a short cut by the back way to Punshions, which was about half-way down the High Street, but Mrs Villars loved the noble curve so much that even at the risk of meeting far too many friends she preferred to take the longer route.

It was a mild sunny afternoon in early autumn and being Early Closing Day there were not many people about. Mrs Villars inwardly congratulated herself, but too soon, for as they passed The Hollies, a pleasant stone Georgian house standing back a little from the street, out burst Mrs Turner with her two nieces who lived with her.

Mrs Turner, who was the very same who had given the Rector half a crown for the British Legion, had been so long a widow that she had quite lost the attributes of widowhood.

Some bold spirits indeed went so far as to say that she had never been married at all and had merely taken the honorary status of Mrs, but this was not true, for she still quietly cherished the memory of the late Mr Turner who had been an unmitigated cad and waster till death with kindly care removed him after a year of married life. By great good luck he had not yet been able to spend all his own or his wife's money, so Mrs Turner found herself quite comfortably off and after a few years of travel, which rather bored her, came to anchor at The Hollies and adopted two nieces whose parents had died of influenza. From The Hollies she radiated ceaseless and benevolent activity, loyally supported by the nieces who showed no signs at all of getting married. So she had hailed with joy the arrival of officers at the Vicarage and made her house into a kind of club where they could play billiards, at which game she herself was no mean performer, turn on the radio-gramophone, thump the piano to their hearts' content, or read the many illustrated papers which she took in, for where papers and magazines were concerned The Hollies was, as Mr Holden said, as good as a dentist's waiting-room with none of the disadvantages.

Mrs Turner greeted Mrs Villars and Mr Holden warmly and said she and the girls would walk along with them, as they were going to see Miss Pemberton about some apples. On learning that the Rectory party were also going to Punshions she said wonders would never cease.

'Ackcherly,' said her niece Betty, 'I'm only going as far as the chemist.'

'Early closing,' said the other niece.

'Good Lord! it happens about twelve times a week,' said Betty. 'Then I'd better come with you, Auntie.'

'You young people go on ahead, then,' said Mrs Turner, such being her simple methods, 'and I'll walk with Mrs Villars. And don't forget the basket, girls.'

As this would have happened in any case, they all proceeded down the street, Betty and the other niece walking one on each side of Mr Holden rather as if he were Eugene Aram, though less because they looked upon him as their prey than because they loyally shared every treat that came their way, from an unattached man to two-pennyworth of sweets. Mrs Villars inquired after the Communal Kitchen which Mrs Turner had started at the beginning of the war and had run herself with the help of her nieces and other voluntary workers ever since.

'We are doing nicely,' said Mrs Turner. 'Quite a lot of vegetables have come in this week and Miss Pemberton has promised some apples which is what I'm going to see her about. Lord Pomfret sent us down some venison from Scotland but unfortunately the name leaked out, and the children wouldn't eat it.'

'So what did you do?' asked Mrs Villars.

'Gave them fish pie next day which they detest,' said Mrs Turner, 'and the day after we minced up the venison and called it shepherd's pie and they all wanted second helpings.'

'Ernie Wheeler was sick afterwards,' shouted Betty, who always preferred other people's conversations to her own, over her shoulder.

'Only because he had cocoa and sardines for breakfast,' shouted Mrs Turner. 'His hostess, Mrs Gibbs,' she added in a gentler voice for Mrs Villars's benefit, 'Gibbs's wife, you know, is so kind, but all her children died young and she really has *no* idea of how to feed little boys.'

'Perhaps that's why,' said Mrs Villars elliptically.

Mrs Turner said she expected she was right and the cortège continued its way.

As they approached the front door of Miss Pemberton's cottage Mrs Villars felt a peculiar sinking of the heart, for innocent as she was of any attempt, or of the slightest wish, to rape Mr Downing from Miss Pemberton's mature care, she felt it in her bones that she lay under suspicion, as indeed did every other woman in Northbridge of suitable social standing, of wishing to destroy that lady's extra-matrimonial peace. True it was a Wednesday, and Mr Downing was always in town during the middle of the week, but one never knew where one might offend. The first time she had visited Miss Pemberton, and that by special invitation, she had inquired how Mr Downing's new anthology, a collection of twelfth-century Provençal lyrics, was getting on; and though Miss Pemberton could talk of little else at the time she appeared to resent the introduction of the subject by her visitor so deeply that Mrs Villars blushed inside herself whenever she thought of the episode, as if she had been guilty of some gross indelicacy rather than a polite inquiry about something that did not really interest her in the least. For who, as she said to her husband the same evening, can be interested in things that say

'Ay! lez moult en fiez donnouro genti'

or words to that effect. To which her husband had replied that he supposed Mr Downing was, and she had kissed the top of his head.

13

'It's all very well,' said Mrs Turner in her loud cheerful voice, as if answering Mrs Villars's thoughts, 'but if I didn't want those apples, I wouldn't have come. I've got nothing to say to a highbrow like Mr Downing, but she looks at me as if I were Venus and Adonis.'

Upon this she pressed the bell with an unswerving finger, remarking that Effie Bunce was always out at the back. The bell rang for what Mrs Villars nervously felt to be at least five minutes. Miss Pemberton's face appeared at a window, looked dispassionately at them and disappeared. Mrs Turner, slightly dashed, took her finger off the bell and Effie Bunce came round the corner of the house with an armful of tea-cloths.

'I was just taking the clorths off the line,' she said, 'and I thought it must be the bell.'

She then retreated, and in a few seconds the front door was opened.

'Well, Effie, how is your father's rheumatism?' said Mrs Turner.

Effie giggled.

'Him and mother had a good old dust-up on Saturday night,' said the undutiful daughter, 'and the radio going on and all. Ruby and me we laughed fit to die.'

'Ruby is Effie's sister,' Mrs Turner explained, with a faint air of pride in her knowledge. 'Is Miss Pemberton in, Effie? I've come about the apples.'

For an answer Effie gave a violent knock on the sitting-room door, threw it open without waiting for an answer, and went back to the tea-cloths, leaving the callers stranded high and dry. Mrs Turner, who in the cause of charity knew no fear, walked in followed by her party, the more sensitive of whom – we allude to Mrs Villars and Mr Holden – wished they had never come, for sitting on opposite sides of the fire, a well-spread tea-table between them, were Miss Pemberton and a spare, grey-haired, intelligent looking man of about fifty-five.

Miss Pemberton rose, for no other word can express her action. Mr Holden saw what was apparently an elderly man with a powerful and slightly unpleasant face, dressed in brown sacking with short grey hair and an amber necklace, but his friends, who were used to this phenomenon, saw that Miss Pemberton would not forgive them lightly for having come to call on a day when by all rights Mr Downing should have been in town. Mrs Villars, pulling herself together and reminding herself that she was the Rector's wife, came forward, said How do you do to her hostess and introduced Mr Holden.

'Mr Downing,' said Miss Pemberton, 'and I always have high tea. It saves supper.'

With which explanation she reseated herself. Taking this as a royal permission to make themselves at home, the visitors also sat down. Mr Holden took the precaution to get as near Mr Downing as possible, feeling that a fellow-man, however Pemberton-pecked, would be a little protection.

'My name is Holden,' he said. 'I'm with Adrian Coates, and we were much honoured by being allowed to publish your little life of Reynault Camargou.'

'I'm afraid it didn't sell very well,' said Mr Downing in a singularly pleasant voice, 'but when an author pays for his own books I suppose publishers don't mind.'

'We would always prefer a selling success of course,' said Mr Holden, 'but it would have been almost an honour to lose on your book. I hear you are doing a Provençal Anthology.

I do hope you will include something of Camargou's. I was fascinated by the little poem you quoted that begins—

'"*En doubx ebaz m'oun dueilliez paréiou . . .*"'

'Would you say it again?' said Mr Downing.

Mr Holden did.

'Ah,' said Mr Downing, 'you follow Bompard's phonetics. There is much to be said for his theory, but I think, though I would not insist, that the Vicomte de Mas-Cagnou got nearer the root of the thing. According to him the spoken verse would run roughly thus:

'"*En doubx ebaz m'oun dueilliez paréiou . . .*"'

'Yes . . . yes . . . I see what you mean,' said Mr Holden, which was a lie, but he had acquired under his head's capable instruction a fine technique of surface knowledge about any book the firm published. 'I have never really read Mas-Cagnou, but the main trend of his ideas is familiar to me. If you could make one or two points clear—'

Mr Downing required no further invitation and the air became melodious with the sound of verses which their makers would certainly never have recognized, whatever the pronunciation.

Miss Pemberton, casting on Mr Downing an eye that augured ill for his peace when the visitors should have gone, munched her high tea and listened to Mrs Turner's reminder about the promised apples. When Mrs Turner had finished, Miss Pemberton, slightly deepening her voice, said:

16

'Harold!'

Mr Downing started, made an apologetic gesture to Mr Holden, and turned to his Egeria.

'Yes, Ianthe,' he said.

'Did you put those apples in the garage?' said Miss Pemberton.

Mr Downing said he had.

'Mr Downing,' said Miss Pemberton, who never spoke of her lodger by his Christian name, 'has put the apples in the garage.'

'Well, the girls have brought their baskets, so we can take them away if that suits you,' said Mrs Turner. 'It is so kind of you.'

As Miss Pemberton made no answer beyond pouring herself out another cup of tea, Mrs Villars threw herself into the breach and inquired if Miss Pemberton's monograph on the altar-pieces of Giacopone Giacopini, detto II Giacopinaccio, was getting on.

'There are only two of them, and they haven't been seen since 1474,' said Miss Pemberton, her face of a depraved elderly cardinal suddenly lighting to a rather fine eagerness, 'and of course Italy is difficult now. But Lord Pomfret has let me look through some of the papers of the Italian branch of his house and I was able to do a most interesting little piece of research, indirectly bearing on my subject.'

'Do tell me,' said Mrs Villars, while Betty and the other niece exchanged glances of despair.

'The family of Strelsa, into which Eustace Pomfret married after 1688,' said Miss Pemberton, 'had an ancestor who owned the castle of Strelsa, not fifty miles from Giacopone's reputed

17

birthplace. I find that a certain Cosimo di Strelsa was exiled and heavily fined for seducing a nun who subsequently gave birth to a male child. The dates are about right and in the absence of any further evidence, corroborative or otherwise, I think we may take it that Giacopone was the fruit of this relationship. As for Bernardo's suggestion that the nun – Violante by name – had already been seduced by the prior of a neighbouring monastery, that on *prima facie* grounds can be ruled out altogether. If you would care to see the notes I made I will gladly let you see them when they are typed, if they would interest you.'

Mrs Villars, in her turn telling a lie, said she would love to see them, and got up.

'Mr Downing,' said Miss Pemberton, 'will show you where the apples are and I will come too.'

So Mr Downing was torn from his Provençal dream and the whole party went to the garage where Betty and the other niece filled all the baskets.

'Thank you *very* much,' said Mrs Turner as they took their leave. 'It is such a help to our kitchen, and everyone is so kind.'

'Wish I could do more,' said Miss Pemberton with sudden gruffness. 'Good-bye. Come again if you want apples. Harold!'

Mr Downing, who was blissfully engaged again with Mr Holden, jumped.

'Clear the tea-things away,' said Miss Pemberton, 'and I will see them out.'

'Oh, good-bye then,' said Mr Downing to Mr Holden.

'Come up to the Rectory some time and have a talk,' said Mr Holden.

Mr Downing looked longingly at Mr Holden, despairingly at his Egeria, mumbled something and disappeared.

Just as they were at the front door Mrs Villars suddenly remembered what she had come for.

'Oh, Miss Pemberton,' she said, 'I am so sorry to bother you, but could you speak to Effie about the Girl Guides. She never comes now and she used to be such a regular member.'

'Effie!' said Miss Pemberton.

Effie appeared with a damp tea-cloth in one hand and a spoon in the other.

'I was just drying my teaspoons and I thought you called,' she said.

'What is this about your not going to the Girl Guides?' said Miss Pemberton. 'Were you christened?'

Effie said Yes, by the Reverend Danby at Southbridge, because she was born over at Grannie's.

'Very well then. You know your duty,' said Miss Pemberton. 'Render unto Caesar. If you don't go to the Guides regularly I shall tell your Aunt.'

Effie dropped the teaspoon with a clang on the brick floor, picked it up and retired hurriedly to the kitchen.

'That's all right,' said Miss Pemberton, who was fumbling in an embroidered bag. 'And here's something for the Guides, Mrs Villars. Sorry it isn't more.'

She thrust half a crown into Mrs Villars's hands and shut the front door.

'Miss Pemberton gave me half a crown for the Guides,' said Mrs Villars to her husband after dinner. 'I know she can hardly afford it. I do wish people could be as nice as they are good. Was there any news to-night?'

'I don't know,' said the Rector, who hated the wireless, and with his wife's full approval had lent their set to the officers billeted with them. 'I did mean to ask Colonel Passmore if I could listen at six, but it was ten minutes past when I thought of it, so I put it off till nine and then it was suddenly nine-fifteen. I could ask if you like.'

'Never mind, darling,' said his wife. 'It will be in *The Times* to-morrow. Oh, here is Mr Holden. Was there any news?'

'Passmore says there was a bomb on Buckingham Palace,' said Mr Holden. 'Did you know, sir, that one of your hens had been killed? Major Spender's dog got into the run and bit her head off. He asked me to say he's most awfully sorry and he has thrashed the dog within an inch of its life.'

'I understand,' said the Rector, 'that the best way to cure a dog is to hang the corpse of the victim round its neck, like the Ancient Mariner.'

'I'm sure Spender would be delighted,' said Mr Holden, 'but he couldn't catch the brute till it had eaten most of the body too.'

Mrs Villars inquired if he knew which hen it was and on hearing that it was the White Leghorn with the pale comb said she was a bad layer in any case.

'There is never any news,' said the Rector sadly. 'Without being impious, I do wish *something* would happen. The war just goes on and on and on.'

'Well, you never know your luck,' said Mr Holden. 'Good night, Mrs Villars. Good night, sir.'

2

Military Lunch

On the following morning Mrs Villars was doing her usual household shopping in the High Street, when at Scatcherd's Stores, Est: 1824, she ran into Mrs Turner who was lamenting the scarcity of soap-flakes.

'Well, madam,' said old Mr Scatcherd, whose incredible mutton-chop whiskers caused many thoughtless people to take him for the original Scatcherd, 'you see we have so many refugees we are quite sold out. If we was to have twice the amount we could sell it twice over.'

To this Mrs Turner spiritedly made reply that the refugees would be gone some day, by which time the old customers would have changed their grocer, but as Mr Scatcherd preserved the bland indifference of one who knows that he will always have as many customers as he wants, Mrs Turner went away without ordering the olive oil, which in any case she could not have got, and taking Mrs Villars with her.

'Come back with me and have a cup of tea,' said Mrs

Turner. 'The girls always want something to drink in the middle of the morning when they have got the vegetables ready. You know,' she continued as the ladies walked towards The Hollies, 'Scatcherd is simply doing a bit of war blackmail. There's far too much about. If you go into a shop and the rich refugees have bought everything up and you complain, you are told there's a war. Blackmail. If you go to a restaurant in town and get filthy food that I wouldn't give my evacuees at the Communal Kitchen and complain, they tell you there's a war on as if you were a Fifth Columnist. Blackmail again. Hullo, Derrick, where are you off to?' she said to a small boy with pink cheeks and rather thin arms and legs who was carrying a large hammer. 'You remember Derrick, don't you? He is my youngest evacuee. He was a dreadful little scarecrow a year ago, but we are getting some flesh onto him at last.'

'Please, Miss, I'm going to smash the tins,' said the little boy.

'That's a good boy,' said Mrs Turner.

Derrick scampered off to where, on a strip of rough grass in front of the almshouses, lay a large, unsightly heap of tins, their variegated labels making a splash of colour in the autumn sunlight. Two or three other small boys were tearing off the labels while an older boy was hammering the tins with the back of a meat chopper.

'I really do not know,' said Mrs Villars, 'why the Council take the trouble to ask people to wash their tins and flatten them before throwing them on the dump, as nobody does. Luckily my maids would far rather do anything than their own job, so they wash the tins and I think Corporal Jackson flattens them with our coal hammer while the maids giggle.'

'I did ask Mrs Gibbs, Gibbs's wife, you know,' said Mrs Turner, 'why she didn't trouble to clean her tins as the Council asked us, and she said this was a free country.'

There appeared to be no answer to this, so the ladies in silence walked up the little gravel sweep and into The Hollies. Here they found Betty and the other niece drinking sherry.

'Have some, Mrs Villars?' said Betty. 'It's ackcherly prewar.'

But Mrs Villars preferred to have a cup of tea with her hostess, that was, she said mechanically, if they could spare it. Mrs Turner said they were well up on the tea ration as the girls preferred to poison themselves with sherry, to which the other niece replied with great good humour that the more sherry they drank the more tea there would be for Auntie, which seemed to Mrs Villars a fallacious argument though she was unable to put her finger on the fallacy. The girls then went back to the Communal Kitchen next door to put the potatoes on and Mrs Villars hoped to have a few quiet moments with Mrs Turner to ask her about one or two matters when Mrs Paxon was seen coming up the drive on her bicycle.

If, as Mrs Villars said later to Mr Holden, she had known what the feminine of *largo al factotum* was, that was Mrs Paxon. There was not a pie in Northbridge in which Mrs Paxon had not one of her very capable fingers, and since the war her fingers appeared to have multiplied with the pies. She dealt with evacuees, refugees, air-raid precautions, auxiliary fire service, personal service; was a pillar of the Red Cross; housed by a miracle of congestion her husband's two aunts and an evacuated mother with twins; collected National Savings; was billeting officer for the Plashington Road, and went to early service three days in the week. Small and wiry, she appeared incapable of fatigue and usually cooked Mr Paxon's supper herself when he got back from Barchester on the six-forty-three. To the attributes of Briareus she added those of Proteus, for in the course of her various activities she had collected almost as many uniforms, and as she was often a uniform behindhand during a busy day it was rather difficult to know in what capacity she should be treated.

'Minnie Paxon is in her Red Cross things,' said Mrs Turner. 'I suppose that means she has come about the personal service wool, or it might be about moving Ernie Wheeler. Mrs Gibbs might have to take her mother-in-law and her sister-in-law from Islington, and as she only has one bed, Ernie will have to move. I told Mrs Paxon I would take him if she couldn't find anywhere else. I could put the little camp-bed in the box-room, which is quite large and has a window, and Derrick Pumper, that is my elder evacuee, and it is extremely inconvenient that they are both called Derrick, can go in there and Ernie can have the other camp-bed in the attic-room with Derrick Farker, that is the little one we met going to smash the tins.'

'What a curious name Farker is,' said Mrs Villars.

'Might be Farquhar come down a bit,' said Mrs Turner, 'but I dare say not. People do have extraordinary names. Good morning, Minnie. You do know Mrs Villars? Is it about Ernie?'

'Yes *and* no,' said Mrs Paxon laughing, which she did so frequently that we shall not often allude to it again. 'I'm so glad to find Mrs Villars, because it will save my seeing the Rector. But one thing after another. About Ernie ... '

The two ladies plunged into the intricacies of Mrs Gibbs's household and Mrs Turner's camp-beds, while Mrs Villars sat idle and wondered if she ought to have brought some knitting. It seemed unfair that a war, besides wrecking everyone's summer holidays and devastating their evenings and mornings with blackouts, should give one a serious guilt-complex if one did nothing for a few moments. However she had not brought her knitting, so she sat back in the wide window-seat and listened vaguely to the discussion. A war is apt to produce, except among the happy few who are doing whole-time jobs and believe that they are of supreme importance, a great deal of almost morbid heart-searching. Mrs Villars considered Mrs Paxon, not well-off, carrying so many burdens, yet always gay and competent and ready to flash her large violet eyes at anything in uniform. She considered Mrs Turner who was certainly not poor, but devoting herself to what Mrs Villars secretly considered those rather dull girls, though so worthy and good-humoured, and to almost as many activities as Mrs Paxon, running the Communal Kitchen without respite and suffering evacuees gladly. And she wondered, as most women do about each other, why Mrs Turner had not married again, and decided angrily that men in general were fools not to notice that agreeably ripe (she could think of no better adjective) figure, that pretty curling hair and that excellent temper. But if it came to that, what men were there in Northbridge? Quantities of nice dull husbands, one or two retired military or naval men well guarded by unmarried sisters, the curate, Mr Harker, who was practically a celibate, and a few young men whose defective health or sight gave them the right to remain at home where they were very disagreeable in consequence. In fact, Mr Downing seemed to be the only possibility in sight, and he could only reach, or be reached, across Miss Pemberton's formidable body. As far as Mrs Villars knew, all her elder billeted officers were married except Mr Holden and somehow she did not approve that combination. In any case, Mr Holden was far too young, for Mrs Turner must be about her own age. So she gave it up and went into a rather moody consideration of herself, blaming herself for so often being contented with her lot when so many people were wrenched and wretched. A very nice husband who after being a successful schoolmaster had been presented to a very good living; an elder son who was a Professor of Engineering at an unusually early age and was required to stick to his job; a younger son in the Air Force entirely engaged on instruction; her house not too full of very quiet well-behaved officers. In fact, nothing to complain of, except that she felt wicked to be so peaceful. She came to the conclusion that to be contented was her cross, just as Mrs Paxon, having thrashed out the question of Ernie and decided that no further step need be taken till it was known whether Mrs Gibbs's in-laws would go to her or to their other son's wife in Surrey, who having two very young children and a baby imminent, was far less fitted to receive them, and would therefore probably be their choice, turned to Mrs Villars and said:

'About spotting.'

'Oh ... yes ... ' said Mrs Villars, staring rather stupidly.

'Your husband said it would be all right, but he had to get permission about the telephone. And, do you know, I am not sure if we oughtn't to have *two* people. I mean it's a long way down if anything happened and *so* narrow on the inside edge.'

'Oh ... of course ...' said Mrs Villars, trying with no success to look intelligent.

'Minnie means spotting on the church tower,' said Mrs Turner in a low violent voice and making a face at Mrs Villars, intended to convey to her that she really knew all about it if she would pull herself together. Unlike most faces, this was a success, and the fictitious intelligence in Mrs Villars's face, the false dawn as it were, was replaced by a dawn of real understanding.

'You do realize about the necessity for two people?' said Mrs Paxon, who had been grabbling about in her bag and had missed Mrs Turner's prompting.

'You mean if one got ill on the top of the tower by oneself,' said Mrs Villars.

'Or if you were alone and *anyone* came up,' said Mrs Paxon, who believed that practically every man in England was, unless she knew him, a German in disguise, with the fellest designs on the honour of England's womanhood. 'There was an appalling man in the train last Saturday. He got in at Southbridge and asked if the train stopped at Northbridge, so of course I made no reply and he looked at me in a way I can't describe. If he had made a movement towards me I would have opened the door and thrown myself down the embankment.'

Mrs Villars wondered if it was her duty as the Rector's wife to say that God's hand was over us even in a railway carriage and decided it was not, so she asked what had happened.

'He never said another word,' said Mrs Paxon. 'He just lighted a cigarette.'

'How rude of him,' said Mrs Villars sympathetically.

'I must say it was a smoking carriage,' said Mrs Paxon very fairly. 'And then he got out at Tidcombe Halt and went off in a most *peculiar* way. Not by the path that goes under the line and down the hill to Tidcombe, but quite in the other direction. Mrs Copper got in there and I told her, quite in a laughing way of course, because I simply *cannot* help seeing the funny side of things. When I was in the South Wembley Amateur Choral Society we did *Hiawatha*, all in costume, and I did Minnehaha, and they all said the name quite suited me. I expect you thought my name was Minnie,' she said, turning to Mrs Turner, 'but it is only that it stuck to me. The conductor was a splendid fellow, but I never let him see me home. Musicians get a bit temperamental if you know what I mean, after rehearsal sometimes. But this man in the train was quite different; more sinister. I must say though I laugh when I think of it.'

Upon which she laughed a merry peal and said would they both put down their names to act as spotters. So they did and Mrs Paxon mounted her bicycle and went away.

'It is no good saying No to Minnie Paxon,' said Mrs Turner resignedly, 'though what good spotters can do, don't ask me. Have you any field-glasses?'

Mrs Villars said no, but she had a pair of opera-glasses that had belonged to her mother, only they were mother-of-pearl, so they didn't work very well.

'By the way,' she said as she left, 'I meant to ask you something. Who is Effie Bunce's aunt?'

Mrs Turner looked curiously at her friend.

'Don't you know?' she said.

Mrs Villars said she was very sorry, but she had only been at Northbridge just over a year, and as her husband had mostly been a schoolmaster she hadn't quite got into Rectory ways yet and thought she would never learn everyone's name.

'You might as well know Effie's aunt's name,' said Mrs Turner, 'because she is your cook.'

'Not Mrs Chapman!' said Mrs Villars. 'No wonder Effie is frightened of her. Even Corporal Jackson can't get round her.'

'No one ever did,' said Mrs Turner, 'except Bob Chapman, but he ran away before they were married and has never been heard of again. Her boy is doing very well in the Merchant Navy.'

'Then she isn't Mrs Chapman, really,' said Mrs Villars.

Mrs Turner said all cooks were allowed to call themselves Mrs, and Mrs Chapman thoroughly deserved it and she must fly to the Communal Kitchen now.

'Well, I am most grateful,' said Mrs Villars, 'for all your help.'

'That's all right, Mrs Villars,' said Mrs Turner. 'Do ask me anything you like. I've lived here for twenty years and I know pretty well all the ins and outs.'

'There is one thing I would like to ask you,' said Mrs Villars, 'and that is not to call me Mrs Villars. I know Verena sounds a very affected name, but I am used to it.'

'Sintram?' said Mrs Turner.

'Indirectly. Heir of Redclyffe,' said Mrs Villars.

'The only trouble,' said Mrs Turner, 'is that my name is so *awful*: Poppy.'

'Well, whenever I say Poppy I shall think of *you*,' said Mrs Villars, and apparently Mrs Turner quite understood what she meant.

To make the catering and serving easier, Mrs Villars had arranged that lunch should be the same for her husband

and herself and the officers. This plan worked very well, as most of the guests had friends in the neighbourhood or went over to Barchester after office hours to the cinema and did not need much in the way of an evening meal. The Rectory dining-room seated ten very comfortably with the leaf in the table and to-day all eight officers were present. Captain Topham who had been to town for the night was a little late, and as soon as he arrived they sat down to lunch.

'And how was London?' said Mr Villars, for whom as an ex-schoolmaster communal lunches had no terrors.

Captain Topham said it was a fearful nuisance that his club had all the windows broken and his tailor had a bomb in his stockroom and didn't know how much he could save. The worst of it was, he said, that the Megatherium was taking his club in temporarily and they were such a highbrow lot and half of them had one foot in the grave.

'I can tell you, sir, it gave me a turn,' said the Captain to his host. 'The first thing I saw when I got inside was an old gentleman being wheeled into the dining-room in a bathchair, and I'd hardly got half-way through my lunch when there was a kind of scuffle over by a window and some waiters brought a screen along and one of them told me an old gentleman had just had a fit. Pretty grim kind of place that,' said Captain Topham, whose pre-war interests had been largely connected with the turf and the stage. 'Good port, though.'

'Talking of port,' said Colonel Passmore, a middle-aged solicitor whose Territorial enthusiasm had brought him back to the regiment in which he had served in 1914–18, 'it will be a shocking thing when we can't get any more good

French stuff. I haven't drunk any German stuff since I was in Cologne in 'nineteen, and hope never to drink any again.'

Lieutenant Hooper, who could not bear narrow-mindedness in his seniors, or indeed in anyone but himself, said we must remember that English wine-merchants had stocks of German wine honourably paid for, and to ban the drinking of German wine would mean ruin for them.

Captain Topham said a good lager was good enough for him and a good glass of port to finish up with.

Colonel Passmore shuddered and mentally marked the Captain as unfit for promotion.

Lieutenant Hooper asked with what he considered to be quiet irony whether lager was an English drink, to which Captain Topham, who was impervious to any kind of Fine Shades, said Barclays had a jolly good one, but he fancied the Danish himself.

'I once went over a large Danish brewery when I was in Denmark,' said Captain Powell-Jones.

As he was a taciturn man, used to sitting in his rooms at Bangor and frightening men who came to him to be coached in Cymric, everyone was interested in his entrance into the conversation and there was a respectful silence.

'It was very interesting,' said Captain Powell-Jones. 'Yes, very interesting,' he added after a short pause for reflection. 'Would you mind passing the cruet, Dutton.'

Lieutenant Dutton winced and passed the salt-cellar.

'Will you have wing or leg, Colonel?' said Mr Villars from the sideboard where he was carving two fine chickens.

'The upper part of the leg if you don't mind,' said the Colonel. 'Much the best part of a fowl.'

At this Lieutenant Greaves, a jovial youth who was the life and soul of any party at which he found himself and would indeed have been sent down from Oxford for excessive joviality had he not gone straight into the army, was inspired to remark to Major Spender:

'Fowl, eh? I suppose we have you to thank, sir. Jolly good show.'

Major Spender, who was thin and sensitive and spent all his spare time writing to his wife and three children, went red all over on being thus addressed.

'Don't be a fool, Tommy,' said Lieutenant Dutton coldly to Mr Greaves. 'The Major's dog ate the whole bird, feathers and all.'

'Who ate a bird?' said Mr Villars from the sideboard.

Regimental loyalty suddenly asserted itself and no one answered. The Rector turned and looked at his company with an expression which clearly said, 'As none of you have sufficient sense of honour to own up to this extremely foolish and ungentlemanly prank, I shall keep the whole form in for an hour every afternoon till the boy who perpetrated it comes forward. This will of course include the afternoon of the match against Harbord's Eleven.'

'I'm most awfully sorry, sir,' said Major Spender. 'It was my dog.'

'I thought Mr Greaves said a bird,' said Mr Villars, handing a plate to Foster, the parlourmaid, and sitting down.

'He did, darling,' said Mrs Villars. 'Major Spender's dog killed one of the fowls quite by mistake and ate it. But she was a bad layer and Mr Holden says the poor dog was beaten.'

'Then it is not the fowl in question that we are eating?' said the Rector suspiciously.

32

'Nothing left of her, sir, except the claws and the feathers,' said Corporal Jackson, who was an admirable underparlourmaid. 'Quite a mangled affair, sir.'

'Ah well,' said the Rector, evidently letting his form off their punishment in consideration of an honourable if tardy confession. 'Birds will be getting scarce.'

'*Rara avis*,' remarked Mr Dutton negligently, but the Rector looked at him over his spectacles as if requesting the rest of the quotation and Mr Dutton wished he hadn't spoken.

'And think of all the partridges and pheasants flying about this autumn asking to be shot,' said Captain Topham mournfully, to which Mr Hooper said quietly that the hospitals would be glad enough of food before long, but his quietness was so provocative that Captain Topham asked him what he meant, only just stopping himself in time from saying what the devil.

'Well,' said Mr Hooper, 'you *may* laugh at the talk of invasion,' and shut his mouth with what he meant to be a snap, though his younger friends hoped it was his teeth falling out as they had once done at the depot.

Again there was a short silence, for the gentlemen present, none of whom except Major Spender were regular soldiers, were not sure whether mentioning invasion in mixed company was the same as mentioning a woman's name at mess.

'That reminds me,' said Mrs Villars to her husband, 'that Mrs Paxon was asking me about parachute-spotters on the church tower and I said I would be one. Is that all right?'

'If Hibberd has found the key I suppose it is,' said Mr Villars, 'but it has been missing for two days. It is most

33

annoying, because I am responsible. I could swear I left it on its usual nail inside the vestry. Hibberd was away last night so I couldn't ask him.'

'Is Hibberd the one with a Newgate frill in the churchyard, sir?' asked Mr Greaves respectfully.

The Rector, recognizing this description of his sexton, said it was.

'Then I'm most awfully sorry, sir,' said Mr Greaves, 'but I've got the key. I'm awfully keen on old churches and things and I asked your man about the tower and he showed me where the key was and I forgot to put it back. It's in my other tunic.'

'All is well that ends well,' said the Rector, who looked favourably on Mr Greaves as a kind of Captain of the Eleven who had no brains but reflected a certain credit on the school.

'What was it like up there?' said Mrs Villars. 'I'm ashamed to say I've never been up.'

'Marvellous!' said Mr Greaves. 'One of those jolly corkscrew staircases, nearly pitch dark and awfully steep. I think there must be a lot of daws' nests in the windows near the top because the steps are covered with dirt,' he said, quickly substituting this for the word muck in deference to the feelings of a lady. 'And a topping view from the roof. That's a splendid lead roof you have up there, sir,' he continued, addressing the Rector. 'I climbed up and sat on the top of it, a sort of pyramid shape you know, and I could almost see over the battlements. And I've never seen so many dead flying beetles as there are round the gutter in my life. They absolutely crunch when you walk on them. I'll put the key back at once, sir.'

The conversation now became general, each gentleman

talking of the subject that interested him most, except Captain Powell-Jones who ate his food and thought but poorly of a place where no one had probably heard of Morgan ap Kerrig, or Crumlinwallinwer, or Mewlinwillinwodd. Under cover of the noise, Mrs Villars thought with considerable repulsion of Mr Greaves's description of the tower and wished she had not let Mrs Paxon hypnotize her into being a spotter, for twisting stairs and insects, dead or alive, were her greatest terrors, not to speak of a very bad head for heights. This she presently confided to Mr Holden who happened to be sitting next to her that day, for the dining-room table was treated as a sort of club, each gentleman sitting where he liked as he came in. They made the interesting discovery that while Mrs Villars was frightened of looking down from a roof or even a step-ladder, she was never seasick, while Mr Holden, a keen rock-climber with a steady head, had almost forsworn the Dolomites before the war because he was not only seasick but airsick.

After lunch Major Spender lingered in the dining-room to make his personal apologies about the hen and inquire diffidently if he might pay for the damage. This his host of course declined, while thanking him for the suggestion, and offered him a cigar.

'About this invasion,' said the Rector. 'Do you think spotters on the church tower would be likely to prevent it?'

Major Spender said that in his experience nothing prevents anything in particular, but roof-spotting might help the civilians to feel useful. It was, he said, hard luck on civilians, because they never knew where they were, whereas in the Army one did.

'By the way, sir,' he added, 'you were at Coppin's School, weren't you? I was there from nineteen eight to nineteen twelve and my two boys are down for it. The eldest will be going next year. Though I say it, he has an unusual gift for writing and has done some awfully good little stories, quite short you know and illustrated them himself. Only child's work of course,' said Major Spender, obviously meaning that it was equal to the work of Balzac and Michael Angelo rolled into one, 'but one can always tell.'

Mr Villars, who was hardened to parents, said sometimes one could and sometimes one couldn't, which led to an account of the linguistic abilities of the second Master Spender and the ballerina-like gifts of Miss Clarissa Spender, aged three. At this point the Rector, who added to his other gifts that of being able to get rid of parents before they knew it, said, 'Ah, well ha!' and so left Major Spender to find his way back to the office.

When Mrs Villars came down about four o'clock, for she was obliged, much to her annoyance, to lie down after lunch to please her doctor, she found Mrs Paxon in the drawing-room. That lady was wearing blue flannel trousers and a frilly short-sleeved blouse and had tied her head up in a kind of orange fish-net, which made Mrs Villars guess that she had been at, or was going to, an A.R.P. gathering. Mrs Paxon apologized for intruding, saying that she ought to have called on the Rectory months ago, but seemed to have got a bit behind-hand with the war and what not, so she thought she would just run in before the rehearsal and hoped Mrs Villars would take the will for the deed, which Mrs Villars was quite ready to do.

'What are you rehearsing?' she asked. 'Is it in aid of something?'

'Oh, dear, no,' said Mrs Paxon. 'Our little dramatic ventures are *quite* a back number now. We are just having a casualty practice. A bomb is supposed to have exploded outside Scatcherd's and the first-aid party are going to do first-aid. Several of us have volunteered as casualties and I am to be a hysteria case, but what I really came about,' said Mrs Paxon, laughing at herself, 'was the spotting. Do you think the Rector will object?'

Stopping herself with an effort from saying the old min was friendly, Mrs Villars said that if Mr Greaves had found the key she thought it would be all right, upon which Mrs Paxon proceeded to develop her plan. The Air Wardens had decided to call upon a number of patriotic ladies to spend two hours at a time on the roof in couples. Their duties would be to scan the horizon, also the spacious firmament above, and report anything suspicious that they saw falling. Any such object was to be reported at once to the Council Rooms. The Home Guard would then be mobilized and set out in small but determined squads for the probable locality where the falling had taken place. It was hoped that the garage would lend a large-scale map, on which the tower-watchers were to mark the direction the Home Guard should take.

'I have a splendid list already,' said Mrs Paxon. 'Yourself and the Rector, Mrs Turner and her nieces, Miss Pemberton who is very keen and Mr Downing, Miss Crowder and Miss Hopgood from Glycerine Cottage, Miss Hopgood's aunt who has a telescope, Mrs Dunsford and her daughter, only they cannot come on Mondays, Wednesdays and Fridays because they have lent the drawing-room at Hovis House for working parties and Mrs Dunsford likes to keep an eye on them, Miss Talbot and her sister from the Aloes. And last, and least, there is my little self.'

Mrs Villars said that it sounded splendid, but she thought it was all to be women. Mrs Paxon said, Of course, because every man was needed at his post.

'But didn't you mention Mr Downing and my husband?' said Mrs Villars.

Mrs Paxon said they were different; a statement which Mrs Villars very sensibly decided to take as well-meant, and began to pour out tea.

'No sugar, thank you,' said Mrs Paxon. 'War-time, you know, and we must all pull together. I couldn't take yours; you have so *many* calls on you.'

With a laugh she fished out of her bag a small tin, once the home of Oxo cubes, opened it and took out a piece of sugar which she popped, for the phrase rises naturally to one's mind in speaking of Minnie Paxon, into her tea.

'Oh, please!' said Mrs Villars. 'We really have heaps, and as Gregory and I don't take it in tea or coffee we can easily spare it for our guests.'

But Mrs Paxon said that many a mickle made a muckle, and being pressed to take a scone said, Not if there was butter on it, for she knew that Mrs Villars with her big family must need every bit.

'But we have heaps,' said Mrs Villars. 'All the officers have their own rations and we do very well. Besides, this is only margarine, I'm afraid. Mrs Chapman won't let us use butter at teatime.'

38

'Margarine is just the same as butter in war-time,' said Mrs Paxon. 'But if I might scrape it off and just have a teeny-weeny bit of that delicious jam.'

However, her hostess managed to persuade her to do violence to her conscience and then Mr Villars came in.

Mrs Paxon said when the Rector came in at the door visitors must fly out of the window and made her good-byes with bright rapidity. At the door she paused.

'Oh, Mrs Villars,' she said, 'I meant to ask you. What about Father Fewling? He used to be a sailor. I know he isn't exactly a woman, but as we are opening our net so wide we might include him. After all, who is more suitable for a roof-spotter than a High Churchman? My little joke. And if you don't mind my asking the spotters to meet at the Rectory on Saturday at eleven-thirty, it would be most kind. I shall leave it to your gentle arts to persuade the Rector.'

And with a farewell laugh she went away.

'Tea, please, Verena,' said the Rector. 'What's all this about Fewling?'

Mrs Villars briefly outlined to her husband the Air Wardens' scheme for women spotters at the church and with some amusement broke the news to him that he and Mr Downing had been provisionally enrolled.

'I suppose the clergy are looked upon as old women,' said he with a half sigh. 'In the last war I was at the front. Well, well. Still it is my own church tower, so I suppose I have a right to go up if I want to. As for Fewling, he is a first-rate man, and though I don't care for his form of worship, plenty of people here do. He can't do much with his asthma and frets a lot. I think to sit on the roof and look for invaders will cheer him up as long as the warm weather lasts. As for Downing, poor fellow, one hardly knows what to say. I suppose Miss Pemberton will insist on his coming up the tower with her in case anyone should try to call on him while she is out. This *is* an amusing village, Verena.'

His wife agreed, but said that Coppin's School had been funny too, and did he remember Mr O'Brien who used to come to the School Entertainment in a saffron kilt because his ancestors had been Kings of Ireland. So they gossiped about old days till the Rector got up to go on to his next job.

'Then it's all right about spotting, Gregory?' said his wife, 'and having a meeting here?'

'They can do what they like,' said the Rector. 'But you are not to overdo yourself. Remember that. If you look tired I shall put my foot down. I will not have you ill again.'

3

Several on a Tower

The casualty practice was a great success in the sense that all amateur performances are successful. That is, they give intense pleasure to those taking part, while the audience is at liberty to stay away, to take no notice, to be bored, amused, or pleased. In this case the audience was mostly either at home, in its back garden, or waiting for the pubs to open, but if Northbridge's A.R.P. workers had been performing in the Coliseum packed to capacity with lions waiting to eat them if they did not give satisfaction, they could not have enjoyed themselves more. Boy Scouts bearing labels marked 'Fractured Thigh' or 'Spinal Case' were bandaged on the pavement, giving advice the while. Commander Beasley, R.N. (ret.), who was a gas case, read a little pamphlet from a society whose tenets he was thinking of embracing which gave a complete prophecy of everything that had already happened founded on a triangle with Cleopatra's Needle as its base, lost his temper and went home before his life had been saved to write to *The Times*. A large white circle with the word CRATER stencilled inside it had been marked on the road outside Scatcherd's, and this the A.R.P. cars and the town ambulance, in private life the Northbridge Hand Laundry's delivery-van, took great care to avoid, so that the traffic coming in the opposite direction, ignorant of the yawning chasm twenty feet across, spouting gas, water, electric light, telephones and drains, were surprised and annoyed to be met by traffic on the wrong side of the road. As for Mrs Paxon, she had managed to be a hysteria case, and never in the best days of the South Wembley Amateur Dramatic had she enjoyed herself so much. Had it not been for six o'clock, an hour which caused all the remaining male casualties (the Boy Scouts excepted) to withdraw, so that the A.R.P. ladies rather lost interest, she would willingly have repeated her performance till midnight.

She then went home, cooked Mr Paxon's supper, rescued the dropped stitches of one aunt and helped the other with her Patience, superintended the bi-weekly bath of the evacuee twins whose mother was on the whole half-witted and did not rightly know who the kiddies' daddy was, though she gratefully accepted a separation allowance from the gentleman, as she artlessly called him, who had taken a father's place. Mr Paxon, a bank-manager in Barchester, was then allowed to help her to do her National Savings books and disentangle the money due to the Government from the housekeeping money, after which she typed a quantity of notices about the roof-spotting, to be delivered by herself on her bicycle before and after early service next morning.

Mr Paxon, who would have preferred to sleep in his own bed, with a spiral spring mattress that represented the ideal of many years of patient drudgery, then helped her to put up the camp-beds upon which he, his wife and two aunts slept in the dining-room. Mrs Paxon put on her Siren suit, a garment differing in few but important particulars from her ordinary trouser suits. Mr Paxon put a bucket of sand and a stirrup pump in the passage with the full and certain knowledge that he would bang against them in the morning, filled the scullery sink with water and went to bed.

As for the mother and the twins, they had a kind of gypsy camp in a little room known as the Back Room, containing three glassfronted shelves of books and an extra sideboard with a fern on it.

Secure in these precautions, the little town of Northbridge slept peacefully.

As the result of Mrs Paxon's labours all roof-spotters knew by breakfast-time that a meeting would be held at the Rectory at eleven-thirty on Saturday morning. A very full attendance was expected, because everyone was interested in Miss Pemberton and Mr Downing, and it was generally considered that as he usually came down on Friday evening, Miss Pemberton, whose patriotism was well known, would have to come to the meeting and would sooner keep him under her eye than expose him to danger by leaving him at home.

Accordingly, Mrs Villars made her preparations and as these included light refreshments, she decided to speak to her cook about them after breakfast.

It was her custom to go to the kitchen about nine o'clock, for the officers were usually at work by that hour, having previously left with Corporal Jackson a list of those who would be in or out for meals. A good deal of her week-end housekeeping had already been done on the previous day, but there were a few last-moment changes to be made. Major Spender had had a wire from his wife to ask if he could get away for a night to meet her to talk about letting their house in Northamptonshire, and Captain Topham was going over to Pomfret Towers to help to stem the rising tide of partridges and anything else fit for a gun.

The spacious Rectory kitchen was full of sunshine and quite empty when the mistress went in. As she looked at the massive built-in dresser and the almost immovable kitchen table which were scrubbed once a week, and the stone-flagged floor which together with the stone-flagged scullery, larder and passages the kitchen-maid insisted on washing at great length every day because she was frightened of Mrs Chapman and did not want to learn to cook, Mrs Villars felt extremely thankful that she had an income of her own and that her husband had made a very good thing out of Coppin's School. With maids so hard to come by, it was not an easy house to run, but what it would have been for an incumbent who had only his stipend to live on and perhaps several children growing up and being educated, she did not like to think. While quite conscious that she could never make a proper Rector's wife, a career almost impossible to those who do not come of parsonage stock, she was sensible enough to realize that if she made a very happy, comfortable background for her husband, as she knew she did, she would be forgiven for not doing her whole duty on committees and charitable works. Besides, when made to lie down after lunch every day, it is not easy to do all one ought to do.

She walked absently across the kitchen into the scullery

and looked out of the door into the backyard. In Victorian days the Rectors of Northbridge had kept their brougham and hunted a little, as the handsome coachhouse and stabling and the brickpaved yard slightly sloping to a drain in the middle showed. The coachhouse now sheltered the Rectory car and several cars belonging to the officers, the stalls were filled with provisions of coal and wood, the maids' bicycles, odd bits of furniture being stored for friends and a heap of sand for extinguishing incendiary bombs, while in the two little bedrooms above Corporal Jackson had installed himself a number of rabbits, to which he was much attached. Mrs Villars had once been up to visit his pets and had determined that nothing on earth would ever make her go there again.

The kitchen-maid, carrying a pail of dirty water, came out of the dark passage that she was scrubbing, saw her mistress and gasped.

'Good morning, Edie,' said Mrs Villars. 'Do you know where Mrs Chapman is?'

Edie, in a terror-struck whisper, said she thought Mrs Chapman had gone down the garden to get a cabbage or somethink for dinner.

'"So she went into the garden to cut a cabbage leaf to make an apple-pie,"' said Mrs Villars aloud to herself.

The kitchen-maid, still more terrified, dropped her scrubbing-brush with a loud clatter. Mrs Villars looked round and saw her flattening herself against the scullery wall.

'What is it, Edie?' she said.

'Please, m'm, the drain,' said Edie. 'Mrs Chapman says not to put the dirty water down her sink.'

Mrs Villars, understanding that Edie had orders to empty

the scrubbing water down the outside drain, moved aside. Her kitchen-maid made a bolt past her into the middle of the yard to empty her pail, at which moment Mrs Chapman, accompanied by Corporal Jackson carrying a basket of vegetables, came round the corner of the coachhouse. At the sight of her tyrant Edie hastily emptied her pail, at the same moment giving a loud shriek.

'What *is* the matter?' said Mrs Villars, approaching the kitchen-maid. 'Good morning, Mrs Chapman. Good morning, Jackson.'

'Please, m'm,' said the kitchen-maid, appealing to Caesar, though she knew she would repent it afterwards, 'it gave me quite a start when Mrs Chapman and Mr Jackson come round the corner and I let the soap go down the drain.'

'Well, it's lucky soap isn't rationed,' said the cook, with the fine indifference of her class to her employer's property. 'Go and get a bit out of my kitchen cupboard and get on with the work. No need to worry yourself, Mr Jackson, Edie likes carrying the pail. I'm sure I never thought you would be down yet, madam, so I thought as Hibberd hadn't brought any vegetables in I'd just go and look, for bring me the best he does *not*, and Mr Jackson said he'd carry the basket.'

By this time they had all arrived at the scullery door, where Corporal Jackson handed over the basket with a gallantry that Mrs Villars much admired.

'"But at the same time a great she-bear coming down the street popped her head into the shop. 'What, no soap,' she said, so he died,"' said Mrs Villars to herself, adding half aloud, 'and I wonder who will marry the barber.'

Mrs Chapman, who was putting on her white kitchen

apron, looked up in surprise, but being used to the gentry kept her thoughts to herself.

The meals for the week-end were finally arranged and a light refection ordered for eleven-thirty to help the spotters to think. Mrs Chapman announced, with ill-concealed pleasure, that though cooked ham wasn't rationed Scatcherd's hadn't got a crumb, nor Fitchett's, nor the Empire and Fireside Stores. Instead of blenching, her mistress said then they must do without and she would order some from London.

'By the way, Mrs Chapman,' she said, 'did you know Miss Pemberton's Effie had stopped going to the Girl Guides? Mrs Turner thinks she ought to keep it up. It will be a pity if she drops out, as she meets a lot of nice girls there.'

Mrs Chapman's large face assumed an expression which made Mrs Villars very glad she was not Miss Bunce.

'Nice girls!' she said scornfully. 'Of course, madam, a lady like Mrs Turner isn't up to the goings-on. I was only saying to Mr Jackson yesterday when he brought the potatoes up that if Mrs Turner knew where Doris Hibberd spends her evening off she'd lose a year's growth. And as for that Edie, all I can say is if she isn't in by ten o'clock sharp on her day out she'll be one of those that are taken Advantage of.'

Mrs Villars said that was dreadful, reflecting the while upon Mrs Chapman's not blameless past.

'Of course you may say,' said Mrs Chapman with surprising candour, 'that my Bert was an accident of Providence, as you might say. But he's a good boy and I was young then.'

Mrs Villars felt unequal to disentangling her cook's morality and gave her final orders for the week-end. As she went along the passage and saw Edie, rabbit-faced, spectacled, with scanty pale hair, on her knees with pail, cloth and scrubbing-brush and the new bit of soap, and remembered how difficult it was to get good workers, she hoped that Mrs Chapman's views on mankind were as imaginative as Mrs Paxon's.

By eleven-thirty-five the Rectory drawing-room, all rights in which had been ceded for the morning by Colonel Passmore, was thronged with potential spotters. Mrs Paxon, in a neat green uniform denoting Women's Voluntary Services, was the first to arrive, bringing with her Miss Hopgood's aunt, complete with telescope, which she carried in a stout leather case.

'Of course you know Miss Hopgood's aunt,' said Mrs Paxon.

Mrs Villars felt that as Rector's wife she so obviously ought to know Miss Hopgood's aunt, at any rate by sight, that she would now never be able to ask what her name was.

'We did meet at the Women's Institute Sale of Work,' said Miss Hopgood's aunt, a large woman in a badly cut coat and skirt, with a great air of competence, 'but you wouldn't remember me.'

To this unfair, though usually very true, statement there is but one reply.

'But of *course*,' said Mrs Villars. 'I was just wondering where it was. How kind of you to bring your telescope.'

'It is a very good instrument,' said Miss Hopgood's aunt. 'My late husband was head of the Matthews Porter Observatory in Texas for the last three years of his life, and I took a great interest in his work. This is the actual instrument that he used when he went out in the foot-hills. For his astronomical work he of course had the forty-foot Zollmer-Vollfuss with a refraction of eighty-five degrees. It was with it that he discovered Porter Sidus in the constellation of Algareb.'

48

Mrs Villars weakly said it was a pity they hadn't got one like it in Northbridge.

'It would be impossible,' said Miss Hopgood's aunt. 'Porterville is on a pocket of basalt. Here you are mostly clay or chalk and the emplacement for a Zollmer-Vollfuss would be immensely expensive and liable to crack. Also the visibility is extremely poor. In Porterville the air is so dry and clear that I have often watched the coyotes at play in the foot-hills fifty miles away with this very telescope.'

Mrs Villars expressed proper surprise, which was weak of her, for she had no idea how far one ought to see with a telescope and did not want to expose her ignorance to Miss Hopgood's aunt, nor until it suddenly came upon her in a flash after tea was she sure what koy-oties were.

By this time Mrs Turner and her nieces had arrived in company with Miss Crowder and Miss Hopgood from Glycerine Cottage. This name may sound improbable, and indeed is, so it is but the reader's right to expect an explanation. Miss Crowder and Miss Hopgood, maiden ladies whose combined incomes were sufficient for their modest wants, were both firmly convinced that they were spiritually French, however English by birth. In pursuance of this myth they saved up every year to go to the Riviera, where they stayed at Mentone (which they always called Menton in a provocative way) in the Pension Ramsden, kept, as the reader has doubtless guessed, by the French widow of a Major Ramsden, late of the British Army, and distinguished chiefly for his success in dropping the word Sergeant from his rank. Here they had cocktails every day before lunch with the other English residents and in the afternoons went on long motor-bus excursions into the surrounding country, being careful to choose such tours as had an English guide. On one of these excursions they were so struck by a white villa embowered in wistaria, bearing the title Les Glycines, that they determined to adopt the name for the cottage they were building at Northbridge. Miss Crowder, who was a linguist and despised dictionaries, having, as she said, picked up all her French on the spot, therefore caused the words Glycerine Cottage to be painted in Gothic letters on the gate and planted a Virginian creeper by the drawing-room window, thus reproducing to her complete satisfaction and that of Miss Hopgood the atmosphere of the Côte d'Azur.

'I hope we aren't late,' said Miss Crowder. 'My watch is slow, and when I heard the church clock striking half-past eleven as we came out of the gate I was quite ah-hoory, and so was chère amie,' said Miss Crowder, who always addressed Miss Hopgood in this Parisian way.

'When my friend and I heard the clock, I said, "We must hurry or we shall be late,"' said Miss Hopgood.

Mrs Dunsford and her daughter now appeared. As they were dressed exactly as a country-town widow and her daughter of good middle-class family and income should be dressed and did everything together, they were practically indistinguishable from hundreds of other quite useful ladies of the same kind all over England.

'You know Miss Hopgood, don't you?' said Mrs Villars to Mrs Dunsford.

Mrs Dunsford said she knew Miss Hopgood so well by sight, but had not yet had the pleasure of meeting her.

'And this is my friend with whom I live,' said Miss

Hopgood, presenting Miss Crowder. It may be added that Miss Hopgood's fondness for the beautiful word 'friend' caused all her less intimate acquaintances a good deal of trouble, as they had to find out for themselves what Miss Crowder's name was.

'I have always admired the front of Hovis House so much,' said Miss Crowder. 'Pure dix-huitième.'

'I am so glad it appeals to you,' said Mrs Dunsford. 'It was in shocking repair when the General took it and we had to reface it altogether. It has an interesting story. The original owner was a wool-stapler called Hover and the house became known as Hover's. Gradually the "r" fell out and the "e" was changed to "i". Hence its present name.'

'You didn't say, Mother,' said Miss Dunsford, 'that Father thought it was a corruption of Offa's, a place-name from a Danish owner.'

Miss Hopgood said it was wonderful the way these old place-names survived.

As it was now a quarter to twelve and everyone had had sherry and cake, Mrs Villars asked Mrs Paxon to explain the object of the meeting, adding that they would not wait for Miss Pemberton and Mr Downing.

'One moment,' said Mrs Paxon. 'I think I see them in the lane with Miss Talbot and Miss Dolly Talbot,' and so it was, and in a few moments they were in the room. Miss Pemberton announced, with no hint of apology, that she had been writing and could not start till after half-past. As for the Misses Talbot, they were always late.

'Well now,' said Mrs Paxon, 'it's like this. We all know about this invasion and I hope we'll get it, as it will mean a jolly good slap in the eye for our friend the Fewrer and make some people here sit up a bit.'

This bellicose beginning caused several of the ladies to pinch their lips, thereby signifying that they knew exactly which member of the Government, or alternatively of the local A.R.P. personnel, Mrs Paxon was alluding to.

'Well,' Mrs Paxon continued, 'as we can't all be in a hundred places at once and parachutists might come down anywhere, we thought if we had people on the church tower to keep a look-out it would be a good thing. We shall want two watchers at a time, for two-hour shifts, and I'm sure we shall get plenty of volunteers. We must have two on the roof always, for various reasons,' she added darkly, leaving her audience to fill in the gap for themselves.

'My friend and I could easily do a watch together,' said Miss Hopgood.

Mrs Paxon said 'Splendid.'

Mrs Dunsford and her daughter and the Misses Talbot spoke to the same effect and Mrs Paxon said That was splendid.

'I am perfectly willing to watch with Mr Downing,' said Miss Pemberton, who had barricaded her lodger into a corner and was sitting slightly in front of him. 'Or if I have one of my bad colds, Mr Downing could take a watch with the Rector, or Father Fewling. Where is Father Fewling? I thought he was coming.'

Mrs Villars said it was St Sycorax's Day, and she thought Father Fewling was having a special eleven o'clock service but she was sure he would soon be there.

'Well,' said Mrs Paxon, 'I think it would be a very good

52

thing if we all went up the tower and had a look. Then we shall know exactly what we have to expect. Can we have the key, Mrs Villars?'

Mrs Villars said with pleasure, adding that her husband was so very sorry he couldn't be at the meeting as he had to go over to Plumstead, but he would gladly take a turn at watching if his other engagements permitted; for she was a good wife.

Accordingly the party walked across the garden, through the iron grille in the brick wall and across the churchyard, at which point in their journey Father Fewling was seen hurrying over the grass towards them.

Father Fewling had begun his career in the Navy and had risen in the last war to the rank of Commander, after which he had felt a call to the religious life and had entered an Anglican order. In figure he was of that peculiarly firm and unbending stoutness which so often goes with the quarter-deck, and this was his cross, for he liked to think of himself as gaunt and ascetic, but was perpetually brought up short by his tailor or his looking-glass. At St Sycorax, where he was a priest-in-charge, a title which gave him deep pleasure, he indulged in a perfect orgy of incense and vestments. Public opinion was strongly divided on the subject, half the church-going population following him with enthusiasm, the other half seeing in him a first cousin at least of the Scarlet Woman. Mr Villars would never commit himself, but said to his wife that if people wanted that sort of thing it was a good thing to keep them in the parish. Meanwhile, Father Fewling worked even harder than he had worked in the North Sea and brought the St Sycorax Boy Scouts to a pitch of perfection in tying knots that made them the envy of all the Scoutmasters in Barsetshire.

As he came flapping over the newly-mown grass of the churchyard, Mrs Paxon said with a laugh that he was just her idea of a monk in the Middle Ages, a remark that was coldly received by the Misses Talbot, who were ardent attendants of St Sycorax and had very definite ideas about the validity of Father Fewling's monkhood, and about the Middle Ages. For their father, Professor Talbot, was a tremendous authority on the medieval church and they well knew that to Mrs Paxon monks meant a picture called 'To-morrow will be Friday,' familiar to the amateurs of early motor-advertisements, and the Middle Ages a limitless period, coeval with The Olden Times and consisting largely of troubadours, serfs (or villeins), and cardinals overeating themselves.

Mrs Villars, seeing all the committee assembled, now led the way into the church, where Father Fewling genuflected in a way that made Miss Hopgood draw in her breath with a hissing sound. Mrs Villars led the party to the foot of the tower stairs and unlocked the door. Darkness rushed out and almost hit them in the face.

'I don't think I could ever go up,' said Miss Hopgood, retreating from the doorway.

'Nonsense, chère amie,' said Miss Crowder.

Mrs Paxon, hovering round, said it was only the sudden contrast of coming from the sunlight into the dim religious light and there were windows higher up the stairs. But Miss Hopgood said she knew there were bats, from which attitude nothing could move her, so Mrs Dunsford volunteered to stay with her while the others went up. After a rivalry of

54

unselfishness between the ladies, Mrs Dunsford won and the rest of the party, led by Father Fewling, began the ascent. Mrs Villars came last, partly from politeness as hostess, partly because she secretly was terrified of being locked into the tower and felt that if she kept possession of the key and was nearest the exit she might be safe. Also by being last she could go at her own pace, and as corkscrew staircases made her feel rather red in the face she was glad to go slowly. Above her the voices of the climbers echoed down in the darkness, with Father Fewling's encouraging remarks dominating the confusion. The awkward corner where the belfry door opened from the little landing all askew was safely negotiated and presently a faint light began to shine from above. A lancet window in the wall came into view, debris of nests crackled underfoot, there was another turn in the dark, light shone again and grew stronger and Mrs Villars, blinking, stood upon the lead roof of Northbridge Church, where she had never yet been.

As soon as her eyes had stopped being dazzled she was able to appreciate Mr Greaves's description of the roof. The walls were high and solid, with battlements or machicolations at about five feet from the ground. Below the walls was a lead path about eighteen inches wide with rain-spouts at the corners. The whole of the rest of the roof was, as Mr Greaves had described it, a leaden pyramid which climbers could scale by means of a kind of hen ladder on the side nearest the door. On its peak a weathercock rode high on an iron rod. Three of the angles were crowned with pinnacles and on the fourth was a larger pinnacle with a flagstaff.

Mrs Villars was a fair height, but only by standing on

tiptoe or jumping could she get any idea of the magnificent view which obviously spread in all directions. As for Father Fewling and Mrs Paxon, they might as well have been in prison.

Conversation of a general kind was not easy, as owing to the narrowness of the path the spotters, hemmed in by the battlements on one side and the pyramid on the other, were strung out and cut off from each other, in addition to which a strong gale, which certainly had not been in the churchyard, was blowing on to the tower apparently from every quarter, carrying away even Father Fewling's voice.

'Regular crow's-nest,' shouted Father Fewling to Mrs Villars, with great enjoyment. 'Reminds me of the Horn. Do you know I have been round in a sailing-ship, one of the last men who has, I suppose.'

Mrs Villars, who had an impression, chiefly gathered from old back numbers of the *Boys' Own Paper*, part of her husband's dowry, that no ships ever did go round the Horn except sailing-ships and that they were mostly wrecked, made violent faces of interest and surprise.

'Better get under the lee,' bellowed Father Fewling, 'if there is a lee up here. Come round a bit.'

He shepherded the party to the flagstaff side where there was certainly less wind, and by bunching together rather uncomfortably they could hear his voice when it was not drowned by the tearing noise of St George's banner which was celebrating St Sycorax's Day by winding itself round the flagpole, fighting for breath and with a rip and a roar unwinding itself again.

'Now, Mrs Paxon, will you tell us the scheme,' said Father

Fewling, who was obviously itching to take the whole thing into his own hands.

'I think—' Mrs Paxon began.

Miss Dunsford's mulberry velours blew over the battlements and disappeared.

'It's all right,' said Father Fewling, who with unexpected agility had hoisted himself half-way up the pinnacle and was looking over the edge. 'It has stuck on the big yew. I'll get it for you when we go down.'

'Oh, Father Fewling, you will be giddy,' said Miss Dolly Talbot, anxiously grasping a fold of his fluttering cassock. Then, abashed by having shown her maiden heart, she retreated behind Miss Hopgood's aunt.

Father Fewling jumped down.

'As I see it,' he said, 'we shall need some kind of platform if we are to spot parachutists. Most of us can't see over the edge. I certainly can't. Is there anything of the sort, I wonder.'

Mr Downing, whom everyone had forgotten or ignored, was heard to say that he had once helped the ringers, and there were some tools in the room where the ropes were. On hearing the word ropes, Father Fewling clattered down the stairs as quickly as Sweet William slid down the cords, and was back carrying a couple of wooden stools before Miss Pemberton could do more than blight Miss Talbot's attempt to engage Mr Downing on the subject of campanology.

'Now,' said Father Fewling, mounting one of the stools, 'that is much better. What a glorious view! I can see right over to Bolder's Knob.'

'Not if you are looking south-west, Father,' said Mr Downing in his pleasant scholarly voice.

57

'I'm looking sou'-west all right,' said Father Fewling.

'But Bolder's Knob – a corruption of course of Baldur's Knob or Hill – is due west,' said Mr Downing. 'Gundric's Fossway runs right under it, past Freshdown, which, as you know, is Frey's Down. Let me show you.'

So speaking he mounted the second stool. Miss Pemberton, half resentful of her lodger's sudden independence, half proud of his knowledge, stood up against the stool, blocking the way from Miss Talbot.

'Well, I believe you are right,' said Father Fewling, just stopping himself saying 'By Jove.' 'I ought to have my bearings better. It was that clump of beeches on the hill that confused me. What hill is it, if it isn't Bolder's Knob?'

Mrs Paxon said if he could see the Plumstead water tower in a line with it, then it was Humpback Ridge, but Mrs Turner maintained that it was rather the Great Hump. Miss Crowder said she thought Great Hump was more over towards Nuffield, but bird's-eye-views always made things look different, adding aloud to herself in French, 'Le ciel est padersoo le twah.'

'Ackcherly,' said Betty, 'it's Fish Hill, because it's stone pines, not beeches. I know because I went up there one day with Bill and Martin and those whatsisnames and we saw a golden-crested mippet.'

'A golden-crested mippet!' said Mr Downing, getting off his stool and even pushing past Miss Pemberton in his excitement. 'I didn't know there was one nearer than Lincolnshire.'

Mrs Villars, who began to feel that her party wasn't a success, said if only they could see if the trees were stone pines or beeches that would settle it, and with a flash of inspiration asked Miss Hopgood's aunt if she could see through her telescope. Without a word that redoubtable woman took her telescope from its case and mounted the stool so recently vacated by Mr Downing.

'Can I help you?' asked Father Fewling, his fingers itching for the telescope.

But Miss Hopgood's aunt had already laid the telescope in the most masterly way on the hill and was taking a sight. Father Fewling, who had let many ladies look through telescopes in his time and knew that they could not see anything without screwing up all one side of their faces, was struck dumb with admiration of a woman who could concentrate on one eye and leave the other open, and immediately fell into a professional conversation on telescopes that threatened to have no end.

'Now we have all seen the roof,' said Mrs Villars to Mrs Paxon in a low voice, for to interrupt Father Fewling and Miss Hopgood's aunt would, she felt, have been like brawling in church, 'shall we go down?'

Mrs Paxon who, occupied though she was, noticed that the Rector's wife looked tired, quite agreed, but at that moment steps were heard on the stair, and Major Spender, stifling an oath as he hit his head on the low lintel, stepped out on to the leads.

'Oh, Mrs Villars,' said he as soon as his dazzled eyes could pick out his hostess, 'I am so sorry to trouble you, but Jackson said he thought you were on the tower.'

'So I am,' said Mrs Villars. 'Could I do anything?'

'I am frightfully sorry to interrupt,' said Major Spender looking nervously about him, 'but Mrs Chapman said you hadn't gone up so long ago, or I'd have waited till you came down.'

'I was really just coming,' said Mrs Villars. 'Can I help at all?'

'It seems awfully rude to bother you,' said Major Spender, 'but the boy is waiting and Foster said you mightn't be down till lunchtime, so I thought you wouldn't mind my coming up.'

'I don't, a bit,' said Mrs Villars patiently. 'Is it something you want to see me about?'

After a good deal more apologizing, Major Spender having by now attracted the attention of most of the party, who were huddled near the door looking over each other's shoulders, explained with every maddening circumlocution that nerves could suggest that his wife, who had meant to meet him in town, had wired to say the hotel she usually stayed at had been bombed and could she come to Northbridge for the week-end instead. Corporal Jackson, who knew more about Northbridge than any of the Rectory inhabitants, had supplied the information that every hotel and inn and lodging was booked up to the brim and the only chance was a bed in one of the council cottages in the Plashington Road.

'Not a room in one of them,' said Mrs Paxon from behind Miss Dunsford. 'I went down there trying to billet some fresh evacuees yesterday. I do wish I could take your wife. Perhaps, if she didn't mind the couch in the drawing-room—' said Mrs Paxon, who had determined from the first day of heavy bombing that it was madness for anyone to sleep in comfort in a bed.

Major Spender looked so full of ungrateful gratitude and hopeless misery that Mrs Villars felt she must do something.

'Do ask your wife here,' she said. 'The room that I keep for my sons when they come here is quite free. It is really my youngest boy's room, but there are two beds in it. We shall be delighted to have her.'

Major Spender went bright red, and mumbling profuse thanks hit his head on the lintel again and disappeared down the staircase. Mrs Villars saw that Miss Pemberton was edging towards her lodger and Betty, and suddenly yielding to a slightly malicious inspiration, begged her to lead the way down, alleging quite truthfully that she was terrified of the descent. Torn between her wish to rescue Mr Downing and the appeal to her strength of mind, Miss Pemberton decided to be a benefactress to Mrs Villars, the kind of woman, she felt, with whom if necessary Mr Downing could safely be left, and plunged into the darkness, planting her sensibly shod feet firmly upon each step as she went down. Instead of following her, Mrs Villars stood aside till Mrs Turner and her other niece, the Misses Talbot, Miss Crowder, Miss Dunsford and Mrs Paxon had gone into the staircase door. From where she stood she could see Father Fewling and Miss Hopgood's aunt deep in discussion, while a momentary lull in the wind let her hear from behind the pyramid the words 'early nester' and 'simply won't look at bird sanctuaries'. Pleased with her social successes, she went down.

The Misses Talbot, who were only waiting to say good-bye to her, went off to the Aloes after issuing a cordial invitation to tea. Mrs Turner, asking Mrs Villars to tell Betty when she came down not to forget to go round by Scatcherd's about the dog biscuits as she had her bicycle with her, carried off her other niece. Mrs Dunsford and Miss Hopgood, who had been sitting in a pew discovering common friends in Hampstead, rose and came forward.

'I am sure my daughter has enjoyed her visit to your beautiful tower very much,' said Mrs Dunsford. 'It was so kind of you to let us come. Barbara dear, I think we must be going. But where is your hat?'

'It blew off, Mother,' said Miss Dunsford, suddenly conscious that she was offending St Paul. 'Father Fewling said it had caught in a yew tree. Perhaps I had better just put my scarf over my hair.'

'I think, dear, it would be better,' said Mrs Dunsford, helping her daughter to adjust her head covering. 'No, not like a turban. I don't think that would be *quite*. Just over the hair and tied behind.'

'It is so different in our dear Abroad,' said Miss Hopgood, 'where the peasant women run in and out of the churches so *naturally*, with their beautiful dark hair just knotted up.'

She sighed deeply, to express her feelings. Mrs Dunsford, who during the roving life of a soldier's wife had remained splendidly immune to Abroad, finding an English church wherever she went, smiled graciously and said she and her daughter would go and look for the hat, as they must be getting home to lunch.

'And did you enjoy the roof?' said Miss Hopgood joining Miss Crowder.

'Very much,' said that lady. 'Such a view! I have never been so frappay by a landscape. A little like the view from the back windows of the Pension Ramsden, only, of course, the sea isn't

62

there. Well, good-bye, Mrs Villars, and thank you very much for letting us come. You must come to Glycerine Cottage one day.'

Mrs Villars, who had realized long ago that one of her war duties would be to make friends with many people whom at other times she would have been able without discourtesy to avoid except as acquaintances, said she would love to come.

As the church was now empty of visitors except for Miss Pemberton, who remained to watch the tower door for her lodger's reappearance, Mrs Villars went into the porch where Mrs Paxon was waylaying her spotters and pinning them down to hours of duty. Mrs Dunsford and her daughter were looking vaguely at the yew tree, hoping to see the mulberry velours.

'Well, good-bye,' said Mrs Paxon, 'and thank you most awfully. I'll catch the others later. I have a splendid list already and I am going to beat up some more this afternoon. Mrs Villars, you'll excuse my saying so, but I don't think you ought to spot. You look so tired.'

Mrs Villars realized the genuine kindness of the suggestion and tried hard to keep out of her voice the slight resentment that it had roused (for what is near the truth is often the most annoying), as she answered that she was really looking forward to taking her turn on the roof and felt quite ashamed that she had never been up before.

'Well,' said Mrs Paxon, 'we can't be grateful enough. And I do hope you will come to tea one day. We'll choose a day when my husband's aunts go to Barchester, and have a real chat together.'

Mrs Villars nearly said, 'If you begin one more sentence

with "Well," I shall scream,' but restrained herself and said she would love to come.

A slight sensation of someone hovering which she had for a few moments felt in her right shoulder now resolved itself into Mr Holden, who suddenly materialized in front of her, holding a mulberry coloured hat in a slightly reverent way.

'I hope I'm not being a nuisance,' he said, 'but I was looking out of the office window when you were all on the tower, and I saw a hat blow off the roof on to one of the yew trees, so I rescued it. It isn't yours, is it?'

Mrs Villars smiled and shook her head, round which she had twisted a scarf before going over to the church.

'Of course not, how stupid of me,' said Mr Holden, suddenly holding the hat with a want of reverence as marked as his previous careful handling had been.

'Oh, there is Barbara's hat,' said Mrs Dunsford coming up with her daughter. 'How very kind of you to rescue it.'

She looked with well-bred questioning from Mr Holden to Mrs Villars, who pulled herself together and introduced them.

'Thank you so much, Mr Holden,' said Miss Dunsford removing her scarf and putting on the mulberry velours.

'Thank you, indeed,' said Mrs Dunsford, 'and I do hope you will come to tea one day. Perhaps Mrs Villars would bring you. I should have called before,' said Mrs Dunsford, turning to Mrs Villars, 'but you will excuse the formality in war-time, I know. I will ring you up if I may.'

Mrs Villars thanked her and expressed pleasure in the prospect.

'May I walk back to the Rectory with you; you do look so

tired,' said Mr Holden, who appeared to Mrs Villars to take a real pleasure in her undoubted fatigue.

'Yes, do, it's just lunch-time,' she said prosaically. 'No, I'm really not tired, thank you, but I was wondering if I ought to wait for the others to come down, because of putting the key back in its place. Miss Pemberton is in the church but the others are up on the roof still.'

'Certainly not,' said Mr Holden, and walked into the church, where he found Miss Pemberton sitting bolt upright on a very small chair in the Children's Corner, which was a kind of nursery chapel with cheap and dwarfish furnishings near the foot of the stairs, and one of the Rector's crosses.

'Good morning, Miss Pemberton,' said Mr Holden. 'Mrs Villars is rather tired and I have persuaded her to go home. She wanted me to ask if you would be so very kind as to lock the tower door when the others have come down and replace the key on its nail in the vestry.'

Miss Pemberton, with a sudden vision of locking the door upon Mr Downing and Betty till they both died of starvation, willingly undertook the task, and Mr Holden went away. But reflecting that Father Fewling and Miss Hopgood's aunt, who were not in any way her rivals, would be involved in this doom, she relented and sat more bolt upright than ever. She had not long to wait, for the church bell striking one brought the loiterers back to the world, and almost at once their feet and voices were heard on the stairs. When they were all out Mrs Pemberton locked the door and took the key to the vestry in a silence which had no effect upon three of the party.

'That's lovely then,' Betty was saying to Mr Downing as Miss Pemberton came back. 'We'll do Fish Hill one day and

65

I'll show you where I found the mippet, and we might see the broad-tailed gallowsbird. Do you know, they call him Jack Ketch round here.'

'Lunch will be waiting,' said Miss Pemberton, ignoring Betty altogether.

'And you must come too,' said Betty amiably. 'I'll tell Auntie to ring you up. She's awfully keen on your books. She's had her name down at the libery for ages.'

She sprinted across the churchyard into the Rectory drive, mounted her bicycle and rode off. Miss Pemberton, conscious that Mr Downing had for the moment slipped entirely from her orbit, looked at him and walked away. Her lodger, who had immensely enjoyed his bird-talk with Betty and looked forward to going to tea with her and her delightful aunt, Mrs Turner, tried to speak lightly as if nothing had happened, but against his Egeria's frozen silence his voice died uneasily away. This dread silence she observed all through lunch, which was spaghetti and tomato sauce out of a tin and some very dull biscuits with the very small piece of cheese that was all Mr Scatcherd could produce that week. If Mr Downing spoke while Effie was in the room Miss Pemberton answered, for the forms of society must be kept up before inferiors, so that Effie was able to report to her sister Ruby that the old cat was in a fine wax to-day, but as soon as Effie had left the room she confined her answers to the monosyllable 'Oh,' pronounced with a want of interest that chilled her lodger to the bone. Not till teatime did she relent, when she uttered the noble words, 'We will not discuss this again, Harold,' and spoke of very little else till bedtime.

As for Father Fewling and Miss Hopgood's aunt, they

walked as far as her cottage, The Milky Way, in deep converse and arranged to meet on Tuesday night to look at heavenly bodies from Father Fewling's sitting-room window. Father Fewling walked up the Plashington Road, at the top of which he lodged with Mrs Hicks, Mrs Villars's head housemaid's mother, with an uninterrupted view of the sky, and there ate a biscuit and two bananas before rushing out to a meeting.

Mrs Villars had waited for Mr Holden, who escorted her back to the Rectory. On the way she broke it to him that Major Spender's wife was coming for the week-end and asked if he knew her. Mr Holden, who had already heard almost more than he could bear of Major Spender's agitation over his wife's telegram, said he knew nothing, but had imagined her as like the Major, thin, quiet and sensitive, to which Mrs Villars replied that she could only see her as short and stout and bubbling. At the garden door they separated.

'You will lie down this afternoon, won't you?' he said earnestly.

'But I always do,' said Mrs Villars.

4

Eye-Witness's Account

Hibberd, the Sexton, who before the war had kept the rectory garden in quite good order, had taken full advantage of the joyous state of chaos produced by a national calamity to withdraw himself gradually from his job, though not from his wages. This was not altogether a misfortune, for he was adamant about bedding out and Mrs Villars was now able to call her flower-beds her own, and so long as he stuck to the vegetables she did not much mind. Mrs Chapman was not the woman to tolerate any hanky-panky about her vegetables, and Mrs Villars felt she could safely leave the matter in her hands.

After she had had the rest that bored her so much, read and answered her afternoon post and given her husband his tea, Mrs Villars went into the garden and began to weed, a form of authorized destruction which, she said, made her understand how nice it must be to bomb churches and knock down hospitals. Rain after a dry summer had at last loosened the soil, and the long-legged weeds which a week earlier had apparently been clamped into concrete emplacements now came up with an alacrity that made Mrs Villars sit back on her heels with a jerk. So absorbed was she in her orgy of uprooting that not till a mighty shadow darkened the sun did she realize that her cook was standing beside her.

'What is it, Mrs Chapman?' said Mrs Villars, rubbing a strand of hair off her face with her wrist.

'I'm sure I didn't wish to disturb you, madam,' said Mrs Chapman untruthfully, 'but it's about the late beans.'

This subject, suddenly introduced and reminiscent of a popular play of some years ago, so took Mrs Villars aback that she only stared.

'I was passing the remark to Mr Jackson half an hour ago,' said Mrs Chapman, 'that beans can't come in of themselves, and he was willing to oblige by getting them in for me, because I really didn't know which way to turn. "You may talk about war, Mr Jackson," I said, "but let me tell you that my front is the Rectory kitchen and I can't be in six places at once like a centipede."'

'So what did Jackson say?' said her mistress.

'Well, we had a good laugh, madam. Mr Jackson's quite a Umorist. So then he said he would get the beans. But that Hibberd was in the potting-shed, where he had no business to be on a Saturday afternoon,' said Mrs Chapman with the scorn of a trades unionist for a blackleg, 'and him and Mr Jackson had words, so I thought you'd like to know.'

'I wouldn't particularly,' said Mrs Villars. 'So what happened to the beans?'

'Edie's stringing them now,' said Mrs Chapman, 'and I hope

she'll not slice half her thumbs off the way she did last time. The sight of blood I can't abide. It's in the family.'

'That's all right then,' said Mrs Villars, forking up a fine bit of groundsel with such energy that her cook went away.

From previous experience Mrs Villars knew that the next thing would be a visit from Hibberd, who presently emerged from the kitchen garden and with the unhurried tread of the professional gardener came up the grass walk and stood in silent disapproval of employers and particularly employers' wives.

'Good afternoon, Hibberd,' said Mrs Villars, and as she was by nature a nettle grasper she added, 'Anything wrong?'

Hibberd said, No, not rightly wrong, and for at least six minutes developed this theme with frequent reference to people that came meddling into other people's gardens calling themselves soldiers. He had himself been a soldier, he said, as everyone knew, in the Boer War, and he knew what soldiers were. Some people that had never seen a gun fired might come taking other people's beans and coming the lah-di-dah over them, but he didn't hold with it, and he would like to see some people, he wouldn't demean himself to say who, having to dig old Mrs Tower's grave while the drought was on same as he had.

'If it's about a grave you had better speak to the Rector,' said Mrs Villars with great presence of mind. 'And I want to have the rest of the late beans this weekend. You always have your late beans later than anyone in the village. I don't suppose Jackson has ever seen them so late.'

Although her back was turned to Hibberd she could feel him being mollified, and muttering something about showing these young fellows what beans really were, he retired to the kitchen garden.

Peace fell again. It was astounding, Mrs Villars vaguely thought as she pulled up her enemies, shook the earth from their roots and threw them into her delightful, deep garden basket on three wheels, how much peace there was about in spite of everything. So many people, herself included, were as yet almost untouched, with the world at war all round them. Money, position, husband, children, house, belongings were so far not in any obvious danger. The common load of anxiety was always there, but Mrs Villars felt almost ashamed, though very grateful, when she reflected how often that heaviness was forgotten. So often she woke up happy, so often she had sudden, absurd, causeless attacks of happiness during the day. She could not defend her position and felt that in common decency she ought to be anxious, nervous, and wearing her own body and temper out in doing good deeds that she wasn't at all fit for or interested in, leaving her husband to an undusted Rectory and cheerless meals while she gallivanted in a uniform. For further self-mortification she thought of Mrs Paxon, who not only gallivanted in five or six different uniforms, but cooked her husband's supper every night and was kind to her aunts, and always laughing. At the thought of all the energy of the women of Northbridge, Mrs Villars suddenly felt so tired that she could have lain down on the newly weeded bed and cried, which drove her to the mortifying conclusion that she was only fit to do what she was doing and had better be humble. Time had flown since she came into the garden after tea. The church clock struck seven and Mrs Villars scrambled to her feet and put her gardening things away. Mrs Spender was due at seven-five at Barchester, where her husband had gone over to meet her and her hostess must be ready to receive the slight, sensitive, or alternately the plump, bubbling and, in any case, not very much wanted guest.

Mrs Villars had her bath, noted with annoyance that as usual she had not greased her nails enough before putting on her gardening gloves, and was down by half-past seven. To make conversation easier, she had invited Mr Holden and Mr Greaves to dine with them, and found those gentlemen already in her sitting-room. Foster brought in the sherry and said the Rector sent word he was writing letters in the study and wouldn't come in till dinner was ready.

'How late is the seven-five apt to be?' said Mrs Villars.

'Not very late on Saturdays,' said Mr Greaves. 'Quite a lot of people from the War Office live round Barchester and they don't like to be late at week-ends. And,' said Mr Greaves, who had an encyclopaedic knowledge of trains, 'I heard the whistle from Tidcombe Level Crossing as I was washing my hands and that means the six-fifty-nine up will be out of the way. I should think they'd be here any time now.'

And even as he spoke Foster let in Major and Mrs Spender.

When we say let in, we do not wish to do any injustice to Foster, who was an excellent servant, having been second parlourmaid at Northbridge Manor for some years, and was particularly good at announcing people. But Mrs Spender, who had a maddening desire to save people trouble, charged in unannounced, followed by Major Spender, who was experiencing the peculiar sinking of the spirits that always overcame him when his wife, whom he loved and admired greatly, turned up.

'You are really a guardian angel,' said Mrs Spender, shaking hands with Mrs Villars. 'I simply didn't know *what* to do, I mean Ockley's Hotel where I always go and all the staff are devoted to me and the manager almost a personal friend if you know what I mean who has known us all for years was blown up practically under my eyes. Luckily, I had parked the old suitcase at Waterloo – and, my dear, *what* a mess there, I mean simply seething – and when I got to Ockley's it simply wasn't there. Not to be seen, believe me. It was a time-bomb, I mean they all got out in time and there were no casualties, but as for the hotel, where was it, I ask you. So I said, "Not for you, my girl," and went to my club and sent a wire to Bobbie over the 'phone. How the telegram got delivered I cannot tell said she in a resigned voice, for one knows what telegrams are now, but I didn't know your telephone number so there it was. However Bobbie for once showed a little sense, the dear old stupid, and sent a wire to the telephone number of my club where, by the grace of God, I was near the desk when the call came through and heard our porter who is such a *pet*, getting into difficulties, so I made a bolt into his little cubbyhole and said, "Give it me, Peters, it's the Major," and that was that. So I got a taxi and sped to Waterloo where my suitcase was quite all right, no thanks to little Adolf with three alerts, *three*, my dear, between lunch and tea, and here I am. Of course Bobbie, like a dear old chump, had to go to the wrong platform, but my porter, a *perfect* gentleman believe it or not said there was an officer on No. 3 platform, so we went to look and now all's well that ends well and I am really *too* grateful.'

During this speech Mrs Villars had had ample time to wonder how the Rector, who had known too many parents to suffer fools gladly, would take it. Once and once only she had let her eye wander to Mr Holden's, expressing what she hoped looked like humorous despair; but meeting in his not the conspiratorial amusement she had expected, but rather a kind of anxious solicitude, wondered if she had gone too far. But there were other and more pressing duties than guessing at Mr Holden's emotions, so she asked her new guest if she knew Mr Holden and Mr Greaves.

Mrs Spender said she was always so glad to meet any of Bobbie's babies, as she always called his subalterns, a remark which Mr Greaves treasured for later use.

'And now let me take you to your room,' said Mrs Villars.

'No, I shan't keep you waiting one *moment* longer,' said Mrs Spender. 'I washed and all that in the train, and in a war time and tide wait for no man, and for no woman either, though I say it that shouldn't.'

'Just as you like,' said Mrs Villars, 'but my husband isn't here yet, so if you'd care to tidy – not that you need it in the least – the parlourmaid will take your things up.'

Mrs Spender, with a loud protest against anyone carrying her luggage in war-time, hurried to the door, where Foster was disapproving of the whole situation, and snatched at her suitcase. But Foster, who was very strong, twisted it deftly from her grasp and saying in an icy voice, 'This way, madam,' led the way upstairs.

'I shan't be more than two little minutes,' Mrs Spender called over her shoulder. 'If you want to be quite angelic have a tinty-winty sherry ready for me when I come down. Bobbie is such a dear old clumsy he always forgets.'

Good manners forbade the immediate discussion of Mrs

Spender, especially in front of her husband. Mr Greaves, whose kind nature was moved to pity by the sight of his Major's depression, plied him with sherry, which left Mr Holden free to approach Mrs Villars.

'I couldn't have believed it,' said Mrs Villars. 'I expect she is really very nice indeed and perhaps a little nervous. People are often funny if they are shy, at least I know I am.'

Mr Holden thought of saying, 'You are never funny,' but rejected it, and so quick is thought that Mrs Villars noticed no gap before he said:

'How long is she staying?'

'Only till Monday, I think,' said Mrs Villars, 'but I expect to be dead before then, so I shan't know.'

'I wish I could help you,' said Mr Holden in a fierce, concentrated sort of way.

Then Mrs Spender came back, and accepted the sherry that Mr Greaves had poured for her in a liberal spirit, disregarding her instructions of tinty-winty.

'Don't let me keep you one moment longer,' she said. 'I'll take my glass in with me, for I know you must all be starving.'

'Please, don't hurry,' said Mrs Villars. 'My husband hasn't come in yet and he so wants to meet you.'

While she was speaking the Rector had entered and was able to study the new arrival for a moment without being seen. He saw a stoutish woman of about forty, not so tall as his wife. She was dressed in an olive-green ready-made suit, known as a three-piece, and had wine-coloured shoes, bag and jumper. Unfortunately, the green and unbecoming felt hat which was secured at the back of the head by a wine-coloured petersham bow, and the wine-coloured gloves to tone had been left upstairs, but this made Mrs Spender's crowning glory of hair all the more apparent. Dark auburn and set in hard waves, it was parted in the middle, dressed low and done in a simple knot at the back. Her dark twinkling eyes showed terrifying vitality. Her colour was high, her large, rather hard, mouth showed a set of magnificent teeth whenever she spoke, which was more often than not, and she had very ugly hands, whose fingers managed to be at the same time coarse and tapered.

'Oh, here is my husband,' said Mrs Villars. 'Gregory, this is Mrs Spender.'

'You have been so good to Bobbie,' said Mrs Spender, giving the Rector's hand a hearty pressure, 'and I really can't thank you enough for having me here. I can't tell you what a time I had in London, I mean you would hardly believe that an hotel could simply not be there. When my taxi stopped I looked out of the window and saw simply *nothing*. What I always say is that it isn't so much the destruction of a house that upsets one as what *isn't* destroyed. I meant the hotel not being there left me, believe it or not, absolutely cold, but when I saw an armchair standing simply on *nothing* half-way up, it makes one realize. So I said this is no place for you, my girl, and went to Waterloo where I had left my suitcase, and it was absolutely a welter, if you know what I mean, but my porter was terrifically sweet and I surged into a carriage and got here almost on time. Of course poor Bobbie, who is really the world's greatest idiot, poor lamb, said she quite in an aside, was on the wrong platform but my porter, who was really rather a pet, found him for me and here I am really simply one mass of gratitude.'

Foster, who had been waiting, and so Mr Greaves afterwards maintained holding her breath all the time, now announced dinner, and Mrs Villars who, as did the gentlemen, found Mrs Spender's habit of speaking a kind of stage directions about herself, prefaced by the words 'Said she,' rather perplexing, led the company into the dining-room.

'Let me see,' said Mrs Spender to the Rector when they had taken their places, 'you were—'

'Just one moment,' said the Rector. 'Benedictus benedicat. Did those letters go by the evening post, Foster?'

Foster said Mr Jackson had taken them himself to the post-office.

'You were saying—' said the Rector, turning to Mrs Spender.

'You were Headmaster of Coppin's School, weren't you?' said Mrs Spender. 'That's what Bobbie wrote to me, but if the dear old pussycat *can* get anything wrong, he does.'

The Rector said that Major Spender was quite accurate in his statement.

'Then I expect you knew my uncle, Fred Brown,' said Mrs Spender.

The Rector said he had no recollection of the name.

'I am sure you couldn't forget him,' said Mrs Spender. 'Besides everyone in Yorkshire knew him.'

The Rector said he had never lived in Yorkshire.

'But you must have,' said Mrs Spender. 'Coppin's is in Yorkshire, isn't it?'

The Rector said Somerset.

'Of *course*. It was Harberton Grammar I was thinking of,' said Mrs Spender. 'We all get like that in the war and I always

77

say one must fight it. I expect Bobbie told you our boys are down for Coppin's. No, I couldn't drink any wine, thank you, not after all that sherry, or really only half a glass. Do you get Empire wine?'

'No,' said the Rector.

'I know people look down on it,' said Mrs Spender, 'but Bobbie's wine merchant, who is really the dearest old thing and practically mad now, I mean the difficulty of getting wine from abroad, though what I always say is, why not bring it in *barrels* because they don't break like glass, says if you don't think of it as *wine* it is quite delicious; just as a *drink* if you see what I mean.'

Mr Greaves threw out the remark that it was a jolly good thing there wasn't Empire beer too, or we'd have to drink that, and was backed by Mr Holden, but their efforts to distract Mrs Spender were in vain.

'Now I do hope,' said the lady, 'that you haven't made this marvellous dinner just for me. I'm really not used to such luxury in war-time. I could tell you some terrifically economical dishes, Mrs Villars. There is one that is a great favourite with us at home, in fact, we call it Daddy's Own, don't we Bobbums,' she said addressing her husband. 'You take anything that is left over and push it through the mincer with some onion and flavouring and warm it up with some gravy and put it into a pie-dish and put some left-over potato on the top, mashed of course, and just a few dabs of marge, and pop it all in the oven.'

Mr Holden said, 'Shepherd's Pie' in a low voice to Mrs Villars, who replied, almost without moving her lips, 'But not a nice one.'

With a great effort Mrs Villars then led the conversation, willingly seconded by Messrs Greaves and Holden, to the roof-spotting plan. The Rector, who saw a trying week-end ahead and was annoyed that his wife should be worn out, as she doubtless would be, by her new guest, also exerted himself and talk became general, which it would not have been had not the Rector suddenly become deaf in the ear next to Mrs Spender, till dessert, when that lady took advantage of a temporary lull to say that she supposed they would soon be hearing the siren, to which the Rector replied that Northbridge had so far been very lucky and only had one alarm, quite near the beginning of the war.

'Touch wood, touch wood,' cried Mrs Spender, 'not that I am superstitious if you know what I mean but you never know, and I knew a man who was a terrible pet and was killed just because he *would* go out when the raids were on.'

'You weren't here, I think, Spender, when the siren began and couldn't be stopped,' said the Rector. 'It sounded for ten minutes till they got a man who understood the working.'

'No, sir,' said Major Spender, cheering up a little at being brought into the conversation. 'But there was that day when we got the general alarm from Barchester and ours was the only siren that wouldn't go off.'

'And what happened?' said Mr Holden, to keep things going.

'We got Jackson to look at it,' said the Major. 'He is a pretty good electrician. But it was really a bit of a bird's-nest in the works.'

'Some people,' said Mrs Spender, 'don't like the siren, but I must say I'm funny that way if you know what I mean.

When I hear it I get so worked up that I could do absolutely *anything*. When I was doing A.R.P. near our home one of our wardens, you know who I mean, Bobbie, Mr Tupper, a perfect pet of an old darling,' she added to the uninitiated, 'so sweet with his little white beard and moustache, was on duty with me one night and the siren went off, but *right* under our noses, my dears, believe it or not, and Mr Tupper was most terrifically kind and offered me plugs to put in my ears, but I don't know how it is I'm just funny about plugs, and I simply shouted at the top of my voice, because, of course, he had his plugs in already and I said, "I *like* to hear the siren, Mr Tupper. I suppose I'm peculiar but when I hear the siren I could simply take a sword and *fight*." And he couldn't hear it stands to reason with plugs in his ears, but he nodded and smiled so sweetly. I do think people are quite marvellous, Mr Villars, don't you?'

Mr Villars said for what they had just received might the Lord make them truly thankful, and his wife got up.

'I'm afraid I must say good night, Mrs Spender,' said the Rector very meanly, 'as I have a good deal of work to do. I wish you a very pleasant sleep. Holden, I leave these gentlemen in your care.'

He opened the door for the ladies. As his wife went out he looked at her with a kind of affectionate apology that she perfectly understood. She had not kept parents off him for many years for nothing and she knew that it was her business to keep Mrs Spender at bay for the next twenty-four hours till her husband had got through what is not a day of rest for the clergy.

Mr Holden and Mr Greaves, left with Major Spender,

nearly went mad owing to the impossibility of discussing that gentleman's wife, but much to their relief he showed symptoms of restiveness at an early stage, so they all went to Mrs Villars's sitting-room, where Mrs Spender was telling her hostess about her children.

'I say, Bobbie,' she said as her husband came in, 'I didn't tell you what Billy said to Nurse last week. I was just telling Mrs Villars, but I know you won't mind hearing it again, will you. I mean Billy is really priceless for only six, isn't he, Bobbie? He's just the sort of boy that a school would give anything to get if you know what I mean.'

She then related a pointless and slightly unpleasant anecdote about her younger son, which her audience were sycophantic enough to applaud.

'Good heavens!' cried Mrs Spender, 'ten minutes to nine! I *must* hear the news.'

She looked wildly about.

'I am so sorry,' said Mrs Villars, 'but Gregory and I don't like the wireless, so we lent it to the officers' mess. I have a little portable that I use just for concerts sometimes and I could easily bring it down from my room if you like.'

'Lord! no, my dear woman,' said Mrs Spender with great good nature. 'Bobbie will show me where the officers are and I shall just hear the news and be back with you before you know I've gone. That announcer I always like so much is speaking tonight. I can't remember his name, but he is such a lamb with a voice that somehow reminds me of a bed of violas,' said she romantically, 'so soft and velvety if you know what I mean.'

While she was thus expressing her views on announcers,

Mr Holden, speaking out of the side of his mouth, requested Mr Greaves as a personal favour to see that old Passmore kept Mrs Spender and her husband down in the mess as long as possible, or he would not be responsible for his actions. Mr Greaves grinned and followed the Spenders from the room. When they had gone Mrs Villars got up and began to tidy cushions and empty ashtrays into the fire. When she picked up the third ashtray Mr Holden took it out of her hand.

'Thank you,' said Mrs Villars, and sat down on the sofa.

'You were going to drop it,' said Mr Holden accusingly.

Mrs Villars shook her head.

'Believe it or not, if you know what I mean, you *were*,' said Mr Holden emphatically. 'You will now rest on the sofa till that she-devil comes back and I shall read *Blackwood*, which is so soothing because it is the one thing unchanged in a world of change, and not say a word. Mr Villars will be quite furious when he sees what that bouncing Blowsabel has done to you,' said Mr Holden angrily, 'and I don't blame him.'

He picked up *Blackwood*, that respectable periodical which the Rector had been meaning to give up ever since he took over an unexpired yearly subscription at his father's death twenty years previously, and sat down by the lamp. As the light was behind him he could look across at Mrs Villars from time to time without appearing to intrude, and was glad to see her sitting back, relaxed, among the cushions. The silence was unbroken except for the church bell, which chimed nine o'clock, a quarter-past, half-past, and a quarter-to-ten. Just as he began to wonder if he could persuade Mrs Villars to go to bed, a noise like the murder of Becket was heard on the stairs, and Mrs Spender surged back into the room accompanied by the Rector, her husband, and Mr Greaves.

'I am afraid you will think me too terribly unconventional,' she said to her hostess, 'but we had such a marvellous talk on the wireless that I had to stay; my dear a simply thrilling account by the third mate of a cargo steamer of a voyage from England to some place he wasn't allowed to mention. And believe you me they were at sea for sixty days and never saw a single submarine. It does make one feel proud of being British, I mean the *courage* of doing a thing like that, said she going all patriotic, and such a terribly sweet Cockney accent. And on the way back Mr Greaves saw a light in the Rector's study and thought we might go in and the Rector was most terribly kind and said I ought to go to bed, because it has been a very long day and seeing Ockley's Hotel just *gone* like that, simply gone, but *fantastic* I mean. So I know you'll forgive me if I just pop quietly off to bed and take Bobbie along with me, as we've heaps to discuss and I dare say we shall talk all night.'

Good nights expressive of the highest esteem and a wish for long and restful sleep were showered upon them from all sides.

'Breakfast is at nine,' said Mrs Villars, 'and I'll have yours sent up to you, Mrs Spender. If you feel like coming to church I shall be here about a quarter-to-eleven and so glad if you will come with me.'

'I'm not what you would call a regular church-goer,' said Mrs Spender, apparently settling herself, to the horror of her hearers, for a good long talk, 'but I always say there is Something if you know what I mean that goes deeper than merely going to church. When I saw the hotel this morning, well when I say saw, of course there was nothing, I mean *nothing*, that sort of thing makes one think. Of course, we know that everything is sort of ordered for the best, but of course we can't take it in and I always say that is where Faith comes in. I'm funny that way, I suppose, but I always say I have a deeply religious feeling and when I saw the hotel simply not there, I mean literally, I could have killed someone.'

With this clear and concise apologia, Mrs Spender said good night to everyone and went away, carrying her husband with her.

'You have all saved my life,' said Mrs Villars gratefully to the men.

'It was really Holden,' said Mr Greaves. 'He told me to get old Passmore on to Mrs Spender and the old man came up to scratch and had her talking away like anything.'

'I am extremely grateful to you, Mr Greaves,' said the Rector, 'for coming into the study; and for winking at me,' he added to Mr Greaves's mingled confusion and delight. 'I haven't dealt with parents for twenty years for nothing and this gave me the chance to persuade her to go to bed.'

'Thanks awfully, sir,' said the gratified Mr Greaves. 'By Jove, Mrs Spender can talk. Good night, Mrs Villars, and thanks most awfully for the party. Good night, sir. Coming, Holden?'

'In a second,' said Mr Holden. 'Greaves and I did our best,' he continued, addressing his host and hostess, 'but if the Rector hadn't helped we could never have got Mrs Spender to bed. Good night, Mrs Villars.'

'Good night, Mr Holden, and thank you for being very kind,' said Mrs Villars, holding out her hand.

Mr Holden much wished that he had foreign blood in

his veins as he could then, he felt, have kissed her hand respectfully, but the habit of a lifetime and the possibility that Mr Greaves was lingering outside the door stood in his way, so he shook hands and followed his brother-subaltern.

'Oh, Gregory, you have saved my life,' said Mrs Villars. 'Can we ever live till Monday? Thank goodness to-morrow's Sunday and you are pretty safe.'

'She can't get into the pulpit – at least I don't think she can,' said the Rector cautiously. 'But I know what will happen. I shall find myself saying Here beginneth the First Lesson believe it or not.'

'Well, I am going to bed, if you know what I mean,' said Mrs Villars, laughing and yawning. 'Don't be too late going to bed, Gregory. You have to be up early to-morrow.'

5

Social Evening

Next morning, being Sunday, Mrs Villars who did not go to early service, partly because she didn't want to, partly because she knew it afforded such ardent spirits as Mrs Paxon and Miss Hopgood so much pleasure to feel that the Rector had got up early for them alone, had her breakfast peacefully in bed at eight o'clock and, as was her custom on Sundays, wrote to her two sons. She then got up and by ten o'clock was dressed for church, meaning to go to her sitting-room and polish off some more letters till it was time for her to start.

As she came out of her bedroom she nearly bumped into Mrs Spender, who was carrying a tray of breakfast things.

'Here you see me, bright and early, doing my little bit,' said Mrs Spender.

'Oh, please don't,' said her hostess, trying to take the tray. 'The housemaid will come for it.'

But Mrs Spender clutched her war work tightly, saying that she knew she was giving a lot of extra trouble and simply

86

must do something to help. Mrs Villars said it was very kind of her, and begged her to put the tray on an oak chest that stood on the landing, which, much to her relief, Mrs Spender did, tilting the tray as she set it down at an angle that quite terrified Mrs Villars. A long trickle of tea ran out of the spout of the teapot on to the linen tray-mat, an orange rolled into the little dish of marmalade and a spoon leapt off the tray, crashed on to the oak chest and fell down behind it.

'Oh, dear, they haven't given you any butter,' said Mrs Villars. 'I am so sorry. It is too stupid for we have plenty.'

Mrs Spender said that nice housemaid had brought her a quite gigantic helping but she had told her to take it down again.

'I would never dream of using other people's rations in war-time,' said Mrs Spender. 'I always take mine with me, even if it's only for a night and then I feel I'm doing my bit if you see what I mean. I must show you my little arrangements,' she said, leading her unwilling hostess towards her bedroom. 'When rationing came in I said to myself, "Now, my girl, this needs *thought*." So this is what I did. I took some little boxes, I always keep boxes because you never know what will come in handy, and we have three each for butter, sugar and tea. It saves such a lot of trouble.'

She then led Mrs Villars, who had an intense dislike of people's bedrooms between the moment the occupants had got up and the moment at which the housemaids had made everything tidy, into the room where she and her husband had spent the night. Everything was very untidy. Mrs Villars wished she felt more tolerant. Mrs Spender pointed proudly to the dressing-table. Various articles of toilet lay about on it, including brushes from which Mrs Villars averted her fastidious eyes and then blamed herself again. Scented face powder was liberally scattered on the white embroidered cloth, some unappetising bits of cotton wool littered the stand of the mirror and the air reeked of the scent of nail polish. Among these rites of civilization were the three boxes of which Mrs Spender had spoken. An ex-cough-lozenge tin, its lid open, showed about half an ounce of tea. A round cardboard box whose lid lay on a pair of stockings nearby, contained six lumps of sugar whose curious pinkish colour was attributable to the remains of face powder that clung to it. Near these was a round box made of what one can only call chemists' alabaster, labelled THE OINTMENT. *To be used as directed upon the irritated surface.* This Mrs Spender proudly opened and showed her fascinated hostess a small lump of butter from which her breakfast portion had evidently been taken.

'There!' said Mrs Spender. 'And I don't mind telling you if everyone did that it would save a lot of bother. When General Binder came to stay with us, he wouldn't go till I gave him three boxes for himself. I often say to people, I really don't know what you mean by talking about rationing, for believe it or not, we have ample. Ample, I say. It is all a question of management and I may tell you I have a pretty good head for managing, or Bobbie and I could never have managed in those early days. My uncle who is in the Service always said he would rather leave things to me than anyone. As for the servants of course they are hopeless, my dear, absolutely hopeless. Of course we are going to win, of that I am as convinced as I stand here, but I often say what servants need is a dose of friend Adolf, not that I say it seriously if you know what I mean but really, to see the way they go on makes me quite Bolshie. I suppose I'm funny like that,' said Mrs Spender, folding up an odd pair of stockings as she spoke, 'you must just see these stockings my aunt in Cheltenham sent them to me, at least this one, for they are not quite a match, and believe you me, I haven't an idea where the others are, I mean the ones that are the other half of each pair if you follow me unless they are in my hat-box, but I simply cannot bear waste, said she coming over all patriotic again, simply *cannot*.'

Mrs Villars, glancing like a drowning man at her watch, said it was after half-past ten and they ought to be thinking of church, and so escaped for a short rest to her sitting-room. Much to her relief, Mrs Spender did not talk in church, and to her hostess's surprise and pleasure, came out with a very pure, true singing voice. After the service Mrs Villars took Mrs Spender back through the garden, and seeing Hibberd pottering vengefully about the border she had weeded the day before, deserted her guest, who in ten minutes had reduced Hibberd's spirits to zero by her display of gardening knowledge. Not that he believed her, but as he never found an opening to reply to any of her suggestions or criticisms, they had to go unchallenged.

In the hall Mrs Villars met Major Spender, told him where his wife was, and escaped to her own room, where she locked herself in till lunch was ready.

Of the rest of the day she subsequently had but a fevered memory. Such of the officers as were in to lunch exerted themselves manfully, these being their instructions from Mr Holden, to keep Mrs Spender amused, and after lunch she announced that she was going to take her husband for a long tramp, saying no one must mind if they weren't back for tea as the daylight was too precious to lose. So Mrs Villars went and lay down, her husband went to sleep in the study while his curate, an uninteresting man called Harker, took the children's service, and the officers scattered to the various houses where they had made friends. Corporal Jackson came to tea in the kitchen, where he made himself so agreeable to Mrs Chapman and the staff that Edie, overcome by his wit, choked and was severely reprimanded, but told the under housemaid when she came in from her afternoon off that she wouldn't have missed it for the world and Mr Jackson was ever so nice.

Fortune further bestowed her favours on Mrs Villars by arranging for Major and Mrs Spender to come in by the back door as she went out to evening service by the garden door. Not that it was usual for guests to use the back door, and Major Spender was as miserable and ashamed as Mrs Chapman was scandalized and outraged, but Mrs Spender, who loved poking about in quaint corners, her phrase not ours, was perfectly happy and insisted upon going straight to the officers' mess to hear the news. Here she lingered so long among her fascinated audience that Mrs Villars was able to slip upstairs to her room after church and stay there till dinner-time.

It was Mrs Villars's habit to have people to Sunday dinner, for she refused to call it supper on the grounds that it made one think of blancmange with a tough skin and took one's appetite away. As her husband was ready to be gently amused after his Sunday work, she usually asked friends who would put him into a good temper and talk easily and quietly. This week-end, greatly daring, she had asked Miss Pemberton and Mr Downing, who to her great surprise had accepted. This, she fully realized, meant that Miss Pemberton considered her as out of the running for Mr Downing, and as she had no feelings about that gentleman one way or the other, she was quite undisturbed. She had also invited Mrs Turner, with her other niece, and when she found a telephone message to say that Mrs Turner was so sorry her younger niece was in bed with a cold but might she bring Miss Betty instead and would Mrs Villars not trouble to answer unless it was inconvenient, she merely thought one niece was as good as another, for she had not realized the passions let loose on the roof of the church tower on Saturday morning. To balance Mrs Turner and Betty she invited Colonel Passmore and Mr Dutton, whose turn it was. She would have liked to ask Mr Holden, but he had dined with them on the night before and she did not like to have more than eight on Sunday evenings.

After the events of the previous twenty-four hours, Mrs Villars was not in the least surprised to see Mrs Spender appear for dinner in a royal blue tea-gown with a divided skirt, which emphasized the contour of her firmly moulded lower limbs. Mrs Spender apologized for her toilette. Her father, she said, who was in the Service, made them all change for dinner every night at home, but in war-time one didn't feel it was quite the thing, so she always slipped into slacks, and then if anything happened, there you were.

'But your hostess-gown is simply marvellous,' she said generously.

Mrs Villars, who was wearing a two-year-old cocktail frock, winced inside herself, blamed herself, and turned to greet Miss

Pemberton and Mr Downing. Miss Pemberton, who was robed in what was apparently sacking of a rich russet tint and a sensible length for walking, and wore several amber necklaces, eyed Mrs Spender malevolently. Colonel Passmore and Mr Dutton followed hard upon, and introductions were made. Sherry and a confusion of talk filled the next two minutes, and then they went in to dinner.

When arranging her table Mrs Villars had wondered if Miss Pemberton would insist on having Mr Downing beside her, so she did the best she could by putting him between herself and Mrs Turner, with Betty on the opposite side of the table. Her conscience was pricking her slightly over her behaviour on the tower the day before, and though it had been fun to manoeuvre Miss Pemberton away from her lodger, she had an uneasy feeling that she had been wantonly unkind, so she put Miss Pemberton between her husband and Major Spender.

As Colonel Passmore was the senior guest in point of ranks, Mrs Villars turned her attention to him and discussed with great interest the question of Christmas leave. She had hoped, though without any particular grounds, that most of the officers would go home, but Colonel Passmore was not encouraging. He pointed out that days would be short, trains full, everyone travelling, weather probably bad, and ended by saying with a certain gloomy satisfaction that any leave that was given would probably be cancelled.

'Invasion?' said Mrs Villars, and at once had a lesson against idle talk, for Mrs Spender, right away in the opposite corner, not finding so much amusement in Mr Dutton as he found in her, had let her attention wander from her partner and at once picked up the conversation.

'Of course, all this is absolutely hush-hush,' she said, 'but I don't suppose our little friend with the moustache is under the table or here in disguise, besides it was all in the *Weekly Messenger* last Sunday. We had the invasion a few weeks ago, but no one knew, except the Navy. My cousin who is in the Service says we were never so near danger since 1066.'

'Which Service?' asked Mr Dutton.

As Mrs Villars had several times wondered the same thing herself and come to the conclusion that Mrs Spender was sprung from a line of admirals, or generals, or perhaps diplomats, but had not liked to ask, she listened with interest.

'Mixo-Lydian,' said Mrs Spender shortly to Mr Dutton, of whom she had no opinion at all, and before anyone could ask for further details she continued, 'Believe it or not, for it sounds too *fantastic*, my dears, if you know what I mean, but the Germans had absolutely millions of boats with no bottoms. I mean they were flat underneath, not spiky, and they filled them, simply *filled* them, my dears, with these poor boys who had never left home before and didn't even know where the sea was. Of course I'm funny that way, but what I say is boys will be boys. My cousin who is in the Service said the sea was like a millpond and all the boats coming across till they were quite near the coast, and then what should appear but one of our warships, but of course I mustn't say which, and she steamed round and round among the boats, simply round and round I ask you and made such a wash that all these poor boys, for really they were no better, were so sick they didn't know what to do and all the boats were swamped. Their officers set them all on fire to try to save them, but not a single one escaped and the shore was one mess of remains next day,

I mean too ghastly for words, practically unrecognizable if you see what I mean. And to this day little Adolf hasn't an idea, I mean not an *idea* what happened.'

Mrs Spender's hearers were so stunned by this epic that no one spoke for a moment. Then Mr Villars, at her other side, said:

'I beg your pardon, but did you say your cousin was a Mixo-Lydian?'

'Oh, no!' said Mrs Spender, 'I am thankful to say. Mixo-Lydian *consul*, and such a lamb, isn't he, Bobbie? One of those people, you know,' she continued, taking the whole table into her confidence, 'that seem awfully gruff and disagreeable, but have hearts of gold, I sometimes joke him about it and tell him he is quite an old bear and he just grunts at me but really, I mean inside you know, I know he would do anything for me.'

The Rector said there were a number of Mixo-Lydian refugees over at Southbridge.

'Oh, but George has nothing to do with refugees,' said Mrs Spender. 'He is simply *consul*. My father, Daddy we always used to call him, was consul before he died, and my uncle, I mean really my mother's uncle if you know what I mean was consul too. It is really all in the family as I might say, though don't ask me why.'

Mr Dutton, who was in private life a young don of the left-intellectual-wing, plumed himself on pinning people down to facts by the Socratic method; by which he meant that he enjoyed asking questions in an unpleasant voice of people who were not familiar with the name or the methods of dialectics and then sneering at their answers. So he simply said 'Why?'

Mrs Spender, good naturedly, said it was such a long story if he saw what she meant. To this Mr Dutton, with the devastating irony for which he was famous in his own circles, said, 'Not exactly,' which, being overheard by Colonel Passmore, confirmed him in a decision which had been simmering for some time to send Mr Dutton back to the depot on the first possible opportunity. And this, we may say, he did within a few weeks, to the satisfaction of the whole mess and of Mr and Mrs Villars. But Mr Dutton, unheeding of his pending doom, was served right by Mrs Spender relating to him, with every divagation that her fancy suggested, the whole history of the connection of her family with Mixo-Lydia from the year 1848, when her mother's uncle had inadvertently helped in a Mixo-Lydian rising and thus acquired the eternal gratitude and honorary consulship of that odious nation, to cousin George, the gruff and disagreeable, who was the present holder of that hereditary office.

Mr Villars was, to his great relief, thus set free to talk to Miss Pemberton who, being truly and unselfishly zealous for the greater glory of her lodger, asked Mr Villars if he would feel like doing a little notice of Mr Downing's Anthology of Provençal Lyrics for the *Journal of the English Word-Lovers' Association*, of which she was secretary.

Mr Villars said he was afraid his knowledge of Provençal literature was too slight to be able to do justice to Mr Downing's book.

'That doesn't matter,' said Miss Pemberton firmly. 'Any scholar of general culture can treat the subject as literature in the broader sense. Of course, Merriman is the obvious man for Provençal stuff, but he has had his knife into Mr Downing ever since Mr Downing reviewed his *Cultural Influence of the Court of King René*. Then I did think of Professor Gawky, but ever since her so-called historical novel, which I don't suppose you troubled to glance at, *Gaily the Troubadour*, I have felt that she could only be classed as a journalist.'

Mr Villars said he must, to his shame, confess that he had read the book in question, though partly, he must say in self-exculpation, because the library sent it by mistake on a Saturday and it lay about the house all the week-end. Was it not, he said, about the Vidame des Egouts who made his wife eat her lover's heart?

'There you hit the exact spot,' said Miss Pemberton. 'Professor Gawky speaks of a heart, but the merest tyro knows that it was her lover's liver and lungs that he served at dinner. To speak of a heart entirely destroys the imagery of the whole story. Women dons! I have no patience with them.'

Mr Villars said he had none either, and they had a perfectly delightful time together running down all forms of organized education for women, during which Miss Pemberton became quite human and even forgot to keep an eye on Mr Downing. It is true that seeing him safely sandwiched between Mrs Turner and Mrs Villars she did not feel any great anxiety and could reserve her energies for defending him against Betty in the drawing-room. But had she known what was taking place in Mr Downing's scholarly soul, she would not have been so calm.

Mr Downing and Mrs Turner at first touched upon birds, about whom Mrs Turner frankly said that she knew little and cared less and would really not mind if she never saw another one again, adding that Betty was the authority and

Mr Downing must have a good talk to her after dinner. But in spite of these sentiments Mr Downing felt that a woman who knew her own mind as thoroughly and unaffectedly as Mrs Turner and could look so charming while she spoke it, was more than a reward for having to come out to Sunday supper with a slightly sulky Egeria. What was curious was that in spite of her avowed dislike for birds she was not unlike one herself; a motherly yet youngish thrush with bright sideway glances, or a very charming, wise, benevolent owl, in the highest sense of the word, dressed in comfortable warm feathers, with no pretensions of any kind; or so Mr Downing chose to think. It then transpired that Mrs Turner's mother and Mr Downing's mother had been at the same school, and though neither of the mothers had ever mentioned the other and indeed had barely overlapped, the fact was felt to constitute a very definite link.

'Betty says you are going to Fish Hill with her one day,' said Mrs Turner. 'You must come back to tea with us and perhaps Miss Pemberton would come too. I have plenty of petrol left and could easily fetch her and take you both back.'

'That is so kind of you,' said Mr Downing, 'and I am sure Miss Pemberton would be delighted. Would you perhaps speak to her about it after dinner, because it might come better from you?'

Mrs Turner, who felt it certainly would, promised to approach Miss Pemberton. And after that they fell into the nicest kind of easy talk, not going very deep and laughing about quite foolish things and Mrs Turner never once remembered that she had spoken of Mr Downing as a highbrow.

As for Betty, she was never at a loss and prattled away to Major Spender and Colonel Passmore about anything that interested her, so that dinner passed away smoothly enough till dessert, when Mrs Spender, a little annoyed by Mr Dutton's lofty attitude towards air-raids, raised her voice in a way that didn't give any other conversation much chance, explaining that no one who had not seen Ockley's Hotel could begin to understand what bombing meant and giving in full her experiences in London on the previous day. Mr and Mrs Villars, who had already heard it all twice at great length, suffered in silence and found on comparing notes afterwards that each had been mentally calculating the exact number of hours that Mrs Spender was likely to remain with them and had thankfully decided that it would not be more than fifteen at the very most, at least nine of which would, they hoped, be spent in her bedroom.

'We have been extraordinarily lucky down here,' said Mrs Turner with a general view to pacification. 'I sometimes feel quite wicked when I see my house safe and sound and sleep in my own bed, but it is very nice all the same.'

'Touch wood,' said Colonel Passmore, whom no one had suspected of such a weakness, 'we have been very lucky indeed and I hope it will go on.'

Betty said that Haw-Haw had said on the wahless the other night that he was only sparing Northbridge because he had good friends there. Ackcherly, she added, she thought there were fifth columnists in Northbridge but wild oxen wouldn't drag it from her who they were. It then transpired that everyone knew exactly who Haw-Haw was. To all Northbridge people it was an article of faith that he was a cousin of a communist ex-M.P. who had amassed a fortune almost simultaneously with having to give up his seat and bought a Tudor house in West Barsetshire; or alternatively, belonging to a family well known in East Barsetshire, and had shown for some years markedly fascist and pro-German views that had caused him to go to Germany not long before the beginning of the war and never be heard of again. Colonel Passmore knew from a legal friend now on important and secret Government work that the fellow was in Russian pay; Mrs Spender said darkly that good ould Southern Oireland was never far away when there was a spot of trouble; and Mr Dutton put the seal on his unpopularity and on his own fate by saying that he for his part would not judge a man, or men, if he was to take as true all he had just heard, who could not answer for himself. As for Major Spender, that depressed officer saw no reason to add his voice to the rest, so he held his tongue and drank his port.

'I'll tell you what we do at home,' said Mrs Spender. 'Nurse and I have a camp-bed and the kiddies have mattresses. We bring them down to the dining-room every night because it has three inside walls and a good strong chimney and I have always noticed that chimneys stand a lot of tough treatment. At Ockley's, believe it or not, the chimneys were as good as new the whole way up, six storeys I think it is, or do I mean seven, well anyway six at least while the rest of the building was absolutely wiped out, I mean it simply didn't exist. I sleep along the wall and the kiddies put their mattresses under the dining-room table and simply adore it. I must tell you what Clarissa said, she's only three and a bit, my dears, but as cunning as a cartload of monkeys. I mean you can't say anything she doesn't pick up. Nurse and I have many a good laugh over her quaint sayings though I say it that shouldn't. It was something too funny, but simply too funny about going to bed under the table. You remember, Bobbie. But Bobbie is such a fuzzy old rabbit he forgets everything. And of course *heaps* of tinned food in the room and a gas-ring to boil milk or anything and an oilstove in case the gas is blown up, and the window *tight* shut against gas, and Nurse puts a piece of paper in the keyhole and we have the greatest fun. If only we had Daddy at home it would be perfect, but we have to remember there's a war on.'

Most of her hearers were by now bursting with questions which civility forbade them to ask, but Betty who had few inhibitions said if it was her she'd put the children near the chimney if that was the safest, and anyway it wasn't any good doing anything about gas because they changed it all the time and if a room was really gas-proof you couldn't breathe at all, and how many raids had Mrs Spender had.

'Oh, none,' said Mrs Spender. 'It is extraordinarily quiet near us because we are right out on the edge of the moors and the aerodrome was moved just before the beginning of the war. I suppose I'm funny about things, but I do say one ought to do one's best about air-raids because after all we're in the same boat if you see what I mean.'

Her voice was then drowned by the rising tide of people saying what they did in preparation for air-raids. Miss Pemberton, it appeared, kept the manuscript of any book she was working on in an American oilcloth bag by her bed and left her bath water in the bath. Mr Downing also confessed to keeping his work close at hand together with one or two books, a grey woollen cardigan, and an alpenstock, to which he was much attached. Mrs Turner and Betty, who were on duty three nights a week for A.R.P. at the Council Rooms, considered this sufficient protection, and beyond having a few pails of sand and water about did nothing at all. Mrs Villars confessed that she put clean underclothes, all her silk stockings and her spare spectacles into a little suitcase every night and had recently added her passport, though she didn't really think it would be much use. Mr Villars, on being pressed, said he packed his old false teeth and the Bible, and then felt he would have done better to put it the other way round.

As soon as the ladies had gone Colonel Passmore moved into Miss Pemberton's place to be able the more fully to discuss with his host the fascinating question of false teeth. They were quickly joined by Mr Downing, so that Major Spender and Mr Dutton were left in a despised minority and had to talk about form MOX/PMMG/12-75-XXX, which was giving them a good deal of trouble in the office.

'I always have such difficulty in keeping mine in,' said Mr Downing plaintively. 'I believe I have a very difficult mouth to fit,' he added with some pride. 'They are all right for six months or so and then quite suddenly, without any warning, they seem to get much too big and I hear them clashing about like cymbals in my mouth. And one can't go on having new ones for ever; it is so expensive. Besides my London man has moved to Chichester and though I believe young Fillgrave at Barchester is very good, I am used to my own man and have shirked doing anything about my uppers.'

Colonel Passmore said his trouble was just the opposite.

His dentist, he said, had told him that his mouth was the best mouth for fitting he had ever come across and had not only taken a cast of it as a permanent record, but had written an article, with photographic illustrations, for the *Monthly Odontologist*, in which his jaw, under the thinly veiled pseudonym of Colonel H. W. P.'s, was extolled as unique and the dentists' *beau idéal*. His only trouble, he said, was that when he had put his teeth in it was practically impossible to get them out, and on one or two occasions he had had to go to his dentist and have his uppers forcibly extracted.

'I'll tell you what you ought to do, Passmore,' said Mr Villars earnestly. 'Take a deep breath, shut your mouth, and blow. You will find that loosens practically any plate.'

'Not mine,' said Colonel Passmore with sad pride. 'Benton told me I would have difficulty, and by Jove, I have.'

'Do *you* go to Benton?' asked Mr Villars eagerly. 'He's a first-rate man. And so kind.'

This remarkable coincidence occupied Colonel Passmore and his host for several minutes. When they paused Mr Downing said his one fear in the case of a bomb exploding near him was that all his teeth would fly out into the street, or, less mortifying but equally disastrous, rush down his throat and choke him.

'You needn't worry about choking,' said Mr Villars. 'I happened to express a fear of swallowing mine to Benton, soon after he had made me my first set, but he pooh-poohed the idea and assured me that my throat could not expand to more than the circumference of a half-penny.'

'Then tell me this,' said Mr Downing. 'Why do they take one's teeth away from one if one has an operation?'

Mr Villars said it might be just to prevent themselves getting bitten by mistake, but his real worry was that the Air-Raid Instructions were not explicit enough. You were told that if you heard bombs you must put a piece of rubber between your teeth, lie down on your stomach and clasp your hands lightly behind your head. This, he said, would be fatal to anyone with a complete set. Not only would holding the rubber between your front teeth entirely upset the balance, as anyone who had tried to bite an apple with false teeth knew to his cost, but to lie on your face with your hands behind your neck was simply asking your teeth to fall out, let alone being blasted out.

'I had thought of that, too,' said Mr Downing, 'as of course it specially affects me. But now they say you must also raise your chest off the ground or the vibration of the explosion will break your ribs. It seems to me that what you miss one way you are bound to get the other.'

So interesting was the point raised that had it not been for the presence of Mr Dutton, all three gentlemen would have been on the floor giving demonstrations of the practical difficulties of the methods recommended and would have invited Major Spender to join them, though in fairness it must be said that such teeth as the Major had were all his own.

So regretfully, Mr Villars led his men to the drawing-room.

Here all was peaceful. Mrs Turner who was good nature itself had taken on Mrs Spender and was listening placidly to her account of her journey from her home to London, and from London, after the sad disappointment of finding Ockley's Hotel simply not there, to Barchester, a journey beside which the ascent of Mount Everest was but child's play. Miss Pemberton, with great cunning, had attached herself to Betty, against whom she had no particular feeling where Mr Downing was not concerned, and was discussing cheap and nourishing dishes for the Communal Kitchen with her, for Miss Pemberton was no mean cook and had lived for some years with rather poor French relations when she was young. Mrs Villars was thus left a little out of it, which she found restful, but when the men came in and Mr Downing came and sat by her she was quite pleased to see him. Groups reformed and there was some talk, but most of the party had work to do on Monday and no one minded when at about ten o'clock Mrs Spender said to Mrs Villars that she was really most terribly sorry but she had to be off absolutely at cock-crow next morning and a little voice told her that she ought to go to bed.

Mrs Villars, who had naturally been longing to know the blessed moment which would release her from her guest, expressed her regrets and asked what time she would like to be called.

'Seven if it isn't too frightfully troublesome,' said Mrs Spender. 'Bobbie is going to drive me to Barchester to get the eight-thirty. And if I could just have a cup of tea and a little bit of toast and not give any trouble that would be perfect. I always think guests are *such* a nuisance. When we have people to stay with us, Bobbie and I dance, literally *dance*, my dear, with joy when they have gone, don't we, Bobbums?'

Mrs Villars said it would be no trouble and there would be breakfast for Major and Mrs Spender at half-past seven, either downstairs or in their room, whichever they liked.

'Oh, well, if it isn't giving a perfectly frightful amount of trouble we'll come down,' said Mrs Spender. 'Or if it's a bother we'll have a tray upstairs, only not a *cooked* breakfast if you know what I mean just a cup of tea really and nothing else. But I expect your housemaid is terribly busy on Monday morning, so much always to do, don't I know it, my dear, said she being a good housewife, so perhaps in the dining-room would really be best. Unless, of course, it's a *trouble*.'

Mrs Villars, with perfect patience, said breakfast would be ready at half-past seven and she would be down to say good-bye, which called from Mrs Spender such a shower of protests that she wished she hadn't spoken.

'Well, I'll say good-bye,' said Mrs Spender, surveying the company. 'Good-bye, Mrs Turner; goodbye, Miss Turner; good-bye, Miss Pemberton; good-bye, Mr Downing. I have so enjoyed our talks, Colonel Passmore. I always feel so at home in an officers' mess, if you know what I mean. Good-bye, Mr Villars, and thank you quite terribly for being so kind, and church and everything which I always say does one so much good even if one isn't absolutely in tune, if you know what I mean, but you can always reverence, even if you don't see eye to eye, and after all in these times it is so nice to know the Church is *there*, said she suddenly coming quite religious, though really that is not the word I mean. I shan't say good-bye to you, Mrs Villars, if you really insist on coming down to-morrow, though I'm sure it's a frightful trouble, but if it isn't of course I shall simply love it. Come along, Bobbie.'

Bearing her husband along with her she left the room, pausing however on the threshold to say with cold politeness, as if she had but just become aware of his existence, 'Oh good-bye, Mr Dutton.'

Mr Dutton tried to carry it off, but his commanding officer said he had better see if those P.L.T. files were ready for to-morrow, so he went back to the officers' quarters, despising everyone.

His exile and the departure of the Spenders sent everyone's spirits up so much that the party took a fresh lease of life and stayed on, discussing in a purely academic way the three guests who had just left them.

'Gosh! she called me Miss Turner,' said Betty, scornfully. 'I thought everyone knew I was Auntie's niece. I never even saw Uncle Turner. Ackcherly I couldn't have, could I, Auntie?'

Mrs Turner, who although she lived on terms of great equality and frankness with her nieces, had a feeling for her late husband that had kept her from telling them that he spent the last months of his life in a home for inebriates, did not answer this question directly, and Betty, who had put it rhetorically rather than from any wish to know, did not press it. Miss Pemberton, having kept her lodger well under her eyes all evening, made no objection when Betty suggested the following week-end for the excursion to Fish Hill, followed by tea at The Hollies, and when Mrs Turner said in that case Miss Pemberton must come too, that lady accepted with a good grace. After some further talk, Mrs Turner said she and Betty must really be getting home. Miss Pemberton said she and Mr Downing would go as far as The Hollies with them and the Villarses went into the hall to help the guests to find their clothes, for in spite of more than a year of war the black-out was not perfect, and Mrs Villars found it safer to have a dark shade over the light.

'It's queer,' said Mrs Turner, 'how last year's black-out doesn't seem to last. Mine was perfect last winter, but when the days began to draw in I found there were lots of chinks. I have really spent almost as much on getting it right as I did last winter when it began.'

Miss Pemberton said she had found that a piece of good thick black material, but one had to pay a good price for it now, hanging by rings from little cup-hooks right against the window was the best. Curtains were all very well, but one's old ones were never thick enough and one needed two or three pairs, whereas with the black stuff stretched tightly over the window and well hooked along the top and along the sides, and coining at least six inches below the bottom of the window, even the servants found it difficult to leave a light showing.

'That is the difficulty, of course,' said Mrs Turner, who was standing on one leg like a stork while she put on a galosh. 'Servants, I mean. If only they didn't think that we had invented the black-out just to have a chance of jumping on them. Still it's war-time and the better we black out the safer we are.'

'Did I hear a bump?' said Miss Pemberton.

Mrs Villars said it might be Annie, the second housemaid, whose footfall was celebrated for its sturdy qualities and had more than once brought the Rector out of his study when she was turning the beds down at night to see if it was an air-raid.

Mr Villars opened the hall door a little way, to prevent any ray of light shining out, and stood by it to speed his guests.

'What's that?' said Betty.

<pre>
                    ? !
                  * * ?
ee-ee-EE-EE-OW-OW ? * * !   OW-OW-EE-EE-
                  * ? !
</pre>

said the siren.

Mr Villars, with great courage, shut the hall door.

The siren repeated its unpleasant remark eight or nine times and sank into its grave with a moan. Colonel Passmore went quietly to the officers' quarters.

'Gosh!' said Betty. 'It's our night for the A.R.P. post. Come on, Auntie, if we don't get there first that awful Dolly Talbot will bag the camp-bed with the extra mattress. Oh Lord, I never brought a net and I had my hair set on Saturday. Well, there it is. Got your torch?'

Mrs Turner routed about in her coat pocket and produced it.

'Oh dear, the battery has run down,' she said.

Mrs Villars offered to lend hers, if Foster had remembered to put it back because she had lent it to her on Friday to go down to the post late. Miss Pemberton said she had hers and would see Mrs Turner and Betty as far as the post, she meant the A.R.P. not the post, and from a bag with bands of Central European embroidery produced a torch the size of a blunderbuss.

'It's more practical to have the big size,' she said. 'They say the small batteries won't be obtainable this winter. Are you ready, Harold? Put your scarf well round your neck; there are probably German planes about.'

Mr Downing took this wise precaution and the party were

just slinking out of the door when a voice from the staircase said:

'And to-night of course, I ask you! They simply *follow* me, my dears. First Ockley's, now here. Where is your refuge, Mrs Villars?'

Everyone looked up. The form of Mrs Spender in a pink, quilted dressing-gown and a pink boudoir cap, followed by her husband, still in uniform, was seen descending the stairs.

'Well, we haven't exactly got one,' said Mrs Villars, 'I mean,' she added, unconsciously adopting her guest's form of speech, 'there *is* a cellar, but it always had a foot of water in the winter and the door only opens from the outside, so no one can get out. But you will catch cold. Come into the study.'

'Come on, Auntie,' urged Betty, opening the front door again. Mrs Turner and her niece slipped into the darkness.

'Are you coming, Miss Pemberton?' said Betty's voice.

'No, thanks,' said Miss Pemberton, who suddenly visualized the possible reactions of a dark night and an air-raid upon Mrs Turner's niece and Mr Downing.

An intermittent hum sounded high in the sky. Miss Pemberton shut the door.

'That's Jerry,' said Mrs Spender.

'Speaking as a layman,' said Miss Pemberton, who disapproved of what she called loose thinking, 'I do not pretend to distinguish one aeroplane from another. I dare say you have special knowledge.'

'Everyone knows,' said Mrs Spender, coming down into the hall, 'that Jerry says, Barum, bar*um*, bar*um*, and ours have one steady roar.'

'Why the German planes should recite Lorraine, Lorree,' said Miss Pemberton, 'is beyond me.'

Mrs Villars, rather wishing that Miss Pemberton had gone back with Mrs Turner, led the way into the study, where a good fire was burning.

'You see,' said Mrs Spender throwing open her dressing-gown, to the great terror of Mr Downing, 'I am always prepared. I keep my siren suit hanging at the foot of my bed and my cosy boots beside me, so all I have to do is to leap out of bed, slip into the siren, pop my feet into my boots, and there I am all ready for the fray. When I tell you that Nurse and I and the kiddies can all be dressed in two minutes from the moment the alarm has sounded – Bobbie! the gas-masks!'

'Oh, I don't think you'll need them to-night,' said Mrs Villars soothingly.

'It's not needing them, so much as the example, if you see what I mean,' said Mrs Spender. 'I mean if everyone carried their masks all the time think of the effect. I hung mine on the handle of the wardrobe, a thing I *never* do, but of course it would happen, just the one night I was unprepared.'

Major Spender said he would go and get it.

'No, dear,' said Mrs Spender. 'Now you are down you had better stay down. No sense in taking risks.'

'I'll get it if you like,' said Mrs Villars. 'I did want a clean handkerchief. I must have forgotten to put one in my bag.'

'If you are sure it is all right,' said Mrs Spender doubtfully. 'I heard bombs then. Bobbie, let's *both* go up. I want you to carry some things for me.'

'Not bombs,' said Miss Pemberton, ignoring the Spenders' departure. 'That was the guns from the other side of

Barchester. They have a peculiar sound, which it is impossible to mistake; ker-*bomp* ker-*bomp*.'

'Ker-blinkety-blunk,' said Mrs Villars aloud to herself, and meeting Mr Downing's eye, smiled.

'I didn't think there was anyone left who knew Uncle Remus,' she said.

Mr Villars said he did not wish to disagree with Miss Pemberton, but the noise sounded to him more like *Umble-bumble-bumble*, in which case it was undoubtedly the rolling mills at Hogglestock, which often, and the more especially when the wind was in a certain quarter, made a sound which might easily be confused with guns.

Mrs Villars said if only it would do it again she could hear better what it said, upon which it obliged with considerable violence, making the loose windowpane in the study rattle slightly.

'Of course there is no doubt at all,' said Mr Downing. 'I remember that noise at Antwerp in 1914. One couldn't possibly mistake it for any other, so plainly did it say – I cannot exactly imitate it, but rather like the lions when they gobbled up Count Hogginarmo.'

'Wurra-wurra-wurra,' said Mrs Villars sympathetically.

'Exactly,' said Mr Downing, gratified in his turn to find his literary allusion so quickly taken. 'Naval guns.'

Mr Villars then remembered that Hibberd had told him that they did say there was a naval gun on a car that went at incredible speed up and down the country.

'Naval gun?' said Mrs Spender, reappearing with her gas-mask slung round her neck and a rug over her arm. 'They put them on a trolley and rush them about on the railway lines.

Put them there, Bobbie,' she said, pointing to a large arm-chair near the fire. Her husband, who had followed her into the room staggering under eiderdowns and carrying a small suitcase, did as he was told. 'If they took them about in cars they would sink right into the road. You see me, quite an old campaigner, Mrs Villars. I make myself cosy in a twinkling. I suppose I'm funny that way, but what I say is, Be comfortable while you can, if you see what I mean. To be uncomfortable is just playing into the Nazis' hands – they are *out* to make us uncomfortable, but I say to myself, Now, my girl, you are fighting on the home front. Now I just wrap the rug round my legs and sit down quietly. The eiderdown over my shoulders, Bobbie, please. And my suitcase here. Has anyone a cigarette? Oh, thanks most awfully, Mr Villars, you are a saint, though you mayn't like the word.'

A long rolling grumble culminating in a dull heavy thud made the loose pane rattle again.

'That was quite close to,' said Mrs Spender. 'Would you like me to go and see if the servants are down?'

Mrs Villars thanked her very much and said she was afraid they never heard anything.

'Well, if anything does happen, I've everything there,' said Mrs Spender, slapping her suitcase. 'Brandy, though I'm not a brandy drinker, if you know what I mean, but one always ought to have it handy; ear-plugs, if anyone wants any, they've hardly been used at all; some chocolate, some cards – now don't be shocked, Mr Villars, but the kiddies and I play rummy nearly every evening in our shelter – I suppose I'm funny about cards, but I say teach children the facts of life *young* and they are all right.'

'Then I suppose your children will never want to play cards again,' said Miss Pemberton, a little snappishly.

'And my little first-aid outfit,' Mrs Spender went on, 'and some concentrated meat tablets and writing materials and, though you may not think it, my knitting. You may have noticed that I haven't knitted while I was here, but I have nearly finished the foot, so I said to myself, Now, my girl, keep it till you really want it, and believe it or not, when we heard the siren I said to Bobbie, zero-hour for knitting. I'm like that, you know, I must have my hands occupied.'

She began to work with practised speed upon a sea-boot stocking about three feet long, fifteen inches in circumference and as thick as a blanket, with a fine smell of natural fat which it wafted about the room.

Mr and Mrs Villars wanted quite desperately to go to bed, but didn't like to leave their guests, so they sat there, trying to keep conversation alive, till another and yet more shattering noise apparently came down the chimney, bumbled round the house and came to rest in the garden.

'Well, if that's the way they are going on, I'm going home,' said Miss Pemberton. 'I shall certainly not let my cottage be blown up while I am out. Put your scarf well round you, Harold, and we will go back and have some Horlick's and finish correcting your proofs.'

'I suppose I'm different from other people,' said Mrs Spender, knitting so hard that with her boudoir cap and eiderdown she made Mrs Villars think of Alice's sheep, 'but I say Ovaltine every time, and Bobbie is *too* funny, what do you think *he* likes?'

'Whisky-and-soda,' said Miss Pemberton, cutting Mrs

Spender short. 'Don't come to the door, Mr Villars, you don't know what might be outside. I know the way. Harold!'

Mr Downing, who was trying with Mr Villars to remember the name of a very bad dentist they both had gone to at Oxford, and who had afterwards murdered his wife while on a holiday in Devonshire, gave a guilty start and followed his Egeria.

'Funny Miss Pemberton saying that,' said Mrs Spender, her fingers twinkling faster than ever, 'because it isn't whisky-and-soda, but they say great minds meet, and what Bobbums really likes for his nightcap is a tinty-winty brandy with some hot water and sugar, or honey does if you know what I mean.'

The laws of hospitality then made Mr Villars get out the brandy and Mrs Villars go to the kitchen, which she was much relieved to find warm, dark and empty and not too many blackbeetles about, and get a small black kettle which she put on the study fire. Glasses and spoons were provided and the unhappy Major Spender, whom brandy always made rather sick, was forced to superintend the making of a jorum in which the Rector said he would join.

'I am so sorry,' he said to Mrs Villars, waylaying her at the door as she came back for the third time with the sugar, 'and I do hope it isn't a bother. I don't really like brandy a bit, but my wife thinks I ought to, and I do like to give her pleasure.'

'Perhaps she would have some,' said Mrs Villars, putting the sugar on the tray.

'I am sure she would,' said the Major. 'You know, Mrs Villars, she really is quite wonderful. When Billy had his appendix she was splendid and when Jimmy had his double mastoid she was with him day and night for ages. And I'll never forget how she nursed me when I had my tonsils in nineteen-twenty-five, and as for Clarissa's leg, when she fell out of the pram at Felixstowe and broke it, she was past all words. You have no idea what a woman she is, Mrs Villars. She has never been in bed a single night when there was a raid on and keeps so bright and helpful all the time.'

Mrs Villars felt that Major Spender once launched on his wife's perfections might go on for ever, and in desperation begged her guests to excuse her if she went to bed.

'Do go, Mrs Villars, you look quite worn out,' said Mrs Spender. 'I shall stay here quite snug and cosy till the All Clear goes and then I'll tiptoe upstairs like a mouse and just pop into your bedroom and let you know you can sleep in safety. I never let raids worry me.'

'Our doctor,' said Mr Villars, coming to his wife's help, 'says Verena ought never to be disturbed between midnight and eight o'clock, as it might upset her seriously; but thank you so much all the same.'

'I quite understand,' said Mrs Spender, who made up her mind from that moment that Mrs Villars was subject to fits. 'I don't know how it is, but I'm funny in that way, I mean psychic things. I understand people's feelings so much more quickly than most, if you see what I mean. Sympathy. So of *course* I won't disturb you, only just open the door a tinty-winty to see if all is well, said she quite the hospital nurse. So don't worry.'

Mrs Villars said something suitable and escaped. Her husband followed her shortly and found her sitting in front of her mirror staring at herself.

'We'll never have any officer's wife here again, whatever

their extremity,' he said. 'I ought to have put my foot down. Go to bed.'

'I am sorry, but I am too tired to go to bed,' said Mrs Villars, articulating each word with extreme clarity.

Her husband told her in the kindest possible way not to be silly and to undress and get into bed at once. He then went back to the study and mixed a strong hot drink, which he carried upstairs, not caring if the Spenders thought he was a secret drinker.

'Drink it up,' he said, standing over his wife.

'I couldn't,' she said. 'Besides, Mrs Spender is coming in to tell me when the raid is over, so I might just as well stay awake.'

Her husband, though he could not bear to see her so worn out, was quite firm. She drank her brandy, which she really enjoyed, and lay down obediently.

'Don't worry,' said the Rector. 'I promise you that woman will not come near you. And you are not to come down till she has gone. I forbid it. Now go to sleep.'

'Well, if you promise, it is all right,' said Mrs Villars gratefully, and already looking more at peace. 'You really do save my life, Gregory.'

'That's what I am here for,' said Mr Villars. 'Besides, you have been saving mine for years, so it is but fair. Good night.'

He went to his own room, but did not go to bed. He lighted the gas-fire and read a thriller. At about half-past one the All Clear signal blasted the night and woke up a great many people who had not heard the original Alert. Mr Villars went to his door and listened, but all was quiet in his wife's room. In a few moments the Spenders appeared, tiptoeing upstairs like mice, as Mrs Spender had promised, but mice that were so burdened under rugs, wraps, gas-masks and suitcases that they rather resembled living pantechnicon vans.

Before Mrs Spender could open her mouth Mr Villars put his finger on his lips in such a very terrifying way that Mrs Spender went straight to her room, where she told her husband that it was like the Murder of Becket or being Excommunicated, and she couldn't help feeling sorry for that nice Mrs Villars, if he saw what she meant. But Major Spender was already asleep, or pretending to be, so hard that his wife believed it.

Mr Villars said his prayers, with a special petition to be helped not to hate people that overtired his wife, and went to bed.

6

The Two Nations

The Spenders duly had their breakfast at half-past seven, after which Mrs Spender gave mortal offence to Foster by insisting upon clearing the plates and tea-cups onto the sideboard. Mr Villars very skilfully cut them off as they came out of the dining-room, said he had used his authority to keep his wife in bed after their disturbed night, and had his guests out of the house before Mrs Villars was even awake.

When her breakfast was brought up at half-past eight she was still half asleep and only recovered her wits when she had drunk some coffee, after which her husband looked in to tell her his engagements for the day and ask how she was. His wife said she was quite well, but would infallibly have died if he had not saved her life last night.

'I shall save it again and again,' said Mr Villars, 'but if you could see your way to being a little sensible sometimes, it would make my path easier. Need you really have invited an unknown officer's wife for a week-end?'

'Not so much an unknown officer's wife as the unknown wife of an officer,' said Mrs Villars thoughtfully, 'if you see what I mean.'

'Prig,' said her husband affectionately.

'After all, Gregory,' said Mrs Villars, 'you brought me up by hand as a schoolmaster's wife and I exercise hospitality without thinking. But I will really change my manner of life and become a curmudgeon, for it is hard on you to have your Sundays devastated: they are bad enough anyway.'

Mr Villars said he was used to working on Sundays, but he could not stand his wife being devastated. So with great affection they separated, he to his work, she to hers.

It was as well that Mrs Villars had spent a peaceful night, for the kitchen and the telephone were seething. The kitchen was divided between resentment at Mrs Spender's gross breach of etiquette in coming in by the back door and trying to help the servants and admiration of the large tip she had left on the dressing-table, tinged, for such is the kitchen code, with contempt for the giver. Edie, flushed with strong tea and the bacon which Mrs Chapman mysteriously managed to get every week through Corporal Jackson, went so far as to stigmatize Mrs Spender as a Nosey Parker, and was severely taken to task by the head housemaid, who said Mrs Spender was a reel lady and if she was a bit of trouble getting her room in a fine mix-up, she knew how a lady ought to behave and there was many who wouldn't give five shillings, let alone ten, which was what Mrs Spender had left. This led to a very interesting discussion of the billeted officers with estimates of their characters founded on the kitchen's personal experiences and Corporal Jackson's *obiter dicta*, and the reader will be glad to learn that while Colonel Passmore and Captain Topham tied for first place and Mr Greaves was thought very favourably of, Mr Dutton was unanimously voted to be a mean sort of fellow and no gentleman.

At this juncture Corporal Jackson looked in and was offered a cup of tea by Mrs Chapman, which he accepted, saying he didn't mind if he did.

'And what did you ladies think,' said Corporal Jackson, pulling up a chair at the end of the table next to Edie, who at once began to giggle, 'of the eerial activity last night?'

'The Milk did say something about some of them German aeroplanes,' said Mrs Chapman, 'but I don't hold with them. I went to sleep with a good conscience, same as I usually do, and when once I go off the Keeser himself marching into my room wouldn't make me so much as wink,' said Mrs Chapman, who appeared to confuse this war with a former one. 'Mother always said I was one for sleeping. Those that have something to keep them awake, let them, but unless it's something like wondering if the meat will go off in the summer, I don't see no call to stay awake.'

'Mr Hibberd said his cottage shook somethink awful,' said Edie.

'That's enough, Edie,' said Mrs Chapman.

'And what were you talking to Hibberd for?' said Foster, who as a head indoor servant was opposed to any courtesy titles for the outdoor staff. But Mrs Chapman, whose peculiar slave Edie was, though she might bully in private backed up her dependant in public and said, quite untruly, that Edie was asking Mr Hibberd about the last cooking apples at her special request. At the same time she threw on

120

Edie a glance full of such pantomimic warnings that Edie, who knew Mrs Chapman was not speaking the truth and could not understand what her faces meant, bolted her tea and fled to the scullery, where she could be heard clanking her pail.

Before Mrs Chapman and Foster could join battle the postman came with the delightful news that bombs had fallen on Barchester aerodrome and made a hole as big as the Cathedral and killed eighteen men. Everyone's spirits were raised to the highest pitch, only to be dashed by the Man About the Blocked Pipe, whose cousin was a ground mechanic at the aerodrome and had rung up his wife that morning about his washing and said they were all fine and he heard Northbridge High Street was in ruins.

'It's all this propaganda,' said Mrs Chapman, rising. 'If it isn't one lie it's another. How do we know there's any such place as Germany? The papers'll say anything.'

Foster said we got it on the wireless, to which Mrs Chapman retorted that she had something better to do than listen to the wireless, and in her young days there was no such thing and her mother had lived to be ninety, and clanked all the tea-things together. At this signal the party dispersed and Corporal Jackson went out by the yard, where he managed to linger till Edie came to empty her pail.

Mrs Villars was rung up by several friends who had all had enemy aircraft directly over their houses but were in entire disagreement as to where the bombs, if any, had fallen. The last to ring up was Miss Crowder, with a pressing invitation to come to tea at Glycerine Cottage during the week. After refusing with an unnecessary amount of explanation for

Monday and Tuesday, Mrs Villars found herself unable to think of any reason for not going on Wednesday beyond the excellent one that she did not much want to go, so she accepted with enthusiasm, hung up the receiver, called herself a coward and went out to do her shopping.

In the lane she found Mr Holden, who asked if she had been worried by the noise in the night.

'Not so much as we were by Mrs Spender,' she said. 'She came down in a siren suit and instructed us about air-raids.'

Mr Holden said he had nearly come to ask if he could do anything, but hadn't wanted to be a bother, so Mrs Villars thanked him very much and said her husband had very obligingly saved her life by sending her to bed and she had never heard the All Clear.

'You didn't miss much,' said Mr Holden. 'I happened to be awake because I was reading and it nearly threw me out of bed, but rather confusing because some alarms were going off in the distance and one really wonders which means what.'

'That must have been Nutfield, right over the other side of Barchester,' said Mrs Villars. 'They get their alarm from Portbury, which is right off our beat. We get the Barchester alarm, so sometimes we have Danger while Nutfield has Raiders Passed, and sometimes it's the other way round. And the other sirens round here take sides, so one never really knows where one is.'

'Rum place, Northbridge,' said Mr Holden thoughtfully.

Mrs Villars said it was, but she expected there were a great many places just as rum at present and she was very fond of it, though she hadn't lived there long.

'So am I,' said Mr Holden, 'very fond.' And he went away into the Bank.

Scatcherd's Stores, Est: 1824, was very full when Mrs Villars went in, for as usual she had put off her shopping till rather too late. There were queues of five or six people before each assistant, so Mrs Villars patiently took her place at the tail of one of them, hoping that she would not see many friends, for she was tired in spite of her life being saved. The customers seemed to her to take longer than usual over their orders. Further up the counter intelligent, alert women handed in neatly written orders together with their ration-books, said 'On account, please,' and walked away. But in her queue the shoppers were dispirited and had lists they couldn't read on dirty bits of paper and had forgotten their ration-books, or insisted on having an order made up of seventeen half-pounds of different groceries given to them on the spot because Cook wanted them for lunch and Mrs Villars thought her turn would never come. Presently a basket began to stick into her and hurt a good deal, so she turned round and saw Miss Pemberton's well-known mushroom hat and olive-green serge mantle.

'Sorry if my basket is in your way,' said Miss Pemberton, 'but everyone behind me is squeezing so.'

She said this in a determined bass voice which in better days had the power of quelling all within its range, but the squeezers, being mostly well-to-do refugees in sham astrakhan jackets, trousers, and high-heeled shoes, lit cigarettes and didn't pay the faintest attention.

'I hope you and Mr Downing got back all right last night,' said Mrs Villars.

'Very comfortably,' said Miss Pemberton. 'I couldn't have stood that Mrs Spender much longer. Besides, I didn't like the idea of my house being alone in a raid.'

Mrs Villars, surprised at this sudden touch of humanity in Miss Pemberton, said 'Of course not.'

'Some like dogs, some like cats,' said Miss Pemberton. 'I don't. And how people who pretend they do can be brutal enough to drag their unfortunate dogs about in shops to be kicked and trodden on, I don't know,' said Miss Pemberton, casting one of her most malign glances on a stout, golden-haired, middle-aged woman in sham ocelot and grey slacks, whose Great Dane was smelling the coats of all the shoppers and twisting his lead round their legs. 'The R.S.P.C.A. ought to come down on them.'

The stout blonde said to her Great Dane that he was Mother's petkins and not to listen to nasty people.

'Go on,' said Miss Pemberton, giving Mrs Villars a friendly push, 'it's your turn.'

Mrs Villars, whose attention had been absorbed by the skirmish, looked up, saw a gap at the counter and moved forward. But the middle-aged blonde was too quick and pushed in before her.

'Excuse me, I was here first, I think,' said Mrs Villars, appealing to the girl behind the counter, and conscious that her voice sounded as horrid as if she were someone else.

'Couldn't say I'm shore,' said the girl, examining her blood-red finger-nails fringed with black, and abstracting herself altogether from mundane affairs.

'One can't be expected to wait for people all day: there's a war on, though some people don't seem to know it,' said the blonde, and opening a notebook began to read aloud an interminable order, each item of which the girl went to look for separately, usually returning from a lengthy absence to report that there wasn't any.

Mrs Villars felt guilty and miserable. She had only asked to have her fair turn and before she knew where she was she was being practically accused of want of patriotism. Realizing that she had no weapon at all against her conqueror she swallowed her anger and waited another ten minutes while the blonde smoked a cheap cigarette. At last the parcels were collected, the blonde shoved her way out and Mrs Villars could give her order. The girl took it down with obvious disdain, and when Mrs Villars gave her name and address said, 'The Rookery, was it?'

'No, Rectory,' said the Rector's wife.

'I thought you said Rookery,' said the girl. 'Lot of queer names we get. Ow, I know what you mean. Near the church, isn't it?'

The Rector's wife said it was.

'Wait for me,' said Miss Pemberton, and before long the two ladies were free of the grocery counter.

'And can we do anything more for you this morning, madam?' said Mr Scatcherd, the elderly proprietor, who was going round the shop keeping an eye on things.

'Well, you could but I'm not going to wait,' said Miss Pemberton. 'People shoving and pushing, the girls as rude as they can be. I don't wonder people send to London for their things.'

'I assure you, madam,' said Mr Scatcherd, his lean grey face puckering as if he were going to cry, 'that I wouldn't blame you. Here are we, making more money than we have made since great-grandfather started the stores, and I declare to you, I would be glad to be making only half the amount and have things as they were. All this rabble, if you'll excuse the word, ladies, coming down from London and behaving the way I hardly know if my shop's my own. Harpies they are, if you take me,' said Mr Scatcherd, who appeared to be labouring under a slight confusion of names. 'Why no later than yesterday there was a lady come in, well as Dad always said to me, "Remember, my boy, every customer is a lady as long as she is in the shop," wanted a fowl and there was only the one left that I was keeping for Miss Talbot, and what does she do but reach right over the counter, grab it and put it on the scales. "I'll have that," she says. "Well, madam," I said, "I am sorry you can't, but it is reserved." "First come, first served," she says. "Remember there's a war on and you can put an extra shilling on the price. Money's no object to me and I'll pay for what I want." She said that, ladies,' said Mr Scatcherd, by now almost in tears. 'And you can't snatch things back, not before everyone. And the girls we get. Here for a week, know nothing, give a lot of trouble, yet say a word to them and they are off to the Army canteens. I don't wonder some of my old customers are getting things from town and the shocking thing is I don't miss their money. But I do assure you, ladies, I miss their good-will.'

There seemed to be no real consolation for this wail. Miss Pemberton, who was an old customer, spoke some brisk words of comfort and said it would take more than a war to make her change her grocer and general provision merchant, while Mrs Villars, a comparatively new comer, vaguely expressed her determination to go down with the ship. Mr Scatcherd looked a little cheered and with a hurried excuse rushed away to stop one of his young ladies giving mortal offence to Lady Betterton, who though she wore the same tailor-made for ever and ever, was immensely rich and had for forty years been one of Mr Scatcherd's best customers.

Mrs Villars and Miss Pemberton walked down the street in silence. In the open-fronted shop of Mr Vidler, the poulterer, a number of ducks and chickens were lying dejectedly on a slab on their backs, their limp necks hanging down. Three very dirty children of tender years were kissing their heads with much affection.

'I don't think that can be good for the children, or the birds, do you?' said Miss Pemberton.

Mrs Villars looked about her. Three ladies in sham fur coats, black patent-leather shoes with white trimmings and a good deal of cheap jewellery were talking and smoking at the corner.

'Excuse me,' said Mrs Villars, approaching them. 'I don't know if those are your children, but perhaps it isn't frightfully good for them to have their mouths near those birds. They've been there all morning and might be rather germy.'

'Well, it's a free country, isn't it?' said one of the women, 'and I'm sure I don't see what harm the kiddies can do. Anyone'd think we was Germans to hear you speak.'

Mrs Villars retreated, unhappily conscious of loud laughter behind her and the words, 'Quite a madam, isn't she,' and was but little comforted to observe from a safe distance that the mother who had spoken to her gave her child a hearty smack and took it away.

'I wish I could be rude,' she said plaintively to Miss Pemberton. 'It doesn't seem fair for everyone else to do the rudeness and us to do the putting up with it.'

'You could be rude,' said Miss Pemberton, 'extraordinarily rude. But those people wouldn't know you were rude, they would only think you were being ordinary. And you would feel so horrid afterwards that it wouldn't be worth it. There is no way of communicating with them, none at all. Ever read Disraeli?'

Mrs Villars said she did, bless his heart.

'You remember the sub-title of *Sybil* then,' said Miss Pemberton. '"The Two Nations". It's as true now as it was then and even nastier. Well, good-bye. You and your husband must come in one evening.'

Mrs Villars said they would love to and would Miss Pemberton ring her up and suggest a day.

'I don't have a telephone, you know,' said Miss Pemberton. 'I found if I had one I only used it, and I couldn't go on affording it. But I'll send a note up by Effie on her day out.'

She walked off down the High Street, leaving Mrs Villars so full of thoughts that before she knew where she was she was half-way home again with her shopping unfinished. Luckily what she had forgotten was only for herself and she would not get into disgrace with Mrs Chapman, so after making an irresolute dash or two in each direction alternately she turned her back on shops and refugees and rudeness and went along the Rectory Lane. When she got back she delivered her basket to Foster; read without enthusiasm several telephone messages which had been received in her absence, and sat down to write letters.

Some people can dash off letters in a fine, flowing, or a bold, illegible (as the case may be) script; lick them up, stamp them, and be done with it. Others, and to this class Mrs Villars belonged, find the actual physical part of writing a fatigue; their thoughts far out-distance their pen, and their pen obstinately refuses to make the lines and curves that their mind wishes to impose on it, so that their handwriting, while it does not in the least represent their mental concept of it, does mirror in a mortifying way their total failure to achieve any result they have aimed at. When you add to this that they go off into rather irrelevant dreamings between or even in the middle of sentences and forget how they meant to finish them; that they find themselves being stiffly pedantic or suddenly pouring out a great gush of emotion whose genuineness they at once doubt; that they quote poetry and are then assailed with doubts which send them rummaging all up and down Bartlett's Familiar Quotations, the Shakespeare Concordance, and the Complete Works of Shelley; that they are irresistibly attracted by anything that will enable them to put off concentrating for a few moments, browsing on newspapers, catalogues, even time-tables, till some of them have to remove every printed article to a distance at which they cannot reach out a hand unbeknown to themselves and pick it up; no wonder that they waste an enormous amount of time over their letters and often tear them up in the end. And so it was with Mrs Villars who meaning to write to a great friend in Norfolk with whom she exchanged periodic news of family events, drifted into such a complication of all the aforementioned difficulties that she might just as well have gone back to the High Street and finished her shopping.

She began easily enough by writing that she was so glad to hear that Freddy was really getting over his influenza at last and young Freddy was getting promotion and how nice it was that Rosemary had got through her School Certificate with eight credits. Looking wildly if subconsciously round for an excuse not to go on she saw that the fire was low, got up and put a log on it and read with some care the various invitation cards to committees and meetings that were on the mantelpiece. She then blamed herself for irresolution and sat down again. Irresolution was, she knew, one of her faults. Again and again she said to herself, I will simply make up my mind and stick to what I have decided to do. But how difficult that was. To begin with, making up one's mind was like a physical pain and even when you had made it up you hadn't really made it up at all. She went hot as she thought of herself that morning at the moment when she had remembered that she had forgotten the rest of her shopping. She had felt a cold hand grip her vitals, turned in quick obedience to it and hastened back towards the shops: at the corner by the bus stop she had reflected that the shopping didn't really matter and turned homewards again: outside The Lollipoppe Shoppe, whose windows now contained nothing but empty sample chocolate boxes, some cigarettes, some fish-paste and some revolting little coloured plaster figures of dwarfs which were being raffled, she had thought how silly it was not to do what she had set out to do and had set her face once more towards the High Street. As she walked she had said to herself, 'Well, I am going to do the shopping or I am not, one or the other, so it doesn't matter what I do, because I'm going to do whatever I'm going to do,' after which philosophical flight she had, for no particular reason that she could remember, with great resolution set her face homewards for the third time and was now there. But whether They (unspecified) had meant her to be so silly, and she had circumvented Them; or on the contrary They had meant her to go straight home and it was she who had done the dithering from Free-will, she could not say.

So she went on to tell her friend in Norfolk that her elder boy was frightfully busy and was going to be twenty-seven in March, which really made one think. But what it did make her think was that Mr Holden had somehow let drop that he would be thirty-four in February, which made him almost exactly seven years older than her first-born, a silly affected phrase, which seemed like a kind of coincidence and somehow made her remember that her black cocktail frock wanted a few stitches in the shoulder seam. ·

She then thought about nothing for quite a long time, till a blob of ink gradually formed on her fountain-pen and fell off on to her letter, giving her a chance of playing that delightful game of watching the ink slowly seep up into a piece of blotting paper torn from the pad. After this she was smitten with remorse for time wasted, and wrote that she was so sorry about the blot and her younger boy didn't think he would get leave for some time but seemed quite happy in Yorkshire. She wondered if she ought to cross out Yorkshire and as she wondered she began to feel wretched and guilty and the remembrance of the odious people in Scatcherd's and outside Vidler's came surging back over her and she thought of several crushing repartees which she said aloud to herself, knowing all the while that she would never have the courage to say them to anyone else.

Miss Pemberton's words came back to her: there is no way of communicating with them. It seemed to be horridly true. She knew that in a thousand years there would be no way in which she could find a common language with the blonde refugee or the people in sham fur coats outside Vidler's. Always she would seem stuck-up and affected to them, conceited, lah-di-dah, a Madam. Always, to be perfectly frank with herself, she would fear and shrink from contacts with them. They didn't want to learn her language; she couldn't learn theirs. The only people as far as she could see who got on with them were people like Mrs Paxon who enjoyed bullying and had a fine streak of imperviousness to mental atmospheres, or people like Miss Talbot and Miss Dolly Talbot, who were saints. And if to be a saint meant dressing like the Misses Talbot or being as dull as they were, she did not feel with all due humility that she could do it.

'No,' she wrote to her friend in Norfolk, 'I haven't seen a single book in the Sunday papers that I wanted to read for ages or I'd tell it you. It is extraordinary how many books there are one doesn't want to read. Mrs Turner, who I must have told you about at The Hollies, was going to lend me one about Peter the Great, but her other niece took it back to the library by mistake.'

Exhausted by this piece of composition, she relapsed into unconsciousness from which, doubtless through the word books, the name of Mr Downing surged up, naturally leading to that of Miss Pemberton. Miss Pemberton was going to ask them in one evening, which might be pleasant, though she had grave doubts as to whether her husband and his hostess would see eye to eye about fires. Miss Pemberton was going to send a note by Effie, because she had no telephone. And she had no telephone because she couldn't afford one. Mrs Villars tried hard to imagine the degree of poverty that would make a telephone an impossible luxury and found it very difficult. That very nice people were really badly off she knew, but they had always said, 'Of course, a telephone one *must* have,' and somehow felt that the fixed rent being what it was, it would be extravagance not to spend as much again on calls. She thought of Miss Pemberton's contribution of half a crown to the Guides and wondered, with shame at her own wealth, what sacrifice of comfort that coin had represented. Thinking very hard, or doing what passed in her mind for thinking, she came to the conclusion that to be kind was somehow easier for poor people because the sums they gave weren't large. If I gave everyone who wanted money for charity a pound, she said to herself, it might look like showing off, and yet I suppose I am quite eight times as well off as Miss Pemberton. It is all so difficult, and giving an order to one's bank to pay one's charitable subscriptions once a year doesn't seem like self-sacrifice, and yet if one didn't give the money away one would buy clothes probably, so I suppose it *is* a little sacrifice.

'We still have our officers billeted on us,' she wrote. 'The wife of one of them was here for a week-end, a very nice woman but a little tiring.'

Exhausted by this flight and at the risk of toppling over chair and all, she automatically reached for the November number of the Parish Magazine, the only piece of literature to hand, and began to read it. By a simple association of ideas the Church news made her think of the church, thus of her husband, then of herself. If one were a proper Rector's wife, she thought, one would be able to deal with people kindly and efficiently. Then she remembered the girl at Scatcherd's who had thought the Rectory was the Rookery and went hot with sudden anger. If no one knew what a Rectory was and the Rector's wife couldn't make any impression on shops where the Rectory had dealt for years (for she had faithfully taken over the old tradesmen when she came), what good was it all. She longed for the days of squarsons, wives like Mrs Grantly at Plumstead, who in what now seemed like the Golden Days of Bishop Proudie ruled her husband's parish by Sunday schools, buns, flannel, tea and sugar at Christmas, and visited the poor with practical benevolence and no idea of equality. It's their fault, it's their fault, she said passionately to herself. We would have been quite happy for things to stay as they were, but they didn't. And now it is all rudeness and trousers and children kissing dead poultry, and one can do nothing at all. And she retired into a nostalgic dream of an age she had never known and many aspects of which she would doubtless have disliked, till the gong disturbed her with a sudden booming and she hurried in to lunch still holding the green-covered Parish Magazine, for the officers would be waiting.

The company to-day was only Captain Topham, Captain Powell-Jones, and Lieutenants Hooper and Holden, the others being away on jobs.

'I hope,' said the Rector to the table in general, 'that Mrs Spender caught her train.'

'All with you there, sir,' said Captain Topham, 'because if she didn't she'd be back here again. I wish you'd heard the Colonel on her at breakfast.'

'Well, well, she was our guest,' said the Rector, though

without any conviction. 'I gather that they live somewhere in the Midlands.'

'Couldn't say, sir,' said Captain Topham. 'Spender did mention that his wife's people were called Williams.'

Mr Hooper said that told one nothing.

'Williams,' said Captain Powell-Jones in a suspicious voice, 'is a good name; a very good name.'

He looked round for contradiction.

'Whateffer,' added Captain Topham carelessly, with his mouth full.

As his remark was officially *sotto voce*, Captain Powell-Jones contented himself with a glare, upon which Captain Topham, raising his glass of water, bowed and drank to him.

'I have been reading the Parish Magazine,' said Mrs Villars, feeling the subject would be better changed.

'May I see it, Mrs Villars,' said Captain Topham. 'I say, it's a top-hole one. I do like the picture on the cover. That's the church, isn't it?' he added, exhibiting to the Rector what was apparently an early woodcut by Bewick in a very bad state and almost buried under printer's ink.

'As a matter of fact,' said the Rector, 'it is St Sycorax. We have two blocks and use them turn and turn about. I know it's St Sycorax because it was the Parish Church in October.'

'I should think this one would do for both,' said the irrepressible Captain Topham.

Mr Hooper said one ought to remember that in war-time one could not expect things to be as they were, and the printing industry, which was really a key industry, had lost what he personally considered to be an unfair proportion of its personnel.

'I dare say you are right,' said the Rector. 'Look how small *The Times* is now. But it wouldn't affect us. Our local man, Sampson, is over sixty, a real enthusiast for his trade, and his nephew who works for him is mentally deficient.'

'I suppose he puts the ink on,' said Captain Topham.

'No, his uncle won't allow him near the ink,' said the Rector, 'but he has that uncanny gift for one thing that the mentally defective sometimes have, and in his case it is typesetting. I don't know what the record is, but I am certain he has beaten it. The ink is unexplained. It has always been like that since I came and I suppose always will be.'

Mr Hooper said the Germans put all their insane mercifully to death.

'Good old Germans,' said Captain Topham, 'but I bet they try out some poison-gas on them first.'

Mr Hooper was just going to say that in many ways the Germans were far ahead of us in social betterment, such being his phraseology, when Mr Holden got in:

'What I do like in Parish Magazines,' he said, 'is the communal bit in the middle. I mean the bit that all the magazines have. Enchanting as I find our local news at the beginning and our local advertisements at the end, give me the middle section every time. There's a splendid serial running just now, Mrs Villars, well worth your attention if you haven't followed it. It takes me back to the finest traditions of the late Dr Gordon Stables and the *Boys' Own Paper*, and believe me or not, as Mrs Spender says, it actually has two bright, golden-haired Christian lads of sixteen and eighteen, a golden-haired girl of fifteen, probably Christian, and a Christian Newfoundland dog called Pilot. If I were

Dr Gordon Stables I'd come back as a ghost and prosecute them.'

'What I like,' said the Rector unexpectedly, 'is the household hints. There was one this week – just a moment, Topham—' and he almost snatched from Captain Topham's hands the magazine which that gentleman was avidly perusing. 'Here it is,' he said.

'Do read it to us, Gregory,' said his wife, seeing that he was going to in any case.

'"Mrs Hilda Swainton writes from Middlesbrough,"' read Mr Villars, '"I wonder if any of your readers find that the finger-tips of their gloves wear out before other parts. Perhaps they would find the following hint useful. You will need a pair of gloves with holes in the finger-tips, a stout pair of scissors, a strong darning-needle with a sharp point, and any odd bits of brightly coloured wool. With the scissors cut off the tips of the fingers about an inch from the top or as far as the holes extend, and the same, if necessary, with the thumb. These, i.e., the fingers, should now be buttonholed round the tops with the wool in any liked combination of colours. For instance, green will look nice on a beige glove, or red on a blue. The gloves can then be worn as mittens, or if preferred, under a loose pair of gloves, thus making the hands nice and cosy on a chilly day. Do not throw away the holey (not holy!) tips as these, if collected in quantities, will come in handy to stuff pillows, etc. for your kiddies' dolls, and many other useful purposes." What do you think of that?' said the Rector proudly.

His wife was loud in admiration, but Captain Topham, in whom the rape of the magazine still rankled, ungenerously said that Mrs K. Pont's advice on making a receptacle for soiled linen from a music-stool with a hinged lid was far better, and what was more, it had an illustration.

'Gregory,' said Mrs Villars, who had managed, *via* Mr Holden, to get possession of the magazine and was idly turning the leaves, 'who censors the magazine? There are all sorts of advertisements of corsets and *most* irreligious things. Do you suppose the Bishop has to give permission?'

'When I look at its general level I sometimes think that the Bishop has written it all himself,' said the Rector, who in common with most of his fellow-clergy in the diocese, looked upon the Bishop of Barchester as the chief stumbling-block to the Christian religion. 'What are your men doing there, Topham?'

Captain Topham looked out of the window and following the Rector's finger saw Corporal Jackson and a couple of privates going towards the churchyard, carrying what looked like a great deal of wire. At the lychgate they halted and the corporal said something in a loud voice, apparently to someone in the sky.

'If Jackson is having visions, the churchyard is quite the right place,' said the Rector, 'but as Rector I must know whom he is talking to.'

Voices, not recognizable as heavenly, replied in broad Wessex from the same aerial region.

'It's the telephone, sir,' said Captain Topham. 'Mrs Paxon said you had given permission to have a line put from the top of the tower to our office so that the spotters could tell us where the parachutists are coming down. Not that they'll get it anywhere within five miles, if that,' he added cheerfully. 'So the A.R.P. people have got the Post Office to fix up a line, and as Jackson is a friend of the head mechanic at the exchange and is a bit of an electrician himself, he said he'd give a hand.'

'What did Colonel Passmore say?' asked the Rector, amused.

'He swore at Jackson and told him if he wanted to make a nuisance of himself let it be on a day when he wouldn't see him and he would be in Barchester all Monday,' said Captain Topham.

Mrs Villars said she hoped the tower wouldn't be struck by lightning, and if so, would it run down the telephone wire into the office and kill anyone.

'Like the end of *Four Just Men*,' said Mr Holden. 'No, I think not. The lightning-conductor will see to all that.'

'Three good things in Britain,' said Captain Powell-Jones, coming out of a Cymric dream.

> '"Wine in the cleric's mouth,
> A sword in the cleric's midriff,
> Lightning on the cleric's rooftree."'

'And many of them, old man,' said Captain Topham admiringly. 'Would it amuse you to go up after lunch and have a looksee, Mr Villars? And Mrs Villars, if it isn't too much for her.'

The Rector, looking at his watch, said he would like it very much, but he had a meeting almost at once. If Captain Topham thought the men would still be at work at, say, three o'clock, he would wait for him in the church porch.

Captain Topham said if he knew anything of Jackson, or

the telephone service, or anything else, they would all be there till five o'clock and probably for the next two days.

Mr Hooper said we ought to remember that in time of war things could not be done as quickly as in peace-time, and the telephones, like everyone else, were working short-handed and against heavy odds. He then rather pointedly reminded Captain Topham of those files that ought to be got off, excused himself and went back to the office.

'Will you come, Mrs Villars?' said Mr Holden.

Mrs Villars said she found the tower stairs a little exhausting and thought she had better lie down. A disappointment leapt to Mr Holden's eyes and he said he thought that was a very good plan.

7

Glycerine Cottage

On Guy Fawkes Day the war was brought home to the youth of England by the fact that for the first, or in the case of those of phenomenal memory the second time in their lives, no fireworks were allowed, except indoor ones, which cannot singe, blind or in any way mutilate, and are beneath contempt; nor was it any comfort to them to be told on the following day that President Roosevelt had been elected for a third term, in future to be known by the adjective unprecedented, as President of the United States, for they did not know what their parents and friends were talking about.

On the following day, which was Wednesday, Mrs Villars had to keep her promise and go to tea with Miss Crowder and Miss Hopgood. Miss Hopgood, whom she had met at the fishmonger's on Tuesday morning, asked her if she would bring one of her officers; 'For,' said Miss Hopgood, 'Father Fewling is coming and we feel it would be nicer if there were another man. Not that Father Fewling, at least I don't quite mean that, but after all they are *different* in a way,' said Miss Hopgood trailing into incoherence.

So Mrs Villars promised she would bring an officer and asked Mr Greaves, first explaining carefully to him what she was letting him in for. But Mr Greaves said anything for a change from tea in the office with Hooper picking on everything a fellow said and his aunt used to go to the Riviera every winter for years, so he expected Miss Hopgood would know her.

Accordingly they set out down the Rectory Lane, along by the almshouses and so into the High Street, whence they continued their journey *via* Cow Street to Cow End, where several retired elderly couples and maiden ladies of straitened means had built a little colony of cottages, all of striking originality and all exactly alike. Passing Tork Cottage, the meaning of whose name no one had ever dared to ask because Commander Beasley was so cross, The Evergreens which as yet had none, and Rooftrees which we conclude had one at least, they came to Glycerine Cottage. A bright fire in the arched brick hearth leapt and illuminated the copper jars on the tiled window-ledge. Through the small horseshoe-shaped window that gave on to the porch at the side of the house the guests could see Miss Crowder laying the tea while Miss Hopgood arranged some chrysanthemums in a pot which said BEVI CARA. Miss Crowder looked up and saw her guests, so Mrs Villars rang the bell.

'You may wonder,' said Miss Crowder as soon as Mr Greaves had picked up some honesty that fell top-heavily out of a Chianti bottle when he put his cap, stick and gloves on the little cassone in the hall, 'why Father Fewling is coming.'

Mrs Villars, feeling that in Ancient Rome this question would have been prefaced by Nonne, said untruthfully that she had.

'You know,' said Miss Crowder, 'that chère amie and I do not encourage his form of worship, if worship it can be called, but her aunt, you know the astronomer's widow, has struck up a great friendship with him over stars, so as she was coming we thought it would be nice to ask him.'

Mr Greaves said if that was the R.C. padre, he liked 'em himself.

'Not *Roman* Catholic, Mr Greaves,' said Miss Hopgood, shocked, '*Catholic*.'

Mr Greaves was so obviously going to ask what the difference was, that Mrs Villars was very glad that the kettle, which was very large and black and hung from a hook over the fire, suddenly boiled over and made a loud sizzling noise among the burning logs.

'Let me,' said Mr Greaves, going to Miss Crowder's assistance.

'I can manage, thanks,' said Miss Crowder, putting on a pair of black bag-like gloves, lifting the kettle off its hook and placing it on one of the brick hobs. 'It takes the skin off your hands as soon as look at you. Isn't it a nice piece? Chère amie and I got it, after really *terrific* bargaining, from an old peasant up behind Menton. We call it Pottofur.'

'Potiphar; that's rather good,' said Mr Greaves, whose French was not colloquial enough to take his hostesses' meaning. 'Jolly good name for a pot.'

And then Miss Hopgood's aunt came in with Father Fewling and tea was made.

If the owners of Glycerine Cottage had intended to leaven their party with their two men – Father Fewling counting as one – they were the more deceived, for the gentlemen flowed together and coalesced like drops of mercury almost from the first. It somehow transpired that Mr Greaves's cousin Percy had been a lieutenant in the destroyer where Father Fewling had been Commander, which made it necessary for them to sit next to each other at the tea-table and ignore the ladies. Moreover Father Fewling, in his pursuit of souls, was no mean judge of the public-houses of Northbridge and though Mr Greaves could hardly approve of padres butting into pubs, a thing which the Dean of Divinity of his college would never have contemplated as remotely possible, he could not but bow to such a knowledge of beer as Father Fewling possessed. Miss Crowder and Miss Hopgood's aunt talked about the new people at 'Rentoul' who had arrived from Golder's Green with three pantechnicons and three cars and were managing to get a garage built in a most unpatriotic way. Mrs Villars would willingly have talked to Miss Hopgood herself, but that Martha was so constantly going into the kitchen for something she had forgotten, or picking up the muffineer from the hearth and handing it, or refilling the teapot and getting the cups mixed up, or suddenly remembering that she must black-out, that Mrs Villars found it simpler to smile occasionally and say nothing, which was also less tiring.

Just as Miss Hopgood had finished the black-out, who should walk in from the kitchen but Mrs Turner's two nieces.

'Hullo,' said Betty. 'You were making such a noise having tea that you didn't hear the bell, so we came round by the back door. Hullo, Mrs Villars.'

Mrs Villars said How do you do, not that she felt priggish about Hullo, but How do you do came more naturally to her, and asked the girls if they knew Mr Greaves.

'Oh, hullo,' said Betty. 'No, I didn't. Is he one of your lot? I say, can we have some tea? We've been all over Cow End leaving leaflets on people about what you do after the air-raid, and none of them could read, at least you'd think not, the way they asked us questions when it was all written down for them.'

Mr Greaves, with a promptitude which Father Fewling as an ex-naval man admired and envied, had got two more chairs and managed to seat himself between the newcomers before Miss Hopgood could refill the teapot.

'Hullo, there's your aunt,' said Betty to Miss Hopgood. 'Did you manage to see that star the other night? I've forgotten its name, but it said about it in the *Daily Mail*. Ackcherly it was an ordinary one, but it was doing something or other. I heard all about it on the wahless.'

Mrs Villars wondered if Father Fewling and Miss Hopgood's aunt would rise as one astronomer and smite Betty to the earth, but they only laughed.

'I saw stars,' sang Mr Greaves in a pleasant tenor.

Mrs Turner's other niece turned on him.

'You could sing at our concert,' she said, fixing him with her dark eyes.

Mr Greaves asked for information. Both the girls leant their elbows on the table and talked at once. Mr Greaves, not a whit discomposed, discovered that the concert, in aid of Comforts for the Barsetshire Regiment, was to be held just after Christmas in the Village Hall, and volunteered to sing, dance, recite, black his face, or do anything they liked. An arrangement was at once made for Mr Greaves to come and rehearse on Saturday between tea and dinner, and the noise was such that the elder members of the party had to stop talking. When things were quieter, Mrs Villars said to Miss Crowder that Mr Greaves's aunt had wintered on the Riviera for years and she wondered if they had ever met.

'If she was on our dear Riviera, I must have come across her,' said Miss Crowder. 'One comes across everybody if one stays long enough at dear Pension Ramsden. Did she ever go there, I wonder. Such *nice* people Madame Ramsden always had. Do you remember the year Lady Horkins was there, chère amie?' she said, turning to Miss Hopgood. 'Such a good-looking woman. She used to go into dear Monte by the bus every day. All the conductors knew her and she had such an amusing word for each. There was one called Isidore, and she used to make a little joke, a jou de mots, on his name. Something about Isidore and Issy dore, here sleeps, you know. So French.'

If her guests thought it a little too French, in the less refined sense of the word, they were too polite to say so.

'I'm sure my aunt would know about the Pension Ramsden,' said Mr Greaves, faltering in his complete assurance for the first time in Mrs Villars's knowledge of him. 'She had a villa at Mentone and used to have lots of English friends. Villa Thermogène – I expect you know it.'

'But that's Lady de Courcy's,' said Miss Crowder.

'She's my mother's elder sister,' said Mr Greaves apologetically. 'She's awfully hard up and had to let the villa quite often.'

The fact that Mr Greaves's mother was sister to a countess cast a faint gloom over Glycerine Cottage. Much as Miss Crowder and Miss Hopgood loved the Pension Ramsden, something told them that Lady de Courcy would never have friends there. Had she ever descended at its shabby portal Madame Ramsden would certainly not have kept silence and the countess's visit would have been added to the Roll of Honour which she loved to recite to newcomers.

'It's not your fault,' said Mrs Turner's other niece. 'We've all got queer relations. Auntie's husband was in a loony-bin or something. Come on, Betty, we've still got four leaflets to leave and it's nearly dark.'

'Ackcherly I've got a torch,' said Betty. 'Don't forget Saturday, Mr Greaves. Oh, bother, it's the day I said I'd take Mr Downing to Fish Hill. Never mind, we'll have plenty of time after tea.'

She and Mrs Turner's other niece got up violently. Mr Greaves got up too.

'Won't you walk back with Mrs Turner's nieces?' said Mrs Villars, seeing in Mr Greaves's candid face a hunger for young companionship kept in check by politeness to an older woman, and liking him for it. 'I've got a torch and shall be quite all right.'

While Mr Greaves's chivalry still kept him undecided Father Fewling said he would go back with her with pleasure, so the three young people went off. Their voices could be heard in laughter and died away.

'Si jounesse savvay,' said Miss Crowder nostalgically.

'Ah,' said Miss Hopgood's aunt, 'but it doesn't.'

Miss Crowder and Miss Hopgood then recovered their

spirits and took their guests to see their kitchen, because it was so like dear France, though Mrs Villars could see nothing French about it except a jar of French mustard on the dresser.

'You see,' said Miss Hopgood, 'mustard for our little supper. The last pot in London, positively. What we shall do without it I can't think.'

'Eat English,' said Miss Hopgood's aunt. 'It's time you got out of your French ideas, Miriam. Enemy aliens.'

'Oh, Aunt Helen!' said Miss Hopgood, shocked. 'Our dear French aren't enemy aliens. They are only *misled*.'

'And all the ones here are Free,' said Miss Crowder, who had a photograph of General de Gaulle pinned up over her writing-table and often wished as she looked at it that she could be a vivandière.

'Aliens then,' said Miss Hopgood's aunt. 'It's all the same. If you girls had scientific minds you wouldn't get into such a muddle. Foreigners can't help being foreigners. Your uncle had a great many foreign scientists to visit him at the Observatory and they were all exactly alike. Not a pin to choose between them. I dare say I have told you about Professor Goblin, a Russian he was. He used *most* underhand ways and actually tried to claim Porter Sidus after using your uncle's Zollmer-Vorfuss. Goblin Sidus he would have called it. It makes one laugh. Now let's hear no more about French mustard, Miriam.'

Wounded in their deepest feelings, Miss Crowder and Miss Hopgood might have retorted, but that the bell rang. Miss Hopgood went to open the door. The firm cultured voices of middle-aged Englishmen were heard and Mrs Villars, who was squashed up against Father Fewling between the kitchen-table and the dresser, saw to her perplexity that his weatherbeaten face was pale and he had a general appearance of having shrunk. In fact, except for the extreme improbability of such a thing, she would have said that he eyed the back door as if contemplating a leap for freedom.

'It must be the Talbots,' said Miss Crowder. 'They often drop in on their way home from the Red Cross at Mrs Dunsford's. Come back into the sitting-room.'

'I am so sorry to trouble you, Mrs Villars,' said Father Fewling detaining her for a moment, 'but would you be so *very* kind as to let me take you home? I can't explain, but if you would make it clear that I have promised to see you to the Rectory, I shall be so grateful.'

Mrs Villars had always been kind to her husband's assistant masters and this seemed to be much the same, so she smiled and said, Certainly. Father Fewling straightened himself and went forward with a bolder step to meet his mysterious doom.

Miss Talbot and Miss Dolly Talbot were two of those undoubted English gentlewomen who would pass unrecognized anywhere in the world. Both had heavy coils of greying hair under felt hats; both had rather battered tweeds that said Prince's Street as loud as print; both had silk and wool mixture stockings and good brogues. Together it was perfectly easy to tell them apart: apart people were constantly mistaking Miss Talbot for Miss Dolly, though, as Miss Dolly used to say with a laugh, it was funny that people never took her for Marjorie. They were, with the Dunsfords, the pillars of the Red Cross in Northbridge and read aloud a great deal to their father, whose mind was not what it had been. This and St Sycorax filled their hard-working and blameless lives.

Miss Crowder inquired after the Red Cross.

'We had a very busy day,' said Miss Dolly Talbot, whose teeth were a little more regular than her sister's. 'Miss Dunsford has had an appeal for pneumonia jackets for the Mixo-Lydian hospital, so Marjorie and I were cutting out till all hours. We rather wished they were for our own gallant boys, but unfortunately there are very few pneumonia cases at the Barchester General.'

'What did I tell you, Miriam?' said Miss Hopgood's aunt. 'Foreigners all over. First the pneumonia and then the pneumonia jackets. There's no pleasing them; they want everything.'

Miss Hopgood's eyes filled with tears.

'Thirty-six we cut out and tacked for machining,' said Miss Talbot. 'Hovis House is delightful, but Mrs Dunsford's dining-room table is really not big enough. We do miss Mrs Keith's room for our Red Cross work, and it is horrid to think of those rather common typists at Northbridge Manor. We heard from Mrs Keith the other day. She is staying with her married daughter at Southbridge for the duration, you know.'

'Any news of Lydia?' said Miss Crowder, who like most people had been fond of Mrs Keith's rather blustering, masterful younger daughter.

'She is in Scotland with her husband,' said Miss Talbot.

'What a miraculous escape he had from Dunkirk,' said Miss Hopgood's aunt. 'I know you won't mind my saying, Father Fewling, that I am an agnostic, though a deeply reverent one, but all the same Dunkirk did seem like a wonderful answer to the Day of Prayer.'

Father Fewling, who privately felt that the Royal Navy was responsible, said, 'Ah, yes,' murmuring softly to himself, 'What God abandoned these defended.'

But Miss Hopgood, who felt as brave as a tigress after wiping away her angry tears, turned on her aunt.

'It's all very well, Aunt Helen,' she said, 'but you haven't a scientific mind. We had the Day of Prayer on a Sunday and what happened on the Tuesday? King Leopold. I thought you believed in cause and effect.' She then went very pink and burst into tears outright. Her aunt, speechless before the accusation of being unscientific, the only charge which could really wound her, had a strong impulse to slap her niece, but her scientific mind, schooled by her late husband, told her she should examine any fact presented to her in the cold light of reason, so she controlled herself and told her niece not to mind.

'I don't wonder she is upset,' said Miss Talbot, with more sympathy than understanding. 'I often feel like crying myself over Heroism. I know we English don't talk about it much, but of course our men are marvellous. You must feel it specially, Father Fewling,' she said, turning mild worshipping eyes on her pastor, 'because of the Navy.'

Father Fewling said the Navy was all right, quickly adding Thank God.

'Well,' said Miss Dolly Talbot, the more practical of the two sisters, 'we mustn't forget why we came here, Marjorie. We are having a special Red Cross meeting on the fourteenth, at Hovis House. A small committee is being formed to see about Comforts for the H.M.S. *Barchester*, you know the city and the district have adopted her. If you could come, Father Fewling, and give us a little talk about life on, or I believe I should say in, a cruiser, it would make all the difference. I must make a little confession,' she said with slightly religious archness. 'Marjorie and I did a little sleuthing. Miss Crowder had mentioned that you were coming, so we looked in hoping to catch you in melting mood. Do say yes.'

Father Fewling said he was more at home in a destroyer, but would come with pleasure.

'Might I ask,' said Miss Hopgood's aunt in an ominous voice, 'for what hour the meeting is convened?'

Miss Talbot said half-past eight and all wishing to help would be cordially welcome.

'If you mean me,' said Miss Hopgood's aunt, 'I did have an engagement for that evening, but as it appears to be cancelled I should like to come.'

'Oh, Lord!' said Father Fewling, quite forgetting himself, 'I *am* so sorry, Miss Dolly, but I have an engagement that evening. Stupid of me.'

He looked deprecatingly at Miss Hopgood's aunt, who said with icy brightness that if he meant their astronomical evening, she quite realized that in war-time things were different and she much looked forward to the meeting.

This made everything so uncomfortable that Miss Crowder in desperation at the fate of her tea-party suggested a little sherry. But the revolting qualities of the Glycerine Cottage sherry, due partly to narrow means and even more to ignorance and a blind trust in the Cathedral Wine and Mineral Water Stores, Branches all over the County, were so well known, even to the ladies of Northbridge, that there was a rush to say good-bye.

'If you wish to explain we can walk back as far as the post office together,' said Miss Hopgood's aunt in a tense voice, pinning Father Fewling into a corner by the door.

Mrs Villars, who was very near them, which it was impossible not to be in a room nine feet by twelve and seven people in it, said, 'Are you ready, Father Fewling? Father Fewling has promised to see me back because I haven't got a torch,' and as she said it, realized with some pleasure that to be the Rector's wife still gave one a little pull among well-brought-up people, for Miss Hopgood's aunt, for all her possessiveness, was well brought up. She accepted her defeat, told Father Fewling they must arrange another night for their astronomy, and went off into the dark.

'What a pity we weren't all going the same way,' said Miss Talbot, who never much noticed what was going on. 'But you come our way, Father Fewling, don't you?'

Mrs Villars tried to think of another lie and failed, so they all left in a bunch after thanking their hostesses warmly for the tea-party. The darkness outside was very thick and the Misses Talbot insisted on standing on the edge of the path for a few moments to get used to it. Mrs Villars could not see Father Fewling's face in the dark, but he had appealed to her once and no underling of her husband's had ever appealed to her in vain.

'Will it be a frightful trouble if you come round by the Rectory, Father Fewling?' she said. 'Gregory did specially want to see you if it isn't out of your way. It's about the Parish Magazine, I think.'

'If the Rector wants anything, his word is law,' said Miss Talbot, who, although she preferred Father Fewling's form of worship, had the greatest reverence for the Rector in virtue of his office and found something inexpressibly elevating in the name of Gregory, as did her sister.

'And you and I must have a nice talk another time about the Thursday Intercession Service,' said Miss Dolly Talbot to Father Fewling. 'Some of us were thinking that if you altered it from four-fifteen to four we could just pop in between the Mothers' Union and tea. Well, good night.'

The couples separated and were swallowed up in the darkness.

'Do you know,' said Mrs Villars, 'that I have told two lies within ten minutes.'

'You ought to be an Admiral's wife,' said Father Fewling, expressing not so much his opinion of the untruthfulness of Admirals' wives, as his admiration for Mrs Villars's resourcefulness. 'Do you know, Mrs Villars, I sometimes wish that I had stayed in the Navy. Not really, because I'm awfully happy here,' said Father Fewling, emboldened by the darkness through which they were walking, 'and Villars is a splendid man to work under and one of the most broadminded chaps I've ever known. But sometimes the ladies of the congregation do get me down. They are so good and helpful and so really religious, but there are such a *lot* of them, and they *will* like me,' said Father Fewling, voicing the unexpressed feeling of nine-tenths of the Anglican clergy, 'and they are so confoundedly interfering. I beg your pardon, Mrs Villars, but they really are. I suppose I was in the Navy too long and haven't quite got the hang of things, but it seems to me that an Intercession Service is a bit more important than tea. And to talk of popping in. Of course I'll do my best, but Miss Talbot and her sister, whom I really do admire very much, and I can't think what St Sycorax would do without them, want to run everything, and there can't be two captains on one quarter-deck – your husband being the Commodore of course,' he added, in case Mrs Villars should think he were arrogating too much position to himself.

Mrs Villars was touched by this outpouring, which reminded her of confidences made to her at Coppin's School and, in her turn finding it easier to talk under cover of the darkness, sympathized very much with her companion. She would go quite mad herself, she said, if she had to put up with the Misses Talbot for long, but she was sure that Father Fewling, both as a sailor and a priest, though she ought perhaps to say a priest and a sailor, would be able to get the better of his very natural feelings of irritation. As for tea, she said, perhaps Father Fewling, who was waited on in the Navy and did not, she knew, mind when he got his meals so long as he did his parish work, did not quite realize how much the ladies of Northbridge were the slaves of their maids.

'I'm lucky,' she said, 'because we are pretty well off and I can have several maids who are paid to bring tea when I want it, but so many of our friends have only one maid who is apt to sulk if things aren't as she expects them. I know that the Talbots manage with a girl who comes daily, and Professor Talbot is apt to be cross if he is kept waiting. It is all so difficult.'

Father Fewling was silent as they walked up the Rectory Lane and then said he was ashamed of himself. Mrs Villars at once felt that she was a prig, and begged him to come in and have some sherry. If he did, it would, she said, make her second lie come true and she would even force the Rector to talk about the Parish Magazine. Father Fewling, a little perplexed by her casuistry, but grateful, said he would like to.

Emboldened by the last of the mantle of darkness before they went into the Rectory door he said:

'Could you do one thing for me, Mrs Villars?'

'Of course,' she said, fumbling for the door handle, for the door was never locked till they went to bed, as the Rector liked people to walk in and out.

'Would you mind calling me Tubby?' said Father Fewling earnestly.

Mrs Villars paused and did not turn the handle.

'I know it hardly suits me now,' said Father Fewling, whose delusion that he was gaunt and ascetic was unalterable; 'but the chaps always used to call me that and there is no one to do it here. If you didn't mind—'

'That is very nice of you, Tubby, and of course I will,' said Mrs Villars opening the door. And how restful, she thought to herself, that Tubby is all he wants, for more than one assistant master, forcing his unwanted Christian name upon her in his youthful ardour, had followed it by an idealizing of herself which she could hardly bear. But here there would be nothing of the sort. Her heart was sorry for the good, hard-working little man, a prey to his female congregation and sometimes regretting his former calling, but doing his duty valiantly all the time. 'Only you must say Verena,' she added.

'It is *decent* of you,' said Father Fewling, his round face getting very red, 'but I don't think I could. You wouldn't think it standoffish, would you?'

Mrs Villars said of course she wouldn't and admitted to herself that his instinct was finer than hers. But what was the use of impulses if one didn't occasionally give way to them? She led the way into the study, where she found her

156

husband writing and Mr Holden sitting on the sofa reading the evening paper.

'I told a lie, Gregory, to save Father Fewling's life from the Talbots,' she said, 'so, in revenge, he asked me to call him Tubby. Give him some sherry, darling. We only escaped Miss Crowder's sherry by the skin of our teeth.'

'It would have taken the skin right off your teeth,' said the Rector getting up, 'from what I have heard of it.'

'I suppose you can't give Tubby any helpful advice about female worshippers,' said Mrs Villars, sitting down.

'Haven't you enough, Fewling? I thought St Sycorax was crammed,' said the Rector.

'It isn't that, sir,' said Father Fewling miserably. 'They will *like* me. You don't know what it's like.'

'Don't say that to any rector, however apparently unattractive,' said Mr Villars. 'You may have the Talbots, but I have Mrs Paxon and Miss Hopgood. Their zeal for the seven o'clock service is only equalled by their absence when Harker takes it. Not too tired, Verena?'

His wife truthfully said no, for the excitement which sustains one through even the dullest tea-party had not yet worn off, and as usual she forgot that fatigue would be lying in wait and was probably crouching in a corner of the sofa waiting for her at that very moment.

'What Tubby really minded,' she said, sitting down by Mr Holden, 'was Miss Dolly Talbot talking about popping in to the Thursday afternoon intercession.'

'It is a bit Romeo and Juliet,' said Mr Holden, putting down his paper.

Mr Villars paused, then laughed. Father Fewling laughed

too, but more because he was enjoying himself than because he knew his Shakespeare.

'By the way, Fewling,' said the Rector, 'as you are here, I will save myself writing a letter and ask you to let me have the list of your services for December as soon as you have fought them out with your organist, because we have to go to press early, as Sampson's nephew has to go up for his army medical examination. It is purely a matter of form, but he is bound to get conceited about it and may have to go back to the Home for a few days, so Sampson will be short-handed.'

'That,' said Mrs Villars lazily, 'makes my lie come true,' but her husband and Father Fewling did not hear her, for they had plunged into parish matters and were agreeing, though without ever putting it into words, how very dull Mr Harker was.

'Let me get you some more sherry,' said Mr Holden, taking Mrs Villars's empty glass.

She thanked him but did not want any.

'You are tired,' said Mr Holden in a low determined voice.

At this point Mrs Villars split into two women, a phenomenon well known to scientists, but always ravishingly new and interesting to the person who is doing it. The first and more important half admitted that it was a little tired, but knew that a glass of sherry and a bath would so restore its strength that it would enjoy its dinner, pass a pleasant evening with its husband, reading and talking, and go peacefully to bed and so to sleep. The second or inferior half was flattered by the interest shown in it and immediately became submerged in a welter of self-pity, overwhelmed by languor and lassitude, and heard itself, to the horror of its better self, saying bravely that it was nothing.

'You would say that,' said Mr Holden in a threatening way and with every appearance of imminent apoplexy. 'Do you *never* think of yourself?'

He got up, cast a darkling glance on his hostess, thanked his host for the sherry and went out.

Mrs Villars, still slightly under the influence of her worse self, continued to sit on the sofa and feel romantically tired. The symptoms were not unfamiliar. More than one assistant master had felt it his duty to protect his headmaster's wife (or in more serious cases to understand her), and sometimes, just for fun, Mrs Villars had pretended to herself that she needed protection, though from whom or what she wasn't quite sure. But never for a moment had she doubted that her husband was quite capable of giving her all the care and understanding that she needed and would always save her life if required, as he had so lately done in the matter of Mrs Spender. She looked across the room at him with great affection. Then her gaze moved on to Father Fewling. A good little man if ever there was one ... She thought of their walk in the dark, his simple confession of his difficulties and his real pleasure when she consented to use his ridiculous name. Then she went hot with the remembrance of how he had put her back on the little pedestal of his superior officer's wife, a pedestal from which he evidently did not wish her to descend. It must have needed courage to refuse her offer, and that quality she greatly admired. In fact, to know that she stood high in Father Fewling's estimation was a very comforting feeling, and at the same time bracing. It had been very pleasant to be bullied into being tired by Mr Holden, but that was not an enduring pleasure. She pulled herself together and sat up, summoning her better self to her assistance. Her inferior self, annoyed by this treatment, turned itself round three times and went quietly to sleep, and Mrs Villars, who had kept an eye on them both, began to laugh.

Her husband looked up at the sound, for he had always liked her laughter, and asked what it was.

'Nothing, darling,' said Mrs Villars, as she reached the door. 'Only sacred and profane love. Good-bye, Tubby, and thank you for seeing me home.'

Father Fewling said good night and went back, much restored, to his lodgings.

8

The Hollies

After a very happy interlude during which Corporal Jackson and two privates aided by Hibberd, the employees of His Majesty's Telephone Exchange, and any casual labour that happened to be passing, carried great loops of wire up the church tower, flung life-lines from the tower to the ground, bellowed at each other from above and below, had alfresco meals on the leads, knocked off with devoted punctuality, mislaid the tower key, trampled on a small variegated laurel, and left the tap of the churchyard hose running, the spotters' telephone was installed. On the roof was a kind of wooden bird-box with a lock containing a small apparatus of the eighteen-ninety-nine model. From it a long line stretched to the lychgate, whence it was conducted to the office. Mrs Chapman, indulging in heavy badinage with Corporal Jackson, said it would do nicely to hang out her clorths on, to which the Corporal, piqued by the frivolous treatment of his handiwork, said some people seemed to wish there wasn't a war on at all.

Edie, her vacant eyes more vacant than ever with romance, said it made her feel ever so, and was sharply reprimanded by Mrs Chapman and told to get on with her brights, upon which Corporal Jackson volunteered to give her a hand, thus making her lot harder than ever, for, as Mrs Chapman truly said, the brights were not a gentleman's work and what girls were coming to she didn't know.

The telephone being now installed, Mrs Paxon summoned her volunteers to a grand opening ceremony on Saturday morning. As she afterwards owned, this was an unwise step, for it was the custom of many Northbridge ladies to take the ten-thirty-five (Saturdays only) to Barchester, walk aimlessly and exhaustingly about Woolworth's, have a cup of coffee and a bun at Puckle's, the old-established linen draper and unofficial Ladies' County Club, just pop into the Cathedral for a few minutes, and get the twelve-forty back, so it was only a small band of helpers who mustered on the tower to inaugurate the Anti-Parachute Corps. So small in fact that Mrs Villars, much against her inclination, felt obliged to attend.

Accordingly, at half-past eleven, Mrs Paxon, Father Fewling, Miss Hopgood's aunt, who had a magnanimous nature and had forgiven him, Mrs Dunsford, Miss Talbot and Mrs Villars assembled on the tower, supported by Corporal Jackson and Mr Holden, who had no business there at all.

'Gregory is on the telephone with the Archdeacon,' said Mrs Villars, 'but he will come as soon as he can, and he said if you would care for him to take a shift, Mrs Paxon, he would be only too glad, but he fears you are full up now.'

'Well, I have got my time-table quite planned,' said Mrs

Paxon, 'but of course I know any of the spotters would retire if it was a question of the Rector.'

'They mustn't dream of it,' said Mrs Villars. 'Gregory doesn't want to be greedy, but if you do happen to be short of a spotter on Thursdays before lunch, or perhaps I had better say alternate Thursdays, do let him know, won't you?'

Having thus saved her husband's life she perched uncomfortably on the little projecting rain-course that ran round the bottom of the pyramid, and was silent.

'You oughtn't to have come up here,' said Mr Holden, who had promised himself the exquisite gratification of seeing Mrs Villars white and panting from the ascent and was determined, although she looked quite well and pink and was breathing normally, to get his money's worth.

'But I have,' said Mrs Villars's inferior self in a slightly provocative way and rather to its better self's alarm.

'Well,' said Mrs Paxon, 'here we all are, at least all of us that are here. There's not much to say except that we are all very grateful to the Rector for lending us his beautiful old tower for National Service and providing such a beautiful day.'

Here she paused to let people laugh, which they did, except Corporal Jackson, who knew his place when an officer was about and in any case saw nothing to laugh at.

'As you all know,' said Mrs Paxon, consulting some notes, 'the shifts will be of two hours each and there will be two persons on each shift, so that if one should be called away there will still be one on guard. The telephone is connected with the Rectory in case of alarm. Perhaps, Mrs Villars, you would speak to the office as a kind of little opening ceremony.'

Mrs Villars said she would like to suggest that Corporal

Jackson, who had been active in helping to instal it, should speak the first words. Corporal Jackson, confirmed in his secret thought that Mrs Villars was a real lady, looked to his lieutenant for permission.

'Carry on, Corporal,' said Mr Holden.

Corporal Jackson, who had for the last two days carried on over the supposedly virgin line intermittent and very coarse conversations with the office typist, an ex-employee of a firm of racing touts, saluted.

'Oh, I have forgotten the key,' said Mrs Paxon. 'The telephone man gave it to me only yesterday and I must have left it in the pocket of my blue slacks.'

'All right, madam,' said Corporal Jackson, who didn't believe in having things locked unless he could get into them, 'I have the duplicate.'

He strode to the telephone-box, unlocked it and took off the receiver.

'What number does one give?' said Miss Talbot.

'Private line, madam,' said the Corporal, not betraying by the flicker of an eyelash his contempt for the question and the questioner. ''Ullo. That Private Moss?'

The voice of Private Moss replied that it blank well was and he was blank well fed up with waiting for the blankety-blank balloon to go up and wanted to go to his blanky dinner.

Corporal Jackson, still holding the receiver, said, 'Telephone all correct, sir.'

'Shall I speak on it?' said Mrs Paxon.

'Hold on; lady wishes to speak to you,' said Corporal Jackson, with the fiendish wish to annoy Private Moss. In this he succeeded so well that he had to hang the receiver up quickly and said to Mrs Paxon the officers were all out, with which she had to be content.

'Well now,' said Mrs Paxon, again consulting her notes, 'we begin our shifts at twelve o'clock to-day, with Father Fewling and Miss Talbot. Well, I am afraid from twelve to two isn't a very convenient time for lunch. I didn't think of that at the time, how stupid of me. But if we made it from eleven to one, then a pair of spotters would have to come on at one, which is almost as bad. What do you say?'

Father Fewling said it was nothing to the dog-watch, and as far as he was concerned he could lunch at any time, but if Miss Talbot cared to go at one he would willingly carry on alone.

'I talked it over with my sister,' said Miss Talbot, 'and we decided to bring our lunch with us on the days when we took duty. With a few sandwiches and some nut-and-milk chocolate I shall be quite, quite happy.'

'Where *did* you get nut-and-milk chocolate?' said Mrs Paxon, deeply interested. 'Scatcherd's had none, nor had Potter, nor the Lollipoppe Shoppe, and my husband tried all over Barchester last week.'

'You would never guess,' said Miss Talbot, flattered. 'I wrote to my married sister in Cornwall and she says that at Pallas Pendrax they have more than they know what to do with. She cannot account for it, but we must be grateful.'

Mrs Paxon said it was just like sardines which turned up in the most unexpected places and who so surprised as she when she found some at the Cow Street Post Office, but ever since the Purified Steam Bakery had taken to selling potted meat and cigarettes *nothing* surprised her.

'I brought a thermos of coffee, too,' said Miss Talbot, 'in case Father Fewling felt thirsty.'

Father Fewling miserably thanked her.

'Well, now I suppose we begin our work,' said Miss Talbot, who having surreptitiously looked at her wrist-watch and seen it was only a quarter to twelve, thought she would get the rest of the party off the roof and enjoy her pastor's society in peace. 'By the way, what do we *do*, Mrs Paxon?'

'Well,' said Mrs Paxon brightly, 'you keep a good look-out – in every direction of course – and if you see anything you tell Father Fewling or he tells you, and you report it to the office. Corporal Jackson will leave you his key, won't you, Corporal? If it is a parachute, you say where.'

'I suppose a rough indication would be sufficient,' said Miss Talbot, suddenly becoming very technical. 'I mean if I saw a parachute that looked as if it were falling down behind Hopper's Spinney, it might have fallen straight into the dewpond or it might have drifted down at Quelter's Farm, or really anywhere.'

'I did bring my telescope,' said Miss Hopgood's aunt, 'in case anyone wanted it, but I left it downstairs. I mean in the south aisle, with my umbrella.'

'I am sure Corporal Jackson will get it,' said Mrs Paxon. 'Oh, I did so mean to bring you a map, but something put it right out of my head. I think it's the war. It really quite upsets daily life sometimes.'

The invaluable Corporal Jackson said he would get the telescope and fetch a map from the office and clattered downstairs.

Mrs Dunsford, who had, as usual, been correctly silent, coughed gently.

'Er – should—' said Mrs Dunsford, and was overtaken by another fit of coughing.

'You oughtn't to be up here,' said Mrs Paxon.

'Should, I was going to say,' said Mrs Dunsford, trampling on the weaknesses of the flesh, 'should the siren sound, what do we do?'

Everyone waited with interest for Mrs Paxon to speak.

'Well,' said Mrs Paxon, 'of course you can't take cover here. If it was gas, it mightn't reach you on the roof, but a bomb on the tower might be a nuisance.'

'I think I know what Father Fewling would say,' said Miss Talbot intimately.

'Ladies go below at once,' said Father Fewling, 'men carry on.'

'Surely,' said Miss Talbot, turning her eyes on him with as childlike a faith as a woman well over fifty can express, 'we are as safe here as elsewhere?'

But the beautiful implications of this remark were entirely lost on Father Fewling, who very sensibly said that a church was an obvious mark for bombs and when the decks were cleared for action all non-combatants must, as far as possible, take shelter. So earnest was he on this point that Mrs Villars expected him to say that they must be battened under hatches.

'Well, you know our siren,' said Mrs Paxon. 'First we get the planes and the bangs and when everything is quiet it goes off like a mad bull.'

'And then wakes everyone up to say All Clear,' said Mr Holden moodily.

'So we'll be getting along and leave you to your vigil,' said Mrs Paxon.

'By the way,' said Miss Talbot, 'would it be quite – I mean I am no great smoker – but it is occasionally a relaxation, but on a church tower I thought perhaps it would not be *quite*.'

Mrs Paxon looked at Father Fewling as spiritual adviser, but he very meanly pretended to be looking at the view.

'I think,' said Mrs Paxon, 'as it is a War Duty, no one could possibly mind.'

Miss Talbot, who had a simple mind, took it that Mrs Paxon had said No One, and felt relieved.

Corporal Jackson now returned, a little breathless, with the telescope and a map which he handed to Miss Talbot, saluted and retired. She unfolded the map. A strong wind which had been biding its time suddenly whipped it out of her hand, tore it in two and carried it away.

'Oh, dear!' said Miss Talbot.

'You can keep the telescope if you like, Miss Talbot,' said Miss Hopgood's aunt. 'I'll be coming on duty at two and I'll take it over then. Coming to supper to-night, Father Fewling? Porter Sidus will be in conjunction with Ferrovia Australis, and if it is clear we ought to get quite a good view.'

Father Fewling thanked her and accepted.

'Oh, I fear I shall not be able to come to your meeting after all,' said Miss Hopgood's aunt to Miss Talbot, with alarming graciousness. 'Father Fewling will show you how to use the telescope.'

Mrs Villars was the last of the ladies to leave the roof. As she left she heard Miss Talbot say to her fellow-watcher, 'I see you don't mind smoking, Father Fewling, so I will join you in a friendly gasper,' and felt extremely sorry for her friend Tubby.

'Let me go down before you,' said Mr Holden, who had lingered near the door. 'It is so dark on the stairs.'

Mrs Villars was suddenly smitten by a memory of Pelléas leading Mélisande down cardboard steps in the rock and began to laugh.

'Why do you always laugh?' said Mr Holden, stopping abruptly at a turn of the stair where, standing a step lower, his face was on a level with hers. Mrs Villars was just going to say, 'Because of something silly I thought of,' when the church clock struck twelve and the noise was so awful that they both hurried down as fast as they could.

'That noise was too much for you,' said Mr Holden accusingly, as they stepped out of the dark stair into the comparative light of the church.

Mrs Villars's lower self nearly said, 'But you were there, so I was not afraid,' but she caught it in time and said pleasantly that she always hoped not to die in a belfry with a face contorted in such a mask of fear as made it impossible to get her into a coffin. The spell was comfortably broken and Mr Holden helped her to embroider upon this agreeable theme as far as the Rectory garden. As Mrs Villars went up the two steps to her door Mr Holden suddenly remembered not to be natural and said, 'You will rest this afternoon?'

'I always do,' said Mrs Villars, and hoped she had kept the exasperation out of her voice.

During her rest Mrs Villars remembered that she had forgotten to give Mrs Turner a book she had promised to remember to give her, which naturally pulled her back from her comfortable half-consciousness with a jerk and entirely spoilt her chances of going to sleep. So with angry determination she got up, found the book and decided to take it round at once before she could forget it again. But what with Mrs Chapman who sent in a special message that she was sure Mrs Villars would like to know Scatcherd's hadn't sent the soap-flakes and one thing and another it was after half-past four by the time she set out. Thanks to Summer Time, the afternoon was not yet dark, but clouds were blowing up and the wind was cold. Mr Scatcherd said he was sorry about the soap-flakes but there was not a packet left in Northbridge and no chance of getting any till the end of next week as the Government had commandeered it all, so Mrs Villars went over to Potter, where she bought two large packets and was told she could have as many more as she wanted.

'Is Mrs Turner in?' said Mrs Villars when the door of The Hollies was opened.

'Yes, m'm,' said Mrs Turner's maid, but with such a puzzled air that Mrs Villars wondered if anything was wrong.

'Could I see her for a moment?' said Mrs Villars.

'Oh yes, m'm,' said the maid, hesitating again. In fact Mrs Villars felt that if she had not been the Rector's wife she would have been turned away.

She turned towards the drawing-room, expecting the maid to open the door, but an anxious voice from the other side of the hall said, 'They've gone in, m'm.' At the same time the maid opened the dining-room door, disclosing the dining-room table and what looked to Mrs Villars like hundreds of people sitting round it.

It then burst upon her mind that she had done something which was against all the tacit conventions of Northbridge. Coming there as she did, fresh from the life of a headmaster's wife, where open house was kept term in term out, it had been some time before she realized that a Northbridge tea party still had a slightly Victorian sanctity about it. Broadly speaking, one did not drop in to tea; one waited till one was asked. As far as Mrs Turner was concerned, Mrs Villars knew that she was welcome at any time, but the maid was evidently conscious of a gross solecism and would probably live on the story of her intrusion for weeks to come.

'It's all right, Doris,' she said, 'it's business,' upon which the maid's face cleared and she went back to the kitchen.

'I didn't mean to burst in, Poppy,' said Mrs Villars, thinking this was as good a moment as any other to use her friend's name for the first time, as it had to be done sooner or later, 'but I knew you wanted *From Cardsharper to Cardinal* back for the week-end, so I brought it.'

She looked round in a friendly way and saw Miss Pemberton, both Mrs Turner's nieces, Mr Downing, Mr Greaves and Captain Topham all making hearty teas.

'How nice of you, Verena,' said Mrs Turner, who also had not yet used the privilege extended to her till the present moment and was glad to make the plunge and get it over. 'Come up here by me.'

'Have my chair, Mrs Villars,' said Mr Greaves getting up.

'Ackcherly,' said Betty, 'you'd better have mine.'

'Have my chair, Mrs Villars,' said Captain Topham, as an entirely new idea.

Mrs Turner's other niece got up, strode a pace to the wall,

seized a chair, dragged it to the table and put it next to her aunt, so Mrs Villars sat down in it.

'Did you have a nice walk?' she said to Mr Downing, who was on Mrs Turner's other side.

'Ackcherly,' said Betty from beyond Mr Downing, 'there was a beastly wind up on Fish Hill, but I showed Mr Downing where the golden-crested mippet's nest was last year and we met Captain Topham up there so we brought him back to tea. In fact he ackcherly saw the mippet's nest first.'

'Oh, come now,' said Captain Topham, 'not till you told me they always nested in wych elms.'

An exchange of persiflage then took place between him and Betty, so that Mr Downing was free to talk to Mrs Turner, and Mrs Villars turned to Miss Pemberton, who was chumping her cake with an expression of satisfaction. What Miss Pemberton's exact feelings towards Mr Downing were, no one had ever found out, partly because Miss Pemberton gave them no encouragement to do so. Nor perhaps could Miss Pemberton herself have told them. Mr Downing had made his way slowly and over a number of years into her rather crabbed literary heart, or perhaps into that part of her brain that counted as a heart. It was collaboration over that valuable and practically unread work, *The Biographical Dictionary of Provence*, that had thrown them together. Both were poor, both were middle-aged, both were solitary. By the time the Dictionary had reached the section Falh-Féau, the publishers decided not to lose any more money on it and Miss Pemberton asked Mr Downing to her cottage at Northbridge to get over his disappointment. She liked him and wanted to help him and had nothing to offer but a lodging and her own indomitable energy. Mr Downing was glad of the shelter and found the energy such a support, being himself a scholar in the most wearing and unpractical sense of the word, that he came back again and again. Without any definite arrangement being made he had finally given up his not very attractive rooms in London, paid Miss Pemberton a good deal less than he had paid to his landlady, and when he went to town stayed at his club.

Under his benefactress's severe eye he worked harder than he had ever worked before and even looked a little less thin, while his books on Provençal literature continued to excite the interest and in some cases the vitriolic criticism of at least two hundred readers. He sometimes resented her yoke and was always grateful for her kindness, showing his gratitude by accepting her rule in every respect, even when it meant giving up some of his friendships. But the way most pleasing to Miss Pemberton in which he showed his gratitude was one which he did not suspect. Like an intelligent domestic animal he took bed, fire and food for granted, never asked where they came from, and had never once wondered if he were any kind of burden on his hostess's slender means.

This suited Miss Pemberton, under whose arid exterior lay the true woman's wish to make a door-mat of herself without any return, excellently. To look after Mr Downing, to keep his nose to the Provençal grindstone, to guard him against possible wives whom he certainly could not afford to marry, became her life's work. Not that Miss Pemberton wanted to marry him herself. The cottage, which was large enough for Miss Pemberton and Mr Downing, would certainly never have held Mr and Mrs Downing, and that she knew. And if anything so unreasonable had ever come into her mind, her common-sense told her that if she had a husband who stayed at home she could not, at her age, do without her little maid in the middle of the week, nor make the economies of food that she practised between Monday and Friday. Being very poor for a long time makes one forget a little how people who are better off live, and if Miss Pemberton imagined her guest as married, it was always to a woman as badly off as herself, but one who would not deprive herself of small comforts for his sake, so she made herself into a dragon and frightened the spinsters of Northbridge away, or played chaperon with such steely and grudging politeness that they gave up any attempts to get Mr Downing to their tea-parties. Whether Mr Downing would have liked to go to their tea-parties we do not quite know, but his gratitude and a certain desiccated chivalry forbade him ever to express such a desire to Miss Pemberton, so the village looked upon them with faint suspicion and on the whole left them alone.

Mrs Turner and her nieces were, as we have seen, tolerated. Mrs Turner had been a widow for so long that it never occurred to most people, and certainly not to Miss Pemberton, that she could ever be anything else, and as for her nieces they had so lately banged and bumped their way out of schoolgirls into hearty young women that Miss Pemberton had not thought of them at all. Nor indeed had either of these young ladies thought of Mr Downing, except for a general impression that he and Miss Pemberton were awfully brainy and about a hundred, and not till the mention of the golden-crested mippet had Betty considered him as a human being at all. Miss Pemberton, quite rightly, felt that to Mr Downing Betty would seem such a child, and an uneducated one at that, that she could afford to relax her vigilance and even go to tea at The Hollies. She now felt satisfied by her bold step. Betty was obviously far more interested in Captain Topham than in Mr Downing, and in Mrs Turner's mild atmosphere everyone could safely relax.

There are many and innocent varieties of snobisme, from the snobisme pur sang which loves a duke to the esoteric snobisme that knows the upper reaches of the Windrush and resents the fact of anyone else knowing them with the same intimacy. Most of these pleasant affectations are quite amusing to the uninitiate. But one snobbery is peculiarly dull to those who cannot feel a passionate human interest in its object, and that is the absorbing snobbery of birds. Only by devotedly loving relations, or people with houses so big and staffs so competent that guests can do what they like without giving trouble, can the bird enthusiasts be tolerated. The most we can hope is that they will take their lunch out with them, even if to do so they borrow your car and take another guest whom you particularly wanted, and that they will be back not too late for dinner. As for the enthusiast who insists on going out after dark armed with a net which he throws over bushes marked down by him during the day, and then flashes a torch on to it, waking up all the inhabitants, frightening them almost to death and causing several of them to lay three-yolked eggs, just for the scientific pleasure of seeing bird life at night and subsequently sending a photograph for publication in *Country Life* of a mother-bird with mad terror in her eye sitting on a clutch of eggs which will obviously all be addled by the morning, as for him we cannot abide him. We are glad to say that Betty and Captain Topham were not of this kidney, but even so their talk was intolerably dull to their hearers. Not that anyone wanted to listen to them, but their voices were so loud and cheerful that it was practically impossible not to. Golden-crested mippets, broad-tailed gallows birds, wych elms, hurtled in the air.

'I am so glad,' said Mrs Villars to Miss Pemberton, 'that Betty has found some bird friends. She is so enthusiastic and no one here is very keen, at least not in her way.'

'Bird-boxes on a rickety pole on the lawn and half coconuts for tits. Bah! I know them,' said Miss Pemberton with some vehemence.

'Oh, do you like birds, then?' said Mrs Villars, interested in a possible new light on Miss Pemberton's rather porcupine-like character.

'I wouldn't mind if I never saw a bird again,' said Miss Pemberton, cutting herself another slice of cake so generously that Mrs Villars wondered if she was making her dinner now, and felt very sorry for her. 'Or dogs; or cats; or indeed any animals. But Betty is a nice girl and that is more than I could say of most.'

And she looked with decided approval at Betty, who had just hit Captain Topham a violent though friendly blow on the arm by way of emphasizing a point she wished to make in connection with the habits of migratory birds.

'Mr Downing stays at home too much,' said the surprising Miss Pemberton. 'It will do him good to get out with Betty and see some birds. When will you bring your husband to see us, Mrs Villars?'

Mrs Villars thought two thoughts simultaneously, as most

176

of us do during any conversation. The first was whether Miss Pemberton were not secretly a little glad to find a safe and suitable young companion for her lodger. More than once she had seen Mr Downing and his hostess setting out for a walk or returning from one and had sympathetically felt tired with Miss Pemberton trudging along a quarter of a pace behind her companion. As Mrs Turner's cheerful but embarrassing central light beat down upon Miss Pemberton's masculine features, untouched by any art, she looked old, and Mrs Villars, whose quick surface sympathy was apt to lead her to form conclusions upon which her imagination could embroider at its leisure, was conscious of the whole immense fatigue of the woman of brains who lives with the artist, even if his talent is only a slight and scholarly one.

This thought she put away in a flash, to think over and discuss later with her husband, whose name immediately brought her to the second of her simultaneous thoughts, if we may be excused the expression, which was how very little Gregory would want to dine at Punshions, how right he would be, and how disappointed Miss Pemberton would be if he didn't. For it was clear that Miss Pemberton felt that in offering Mr Villars the treat of spending an evening in company with Mr Downing she was offering something very valuable, and that was the measure of her regard for the Villarses, a regard which Mrs Villars found flattering and which naturally softened her heart towards Miss Pemberton.

All these things went through her mind in a flash and were immediately overlaid by a third thought, namely that she must answer Miss Pemberton. So she said that they would be delighted to come, and would Miss Pemberton suggest a day.

'I must ask Mr Downing when he is free,' said Miss Pemberton, who always did her best to impress upon people that Mr Downing was the more important of the household, though with but little success.

The party now began to disperse. Betty dragged Captain Topham off to her sitting-room to look at some old coloured engravings of birds, while Mrs Turner's other niece and Mr Greaves went off to the drawing-room to practise songs for the Comforts for the Barsetshire Regiment Concert, taking turns most good-humouredly in pushing each other off the piano-stool to show how it ought to go.

Mrs Villars found herself in the hall with Mrs Turner and what she was apt to call to herself the Pembertons.

'Harold,' said Miss Pemberton, 'I want to arrange an evening for the Rector and Mrs Villars to dine with us. Will Friday fortnight suit you?'

Now it was tacitly understood that such a question was publicly put to save Mr Downing's face and keep up the fiction that he was master at Punshions. So what was Miss Pemberton's astonishment when her lodger said:

'Mrs Turner has just asked us to come in for coffee that evening, Ianthe, but Saturday fortnight would be all right if Mr and Mrs Villars are free.'

And this appalling and subversive remark he made as if it were a matter of course that his engagements should take precedence of Miss Pemberton's, so that between her public convention that his plans were to come before hers and her inner determination that her plans should always come before his, her mind was sorely upset and exercised. The immediate effect of this was to make her go a dull brick-red, thus terrifying her unfortunate lodger who had not seen this phenomenon since the day when he suggested bringing his publisher's secretary down for a week-end three years ago.

'What is it, Ianthe?' said the wretched Mr Downing.

'Nothing,' said Miss Pemberton, to which, of course, Mr Downing's only possible answer was, 'But what is it?'

'Simply,' said Miss Pemberton in as cold a voice as an elderly woman who is shaking with rage can manage, 'that I thought of asking the Rector and his wife that night. That is all. It does not, of course, matter in the least, but it would be easier if you would sometimes, only *sometimes*, let me know what you want to do before I make an utter and complete fool of myself. That is all. And you may or may not remember that we were going to revise your proofs that Saturday. Possibly you would prefer not to revise them. It does not matter in the least, but I thought I would mention it. That is all.'

There is something about the words 'That is all' that strikes terror to the bravest heart and Mr Downing was not very brave. Mrs Turner and Mrs Villars, who were both passably courageous in social matters, blenched at them, though their blenching was combined with a schoolgirl wish to giggle. Their position was not comfortable. Miss Pemberton, carried away by a just wrath, had apparently not the slightest consciousness that her low, fervent accents were ringing through the hall and Mrs Turner and Mrs Villars would gladly have slipped through a crack in the floor or flown up to the ceiling, as indeed would Mr Downing.

Mrs Turner did go so far as to say that any day would do as well as Friday, much weakening her position by the afterthought or rider that Sunday, of course, wasn't much good, Monday and Wednesday were her A.R.P. nights, and on Tuesday Father Fewling was going to speak to the Red Cross about First-Aid in Dockyards, and she knew there was something which she couldn't remember but it would doubtless come back to her in a moment on Thursday, after which her voice died uncomfortably away under Miss Pemberton's entire want of attention.

As Mrs Villars was the only one who had not spoken, it was obviously her duty to speak, partly to keep the ball, though it was more like a large lump of lead with spikes all over it, rolling, partly because after all she was the Rector's wife. Other Awful Scenes flitted through her head as she madly searched for something that would meet the situation. The day when the School butler had turned up at a cricket match wearing one of her husband's clerical collars under the cumulative influence of having abstracted port in small quantities from the cellar over a number of years; the day when a very unpleasant parent had hinted at benefactions to the school if his equally unpleasant son were Captain of the Eleven; the day when the junior science master had become engaged to the matron, and the far worse day a week later when they had both appealed to her about a quarrel they were having and had broken the engagement off in her drawing-room just before the school play. But in all these social straits she had had her husband's support and authority, while here she stood alone, representing Society and the Church. So she made a mental sacrifice of her husband's feelings and said to Miss Pemberton:

'I don't know if you would allow my husband to look at the proofs if we came on the Saturday, Miss Pemberton. He has enjoyed Mr Downing's other books so much and I know that to see this book before it comes out would really be a great treat for him. Not that it is really his subject, but he is so interested in any kind of French literature. Only if it suits you and Mr Downing, of course.'

Even as she spoke she was aware how very silly her words sounded, but to her intense relief they appeared to be having a good effect. Mr Downing's thin scholarly face softened and assumed an air of gentle fatuity, while Miss Pemberton, her massive head a little on one side like a reflective elephant, appeared to be considering the suggestion with some approach to reasonableness.

'Well, Harold,' said Miss Pemberton, not unkindly, 'how would it be to ask Mr and Mrs Villars on Saturday? You could read those two last chapters aloud.'

Mr Downing, who thought it wiser not to remind his Egeria that Saturday had been his own original suggestion, replied:

'Certainly, Ianthe. And I could ask Villars his opinion of the footnote on the *Andalhou* of Guibert le Biau.'

This was a calculated piece of meanness on Mr Downing's part, for Miss Pemberton had strenuously and hitherto successfully opposed the recognition of the *Andalhou* (a very dull and prolix little work on the twenty-five different qualities of *Amitié par Amour* as opposed to *Amour par Amitié*) attributing it, and we think on valid grounds, to an ardent Félibriste, *maire* of a small commune near Lille, known in literary circles as Numa Garagou. But after the shattering conditions of the last three minutes, for all we have recounted took no longer, she was willing to make any concession that would restore Mr Downing's apparently wavering allegiance, so she swallowed his treachery, though without any intention of forgetting it, and said to Mrs Villars with some dignity that if Mr Villars would really be so kind as to criticize Mr Downing's two last chapters it would be a great pleasure to see them both on Saturday fortnight at half-past seven. And then her conscience, for she was a thorough gentleman at heart, smote her for discourtesy to Mrs Turner, so she smiled her rather alarming smile on her and said she and Mr Downing would like very much to come in for coffee on Friday.

'And now, Harold,' she said, 'if you have your torch we had better be going.'

Mr Downing's brief sense of triumph and authority fell from him in an instant as he confessed that he had forgotten the torch.

Mrs Turner offered to lend one, but Miss Pemberton, uttering the awful words, 'It doesn't matter,' took Mr Downing by the arm and left the house.

Mrs Villars and Mrs Turner looked at each other.

"'Heaven pity all poor wanderers lone!
Hark to the wind upon the hill!'"

said Mrs Villars reflectively. 'Good-bye, Poppy. I must break the bad news to Gregory. Poor Mr Downing.'

'And poor Miss Pemberton,' said Mrs Turner, which shows what a very nice and understanding woman she was.

9

Air-Raid Shelter

It is sad to have to relate among other and more important events that with the approach of winter the roof-spotting inaugurated amid such éclat had gradually died a natural death. For a month or so the relays had succeeded each other with feverish punctuality, rivalry for the telescope had been bitter, and several watchers had brought miniature opera-glasses, relics of their mothers' or aunts' younger days and warranted to show two separate circles each containing a blur. Much to Father Fewling's relief the Misses Talbot began to slacken in their devotion about this time, partly on account of the weather, but more largely because they had discovered at Nuffield a clergyman whose Practices, as Miss Hopgood called them, were even more ultramontane than Father Fewling's, going so far as a crouching before the altar and a gentle banging of the forehead upon the floor that brought inexpressible balm to the soul of the devout. Not that the attendance at St Sycorax suffered in consequence, as our readers will be glad to hear, for Father Fewling was so much liked and respected that a great many people went to his services out of friendship, which is perhaps as good a way as any other. As for Mr Villars, he liked people to enjoy themselves in their own way so long as they did not brawl, and as his definition of brawling did not include the ritual of St Sycorax (though it included root and branch the goings-on at Nuffield) all was concord.

No one denied that excellent work had been done by the roof-spotters, from Betty, who distinctly saw with Miss Hopgood's aunt's telescope a pied gobble-belly trying to nest out of season on the Rectory roof and making a bad job of it, to Miss Dunsford, who having laid the telescope onto the roundabout was able to give valuable evidence in the matter of a mild collision between Captain Topham's little car and an army lorry which was pulling at a highly illegal speed and on the wrong side of the road a trailer containing an immense wooden triangle of national importance though nobody knew what. By the time that the black-out was covering two-thirds of the twenty-four hours, and fog or mist, alternating with gales, the remaining third, the roof-spotting was doomed, much to the relief of Mrs Paxon to whose fertile imagination it had occurred that the one end and aim of any German parachutists would be to land on the church tower and Get her there. So after the telephone wire had been twice blown down and twice restored by the minions of His Majesty's Telephone Service, under the direction of Corporal Jackson, the scheme came quietly to an end.

It is possible that a small subversive element in the A.R.P., headed, we regret to say, by Mr Clifford, the village schoolmaster, and Hopper, the less popular of the two cobblers, might have been disagreeable over the roof-spotting business, owing to a passion for notoriety which they saw no other way of gratifying, but that by great good luck there was the best part of a week of torrential rain. Not that they were drowned, though that would, broadly speaking, have been an excellent thing, but the great affair of the A.R.P. shelter was thereby brought to a head and occupied Northbridge so furiously that the condition of Europe, the disappearance of onions subsequent to price-control, and even the possibility of invasion by parachute paled before it.

The facts were briefly these. During the early autumn the authorities, usually referred to as They, because no one really knew who they were, caused to be excavated from a piece of waste land called Hooper's Platt a deep trench some thirty yards long, six feet wide and six feet deep. This trench was then roofed with semi-circular sheets of corrugated iron (if we make ourselves clear), which in its turn was covered with most of the earth taken out of the trench, thus presenting a very impressive and humpy appearance. At one end of the trench a flight of concrete steps was built and at the other a stove pipe stuck up into the air to ensure ventilation. At the entrance to the shelter, which had a plank seat fixed along each side, a post was erected carrying a white board with the letter S painted in black upon it, reminding Mrs Dunsford of the Siege of Lucknow. Not, she explained, that she was a Mutiny baby, for that was her Aunt Louisa who was rescued by a faithful ayah and so stained with one of those wonderful Indian dyes that her own parents positively could not recognize her when she was restored to them, but that it made her think of those wonderful lines of Kipling's, wasn't it, about Ever upon our something roof the banner of England blew, or flew, she wasn't quite sure which.

A dump for scrap metal was then begun by Them, forming a pleasant adjunct to the shelter. Here such rubbish as the dustman would not take lay and rusted very happily in a tangle of old bedsteads, locks, broken lawn-mowers, saucepans with the bottom burnt out and birdcages.

For a few weeks this magnificent national effort gave great pleasure to the schoolchildren, who were repeatedly late for afternoon school owing to its attractions, stole any small pieces of metal that they could carry, and adorned the walls of the shelter with a number of very unoriginal graffiti. Then a piece of the roof fell in, most unfortunately not killing two very rude little girls whose habit it was to stand by the entrance shouting,

'Squint-eye, square-eye,
Can't catch a butterfly,'

at harmless passers-by and then darting into the tunnel, so the entrance was barricaded except during school hours with some stout barbed wire. This was largely at the instance of Mrs Paxon, who did not care if the little girls were killed or not, but saw in the tunnel which had no second exit alarming facilities for people Getting each other, even going so far as to say this to Miss Hampton, who had come over from the Southbridge A.R.P. to see what the Northbridge A.R.P. was doing. Miss Hampton, who was in her tailor-made grey tweeds, black leggings and a very smart black tricorne, removed her cigarette and its eight-inch amber holder from her mouth, blew a smoke ring and remarked:

'Do 'em good. If I were the Government I'll tell you what I'd do after the war. Have all the air-raid shelters officially recognized. Charge a penny for admission. People don't value what they get for nothing. Get all the inhibitions out of people's systems like anything. Come and have a drink.'

After which she had carried Mrs Paxon off to the Mitre where she expounded her plan to an admiring, if puzzled, audience in the Saloon Bar, while Mrs Paxon, whose ideas on what she vaguely called 'that kind of thing,' were extremely ill-defined, felt she was indeed seeing life and didn't quite like it.

When the heavy rains to which we have alluded began to fall, the ground about the shelter, being of heavy clay, began to get very slithery and several children fell down the steps. Gradually the wet percolated the soil, baked to the hardness of bricks through the long dry summer, and began to appear like beads of perspiration on the walls of the tunnel. As the days went on the beads ran together and became blotches, the blotches turned to rivulets, and by Thursday the floor was a foot deep in water, a rat was found drowned, and every one of Mr Clifford's scholars came to school with their clothes torn by the barbed wire, their boots soaking wet and clay-daubed, and most annoying of all not one of them caught cold.

A frightful row then took place among Them as the result of which nothing at all was done. Some of the water gradually sank away, some was belatedly pumped out by the contractor who was at work on the Government huts over at Plumstead, and the rest froze. As the barbed wire had by now been trampled into uselessness or removed piecemeal, the schoolchildren thus had access to a free skating-rink until Jimmy Hopper, the cobbler's little boy, broke his leg, when They nailed some strong planks over the entrance and peace was restored.

It was on the Saturday which followed the official closing of the shelter that Mr and Mrs Villars were due to dine at Punshions, and it is difficult to say which of them was looking forward to it the less. Mr Villars knew that he would be cold and probably have a bad dinner, but looked forward to a talk with Mr Downing. Mrs Villars disliked the cold mortally, but was better able to bear with bad food. On the other hand, she could think of nothing to say to Miss Pemberton that would take more than a quarter of an hour. Provençal poetry was not her line, Elizabeth Rivers she vaguely confused with Jane Shore, and as for early Italian painters she could hope no more than to look intelligent and not overdo it. And as for Mr Downing, quite apart from Miss Pemberton's views on the subject, she well knew that the gentlemen would grapple each other to their souls with hoops of steel and never stop talking as long as they were together.

It was a clear, cold, starlight night when Mr and Mrs Villars set out at about ten minutes past seven on foot for Punshions. Instead of going by the High Street, as Mrs Villars did when we first met her, they took the back lane that went through Northbridge's slum area, a row of little two-storey cottages that had sunk into disreputability since the beginning of the century. It then crossed a trickle of water, tributary to the river, skirted the churchyard of St Sycorax and debouched into the High Street just by Miss Pemberton's cottage.

As they passed St Sycorax, Father Fewling came out accompanied by someone whom they did not at first recognize in the starry darkness and walked across the lane toward a piece of land which had for some years been for sale as a building plot. From the direction in which they were going a mysterious line of light could be seen, very distinct, yet throwing no beam.

'What is it, Gregory?' said Mrs Villars. 'Spies?'

Mr Villars expressed the opinion that it was the St Sycorax new Air-Raid Wardens' Shelter, rumours of which had reached them, and began to walk very slowly, an action which his loving wife interpreted as curiosity to see what the shelter was like, so she said would there be time to look at it.

'It can't be more than twenty past,' said the Rector. 'I heard the church clock strike the quarter as we passed Faraway Corner. We will go and look if you like.'

Accordingly, they crossed the road and approached the line of light. As they came near it broadened for a moment and a man came out whom they recognized as Mr Downing.

'Good evening, Downing,' said the Rector. 'Is this your new Wardens' Shelter?'

Mr Downing said not exactly his, but he was on duty there on Mondays and Thursdays if the siren went. It was really Father Fewling's, as he and his fellow Air-Raid Wardens, who were mostly ex-Scouts, had constructed it and furnished it. He then asked Mr Villars, rather diffidently, if he and Mrs Villars would care to look at it.

'We'd love to,' said Mrs Villars, voicing her husband's wish, 'only we mustn't stay long.'

'Oh, you can see it all in two minutes,' said Mr Downing.

'I was just going back myself so we can go together. Miss Pemberton is always very punctual. Come down.'

He flashed his torch on to a new little flight of brick steps, down which, with an apology, he preceded his guests. The line of light turned out on a closer view to come from one side of a stout curtain which Mr Downing pulled a little aside, saying, 'Fewling, visitors.'

Father Fewling's stout form came bustling forward from the far end of the shelter.

'Come in, come in,' he cried, holding back the curtain and at once letting it drop again behind his guests. 'How nice of you to come and look. We are pretty ship-shape here, aren't we?'

'Indeed you are.' said Mrs Villars admiringly.

The wardens' shelter was indeed a charming abode. Its rounded roof of corrugated iron was neatly whitewashed, as were its wooden supports. On each side was a two-tiered bunk made from old wooden crates, with considerable skill, pillow and rugs laid on each bunk as neatly as if a ship's steward had been there, and at the head of each was a small electric lamp. The floor was raised a little on a kind of duckboard. Between the supports and above the bunks wooden portholes, painted white, were fixed to the walls, and at the further end was a ship's wheel with a Union Jack hanging above it. In the middle of the ceiling was an electric fan.

'Tell them about the ventilation, Fewling,' said Mr Downing, still with his air of diffidence which Mrs Villars was now sure concealed great inward pride.

'If it won't bore you—' said Father Fewling, also with the diffidence of the lover in discussing his beloved.

'By no means,' said the Rector. 'Tell us all about it, Fewling. You naval chaps do know how to do things.'

'Oh, I don't know,' said Father Fewling modestly. 'We have to be able to turn our hands to this and that. You know Downing was in the R.N.V.R. in the last war.'

'No, I didn't,' said the Rector, eyeing his friend with new interest.

'Well, not really,' said Mr Downing apologetically. 'I was invalided out in 1916, but I learnt a lot, at least I forgot a good deal of it, but Fewling let me give him a hand.'

'Rubbish, my dear chap,' said Father Fewling. 'It was your idea to put up the portholes.'

Mr Downing blushed, as far as one can see a blush by electric light, and begged Father Fewling to show the ventilating system, as he and Mr and Mrs Villars had only a few moments to spare and must not, he said with an uneasy glance towards the door, be late.

'Well,' said Father Fewling, 'we started with a large drainpipe from the roof, forrard there, up to the outside of the mound, but the boys would throw stones down it; my own choirboys, I'm afraid. So I put two thicknesses of wire netting across the top and fastened them down tight. The young imps did put some sand down and one of them tried water, but my scouts happened to be about and gave them an awful hiding and made the whole lot join the Troop, the First St Sycorax. We'll have to have a Second St Sycorax soon, our numbers are so large. Young Scatcherd will make an excellent troop leader. You know, by the way, what my name is?'

He paused, and luckily before Mr Villars could say 'Fewling,' he went on, '"Great Black Bear". Good, isn't it.

My black cassock, you see, and then a bear is a stupid kind of fellow like me. I assure you I was as pleased when the boys gave me that name as I was when I got my first promotion – or was ordained,' he added hastily.

'Hurry up, Fewling,' said Mr Downing. 'I don't want to keep Miss Pemberton – or Mr and Mrs Villars – waiting.'

'All right, old fellow,' said Father Fewling. 'So then you see, Mrs Villars, we found that a ventilating drainpipe wasn't enough, because there wasn't any draught, so you see what I did. Look there.'

He pointed dramatically upwards as if the ceiling were twenty feet high instead of just clearing Mr Villars's head.

'An electric fan. Young Hibberd, your sexton's grandson, wired the place. A bright lad he is. He put up the lights over the bunks. But the best of all were the drains. When we dug this shelter I saw we would be flooded out lying on the lower slope as we do, and drains aren't much in my line. Scuppers, yes; drains, no. But young Fitchett, Fitchett the grocer's son, who is with Trowel the builder, had the idea of using the slope to carry superfluous water away into the stream. Did you know, Villars, that the stream was called Hallbrook?'

The Rector said he never knew it had a name.

'Nor did I,' said Father Fewling, 'but Trowel came down to help his lad one day and told us his grandfather used to call it Hallbrook, so Downing here looked it up in some old books in London and found this bit of land used to belong to a thane or someone, like Ivanhoe, you know, called Haella, and there's the whole history. And all our overflow goes into old Haella's brook and away down into the river.'

While Father Fewling was speaking the sound of the church clock striking the half-hour was distantly heard.

'I can't tell you how interesting it has been,' said Mrs Villars, 'but Miss Pemberton will be waiting.'

'Of course, of course,' said Father Fewling. 'Just look at my ship's wheel before you go. You'd never guess what it is. The wheel of the old *Scrapiron*. I was in her when Phelps, you know Admiral Phelps over at Southbridge, was commander, and when I heard she was being broken up I managed to get the wheel through a friend, and then I hung the Union Jack over it. I don't think anyone would mind, do you, sir?' he said to his Rector.

The Rector, guessing that Father Fewling was appealing to him as to any possible jealousy from higher powers, about which he as a Rector would presumably know more than a priest-in-charge, took it upon him to approve the arrangement wholeheartedly, at which Father Fewling beamed.

'I did rather wish,' he said shyly, 'that I could have had a little ceremony here, a kind of blessing on our work, but I wasn't sure if the Bishop would approve and after all he is my superior officer. However,' he added, brightening, 'Downing has fitted up the most ingenious locker under the bunks for food and books. All sorts of tin things we have, and soda-water, and one of those very small bottles of rum just in case. And a little upright locker here, at the foot of the bunks, for our brooms and cleaning materials, you see. And I can make coffee on this little stove. It was Downing's idea to have it in a biscuit tin to prevent any danger from fire. The only thing we haven't got is water laid on, but as young Trowel said to me the other day, where water is drained off a chap can lay it on, and I believe he is right. In fact,' said Father Fewling wistfully, 'if the war would only last long enough this will be the best Air-Raid Wardens' Shelter in Barsetshire, or in the whole of England. But I mustn't keep you, I know.'

So saying he held the curtain aside and Mr and Mrs Villars followed by Mr Downing, who was each moment more ill at ease, passed out into the starry night, confusingly dark as yet to their eyes after the light below.

'Oh, one thing you haven't seen,' said Father Fewling, turning a torch on to the top of the flight, 'our gate. To keep dogs out. A neat piece of work. And the brass plate with No Admittance on it. One of my lads who is in the ironmonger's shop got that. And a nice little bolt. But I know you have an appointment.'

The Rector and his wife shook hands and thanked him warmly, to which he replied that they would be welcome any Tuesday, Thursday or Saturday if they cared to drop in.

'Or if you are passing between ten and eleven in the morning,' he added, 'you will see all the bedding out to air, if it is a fine day, of course. Take care where you go,' he said, steering Mrs Villars away from a low skeleton erection which was about to trip her up. 'That's a frame to hang the bedding on. Downing again. And next to it the rack for bicycles. We added a tin roof to it the other day which greatly improves its appearance besides keeping the bicycles dry. Oh dear, a quarter to eight. I am so sorry. And just one more thing; Mrs Hopgood has kindly, *most* kindly, offered to lend me her telescope and a tripod if there is anything of special interest when I am on duty. So good of her.'

'Mrs Hopgood?' said Mrs Villars.

194

'Yes. Miss Hopgood's aunt,' said Father Fewling.

'Oh!' said Mrs Villars, adding much to her friend's confusion, 'I never thought of her being called Hopgood.'

'Professor Hopgood was Miss Hopgood's uncle,' said Father Fewling,

'Of course, how stupid of me,' said Mrs Villars. 'Good night, Tubby, and thank you very much for a lovely visit. I adore your shelter. Gregory, we must fly.'

'Don't hurry,' said Mr Downing with the coolness born of despair.

So Mrs Villars walked as fast as she could, reflecting as she went how lucky it was that she had at last discovered Miss Hopgood's aunt's name and wondering why the simple solution hadn't occurred to her before.

'Do you think, Gregory,' she said to her husband, as they turned the corner by Miss Pemberton's cottage, 'that people's aunts are more often real aunts, or by marriage?'

The Rector said it would depend.

'And even then they needn't have the same name as their nieces,' his wife continued, following her own muddled train of thought 'I mean any of one's real aunts who got married would change their names whoever they were.'

'Unless of course they married a cousin of the same name, or a complete stranger who happened to have the same name as their own,' said the Rector, who hadn't the faintest idea what his wife was talking about but enjoyed her divagations and encouraged them.

'Perhaps Professor Hopgood and his wife were cousins,' said Mrs Villars, and was going to enlarge upon this fruitful theme, but was brought up sharp by Miss Pemberton's front gate and a consciousness that Mr Downing was waiting to speak.

'I beg your pardon; I was just going on talking,' she said apologetically to him.

'Oh, not in the least,' said Mr Downing, 'I was only wondering if I had better use my latch-key or ring. You see, we are a little late.'

At his words the Rector and his wife stood silent, to tell the truth a little alarmed themselves. But before Mr Downing could make up his mind the door was opened, a depressing blue light showed in the little hall and the party walked inside. Miss Pemberton, for it was she who had acted as portress, shut the door behind them and without taking any notice of her guests said to her lodger:

'Doubtless you will wish to wash, Harold. We can wait.'

She then regretted the sibilance of her greeting and that she had not said 'want' rather than 'wish,' and helped Mrs Villars to take off her coat and generally unmuffle herself, while the wretched Mr Downing slunk away to wash the contamination of Father Fewling's shelter from his hands.

Miss Pemberton led the Villarses into the living-room, where, before a spare fire, Mrs Turner and Mr Holden sat in amicable converse. Mrs Villars greeted them and made profuse apologies and explanations to her hostess, who received them with a readiness which made it but too obvious that she was saving up her resentment for her lodger. So everyone felt uncomfortable.

'Quite a surprise to see you here, Holden,' said the Rector.

Mr Holden said Miss Pemberton had asked him a week or so ago, but he had, as the Rector knew, been away and wasn't sure if he could get back in time, so Miss Pemberton had very kindly allowed him to leave it open, and he had just got back from town, though with so narrow a margin that he had not been able to call in at the Rectory or he would have offered to drive them. If, he said, he had realized that they were going to be detained he would have hurried to the Rectory and fetched them, as he was sure Mrs Villars must be tired.

Mr Downing came in at this moment, so Miss Pemberton pretended she had not noticed him and said it was a great pity Mr Holden had not gone straight to the Rectory and brought Mr and Mrs Villars along, as they would not then have been kept by Father Fewling to look at the new Air Wardens' Shelter. 'Washed, Harold?' she added.

'Not exactly, Ianthe,' said Mr Downing. 'You see, there isn't any soap in the cloakroom. I meant to tell you this morning, but I quite forgot. I am so sorry. Shall I get the piece from upstairs?'

Miss Pemberton, casting on his quite presentable hands a glare whose malignity should have blackened them at once, said as dinner was already spoilt he might as well. The wretched scholar went up the uncarpeted oak stairs and could be heard through the thin ceiling plunging about overhead.

Mrs Villars said that it was quite extraordinary how soap simply melted away sometimes and Mrs Turner capped her remark with a very rambling story about a bit of soap that had stuck to the sole of someone's shoe and so been completely lost till whoever it was slipped and her shoe fell off. On this anecdote Miss Pemberton made no comment and the two other gentlemen basely talked politics in a corner.

'Washed now, Harold?' said Miss Pemberton with hideous

patience as her victim reappeared. 'Then you might tell Effie dinner. She is staying on till half-past eight to oblige, so we might as well use her while she is here,' she added, for the information of the company.

She then rose, and gathering up her dress, which was a green sack worn under a kind of art burnous of a dull purple woollen material and set off by some rough silver necklaces, moved with a certain toad-like majesty to the further end of the living-room where an oak table, too high for human nature's daily food, was spread with peasant-edged linen mats and dull Swedish silver. When we say dull we allude not only to the design, though that might more suitably be called affected and silly, but to the surface which if you polished it ever so, as Effie Bunce frequently complained to her mother, it didn't seem to get not a *reel* shine. Two unshaded candles in candlesticks of twisted wood, birch-wood salt cellars, a birch-wood pepper mill and four thick art tumblers with warts on them completed this melancholy scene.

The company seated themselves and Effie placed a large bowl of very good thick vegetable soup before each guest. No one liked to be the first to speak, so Mrs Villars began to say something, collided in her speech with Mr Downing, begged his pardon, and retired.

'Well, Harold?' said Miss Pemberton.

'What good soup, Ianthe,' he said, stammering a little in his nervousness.

'It is what we usually have,' said Miss Pemberton, showing faint signs of relaxation.

'And not burnt this time,' said Mr Downing, snatching eagerly at any sign of returning grace.

So horrified were the other guests by the gulf that his remark opened that they all began to talk at once and did not apologize or retire. Mrs Turner and the Rector discussed the pronunciation of Argyrokastro (both being subsequently proved to be wrong by Colonel Passmore, who had surprisingly been there in 1919) while Mrs Villars said madly to Mr Holden how sorry she was she hadn't known he was corning, but she had quite understood when he went away that he wouldn't be back till late that night, so she had had the sheets changed.

'As a matter of fact,' said Mr Holden, 'I only got Miss Pemberton's invitation while I was away, so I asked her if I might leave it open and do my best to come. I knew you were coming.'

When Mr Holden began to speak he had intended to throw into his last sentence a wealth of meaning which would rouse in Mrs Villars's eyes a lovely look of surprise and gratitude, but somehow as the moment approached his self-confidence waned and with great presence of mind he shied away from the kind of voice he had meant to use and got through what he had to say with nothing worse than a small choke which Mrs Villars, if she thought about it at all, probably attributed to a spoonful of soup going down his wrong throat. Meanwhile, Miss Pemberton and Mr Downing sat like spectre brides at each end of the table in the silence, respectively, of rage and despair.

Miss Pemberton now terrified everyone by getting up and walking towards Mr Downing, but to the disappointed relief of her guests not so much with the intention of murdering him as of going to the kitchen door to which his seat happened to be nearest. Effie came in to take the soup basins away and tension relaxed.

'You've left your soup, Mr Downing,' said Effie, pointing, with the corner of her laden tray to Mr Downing's bowl.

'Oh, dear,' said Mr Downing, and after casting a nervous glance backwards, he began to eat it as fast as possible.

'Miss Pemberton does have good soup,' said Mrs Villars.

The rest of the party executed variations on this theme.

'That'll do,' said Effie, taking pity on Mr Downing, and removing his bowl she tipped the rest of the contents into the other bowls, winked at the guests and went into the kitchen.

Miss Pemberton now returned carrying a bowl of grated cheese, and sat down. Effie followed her carrying a large dish of some smoking and savoury-smelling mess which she set down in front of her mistress with such hearty good-will that a great dollop of it splashed over on to the table.

'There now!' said Effie.

'Cloth, Effie,' said Miss Pemberton unmoved. 'No, Harold, stay where you are.'

She then pulled up the draperies on her right arm and rapidly served and passed large helpings of the dish. Effie wiped up the mess and the guests set to. The food, whatever it was, was perfectly delicious and everyone talked about it with their mouths far too full.

'I must congratulate you on your excellent war cookery, Miss Pemberton,' said Mr Villars. 'This would make Mrs Chapman jealous, Verena.'

'Indeed it would,' said Mrs Villars, knowing full well the measure of her excellent cook's contempt for anyone's cooking but her own. 'May I guess what's in it, Miss Pemberton? I have found rice and mushroom and little bits of bacon and tomato, I think, and I suspect paprika?'

Miss Pemberton smiled grimly.

'And I would have said the rice was cooked in veal stock, but I know Fletcher had no veal this week, nor had Bones,' said Mrs Turner.

'Stock from a rabbit,' said Miss Pemberton less grimly.

'And the cheese with it!' said the Rector. 'I understand from Verena that cheese is unprocurable in Northbridge.'

'Hoarded. For guests,' said Miss Pemberton, softening yet more.

'And prunes! And carrots!' said Mrs Villars.

'And *where* did you get onion?' said Mrs Turner.

'Old Bunce sent me some from his allotment,' said Miss Pemberton, not too proudly.

'Pickled walnut!' Mr Holden exclaimed.

Miss Pemberton bestowed on him the approving glance that one connoisseur might give to another who had detected the vineyard at the first sip, the vintage at the second and the exact year of re-corking at the third.

'There is something else,' said Mrs Turner, 'but I can't quite spot it. You ought to write a cookery book, Miss Pemberton.'

Warmed by these tributes, Miss Pemberton became her usual not very gracious self. Conversation flowed.

'I found a very good recipe for a pudding the other day,' said Mrs Turner. 'It was among some recipes I had cut out of the papers and I found it when I was tidying a drawer. It is very simple and used to be a great success. You stew some apples, very slowly, in their skins, with loaf sugar and vanilla. Of course, the sugar part is rather difficult, but lots of people like their fruit not very sweet. Oh, and there ought to be butter with the apples, but of course one would just leave that out. Then you put the apples through a sieve.'

'What about the core?' said Mrs Villars.

'That all stays behind when you sieve them,' said Mrs Turner. 'At least, I don't sieve them. I have one of those things that you turn a handle and it comes out all squelching underneath.'

She paused; but as everyone appeared to understand what she was saying, she went on.

'Well then, you take some sponge cake and crumble it, and fry it in butter with cinnamon and brown sugar; it must be brown. Of course, one can't manage the butter, but heaps of people prefer things fried in oil, and if one can't manage brown sugar one just can't. One could manage a little castor perhaps.'

'Scatcherd's have had nothing but granulated for a fortnight,' said Mrs Villars.

There was a short silence in memory of brown sugar.

'And then,' said Mrs Turner, striking a slightly artificial note of gaiety, 'you put the apple purée in a glass dish, or a bowl, it doesn't really matter, and squash the cake crumbs down on top of it and when it is cool it is like a perfectly delicious Viennese thing – you know, the sort of things one used to get at the Vienna Café before the last war – with a delicious scrunchy top. And it is so easy to make, except of course for the butter and the sugar.'

The three ladies now talked rationing while Effie brought in slices of tinned pineapple in honey, all very hot and brown, and though the Rector preferred savouries he ate it without a murmur and had some more.

The repast having come to an end, Miss Pemberton got up and went to the kitchen to prepare the coffee herself while Effie hurled everything on to a tray. The party, overcome by her whirlwind presence, withdrew to the fire, which was almost dead.

'Oh, dear,' said Mr Downing. 'And no wood. I will just go to the garage and get some. Though why garage, one hardly knows, as neither I nor Miss Pemberton have ever had a car.'

The visitors discussed the excellent war food, though Mr Holden was noticeably silent.

'You know, it's rather pathetic,' said Mrs Turner, looking round to be sure that neither hostess nor host were within hearing. 'They came into coffee last night and I gave them some Benedictine, because I had some in the cellar and what I say is why make two wants of a thing, one when you have it and one when you haven't. And Miss Pemberton told me, because Betty had taken Mr Downing to her room to see one of her books about birds, that one of the few things she minded was not being able to give drinks to her friends, but she said if one once begins anything, only as an occasional treat, one does it again, and the only way, she found, to save money on drink was never to have it at all.'

Her audience felt a little dashed by this story of their hostess's rigid self-discipline and fell silent for a moment. When talking the party over afterwards, Mrs Villars said she felt thoroughly ashamed of herself for not having to think twice before having some claret, as long as the stocks lasted, or some beer; while Mr Villars said that for his part he felt nothing but gratitude to a Providence which, or rather who, allowed him to be able to afford a glass of decent wine with his dinner. Mrs Turner wondered if she could give Miss Pemberton one of her remaining bottles of Benedictine for Christmas, but feared a rebuff, so she asked the Rector's advice. Meanwhile, Mr Holden, who had luckily had a pint of Old and Mild at the Mitre with an R.A.S.C. sergeant to whom he had given a lift from the other side of Barchester, said to Mrs Villars that he knew she usually had wine at dinner and thought she looked tired.

'Indeed I'm not,' said Mrs Villars, rather resenting the suggestion that she was only kept alive by strong liquor.

'I ought to have gone straight to the Rectory,' said Mr Holden, enjoying his self-castigation. 'Even if I hadn't got there in time I might have picked you up on the way back. You must be tired.'

Mrs Villars would have liked to reply that if he mentioned the word tired again she would bite him, but the usages of society prevailing, she said:

'It is so kind of you, but you couldn't have brought your car round that way because there is that narrow bit with the posts across it near Faraway Corner, besides the little footbridge just before St Sycorax. But perhaps you'll drive us home.'

And then Miss Pemberton came in with extraordinarily good coffee and a generous supply of loaf sugar, and all our readers will be glad to hear that Mrs Turner was the only one who liked sugar in her coffee and she only took one small lump. Mr Downing brought in a basket of wood and as he had thought of bringing some small sticks for rekindling, his gaoleress was unable to find fault with him. The fire was soon crackling, then roaring, and finally settled down to burn steadily and, for those who were nearest to it, almost warmly.

'Thank you so much, Mr Downing,' said Mrs Turner in a soft, grateful voice to her host who was on his knees tidying up the brick hearth. 'How nice a fire is.'

'You ought always to have a good fire,' said Mr Downing, looking up and dusting his hands lightly together to remove bits of bark and powdery wood. 'You are a goddess of the hearth.'

Mrs Turner suddenly felt very sorry for Mr Downing who had only someone else's hearth to warm his spare form at, and wished she could somehow subscribe for an extra waistcoat or central heating for him.

'Come to The Hollies whenever you want a good fire,' she said, carried away by her wish to make everyone comfortable.

She had not meant to speak in a very low voice, but somehow her words reached no farther than Mr Downing's ears and his thin face lighted with pleased surprise.

'Well now, Rector,' said Miss Pemberton, who with awful disregard of a stone floor and a draught under the four-hundred-year-old door had established herself in an ancient basketwork chair on the very outside of the little circle, 'we are going to hear your opinion on the last two chapters of Mr Downing's book. We want your criticism, and Mr Holden's too. Will you read it, or shall I, Harold?'

Now it had been arranged between Miss Pemberton and Mr Downing, or rather by Miss Pemberton with Mr Downing not daring to oppose her, that she should read the typescript. This was perfectly reasonable, for Mr Downing, being longsighted, had to wear very strong glasses for reading which made him hold the print near his face, and also read in a very gentle, diffident voice or, as his benefactress put it, mumbled.

But when Miss Pemberton put her question Mr Downing's head was full of the thought of a warm fire at The Hollies and even, most treacherously, of how much nicer a fireplace with hideous strawberry pink tiles and a revolting brass fender with knobs and six or seven brass fire-irons in it were than a clear (brick) hearth and the rigour of an iron hand-wrought kind of devil's pitchfork which did the combined duties of poker, shovel, tongs and hearth brush. The consequence of all this was that he said:

'Certainly, Ianthe. I'll read it myself. Say if it gets dull,' he added, appealing to his audience.

All his hearers assumed the lively air of interest suitable to hearing someone read aloud very indistinctly something one doesn't want to hear, and Miss Pemberton, crossing her fine arms upon her square and massive bosom, gave a spirited rendering of a Spanish grandee suspected of leanings towards heresy proving his devotion to the Church by watching several of his friends and relations being burnt alive and determined to make the best of it.

Mr Downing went to a table, opened a drawer and took out a bundle of galley proofs. An annoying noise had been going on for some time. It was a noise that sent a ghost of itself as herald, then made itself manifest as a loud, tearing, roaring in the dark night, and gradually died away to an echo which lingered in an unpleasant persistence till the listener realized that what he had taken for the end of the old noise was also the beginning of a new one. An occasional dull thud diversified the noise, or a heavy sound of guns in the distance, but all the time it kept up its inhuman note in waves of roaring, tearing drone.

'What is it, Harold?' said Miss Pemberton, for Mr Downing had paused and stood suspended. 'Those planes,' said Mr Downing, listening. 'If hate could kill men, Brother Lawrence,' said Miss Pemberton abstractedly.

'But it can't,' said Mrs Turner. 'And what is so annoying is that one can't even really hate, only dislike and despise.'

'And what is even more annoying,' said Mrs Villars, 'is that one mostly forgets to do either. I mean things like what pudding to have and remembering to collect the servants' National Savings money and hunting for sardines or onions make one quite forget the war.'

'I was going—' Mr Downing began, when a very loud rumble ran from the surrounding darkness upon the house on all sides, trembled through floor and ceiling and ran away with equal speed.

'And right over the cottage,' said Miss Pemberton indignantly. 'Night after night he has to choose this particular place to fly over. Pretentious little man is what he is. Well, Harold, as you are going to read you had better begin.'

Thus encouraged, Mr Downing sat down and put on his glasses.

'Well do you know, Harold,' said Miss Pemberton, striking awe into her hearers by this inverted and rather Plornish-like phrasing, 'that see in the dark you cannot. Get nearer the light.'

Now when Miss Pemberton took Punshions, electric light was not laid on, so she determined to economize by using lamps and candles. Whether they are really an economy no one has ever yet determined, but they have at least a discouraging effect which makes people go to bed early and not try to read when they get there. Mr Downing obediently moved nearer to the lamp and turned it up.

'I shall be most grateful to you for any suggestion you may make, Villars,' he said to the Rector, 'and to Holden too. These are your galleys, Holden, and I'm afraid I've knocked them about a bit, but I hope to be able to pass the page proofs almost without correction. I want to know if you think the chapter I am going to read too daring. If so tell me. I have handled Fyffe-Thompson's last book pretty severely. In fact, the opening sentence refers to him. "Shakespeare has said," I have written, "that it is sharper than a serpent's thanks" – no, no, serpent's tooth it ought to be. I am so sorry, but has anyone a pencil?'

Mrs Villars and Mrs Turner said with one voice that they *always* had a pencil in their day-bags but had none this evening. Mr Villars made a pretence, which deceived no one, of looking for one in his waistcoat pocket, and Mr Holden silently produced a fountain-pen and handed it to the author.

'Thanks so much,' said Mr Downing, crossing out 'thanks' and substituting 'tooth'. 'What a very nice nib, Holden. I can never get a nib that suits me.'

Mr Holden said it was a Potman eighteen-carat with a platinum tip and only cost twenty-seven shillings and sixpence.

Mr Downing, who privately thought this very expensive, thanked Mr Holden again and handed it back.

'You'd better keep it,' said Mr Holden. 'You will have some other corrections probably.'

Mr Downing thanked him once more and continued in a gentle monotonous voice, '"to have a thankless child, but we must confess there are thankless tasks to be performed in the realm of criticism that are even sharper." Do you think that quite makes sense?' he added anxiously.

'No,' said Miss Pemberton.

'I think you are right, Ianthe,' said Mr Downing, and made a large cross against his opening sentence, saying he would recast it later.

'Excuse me, Downing,' said the Rector, 'the lamps.'

A thick column of black and stinking smoke was coming out of the chimney, as everyone but the author had for some minutes been aware.

'Oh, dear!' said Mr Downing, and turned the wick higher.

'I think the other way,' said Mrs Turner. 'Shall I?'

Mr Downing thanked her and their fingers met for a moment on the little thing that one turns lamps up and down with (for though there is doubtless a technical name for it, and quite probably a word in Gaelic which expresses in two syllables and a great many superfluous consonants what we have taken eleven words to say, we are not familiar with either), in a very romantic way.

'I'll tell you one thing about Fyffe-Thompson,' said Mr Villars. 'His brother's younger boy has just passed his School Certificate at fourteen. Extraordinary how brains run in that family. But F-T was always apt to go off at a tangent. I look forward to hear you demolishing him, Downing.'

Mr Downing looked gratified and took up his proofs.

'If anyone wants to hear the news,' said Miss Pemberton, 'it's twenty past nine, so it's over.'

Mr Villars said if he had a curate, and heaven knew they were bad enough, that talked like a B.B.C. announcer he would get him unfrocked.

'You had better go on, Harold, if we are to hear it,' said Miss Pemberton, 'or give it to me.'

'When Professor Fyffe-Thompson,' continued Mr Downing, 'whose research into Provençal origins must by nature of its very thoroughness deserve our respect if not command our approbation, goes so far (in his *Values and Virelais*) as to state—'

Here the galleys, eel-like creatures at best, gave a kind of plunge and fell onto the floor, one or two of the long sheets becoming detached as they did so.

'Excuse me one moment, Downing,' said Mr Holden. 'The word Virelais somehow reminded me of it. Oatmeal! I knew it would come to me.'

His hearers looked at him with stupor, but Miss Pemberton, whose mind was very acute, allowed her face to relax into an expression not remotely connected with approval.

'You are right, Mr Holden,' she said, 'I thickened the stock with it.'

'By Jove! I knew there was something,' said Mr Holden. 'Look here, Miss Pemberton, you simply *must* do a cookery book for us. I know Coates would jump at it. May I put it up to him and get him to write to you? If you can do it as a series of articles with a literary flavour and some good quotations, we could get them into a high-class women's magazine first, and then publish in book form. Will you consider it?'

'It depends what you offer,' said Miss Pemberton. 'We will talk about it later. Will you go on, Harold?'

It was a lucky thing for Mr Downing that Mr Holden had so unceremoniously interrupted him, for Miss Pemberton, annoyed though she was with her lodger, had the soul of a true gentleman and would not see the weak oppressed except by herself. Though she was quite frankly interested in Mr Holden's offer, she would have turned it down for good if necessary sooner than have Mr Downing put in the position of being slighted. Mr Downing vaguely felt this and with a grateful look in her direction he picked up his proofs. The brutal roaring and tearing overhead had at last died away and he was able to read the rest of his chapter aloud undisturbed. When he had finished, the Rector, who hadn't been warm enough to go to sleep, tackled him on one or two points and while they were deep in argument Mr Holden again approached Miss Pemberton.

'I'm afraid we can't do much in the way of an advance as things are at present,' he said. 'Say fifty pounds. I know it's not much, but your money is just as safe, and you'll get it later. We will pay you what you have earned up to the date of publication, if you like; unless of course the advance would be a help.'

'I think not,' said Miss Pemberton with dignity. 'You see, Mr Downing does not get an advance on account of royalties, or only twenty pounds, I think, and I would not like him to feel that I could earn more by a cookery book than he can by his real brainwork. Tell Mr Coates payment on publication will suit me perfectly.'

And she looked with a kind of stern affection towards her lodger.

Mrs Villars now earned everyone's gratitude by saying she must take Gregory home because of Sunday. From the fire-station down the road the siren began to howl its unmelodious chromatics.

'That means we're all right for to-night,' said Mr Holden. 'They never let her rip till the aeroplanes have gone for hours.'

'So long as they don't wake me up with the All Clear, they can do what they like,' said the Rector ungratefully. 'Sirens and the B.B.C. No peace anywhere nowadays. Holden, you are driving us home, aren't you? Mrs Turner, we will drop you.'

While the Rector and Mr Holden were putting their coats on and Mrs Villars was saying good-bye to the hostess, Mrs Turner approached Mr Downing.

'I did enjoy it,' she said with obvious sincerity. 'Having it read aloud off those funny-shaped bits of paper makes the Troubadours come quite alive. I wish the girls could have heard it. Will you come to tea and read some of it to us one day? I was at school with Professor Fyffe-Thompson's sister. It has only just come back to me. An odious girl in a blue serge skirt and red flannel blouse with white spots on it, very good at hockey and so popular. Ivy, her name was. I loved the way you went for the Professor.'

Intoxicated with reading aloud and Mrs Turner's bright, admiring eyes, Mr Downing said he would like to come to tea next week. Miss Pemberton was going to stay at the Deanery in Barchester for the night, and when the day was settled he would let Mrs Turner know. To this she agreed with alacrity and said no one else should be asked. Then they all packed into Mr Holden's car and went back to the Rectory, dropping Mrs Turner at The Hollies on the way.

'Thank you so much,' said Mrs Villars to Mr Holden in the hall, stifling a yawn. 'Walking there was nice, but I didn't so much fancy walking back.'

'I shall always blame myself for not coming here to look for you,' said Mr Holden, suddenly assuming his voice of dark passion. 'You must be tired past words.'

'Well, I'm NOT,' said Mrs Villars, quite snappishly.

Mr Holden murmured something about a woman's courage, and went to put his car away. Mrs Villars had a comfortable yawn, kissed her husband very affectionately and went to bed.

Tea and Troubadours

Christmas, bad enough at the best of times, now began to cast an even thicker gloom than usual over the English scene. No one has ever yet described with sufficient hatred and venom this Joyous and Festive Season. As the Rector when off his guard so truly said, the war was little but an intensification of Christmas in that it either separated families that wanted to be together, or far worse, herded together families for whom normally twelve counties were not large enough. Outwardly, he said, on the Third Sunday in Advent, that once again families were drawing together at this season and not only finding in the companionship of fathers, mothers, sons, daughters and many others a joy they had never felt before, but rejoicing also in the privilege of having among them some less fortunate than themselves, victims of one of the most terrible crimes known in the history of our so-called civilization. Everyone said what a nice sermon the Rector had preached, and went home to lunch.

What with Christmas and one thing and another, Northbridge was beginning to bubble like a boiling pot. Nearly every house, though most of them were already packed to bursting point, had extra refugees or evacuees, or was housing relations that no one wanted but didn't like not to ask. Most of the unwelcome visitors had forgotten or mislaid their ration-books, and made but little effort to get them or to procure new ones.

The whole of England, having decided earlier in the year that it would not celebrate Christmas by the heathen and unsuitable practice of overeating and giving presents during a war, executed a *volte-face* and said that in a war we must above all keep up the spirit of Christmas, only to find that there was practically nothing to give or to eat. Rabbits, herrings, sausages, onions, lemons, oranges, biscuits and chocolate, which had been variable in supply, vanished entirely from the market, in many cases owing to their prices being controlled. The price of turkeys and chickens reached fever-point. Various stout-hearted ladies went up to London by the early train, were decanted at a station ten miles from Waterloo, had to take a bus, another train and a tube, shopped all day, and came back from another station by a train, a quarter of a mile's walk to a motor-coach, and another train, This misfortune they attributed variously to A Bomb on the Line, Enemy Action near the Reservoir, A time-bomb near that big gasometer, A gas main bursting of itself, A Giant Aeroplane wrecked just over the junction, The Germans, You know Who, and The Rolling Stock being all worn out, my dear.

Whatever the reason, they all united in saying that there was nothing in the London shops and went to Barchester, descending like a flight of locusts upon Woolworth's who had nothing but goods which, if we describe them as Empire, will unfortunately be sufficiently described. The result was that the remaining store of scarves, handkerchiefs and stockings in Northbridge was bought up, and Messrs Gaiters & P. B. Baker & Son Ltd sold more Book Tokens and Gift Tokens than would have bought a Spitfire, though even this was not really satisfactory, as the young ladies at these establishments when interrupted in their conversation with each other, or their manicure, said coldly in answer to inquiries for current books that (a) they weren't out yet, (b) they were out of print, and (c) the publishers weren't doing any new books now.

Perhaps the repercussion of Christmas was least felt at Punshions where Miss Pemberton could not afford to spend much extra money on food or presents. Luckily she had got about fifty cards left over from last year with the words: 'With good wishes for a happier Christmas and better things to come in the New Year,' printed in clear Roman type with her name and Mr Downing's and their address in italics in the bottom left-hand corner. So she gave twenty of these to Mr Downing, personally supervised his list of recipients so that it should not overlap hers, and kept thirty for herself.

'And do not forget, Harold,' she said on the afternoon that she left for Barchester, there to spend a night at the Deanery and give a lecture on Giacopone Giacopini to the Choristers' Parents' Club, 'that those cards must be posted to-day. We are asked to post by the 18th at latest. Effie is leaving your supper out for you. You can light the oil-stove as I know you'll let a fire out. The casserole will be in the hay-box and the coffee will be in an enamel saucepan ready to heat on the oil-stove.'

She then put on a brown raffia hat and a kind of black mantle with embroidery on the fronts, took her striped canvas bag with which she went away for the night, slung her gas-mask in an imitation patent leather case across her right shoulder (for she was a good citizen) and walked down to the Mitre where she took the bus to Barchester.

Mr Downing was now left entirely his own master for the next twenty hours, for it was now three o'clock and Miss Pemberton was to return by the morning bus that got to Northbridge at eleven. There had been a terrible moment when Miss Pemberton had said she would not go till the four-forty-five bus and he did not dare to tell her that he was due at The Hollies at four-thirty, but most luckily she had remembered that she wanted to look up something in the Barchester Free Library and had taken the two-forty-five. There was no reason that he should not have told her, for as we know she approved his friendship with Mrs Turner, but after years of telling Miss Pemberton his every movement he had a sudden wish to have a secret life of his own, if only to the extent of one tea-party.

Having shut the door behind his Egeria, he went back to his work and was soon so absorbed in making his index, for he prided himself on his very complete indexing with every possible cross-reference, flattering allusions to which were frequently made in reviews, that time slipped by unheeded and it was half-past four. Rather flurried he quickly did the black-out, washed his hands and brushed his hair, put on his old grey tweed overcoat, rammed his proofs into one of its big pockets and the Christmas cards into the other, took up his gentlemanly, shabby, grey felt hat and left the house, taking care to bang the front door behind him as the lock was not in very good order. A few moments' brisk walk brought him to The Hollies, where he was rather alarmed to find several cars in the gravel sweep, but remembering that Mrs Turner had expressed a wish to hear his two last chapters again, he rang the bell.

From this moment he was so happy that the visit, when he looked back on it, seemed to him a peculiarly delightful and soothing dream. The front door was opened by Betty with a large piece of cake in one hand.

'Hullo,' she said, with her mouth full. 'We thought you were dead. Come on in. You're going to read us something about the Troubadours, Auntie said. I adore them. I read a play by someone about one that fell in love with someone he'd never seen and when he got there he died. I simply wept buckets. All in French it was. Delia Grant lent it me, the one that she was Delia Brandon, you know. Put your coat and things on the chest. Auntie, here's Mr Downing.'

So speaking, she propelled Mr Downing into the drawing-room, which was a blaze of comfort. The black-out had already been done, a wood and coal fire was throwing out grateful heat, all the lights were on and the room was full of laughter, smoke and noise. Mrs Turner, sitting on a sofa before a low table, was pouring out tea. Her other niece and Mr Greaves were sitting side by side at the piano with a large plate of cake and two cups of tea by the music stand, singing a duet and sharing the accompaniment. Captain Topham and Father Fewling were sitting cross-legged on the bearskin hearthrug toasting scones. Mrs Paxon, in a red coat and skirt and a bright green halo hat, was near the tea table having a violent flirtation with Colonel Passmore, and Mrs Turner's two good little evacuee boys, Derrick Pumper and Derrick Farker, were sitting under the piano dressed as Red Indians, with a third little boy, wearing a mask with a dog's face, whom Mr Downing subsequently discovered to be their cousin who had been invited for Christmas because his mother had a new baby. All three little boys were gently playing mouth-organs, someone had left the wireless on at full blast in the dining-room, Captain Topham and Father Fewling were arguing about Gilbert and Sullivan with vocal illustrations, and Mr Downing wondered how long he could bear it.

But Mrs Turner, holding a hand out across the table, gave him such a welcoming grasp and smiled so kindly that he plucked up courage and worming his way past Colonel Passmore and Mrs Paxon sat down beside his hostess.

'The girls and I wondered if you had forgotten us,' she said. 'Betty was quite sure you had, but I said you had promised to read us about the Troubadours. Do you like a big cup?'

'Very much,' said Mr Downing, who cherished fondly an outsize cup with a mournful cock on it that Miss Pemberton would not let him use. 'It's like being at Oxford again.'

'What a lovely place Oxford is,' said Mrs Turner, 'and all the colleges. I've never been to Cambridge, but I believe it is lovely too. Topsy, have you a scone for Mr Downing?'

Captain Topham rose from a cross-legged position to his feet in one movement, presented a toasted scone to Mr Downing at the end of a toasting-fork and sat down in the same flexible way.

'Dear, dear, how I wish I could still do that,' said Father Fewling enviously.

'Your legs are too short, Padre,' said Captain Topham, 'and

a bit too much round the old waistline. I thought you High Church johnnies fasted and all that.'

'I do,' said Father Fewling mournfully, 'but it doesn't have the slightest effect. I don't mean,' he added hurriedly, 'that I fast for that reason.'

'Flies to the figure, eh?' said Captain Topham sympathetically. 'I know a fellow like that, a good horseman too, but whatever he eats runs to flesh. Died of 'flu last November, now I come to think of it. Now what was his name? Hi! Tommy!' he shouted to his brother officer. 'What was that fellow that spoke to me at Ascot two years ago the day you and I went down with Jimmy?'

Mr Greaves interrupted his song to say he didn't know.

'Ah, well,' said Captain Topham. 'Have another scone, Mr Downing.'

'Do,' said Mrs Turner. 'And some more cranberry jelly. The girls and I made it.'

'And some more butter,' said Betty, perching on the arm of the sofa by Mr Downing. 'At least it's marge, but we've got heaps. I say, Colonel Passmore, do you know the beagles are meeting at Fish Hill on Boxing Day? Are you going?'

'Well, I've got a car and some petrol, but who is there to go with me?' said Colonel Passmore, who liked the society of ladies.

'If you mean me, I can't go unless you ask me,' said Mrs Paxon, rolling her fine eyes at the Colonel.

'Well, these young ladies will need a chaperon,' said the Colonel, heavily jocose, 'so suppose I take you all.'

'I say,' shouted Betty to Mrs Turner's other niece at the piano, 'Pops is going to take us beagling on Boxing Day.'

'Good for Pops,' shouted the other niece back again.

There was a violent scramble under the piano and the two Red Indians emerged.

'You say, Derrick,' said the smaller boy, pushing the other.

'No, you, Derrick,' said the larger boy.

The smaller Derrick came up to Mrs Turner.

'Please, Miss,' he said, 'can me and Derrick go to the meet? We saw the meet on Guy Fox Day and we ran moiles and moiles.'

'You'd better ask Colonel Passmore, Derrick,' said Mrs Turner.

'All right, young man,' said Colonel Passmore. 'That's the young ladies and their chaperon, and two Red Indians. I suppose you can all manage to squeeze in.'

'And please, sir, can Ron come too,' said the smaller Derrick, dragging the little boy in the dog's mask from under the piano. ''E's got a new sister and he ain't seen 'er, 'cos she's in London.'

The little boy began to cry.

'That's all right, my boy,' said Colonel Passmore, alarmed. 'You can come too. Mind you put your thickest boots on.'

Mrs Paxon darted from her chair, and was down on her knees by the unhappy Ron and had his mask off in a twinkling.

'Blow your nose, hard!' she said, producing a large handkerchief. 'That's right.' And she carefully put the mask on again.

'Now you must all go to bed,' said Mrs Turner. 'It's bath tonight, and, Big Derrick, don't let Little Derrick and Ron stay too long in the bath. Good night, boys.'

'Good night, Miss,' said the three little boys and went off.

'It's a bit early,' said Mrs Turner, 'but they do get tired and then they have their supper in bed after their bath.'

'How curious it is,' said Mr Downing, 'to observe the recrudescence of the cockney "oi". It had apparently gone out altogether within my lifetime in favour of "igh", or as near as I can pronounce it. But I have noticed the older form among many of the evacuee children here.'

Mrs Turner said it was very funny and children did say such amusing things, and then Mrs Paxon said she must be going.

'Can I drop you, Mrs Paxon?' said Colonel Passmore. 'I've got my car outside.'

'If it's a lift you're after meaning,' said Mrs Paxon, with an accent reminiscent of the season she took the part of the Widow O'Brien in a one-act play with the South Wembley Amateur Dramatic, 'sure it isn't dhropping me you'd be and you a great soldier man wid the fine little car.'

'Well, come along and we'll see what I mean,' said Colonel Passmore, to Mrs Paxon's delight, and they took their leave.

'Now we are nice and quiet,' said Mrs Turner, 'we must hear about the Troubadours. Clear the things away, girls.'

Her two nieces, with the assistance of Captain Topham and Mr Greaves, put all the tea-things on to a trolley and Mr Greaves earned great applause by shouting 'Mind your backs!' as he pushed it through the hall and into the pantry,

'Come and sit in a comfortable chair, Father Fewling,' said Mrs Turner. 'Cigarettes are just behind you. Mr Downing is going to read to us about the Troubadours. Have you got it, Mr Downing?'

Mr Downing said he had left the proofs in his coat, and

was Mrs Turner sure she really wanted to hear a chapter. On being assured that she did, he went into the hall where he was nearly deafened by the noise of the tea-things being put away by four able-bodied and able-voiced young people, got the proofs out of his coat pocket and returned, shutting the drawing-room door firmly behind him.

'But you had long ones the other night,' said Mrs Turner, disappointed.

Mr Downing explained that those were galley proofs, but they had been corrected and his book was now in page proof.

'Just like a little book,' said Mrs Turner admiringly.

'Talking of galleys,' said Father Fewling, 'reminds me of the *Scrapiron*. Our cook was a bit of a petty tyrant and used to bully his boy like anything, and Frobisher, our second loot, used to call the boy a galley-slave. Neat, wasn't it?'

Mrs Turner much admired Mr Frobisher's wit and said didn't Father Fewling miss the Navy.

Father Fewling said he missed it like anything sometimes but that was ungrateful of him, because no one could be happier than he was at Northbridge with so many friends and so much to do.

'Besides,' he added with great simplicity, 'I'd probably have been axed long ago.'

The younger members now came back in very good spirits, demanding to play rummy.

'You won't mind, will you, Mr Downing?' said Mrs Turner. 'Just one game and then we'll have the Troubadours.'

Mr Downing did mind rather, but said he didn't. A round table in the window was cleared of books, photographs, and knitting and dragged into the middle of the room; cards and ash-trays were produced and the party managed to squeeze itself in.

'Oh, dear!' said Mrs Turner, just as they were settled, 'I believe this is the pack with the Queen of Clubs missing. Just count them, Betty, And we might as well have the drinks now,' she added to her other niece, who at once got up and went to the dining-room, followed by Mr Greaves.

Betty, flipping the cards out in an expert way, said the Queen was missing all right and where the new pack was she couldn't think. A fruitless hunt in various drawers took place. Mr Greaves and the other niece came back with the tea-trolley laden with drinks and were told about the missing card.

'That's all right,' said Mr Greaves. 'Can I have this, Mrs Turner?'

And without waiting for permission he took from the mantelpiece a card on which the Headmistress of the Barchester High School requested the pleasure of the company of Mrs Turner and friends at a meeting on January 15th, in aid of the Mission to Relapsed Hottentots.

'Scissors, forward,' he said.

Mrs Turner said, on her writing-table in the red leather case. Mr Greaves sat down and in a few moments had cut a card to the correct size and shape, and rapidly inked in a Queen of Clubs, whose small black moustache and negligent coiffure bore a striking resemblance to a person much in the news. This brilliant effort was greeted with shouts of applause and the game began.

Mr Downing, who hated cards, abhorred gambling, and had not been known to raise his voice since he shouted for the Paul's boat in Eights Week about 1907, at first sat silent, confused and suspicious. But the complete friendliness of the atmosphere so put him at his ease that he rapidly acquired the principles of the game, madly staked his small change, and showed such a grasp of strategy and cheating up to the final limits of the conventions that Captain Topham and Mr Greaves, no mean exponents of card-playing, congratulated him warmly on being a dark horse.

While a fresh round of drinks was taken and Mr Greaves shuffled the cards by whirring them backwards and forwards with a sound like the rapid fluttering rise of a flight of pigeons from the lawn where they have been eating grain, the drawing-room clock struck seven.

'Oh!' said Mr Downing. 'I must go.'

'You can't, sir,' said Mr Greaves reproachfully. 'You've got two-and-eightpence of mine. I must have my revenge.'

'But my supper will be waiting,' said Mr Downing.

A rapid cross-fire of questions from Mrs Turner's two nieces made him confess that when he got back he would have to light an oil-stove in the sitting-room, take a casserole out of the hay-box, put his coffee to warm on the top of the oil-stove to economize gas, eat his meal alone, stack everything ready in the kitchen sink, and sit reading or writing by an oil-lamp till he went to bed. Mrs Turner, with a vivid memory of his ineffectual dealings with the lamp, said he must stay to supper.

'You are very kind,' said Mr Downing, 'but I really couldn't.'

'Nonsense,' said Mrs Turner. 'Father Fewling is staying and these boys. That will just make us a round number.'

Vanquished by this appeal to science, Mr Downing gave in, nor did it occur to him till much later to wonder why seven should be a rounder number than six.

'Besides,' said Mrs Turner, 'we haven't had the Troubadours yet,' and to an author this argument was sufficient lure, without the thoughts of a good supper and a warm fire which became more and more seductive.

As the maid was out, Mrs Turner's nieces got supper ready in a leisurely way, much impeded by Captain Topham and Mr Greaves, who said they were the Free French and certainly behaved as such, while Father Fewling and Mr Downing talked very happily about Malta, where Mr Downing had once spent a winter with a cousin who had married an admiral.

By eight o'clock or so they sat down to soup nearly as good as Miss Pemberton's, a gigantic vegetable curry, and a large cheese sent by the ex-nurse of Mrs Turner's nieces, now a farmer's wife in Westmorland. Beer flowed and harmony prevailed.

Mr Downing could not understand why he was enjoying himself so much. Everything in his surroundings was antipathetic to him. Ascetic and fastidious by nature, preferring the cultured conversation of scholars and their uninteresting food to a banquet of Lucullus, disliking bright unshaded lights, card-playing, drinks (except Falernian slowly sipped in a senior common-room), loud laughter, soldiers, young girls, High Churchmen and uneducated women, he found himself perfectly at home with them all. He reproached himself for using the word uneducated of his hostess, whose hospitality and bright kind eyes put her above all criticism. That she had little or no education in the sense that Miss Pemberton had could not be denied; but apart from that she seemed to have every virtue, every grace: sweet-smiling, softly-spoken Lalage.

Just as they were finishing supper the familiar yelp of a siren with its tail caught in a door rose to the cold skies and Father Fewling got up.

'Oh, don't go, Tubby,' said Betty, for during the evening he had begged his hostesses to use this nostalgic name. 'Ackcherly, it's not your night on, is it?'

'I have to go if the siren sounds,' said Father Fewling.

'If you ask me,' said Captain Topham, 'I think it's Commander Beasley. He's been mad to work the siren ever since he sprained his ankle and can't patrol with the Home Guard.'

Father Fewling said wistfully that he would like to work the siren himself and hurried off to his Wardens' Shelter. The young people cleared supper away and Mrs Turner took Mr Downing into the drawing-room. Here, by the roaring fire, with only one reading-lamp on, Mr Downing spent a blissful half-hour, quite relaxed, full of food and beer and warmer than he had been for several months, telling Mrs Turner about himself and how his mother had died six years ago at the age of eighty-one, and how poor a grasp Professor Fyffe-Thompson had of the elements of Provençal literature. Mrs Turner listened with the greatest appearance of interest and thought wistfully of the late Mr Turner and what a frightful bore he used to be about his mother when he had had too much to drink, and came to the conclusion that writing books and drinking had much the same effect upon people: and indeed there is something to be said for her idea. Looking at his thin nervous face, his distinguished if thin grey hair and his spare form, she felt that a little cosseting would do him no harm, and determined, to this end, to keep on the best possible terms with Miss Pemberton. There was something about Mr Downing that made her want to give him a pat on the back as if he were a good dog, but she took no steps in the matter.

Mr Downing, slightly intoxicated by talking about himself and the delightful evening he was having, had a curiously empty feeling in the arm nearest to Mrs Turner and was vaguely conscious that the one thing that it needed was something exactly the right size to go round, say something about the size, shape and consistency of his hostess, but this thought did not get beyond a very nebulous and unpractical stage.

Then the girls and the young men came back and turned up the lights and broke the dream.

'Now, be quiet,' said Mrs Turner, 'all of you. Mr Downing has written a book about the Troubadours, and he's going to read some of it to us.'

'I say,' said Mr Greaves, 'you aren't *the* Downing, are you, sir?'

This ingenuous tribute made Mr Downing swell with pride inwardly, though outwardly he said he had done a little work on Provençal literature.

'That's it!' said Mr Greaves. 'I was reading Modern Languages till I got sent down, at least I would have been, only the Army got in first, and we had to do a lot of awful rot about the old French and my tutor said yours was much the best book. It was jolly lucky I got into the Army or I'd have had to read it, and another chap, who is awfully brainy, said it was jolly stiff. But I never thought I'd meet you.'

In spite of this very mixed compliment, Mr Downing had

rarely felt so flattered and stammered violently in his attempts to acknowledge Mr Greaves's tribute.

'Played the guitar or something, didn't they, sir?' said Captain Topham.

'Ackcherly it was the lute or something,' said Betty. 'Did you ever read that play, Topsy, about a troubadour that fell in love with a princess he'd never seen and when he did see her he died. I wept simply pints when I read it.'

Mr Downing, who could hardly bear to hear this unsympathetic précis of a charming piece of sentimentalism for a second time, said with a slight tinge of impatience that he supposed she meant *La princesse lointaine*.

'That's the one,' said Betty, 'but that wasn't ackcherly her name. And I've forgotten his name.'

'Geoffroi Rudel,' said Mr Downing coldly and, we must confess, with an accent that betrayed acquaintance with books rather than with our formerly lively neighbours the Gauls.

Captain Topham suddenly roared with laughter and then apologized, saying that he was sorry, but Roodle was such a rum name that he couldn't help it. Frenchmen did have funny names, he said, like old what's-his-name that did liaison before we got hoofed out of France, Petitot, that was it, but Roodle was even rummer. As he spoke, the siren, lifting its voice from the cellar to the attic, blared the All Clear.

'Poor Tubby,' said Mrs Turner's other niece. 'Just as he had got to his shelter, I expect. I do think Commander Beasley's the limit.'

'Well, now,' said Mrs Turner, 'we are quite ready, Mr Downing.'

Mr Downing opened his paper-bound page-proofs.

'Golly!' said Mrs Turner's other niece, 'it's nine. Quick, Tommy.'

Thus adjured, Mr Greaves sprang to his feet and switched on the radiogram. A refined and fluting voice remarked, with the air of one bringing tidings of comfort and joy, that our forces in Northern Africa were progressing according to plan, the Foss Agency reported rioting in Salaam-el-Backsheesh, unconfirmed reports of martial law in Crsjek had been received in Bucharest, an important announcement on Seville oranges would be made in the midnight news, a cloudburst in Poncho City, Mexico, had rendered thousands homeless, and a talk would follow by Mr Evan Glendower, the Minah Lyric Writah – *Minah*, he said with a golden laugh, not Minah: Mr Evan Glendower.

'Filthy little brute,' said Mr Greaves. 'Never down a pit in his life. All long hair and legs too short for his body and inferiority complex. He spoke to the Propylaeum Club the term before I was sent down, and got ducked in the river.'

The front door bell rang.

'Turn it off, Betty,' said Mrs Turner. 'Topsy, be an angel and see what it is. Doris isn't back yet.'

Captain Topham went out. A joyful noise of reunion was heard in the hall and he came back with Father Fewling who explained that the All Clear had gone while he was getting into his gumboots, so he had come back and hoped that was all right. Everyone was glad to see him. Betty fetched a bottle of cheap claret, a saucepan, a little sugar and some cinnamon and made mulled claret over the drawing-room fire and they chatted till half-past ten when Mr Downing tore himself away.

'I can't tell you,' said Mrs Turner, holding his hand for a moment as he said good night, 'how frightfully disappointed I was not to hear about the Troubadours, but time seems to go so fast in war-time. You must come another day and read us your book.'

Looking into her kind sparkling eyes Mr Downing said he would love to, and went away. For at least three minutes of the walk home he trod upon air, thinking of the treat he had had and the further treats in store. Opposite the Mitre doubts began to assail him, and by the time he got to Punshions he wondered, as so many of us have, whether the pleasure of the evening was going to be too dearly bought by the aching emptiness it would leave behind and the difficulty of concealing where he had been from his benefactress, from whom he had never succeeded in hiding anything yet.

He opened the front door and went in, slamming it hard after him because of the lock not working well. When he had taken off his hat and coat he saw under the ill-fitting sixteenth-century door of the sitting-room a yellow line of light. His heart gave a bang. The great fear of his life, one which he had been ashamed to confess to anyone, was burglars, and now here they were. They had broken in, lighted the lamp, probably caroused on his uneaten supper, pocketed the very few articles of value in the sitting-room and were now waiting to sandbag him. Valour told him to go on tiptoe upstairs, get into bed and pretend to be asleep: discretion said that after the way he had banged the door it was impossible to pretend that he had not just come in. He stood in an agony of indecision.

*

Meanwhile, on the other side of the door Miss Pemberton, who on finding that the Dean and his only unmarried daughter were in bed with influenza and Mrs Crawley obviously sickening for it, had refused to stay the night and taken the last bus back to Northbridge, was sitting in the icily cold sitting-room by the light of the oil-lamp, waiting for her lodger's return and an explanation of his truancy. No doubt as to his safety assailed her for she was not given to imagining, but a deep and growing wrath gnawed her vitals. Not only was he absent without leave, but the untouched casserole in the hay-box, the unwarmed coffee on the unlit stove, showed that he had been out for some time. She had been waiting for him for thirty-three minutes and was prepared to wait till next morning if necessary. The colder she got the angrier she would be, so she sat and got steadily colder till she heard a key in the lock, the footsteps of the wanderer and the slamming of the front door. She smiled grimly. The footsteps ceased. He must not be allowed to sneak upstairs.

Mr Downing with stealthy movements hung up his coat and took his proofs from the pocket. Feeling in the other pocket for a handkerchief that he thought he had left there he came upon the Christmas cards which he had naturally forgotten to post. He drew them out and stood wavering between bed and safety or burglars and being sandbagged.

'Come here, Harold,' said a voice from the sitting-room.

Mr Downing then lost all human consciousness. Holding the cards in his hand he opened the sitting-room door.

'I see you have not posted my cards, Harold,' said Miss Pemberton.

11

High Tension

Christmas, so long looming over everyone's head, finally surged up, buried everyone alive and ebbed away, leaving its victims distinctly cross. Mr Downing, meeting Mrs Villars at half-past five on Boxing Day near The Hollies, said the epithets given in the *Arabian Nights* to death, namely, the Separator of Companions and the Terminator of Delights, seemed to him as applicable to Christmas as any others. Mrs Villars said sympathetically that she had always thought the words peculiarly suitable to sea voyages, but then as a clergyman's wife she was able to take Christmas as a matter of business and so minded it less. They walked on together. Mrs Villars thought Mr Downing looked poorly, but naturally attributed it to the season, so for want of anything better to say she asked if he was going into The Hollies.

'Yes,' said Mr Downing, 'oh, yes. That is, I have a message from Miss Pemberton for Mrs Turner, so I thought I had better give it. Not that I was particularly going to The Hollies, but as

Miss Pemberton had a message and I was going this way, she asked me to take it.'

His manner was so strange and uncomfortable that Mrs Villars, always too susceptible to atmosphere, began to feel uncomfortable herself, and said in a distracted way that she had just come out to post some letters at the Post Office, because her husband had a conviction that the pillar-box at the end of the Rectory Lane was only cleared on Quinquagesima Sunday, if then, and in any case she could never remember if there was a collection on Boxing Day or not.

'I hope your husband is quite well after everything,' said Mr Downing, wondering as he spoke whether that was the way to talk of the Christmas Day celebrations. 'Not too tired or anything, I mean. Of course, I know it is child's play to him, but even so it must be tiring.'

'Thank you so much, yes, he is quite all right,' said Mrs Villars. 'He and Mr Harker and Father Fewling have really worked like *demons* all this week, but the work is over and I left him writing to all the Old Boys who sent him Christmas cards. Give my love to Mrs Turner.'

With considerable relief she escaped, and Mr Downing, who had by now overshot The Hollies, retraced his steps, and between blissful anticipation and a faint sense of guilt opened the door, for friends of the family never rang, and went in.

On the horror-stricken evening when he had found his benefactress sitting up for him no questions had been asked, and since then Miss Pemberton had shown a stony and cheerful abstractedness from his doings which was more alarming than any curiosity or anger. Of course, Mr Downing, hypnotized by his benefactress's serpent eye, had faltered out an incoherent and self-exculpating account of his evening, to which Miss Pemberton had replied by saying, That was very nice, and it was high time they were in bed, walking, as Mr Downing told Father Fewling during a vigil in the St Sycorax Wardens' Shelter, straight through him, and leaving him to put out the lamp and lock the door, duties which she always performed herself, having no opinion whatever of her lodger's capacities in practical things.

What Miss Pemberton's hidden feelings were it is difficult to say, for she had little power of self-analysis, being one of those people in whom a tradition of breeding and great if narrow culture hide almost primitive emotions. As we have seen, she was very possessive about Mr Downing, but I think this was rather because she wanted something very silly and defenceless to look after than because she really wanted him for herself, and as we know marriage did not enter her head. After protecting him violently against most of female Northbridge she had made a few exceptions. Mrs Villars of course was one, and lately she had added Mrs Turner and her nieces to the favoured few. In Mrs Villars she recognized someone who would never want to encroach. In Mrs Turner and her nieces she thought she had found a surrounding where Mr Downing would be amused, taken for walks to see birds, and well fed when he went to tea. With silent stoicism she had recognized that she could no longer be a companion for her lodger's tramps and could not afford to give him the physical comfort which she despised for herself, and at The Hollies the fellow-walkers and the comfort could be found. But more than Mr Downing's physical well-being to her was his work. Under her goad he had done more in the last few years than his friends thought possible. She knew it was largely her doing, was fiercely proud of her work and determined to keep Mr Downing up to the mark. She knew his temperament and constitution by heart. He could go for long tramps, or spend days in a library, but what he could not stand were late nights and food to which he was not accustomed. Except for a very occasional orgy at Oxford, she had kept him on a tight rein since he came to live with her and had had much inward satisfaction from the results. Now, like a fool, she had pushed him into the arms of people who might in their wanton kindness lure him from the trodden paths in which he had walked so safely.

She spent a very unhappy night thinking of these things, half hoping with some viciousness that Mr Downing would have a bad headache and a worse stomach-ache and come penitent to her altar, half praying that he wouldn't, for his work would suffer at once and through it her pride.

For the next two days she avoided the subject so ostentatiously that Mr Downing did not dare to approach it. From time to time he was conscious that she was observing him closely and felt extremely uncomfortable, not knowing that her anxiety at the moment was almost entirely for his physical health. At the end of this period he was still quite well, but beginning to look so unhappy that Miss Pemberton's withers were wrung, for she loved her Downing in her own peculiar way. After another very unhappy night she made up her mind. Her pride would not let her speak to her lodger on the subject, or admit that she had been unfair, but she determined to give him every opportunity to visit The

Hollies, to walk with Betty and to sun himself in Mrs Turner's kindness. To this end she not only accepted all Mrs Turner's invitations, but gave herself great trouble to invent messages for Mr Downing to take, even going so far as to send him on very flimsy pretexts about four o'clock so that he might stay on to tea which he always did. The only comfort she got out of the whole affair was that no one but herself knew how much she was suffering, but those who have some Pemberton in their natures will realize that the comfort was very real.

Mr Downing, uneasy, perplexed, obedient, found himself going to The Hollies almost every day. He still could not think why he enjoyed it so much. His new friends had none of the things he valued. The house was hideous, the furniture, though fatly comfortable, revolting. There were no books except a set of Chambers' *Encyclopaedia* with some of the volumes the wrong way up and packed so tightly that it was clear they were never used, under a kind of ecclesiastical chiffonier in the hall, and a few odd volumes lying about which involved a daily ritual known as Changing the Libery Book. All the lights were unshaded and of million-candle-power. Piano, radiogram, mouth-organ poured out cheerful unmusical sounds. Nothing could be done without a great deal of noisy discussion. Strange young men full of strange talk were always about the house, treating him with respectful want of interest. Everyone was incredibly ignorant from his point of view and perfectly pleased to be so. But among it all moved Mrs Turner, incredibly efficient, dealing with evacuees, communal kitchens, committees; knitting, cooking dispensing boundless hospitality, on excellent terms with her nieces and all their young friends and always with a welcome that warmed his heart and enchanting friendly looks from her lustrous eyes.

Even as he went into the drawing-room in this late afternoon, the delightful, familiar, rather overpowering atmosphere closed round him. As he entered, his innermost self sent him a warning that this, however enchanting at the moment, was not his life, but when he had shaken, or rather pressed, his hostess's hand, he was as one who had fed on honey-dew and resigned himself to the circling charm. Seven or eight young people were making a good deal of noise.

'Who's that?' said a young man in the Air Force to Mrs Turner's other niece, indicating Mr Downing with a backward jerk of a cocktail glass.

'Oh, that's Auntie's new boy-friend,' said the undutiful niece. 'He's a perfect pet and frightfully highbrow. He's written a book about Troubadours.'

'Well, here's mud in their eye,' said the young man in the Air Force, finishing his cocktail. 'What about a spot of dancing?'

This suggestion met with approval. The carpet was turned up at the other end of the long drawing-room and the young people danced, managing to smoke, drink and talk at the top of their voices all the time.

'You are quite a stranger,' said Mrs Turner to Mr Downing; not that she meant anything by it, but it was a remark she often made.

Mr Downing, a stickler for precision in thought and speech, said she had doubtless forgotten that he was there on Christmas Day to tea, on Christmas Eve after tea, on the Monday when he helped to put up the decorations, and on

Sunday before lunch when those two young gunners came in for drinks.

'Oh, Jimmy and Hoots,' said Mrs Turner. 'But I don't call that a real visit. I mean like the day you read to us about the Troubadours. I did enjoy it so much.'

Mr Downing said he had not actually read to her, though he had come quite ready to do so if she wished it, and then shuddered at his own use of Betty's favourite word.

'Well, you know what I mean,' said Mrs Turner, 'and mind I don't intend to let you off your promise. And how's Miss Pemberton?'

This reminded Mr Downing of Miss Pemberton's message which he delivered.

'Tuesday?' said Mrs Turner. 'Yes, I think we'd love to. Betty!' she called as the gramophone ran down for a moment, 'can we go to tea with Miss Pemberton on Tuesday?'

'Well, the boy-friend Beasley's coming that day,' yelled Betty, 'but if you want to go we'll take him on.'

'The girls will call Commander Beasley my boy-friend,' said Mrs Turner, laughing. 'He's an old dear, but I have seen such a lot of him lately. He's always popping in. I'll tell you what, I'll let the girls look after him and come along to Punshions. Will you give Miss Pemberton my love and thank her very much?'

Now a fortnight or so earlier if any woman of Mrs Turner's or indeed any other age had called an elderly retired naval commander her boy-friend and spoken of his popping in, Mr Downing's face would involuntarily have assumed a pained and almost supercilious look. But somehow when Mrs Turner used the expression it became one with her own charm and gave Mr Downing quite a young and dashing feeling. He thought with some contempt of the kind of people who would take exception to a word or a phrase just because it was slangy, and gloried in this brave new world of modern phrase that was opening before him. If only, he thought, he had known this world earlier in his life how free he would have been; not a thin grey scholar, but a dashing man of letters who could talk with charming widows as man to woman.

Mrs Turner, mistaking the shade of regret that passed over his face for boredom, for she knew that Mr Downing was too brainy to really enjoy talking to her (the adjective and the split infinitive are hers), said she would like to show him some photos of the girls when they were little, an offer which Mr Downing, whose inner self shrank from the word photos as shudderingly as it did from the word snaps, accepted with alacrity.

There is no need to describe the photographs which were inserted at all angles into a large green book with a bunch of poppies embossed in red on the cover and the words 'Happy Moments' in art lettering, for Mrs Turner did all the describing, with a wealth of irrelevant and circumstantial detail that her audience found quite enchanting. One or two pages she turned rather quickly, so that Mr Downing had but a fleeting glimpse of a young man in a deck chair with a small child, presumably one of Mrs Turner's nieces, sitting in a sunbonnet on the grass beside him. Then Mrs Villars came in to borrow Mrs Turner's pinking scissors for her Working Party, and Betty, who was an excellent hostess with an eye for every guest, came and took her aunt's place for a while.

'Has Auntie been showing you her old snaps?' said Betty, idly turning the pages. 'What an awful kid I must have been.

In a sun-bonnet, too. Just look at that of me and Uncle Cecil.'

She showed Mr Downing the photograph of the young man and the child. Quite a good-looking young man in the 1920 style, thought Mr Downing.

'You'd never think he drank to look at him,' said Betty, 'would you? Of course I was too small to know about it, but Auntie must have had a pretty rotten time.'

'Do you mean that is Mrs Turner's husband?' said Mr Downing.

'That's right. Uncle Cecil,' said Betty. 'Auntie told us he died of pneumonia, but of course he drank like a fish and was in a home for drunks or a loony bin, I forget which, and died there. She is such a dear old ostrich, but of course I found out years ago. Oh, I must show you the one of me when I was thirteen. I think it's a crime for anyone to keep snaps of anyone who's as fat as I was then. Gosh, did you ever see such a ghastly kid?'

Then Mr Holden turned up and Mrs Villars vaguely wondered if his seemingly careless inquiry at lunch as to what she was doing in the afternoon had this end in view: for of late he had taken to arriving at tea-parties after his work and escorting her home through the black-out. Not that she minded this, but it seemed to her a pity that he hadn't someone a little younger to dance attendance on.

'I say, Downing,' said Mr Holden. 'I want to see Miss Pemberton soon about that cookery book. Coates is frightfully keen on it. When would be the best time to find her?'

A fortnight ago Mr Downing would have been so torn between his wish to please Mr Holden and his natural terror of making any engagement for his patroness of which she might not approve that he would almost have curled up like a woodlouse with shyness and Mr Holden would have got no satisfaction at all. But how changed were the times and he in them. With diabolic Machiavellianism he considered Miss Pemberton's future engagements. On Tuesday she was, by her own invitation, having Mrs Turner to tea. Mrs Turner's nieces had intimated their intention of staying at home, and no one else, as far as he knew, was to be asked. Therefore, if he could get Mr Holden to come on Tuesday and hold Miss Pemberton in talk, it was more than probable that he himself would be able to talk to Mrs Turner. Not, it is true, so comfortably as he could have done in her own drawing-room, but he could show her one or two books that he felt (though quite erroneously) might interest her and perhaps read her a little translation he had lately done of a poem beginning:

'Cuens di moult cor mi mailhez en les oeilz
I cuy di cor lounguesco por li sangz.'

With these things in mind he said to Mr Holden that he knew Miss Pemberton would be at home on Tuesday, which was New Year's Eve, about tea-time, and delighted to see him. Mr Holden said he would certainly come, and then Mr Downing went back to Punshions where with immense duplicity he said not a word to Miss Pemberton about Mr Holden's projected visit.

Meanwhile, Mr Holden and Mrs Villars walked back to the Rectory in the dark and talked of this and that very pleasantly and laughed a good deal. Mrs Villars said how disappointed she was that her eldest son could not come to them for part of the Christmas vacation, but he had written to say that he had influenza and so much work to do that he would have to put off his visit till Easter. Mr Holden said he was so sorry. On the other hand, said Mrs Villars, her youngest son was likely to get leave any time during January, so that would be delightful. Mr Holden said, indeed it would be, and he looked forward so much to meeting him.

'I wish,' said Mr Holden, who felt obliged to feel noble and let Mrs Villars know it, 'that you could get rid of us all and have your son to yourself. I often wonder how you can stand us all. Would it be any help if I could get leave then?'

'How nice of you, but no help at all,' said Mrs Villars. 'John will love to find you all here. He doesn't come to see me or Gregory in the *least*,' she added proudly, for mothers can always find something to be proud of, even in the fine dashing spirit which has made their sons be had up at Vine Street on Boat-Race Night, or get seven years for a peculiarly brilliant fraud. 'He wants to get a lot of clothes mended and take a lot of Gregory's cigars and go up to town and have all his friends in for drinks and go to some dancing places. He will simply love finding a lot of men in the house, because he is used to living in a crowd.'

'There must be very few mothers like you,' said Mr Holden with dark passion.

'Lots, I should think,' said Mrs Villars, a practical woman in matters of the emotions. 'Only born fools would expect their sons slopping all over them. One of my aunts boasts that her grown-up married sons come in to see her every day on their way home from business. If my boys did that I'd go mad. Fancy having to be in every day of one's life because Tom, Dick or Harry were coming in to see you.'

'I know you don't mean it,' said Mr Holden, 'but one can't help admiring your attitude.'

They were by now half-way up the Rectory Lane, where the path to the kitchen yard turned off. Owing to the moon being well into its last quarter and what there was of it not rising till next morning, not to speak of a cloudy night, the darkness under the laurels was deep. Mr Holden switched on his torch, directing its ray, like a good citizen, upon the ground, and bringing suddenly into view the lower portions of two human figures, one in boots, the other in very unsuitable high-heeled shoes. Mr Holden quickly switched his torch off again.

'Oh dear, Jackson and Edie,' said Mrs Villars as they walked on. 'I do hope it's all right.'

Mr Holden, faintly shocked that so ethereal a creature as he had made up his mind Mrs Villars was should notice these grosser manifestations of human nature, said he must have a word with Jackson.

'Oh, no, pray don't,' said Mrs Villars. 'Colonel Passmore says he isn't married and is most steady and respectable and it would be a splendid thing for Edie, who is the sort that might have an illegitimate child any day through sheer want of intellect, which is so peculiarly awkward at a Rectory. But I will tell Edie they had better not stand *just* in the lane, only she is so stupid that she rarely understands anything one says.'

'I wish I hadn't turned my torch on them,' said Mr Holden.

Mrs Villars said it was a very good thing, as otherwise they might have fallen over Corporal Jackson's boots.

'You have the courage to laugh at anything,' said Mr

Holden, 'but I can't help thinking how this added burden will tire you. You already have so much to carry.'

'On my frail shoulders,' murmured Mrs Villars, very ungratefully to herself, and they went into the house.

'Verena, is that you?' said her husband from the study. 'Come here a moment and shut the door.'

His wife did as she was asked.

'Not John?' said the detached mother, suddenly feeling her face go stiff.

'Of course not, dearest,' said the Rector. 'But worse in a way. Corporal Jackson came to see me to-day about having his banns put up.'

'Edie!' said Mrs Villars.

'Yes, Edie,' said the Rector. 'That's all right. She is twenty-one and as she seems to be mentally defective and you tell me she is a good worker, I dare say it's all for the best. But Jackson seems to think that Mrs Chapman may forbid the banns.'

'Oh, Lord!' said Mrs Villars. 'And she is such a good cook.'

'Well, I thought I'd better tell you,' said the Rector very meanly. 'The banns won't be read for the first time till Sunday week, so they may break it off, or Mrs Chapman might have a holiday or something.'

Mrs Villars said Mrs Chapman would certainly not take a holiday while Corporal Jackson was about the place and if this was the war she wished to goodness it would stop. But seeing that her husband looked alarmed she choked back a few tears of fatigue and annoyance and felt all the better for the exertion.

'By the way, Gregory,' she said, 'oughtn't we to have the officers to something on New Year's Eve or New Year's Day?'

'Of course,' said her husband. 'Ask them to sherry on New

245

Year's Day, and get a few other people. Spender is going home for a week, but I believe all the others will be here. Anyway, you arrange it.'

Mrs Villars went to dress for dinner. Half-way up to her bedroom she stopped.

'Yes!' she said aloud, to any listening power. 'I *have* left the pinking scissors at The Hollies. I would. And now I hope you are pleased. War, indeed!'

And having thus put Providence in its place she continued her journey upstairs.

According to plan, Mrs Turner walked down to Punshions on Tuesday about tea-time and was received by Miss Pemberton and brought into the sitting-room.

'I expect you are looking for Mr Downing,' said Miss Pemberton as her guest's eye roved round the room.

Mrs Turner could not tell the truth, namely, that she was thinking how horribly uncomfortable everything looked compared with her own warm, bright, over-furnished house, so she said she knew he had a lot of writing to do.

'He is at the Wardens' Shelter with Father Fewling,' said Miss Pemberton, 'but he will be back by half-past four.'

Mrs Turner said she was afraid she was terribly early.

'Not at all,' said Miss Pemberton, conveying with the utmost clarity that four-twenty was not half-past four.

Then she was ashamed of herself and made a real effort to be nice, to such effect that when Mr Downing came in at a quarter-to five he found the ladies talking in a very technical way about tapestry stitches and not in the least interested in his arrival.

246

'Put the kettle on, Harold, while I finish showing Mrs Turner my Louis XV piece,' said Miss Pemberton, affectionately fingering a piece of delicately faded, exquisitely fine *petit point*.

'Yes, Ianthe,' said Mr Downing. 'By the way—'

He stopped nervously.

'Yes?' said Miss Pemberton. 'How they could see to do that stitch I cannot think.'

'I have done one as fine as that,' said Mrs Turner, 'but never again, and I won't let the girls try. It simply ruins one's eyes.'

'It wasn't really anything,' said Mr Downing miserably.

Miss Pemberton looked up with infinite weary patience.

'Only Father Fewling is coming to tea,' said Mr Downing, stammering a little. 'He asked to come, and I didn't know what to say, so I said Yes. He is washing his hands because we were clearing out the Shelter.'

'That will be delightful,' said the hostess graciously. 'One more teaspoon in the pot then, Harold, and we shall be ready for our tea as soon as you can bring it.'

Mr Downing thankfully slunk into the kitchen. Mrs Turner felt sorry for him, yet a little mortified that so highbrow an author should have so poor a spirit; which may have been Miss Pemberton's intention. Father Fewling came in and fell headlong into the needlework.

'What a ripping bit, Miss Pemberton,' he said, examining the work with loving finger-tips. 'I did a lot of *petit point* when I was at sea, but I haven't much time now. I'd like to show you a stool cover I did of Gibraltar and the old *Scrapiron* lying out in the harbour. Every detail correct. And I did a firescreen of Cape Town and Table Mountain that you might like. Our paymaster calculated that I must have put about six hundred thousand stitches into it. You must come and see it some day if you will excuse my very simple lodgings, and Mrs Turner too.'

Both ladies accepted with enthusiasm and when Mr Downing brought in the tea no one was in the least interested in him.

'Did you stir the tea, Harold?' said Miss Pemberton as she took her seat at the tea-table.

'Yes, Ianthe,' said her lodger.

'Spoils the tea,' said Miss Pemberton.

She then showed quite fiendish ingenuity in turning the conversation to matters of which Mr Downing was ignorant and if ever he got a foothold in the talk dismissing him to fetch more milk or put another log on the fire, so that he made but a poor showing. Mrs Turner was sorry for him, but again felt a certain mortification that her friend should be so under the thumb of Miss Pemberton. And yet, for such is the female mind, her opinion of Miss Pemberton rose. I leave this for more subtle minds to explain.

Before they had finished their tea Mr Holden dropped in. Room was made for him next to Miss Pemberton and before long he had brought up the subject of the cookery book. Under his skilful flattery, for his chief, Adrian Coates, had trained him well in the art of angling for authors, Miss Pemberton began to melt and said she would do her best to provide a book of easy and unusual war-time recipes embedded in literary essays in time for autumn publication. Mr Holden, on his side, promised to pull every string to get her articles used by a well-known women's monthly before they came out in book form, and we may say now that the arrangement was made, and that if everything goes well Miss Pemberton's articles and her book will have considerable success and bring in more money than her more serious works have ever made.

While this business talk was going on Mrs Turner and Father Fewling talked together very easily at the other end of the table. Mr Downing, although his plans for getting Mrs Turner to himself had been innocently thwarted by Father Fewling, found that he was not at all discontented. To sit and watch Mrs Turner being kind, as always, to Father Fewling, to admire the competence with which she took his ideas for evening classes for evacuees in the St Sycorax Church room and gave them a more practical turn, made a pleasant background across which he could, for the old Adam was strong in him, listen to Mr Holden's conversation with his hostess; and sometimes it was all he could do to keep himself from plunging into it. But as far as he could hear, the terms Mr Holden was proposing to her were fair enough, so he had no excuse.

Mr Holden, having got what he came for, said that he would get into touch with Adrian Coates and a proper contract should be sent to Miss Pemberton, and he was so sorry he had to get back to the Rectory. So he went away and after a few moments of desultory talk Mrs Turner said the girls had some friends coming in and she must go home.

'Come back and have a drink, Father Fewling,' she said. 'It's on the way if you are going back to your rooms.'

But Father Fewling with many thanks said he wanted to speak to Miss Pemberton about his evening classes for evacuees, if she had a few moments to spare. Miss Pemberton, true to her plan of giving Mr Downing as much rope as possible, said he had better see Mrs Turner home through the black-out while she heard about Father Fewling's plans, and so it was arranged.

Father Fewling, left alone with Miss Pemberton, at once embarked upon the subject of which his unselfish mind was at the moment full.

'I wonder, Miss Pemberton,' he said, 'whether I could interest you in a plan I have for our evacuee boys from the secondary schools.'

Miss Pemberton motioned him to proceed; for no other term can adequately express her distracted majesty.

Father Fewling, after a look at her, embarked upon his plan which was, roughly, to catch boys from twelve upwards and collect them for classes in various handicrafts at the St Sycorax Church room, in the hope that a certain amount of religious instruction would also soak in. His appeal to Miss Pemberton was especially as an embroideress, for he felt certain that several boys would be amused and interested in the art of embroidery, and if the only result was a kettle-holder with a portrait of a kettle on it, that would be better than hanging about in the dark or being a great nuisance to their hostesses.

Miss Pemberton listened, her heavy masculine face set in brooding lines. When he had finished what he had to say she was silent. Father Fewling wondered if he had asked too much. Then she said abruptly:

'Of course, I don't believe in religion.'

'That's all right,' said Father Fewling cheerfully, 'lots of people don't. But they really do.'

'And I certainly don't believe in confessing,' Miss Pemberton continued, her massive face moved and troubled.

Father Fewling said nothing and was very sorry for her, for he felt that she was in need of comfort.

'Do you think,' said Miss Pemberton, going on as if she had not noticed any pause, 'that one has any right to try to influence other people's lives?'

Father Fewling could not answer this question at once.

'Because,' continued Miss Pemberton, 'I have been trying for some years to influence a certain person for good. I may or I may not have succeeded. Now that person seems to have come to a cross-road. I know what I want for that person, but I do not know what will be best for that person. Should I try to make that person go in the road I think best, or should I stand aside? I don't know. Can you help me?'

Father Fewling was not unobservant in spite of his simplicity. There was little doubt in his mind who the person was. He had seen Mr Downing at Punshions and he had seen him at The Hollies, and had drawn his own conclusions. But in spite of the bond that unites man and man against woman, he felt very sorry for the hitherto indomitable Miss Pemberton. If she had consulted him professionally in his own church it would have been simpler, but for an ex-naval officer to tell a distinguished literary lady how to order her life was not easy. Father Fewling was not wanting in courage, so he spoke his mind.

'If you insist that you do not believe in religion, Miss Pemberton,' he said, 'not that I think you know what you are talking about, I don't see how I can help you. But if it is a question of one human being helping another, I will do anything I can. Anything.'

Miss Pemberton looked at him with a kind of despairing gratitude.

'I think,' said Father Fewling, 'mind you, I say think, that only in very exceptional cases and if one sees real danger to the soul, or the mind, if you prefer, should one interfere. My advice as an outsider would be to leave the person to whom you allude to go his or her own way. If it is the right way it can't be wrong. If it seems to you the wrong way it may be right for the person you are thinking of. I wish I could be more helpful.'

Miss Pemberton still remained silent. The lines on her face looked deeper, or perhaps Father Fewling's imagination saw too much. She moved once or twice impatiently. Father Fewling looked at her with the same keen look that he had learnt at sea, concentrating on the one job on hand and forgetting self.

'All right,' said Miss Pemberton suddenly. 'I'll come and see what I can do about your boys. I've got plenty of wool, canvas and needles. Tell me when you want me and I'll turn up. Mind, those boys will have to work.'

Father Fewling felt that he and Miss Pemberton had both been answered. What answer she had found to her question he did not know, but he had observed her face and did not think the answer could be wrong.

When Mr Downing, after seeing Mrs Turner home, having a small drink of sherry and listening to a great deal of nonsense from the young people who were there, got back to Punshions about half-past seven, he found the table laid for supper and Miss Pemberton in the kitchen. During their meal his benefactress was neither more nor less prickly than usual, but when she had cleared the things away and they were sitting by the fire with their work, he fancied that she looked at him in a peculiar way from time to time.

'A very pleasant tea-parry, Ianthe,' he said to break the silence. 'Did Fewling stay long?'

Miss Pemberton at first made no answer, which frightened him very much.

'I have been thinking, Harold,' she said suddenly, thus frightening him more than ever, for this remark usually prefaced some trenchant criticism of his work or ways, 'that it is very dull for you here.'

Mr Downing took his spectacles off and stared.

'Looking dispassionately at myself,' said Miss Pemberton, 'I admit that I am not as young as I was, nor so active, nor can I give you certain comforts and luxuries that you would like to have.'

Mr Downing mumbled that he was very comfortable indeed.

'I cannot,' Miss Pemberton continued judicially, 'go for the long walks that I used to be able to take, my eyes are not so good at seeing birds as they used to be, I am not perhaps very good at making new friends. I do not take pleasure in filling the house with noisy young people, nor,' said Miss Pemberton, determined to drink her cup to the dregs, 'would they take any pleasure in coming, as I have neither a gramophone nor a cocktail bar.'

Mr Downing nearly said: 'Mrs Turner hasn't got a cocktail bar,' but just had the sense not to.

'So putting all these things together in my mind,' said Miss

Pemberton, 'I have come to the conclusion that I am perhaps standing in your way.'

'Ianthe!' said Mr Downing.

'Don't contradict me,' said Miss Pemberton with a flash of temper reassuring to her lodger who was beginning to fear that such angelic self-depreciation meant a failing mind. 'I have wanted for some time to say this to you and now I have said it. Don't answer me, Harold. If you find that other ways which are not mine are to be your ways I shall not try to stop you. You understand me. I shall thoroughly approve of anything you do so long as you really want to do it. I will not discuss this question. We will go on exactly as before. If and when you feel that a change must come, you will tell me. And in any case I shall always be ready to help you with your work. That lies quite outside what I have been talking about. Good night.'

Miss Pemberton put away her books and papers in a silence which Mr Downing would have given the world to break, but he found such unaccountable difficulty in speaking that he nearly swallowed his own tongue and said nothing. His patroness lingered for a moment, perhaps hoping for a word, but as none came she went to the door. With her hand still on the latch she turned and looked back.

'I have always known that your work was better than mine, Harold,' she said, and then went upstairs, where we shall not follow her.

Left alone, Mr Downing became a prey to such mingled feelings as his gentle, slightly desiccated mind was not accustomed to. So might a mild duckling brought up by a retired hen of literary leanings feel when suddenly shown the wide expanse of the duck pond, covered with dazzling green weeds, rich in alluring mud. So might he feel the lure of the fat comfortable lady duck preening herself on the bosom of the water, her bright eye beaming a not very intellectual greeting, her figure warmly clad in becoming speckled feathers. So might he linger by the margin of that green and slimy Paradise, longing and fearing, resentful of his foster-mother yet secretly afraid to leave her severe regimen. And so might he shriek and cackle when that lady, tired perhaps of her responsibilities, went so far as to give him the push that would send him into his natural element But here the parallel fails. For whatever Mr Downing's admiration or even deeper feeling for The Hollies, that was not his native air and inside himself he knew it. Gratitude, fear, love of a rather milk-and-water kind, fascination, remorse, so jumbled about inside him that he felt he would shortly perish like Sir Brian de Bois Guilbert, a victim to the violence of his own contending passions. Miss Pemberton's generous offer of help with his work whatever might happen moved him profoundly, although her possessive dictatorial ways had sometimes driven him almost to open rebellion. Mrs Turner's delightful sympathy and interest stirred his gentlemanly heart, even if his acuter brain told him that she would have brought exactly the same bright interest to a cricketer, a gentleman rider, a jazz-band leader, or even, though he was perhaps judging her harshly, a B.B.C. announcer. What he frightfully wanted was for things to go on exactly as they were for ever. Miss Pemberton appeared to be determined to precipitate a crisis. His feelings swung to the hospitable easy-going ways of The Hollies. He thought of an atmosphere of eternal radio, cocktails and cigarettes, and the cloistered repose of Punshions with a dish of herbs and pulse seemed like Paradise. One should be very sorry for people whose heads are more intelligent than their emotions, for when their emotions do occasionally get the upper hand they are apt to hold a Soviet in their hearts and go quite mad.

Poor Mr Downing might have sat there all night, getting colder and colder, while he wrestled with problems so new to him, but habit is strong. Half an hour was the utmost latitude that Miss Pemberton conceded from the time of her going up to bed and that period he had already exceeded by five minutes, so he retired to his couch and dreamt that he was Ghismond Beauxcilsz who left the Dame d'Aiguesdouces and sought the favours of Madon lou Cabrou and was found dead on the Puy des Stryges with a cloven hoofmark on his chest. But dreams notoriously go by contraries.

12

Rectory Sherry

What Mr Downing and possibly Miss Pemberton would have liked would have been a kind of week of retreat in which to examine calmly their own feelings. Even a day or two of complete calm, correcting the final proof of Mr Downing's book, might have been of some help, but this was impossible, for New Year's Day was the Rectory sherry party and as everyone knew exactly who was coming any absence would have been noticed and commented on. Miss Pemberton and Mr Downing wished each other a Happy New Year at breakfast and then kept out of each other's way as much as possible. Miss Pemberton was helping at the Communal Kitchen, so she had her lunch there (bean-and-rabbit stew, potatoes boiled in their jackets which most of the evacuees wouldn't eat, and steamed carrot pudding which the more refined spirits messed about with their spoons and said they didn't fancy), leaving Mr Downing to shift for himself (for Effie had the day off to go to what was known in film circles as

Pin-oak at the Barchester Odeon early session), which he did with brown bread, margarine, shredded cabbage, a very small tin of sardines and some cocoa, which he didn't stir enough and then allowed to burn.

Meanwhile the whole of residential Northbridge began to think of the afternoon's treat and rouse itself from the combined depression and torpor of Christmas week.

Mrs Paxon had been invited to the Rectory party with her husband, but though the card said 'Mr and Mrs Paxon' it was somehow understood without a word or a look passing that Mr Paxon would not come. Mrs Paxon, having as it were risen from the ranks owing to her valiant services, was welcome anywhere, but Northbridge prided itself on its feeling for the fine shades and when Mrs Villars, a newcomer, invited the Paxons, there was no doubt about who would go, though Mrs Paxon accepted in both their names; so the Empire stood firm.

As for the Misses Talbot, they did not even tell their father that his name was on the invitation, for it would have been no holiday for them if he had come too. Ever since the 20th of December they had been domestic slaves not only to old Professor Talbot, who was eighty-three, but to his brothers, Sir Alwyn Talbot, K.C.M.G., ex-Principal of the Board of Tape and Sealing Wax, who was eighty-six and deaf, and Dr Tufnell Talbot, F.R.P.S., aged eighty-eight, who had been a widower for fifty-two years and liked to complain of loneliness. All three brothers had no fraternal feelings whatsoever except loathing, contempt, and total disagreement on any subject that Miss Talbot or Miss Dolly Talbot cared to mention. On every single day since the fatal 20th, the Misses Talbot had done most of the housework, for they only had one maid, and taken two of the old gentlemen for a turn in the village. After lunch one of them read aloud to Uncle Alwyn from *The Times*, and the other to Uncle Tufnell from the *News Chronicle*, while Professor Talbot had his nap, and then took it in turn to read *The Journal of Oecumenical Studies* to Professor Talbot while his elder brothers dozed. They then gave the three flushed, cross old gentlemen their tea and played bezique and backgammon alternately with their father and Uncle Tufnell, while Uncle Alwyn played patience; got most of the supper ready for their greedy and critical charges; listened to the wireless to please Uncle Tufnell, turned it off to please Uncle Alwyn, and turned it on again for their father, who said 'Fools!' to everything that came out of it. Finally, having got the old gentlemen to bed with hot milky drinks, and waited up for the maid, who was late every night 'because it was Christmas,' an excuse which the Misses Talbot supposed it would be ungracious, even un-Christian, not to accept, they went to bed wishing that they lived in very uncomfortable lodgings so that their uncles would not spend Christmas with them.

For several days the Misses Talbot had feared that they would be detained in the ogres' den, or give such offence by going to the party that they would have done better to refuse, but by astounding good luck the three old gentlemen had a resounding row about the rebuilding of Europe and both uncles left three days earlier than they had intended, and we must say for them that though they united in condemning their youngest brother as a damned young fool, they each gave their nieces five pounds and said they didn't think Armorel (for this was Professor Talbot's unaccountable name) was long for this world and young men had no kick in them now. Professor Talbot then had a slight stroke, but no danger, and the District Nurse, a very nice woman indeed, promised to spend the afternoon from five-thirty to seven with him and stay to supper. So it was with a sense of freedom and elation that Miss Talbot put on her wine-coloured tailor-made and her stitched beret, while Miss Dorothy Talbot got out her nice blue coat-frock and her blue felt that went with it, and they set out for the Rectory.

Miss Crowder and Miss Hopkins, in search of the local colour of their beloved South, had offered Yuletide hospitality, as they put it, to some Free French consisting of Madame Duval, Madame Henri Duval and Mademoiselle Marie-Clair Duval who did nothing but talk about the probable fate of their grandson, son and nephew (these three persons according to French usage being the same) who had last been heard of ten years ago in Algeria. They also rightly despised, in no uncertain tones and in a hideous Meridional accent, the cooking, beds, housekeeping, climate and language of the country which had perfidiously given them shelter. Their hostesses had hardly hoped to be able to escape for an hour, but by great good luck a daughter-in-law, husband's brother's wife and sister-in-law, again surprising in one person these three relations, had sent for them on New Year's Eve to come and live with her in a large house near Wimbledon where they would have the great advantage of five other relations, this time five in person as well as in name, to quarrel with.

These are but examples of Christmas discomforts in Northbridge, and indeed all over England, but the reader may take it for granted that everyone who came to the party was equally uncomfortable and that most of them were being extremely good and cheerful about it.

At a little before six Mrs Villars was in the drawing-room to see that everything was all right. Corporal Jackson, through the medium of Captain Topham, had offered his services as barman, and though the bar only consisted of sherry, lemonade and whisky and soda, Mrs Villars had gratefully accepted. By an inspiration she had then remembered some claret that her husband had bought by mistake at the beginning of the war and regretted ever since, and decided to mull it, for an instinct told her that something hot, sweet and gently intoxicating would suit most of her guests very well. Accordingly she mentioned her idea to Mrs Chapman, who thoroughly approved, saying Christmas didn't seem Christmas without something hot, and the New Year the same it stood to reason, and produced her granny's recipe for mulling. After a reduction, to placate the war, had been made in the quantities of sugar required and a reduction, to please Mrs Chapman's taste, in the quantity of water to be added, she made a trial jorum which was sipped, approved and finished by Foster, Corporal Jackson, two friends of Corporal Jackson's, the postman who happened to come to the back door with the afternoon post, and herself. Corporal Jackson said it reminded him of France, which was a tribute to the nastiness of the claret rather than its intoxicating qualities, but Mrs Chapman said she could do with a bit more and Edie, who was allowed to finish the jug in the scullery, flushed to an almost becoming pink and was stigmatized by Mrs Chapman as being tiddley, so that she went about looking more like a March Hare than ever.

'Do you good, Edie, to get a bit merry,' said Corporal Jackson, catching her alone in the scullery for a moment while she was washing up. 'When you're Mrs Jackson you shall have half a pint every day with your dinner. Do you good.'

'Ow, Mr Jackson,' said Edie, her protruding eyes damp with mulled claret and devotion.

'You've not said a word to Mrs C?' said the Corporal. 'Not about us?'

'Ow, no, Mr Jackson,' said Edie.

'There's a good girl,' said the Corporal.

When Mrs Villars came down to the kitchen next morning Mrs Chapman had been able to report that the mulling had been a complete success and when she made it for the party she would put a little less nutmeg and just a taste more cinnamon.

'How many bottles would you wish me to use, madam?' she asked.

Mrs Villars inquired how many there were.

Mrs Chapman said nine, not counting the little bit she had used yesterday to see what it was like, so her mistress told her to do six and stand by in case more was wanted.

The first guests to arrive were those billeted officers who were in residence. Mr Dutton had before this been returned to the depot to nobody's sorrow or interest, and Major Spender had gone into Barchester to meet his wife and take her on to stay with friends near Nutfield, but Colonel Passmore with Captains Topham and Powell-Jones, supported by Lieutenants Holden, Greaves and Hooper, were there in full force, prepared to show gratitude to their host and hostess by talking, drinking and handing drinks. As they had all met at lunch there seemed to be no particular reason to stand on ceremony, but Mr Hooper, who knew etiquette very well, administered a silent rebuke to his fellow-officers by shaking hands with the Rector and Mrs Villars.

'Oh, how do you do,' said Mrs Villars. 'Will you have sherry, or mulled claret?'

Mr Hooper, who knew that sherry was correct, said, 'Sherry, please,' upon which all his brother officers within earshot asked for mulled claret.

'Excellent idea, Mrs Villars,' said Colonel Passmore, 'especially if the claret isn't too good. Pity to waste the best.'

Mrs Villars said she thought theirs was quite bad and no one must be alarmed if it appeared to be one mass of sediment, for this would not be lees, but the nutmeg and cinnamon.

'I did tell Mrs Chapman to strain it,' she said, 'but she didn't hold with straining.'

'That's all right, Mrs Villars,' said Captain Topham. 'Gives it more body. Jove, it reminds one of Shakespeare and Ivanhoe and all those old fellows. Burnt sack, what?'

'Hardly sack, my dear fellow, under the Normans,' said Mr Hooper. 'Mead, or perhaps ale.'

'Or a stoup of right good malvoisie,' said Mr Greaves, who disliked Mr Hooper and upon whom his University education had not been entirely wasted.

'Ale from an ox's horn,' said Captain Powell-Jones defiantly.

'And wine from gold, Gwyn o eur,' said Mr Holden who had lately been re-reading his Peacock. 'And something else

263

for luck because it has to go in threes, but what I cannot remember. You know, Powell-Jones.'

Captain Powell-Jones, who had been about to embark on a triad himself, looked darkly at Mr Holden and moved away.

Father Fewling now came in, very cold after a nature walk with the Wolf Cubs, and gratefully accepted the mulled claret. He then fell into conversation with his Rector on the layout of page two of the Parish Magazine and whether there would be room for an account of the last Mothers' Union meeting at which Miss Hopgood had spoken on A Cruise to Madeira. The officers also fell into shop among themselves. Mrs Villars thought how delightful it would be if all one's parties consisted of men, and those men engaged in the same job, so that a hostess would sit back and not exert herself. But just as she was sitting back very comfortably Mr Holden, who had been eyeing her with black devotion for some time, came and sat down by her.

'You will be tired to death after this,' he said.

Mrs Villars was conscious of her usual impulse to a double entity, but pushing her lower self away under the sofa said parties did her a great deal of good and took her out of herself.

'They may take you out of yourself but they cannot free you from yourself,' said Mr Holden, who before speaking had had an idea which he thought rather remarkable, but found to his annoyance that it made little or no sense if expressed in words. 'Don't try to change yourself. To be what you are is what you were meant for.'

'Yes, I suppose it is,' said Mrs Villars, interested at once by an intellectual conversation about herself. 'I mean, it's all very well to think one can change oneself, but whatever one turned into it would still be oneself and probably what one was meant to be, so it hardly seems worth taking trouble, does it? Of course, it is rather depressing to think that one will still be oneself when one is dead, but I dare say one won't be so critical then. And how is your mother?'

Mr Holden said his mother was very well and his second sister had just had her third baby there, so his mother was very busy and happy.

'By the way,' he added, though it did not seem to be by any particular way, 'I am about due for my captaincy and I expect to be moved at any moment.'

'Oh, I *am* sorry,' said Mrs Villars with genuine feeling. 'I mean about your going away. Where will it be? At least I don't mean that, as it is careless talk and costs lives.'

'I'd tell you if I knew,' said Mr Holden, underlining the 'you' in a way that made Mrs Villars feel she ought to do something silly like Brutus's wife to show she could keep a secret, 'but I don't. Nor,' he added, 'do I greatly care.'

This sentence sounded so well that he said it again in a musing way.

'But,' he continued, bracing himself, 'I shall only tire you if I talk like this. You must not let me be so selfish.'

On this theme he would doubtless have discoursed at greater length but that Foster suddenly let loose a flood of guests into the room and Mrs Villars had to play her part as hostess. Mr Holden stood darkly aside for a moment, marvelling that one so frail and exquisite (which Mrs Villars, though she was rather easily tired and very nice, certainly was not) should bear her burdens (which Mrs Villars would have been the first to admit were as light as any Rector's wife's could be) with so brave a smile (which was simply Mrs Villars smiling as a hostess normally does). After which he devoted himself, for he was really kind as well as rather romantic, to Miss Hopgood's aunt who seemed a bit out of it.

Mrs Paxon, who came as a kind of fireman, with a red scarf round her newly-permed curls, at once turned the battery of her fine eyes upon Colonel Passmore, who joyfully accepted the challenge and finding two seats in a corner there told her all about his grandchildren, while Mrs Paxon said at intervals that no one would believe he was a grandfather and described her troubles in collecting the National Savings every week. She and Colonel Passmore had done wisely to secure seats, for in ten minutes the room was packed with people, all delighted to be at a party and working themselves up to parrot-like screams as they talked. Miss Pemberton, who knowing that Mrs Turner would be present had sacrificially brought Mr Downing so that he might enjoy himself, wished she had had the strength of mind to send him alone, for noise and crowd were what she could not bear and she knew her head would ache for two days afterwards. But she could not resist the wretched pleasure of seeing her lodger's happiness, though she had done little to promote it by alluding steadfastly to Mrs Villars's party as 'that party we have got to go to,' and insisting that Mr Downing should take a large handkerchief drenched in eucalyptus as there were so many colds about.

But although she had determined not to stand in Mrs Turner's light, she saw no reason to allow any other women the privilege of Mr Downing's society, so she hemmed him into a corner, as she had hemmed him at the first meeting of roof-spotters, until she could collect Mr Holden and Father

Fewling, when she released her lodger on a string, as it were, to talk to these safe companions. Mr Holden, who had been trained by Adrian Coates to strike repeatedly while the iron was hot, was not unwilling to have a few words with Miss Pemberton. With her usual energy and orderliness she had already sketched a plan for her cookery book and submitted it to Mr Coates, who had returned it with one or two suggestions that she wished to discuss with Mr Holden. Parking herself in front of Mr Downing, and seeing from the tail of one eye that he was peacefully engaged with Father Fewling, she tackled Mr Holden on the chapter about vegetable soups, and such was her eloquence that he saw her point at once and promised to support her.

'This mulled claret is practically a vegetable soup,' said Mr Holden, 'if nutmeg and cinnamon count as vegetables, but a very good idea.'

'I should say Mrs Villars was a person of excellent ideas,' said Miss Pemberton.

'She is,' said Mr Holden fervently. 'Miss Pemberton, you are an old friend of hers. Do you think you could persuade her to do a little less? She wears herself out with thinking of others. Look at her now. She will be a wreck by to-night.'

Miss Pemberton made no answer but looked piercingly at and at the same time through Mr Holden in a most disconcerting way. She liked Mrs Villars very much and what is more she trusted her, but she could see no reason to pity her. Mrs Villars had a nice husband, enough money, two successful sons, a fine old Rectory; and Miss Pemberton, while envying her none of these things, felt that she did not need Mr Holden's sympathy as well; nor, to do Miss Pemberton justice, did she think Mrs Villars wanted it. She knew well enough from experience the lines and shadows that are set in a face by a ceaseless struggle with narrow means, or by much anxiety for one's nearest and dearest, and of these she could find nothing in Mrs Villars. Mr Holden, looking at her, thought he had never noticed before how unbending her expression could be.

'Fiddlesticks,' said Miss Pemberton suddenly, making Mr Holden jump with surprise at hearing an expression which he imagined to be purely literary. 'There's nothing heartbreaking there. You young men will imagine anything. A very nice sensible woman and not an old friend. They only came here just before the war.'

To hear one's admired hostess called nice or sensible is enough to make anyone cross and only his strong professional feeling kept Mr Holden from saying pettishly that Mrs Villars was neither, so instead he inquired how Mr Downing's proofs were getting on. Miss Pemberton said they were finished and the book would be out about Easter, all being well.

'I suppose one has to say that about everything,' said Mr Holden, 'even if it is a bit depressing.'

'Of course one has to say it,' said Miss Pemberton stoutly. 'If there are a lot of Germans all over the place there will be no great demand for books on Provençal poetry. One must face these things.'

'Hullo, Miss Pemberton,' said Betty, who had just arrived.

This is a difficult greeting to acknowledge, unless you say 'Hullo' back. To say 'Good morning' or 'Good afternoon' in acknowledgement sounds like criticism. But while Miss Pemberton was fumbling for the *mot juste*, Betty, who never noticed anything except what she saw, suddenly caught sight

268

of Captain Topham and considering she had done her duty by Miss Pemberton forged her way through the press towards him, leaving standing-room for one behind her, which was at once filled by Mrs Turner.

'Good evening, Miss Pemberton,' said Mrs Turner, who was looking more ripe and sparkling than ever. 'Isn't it nice of Mrs Villars to throw a party and cheer us all up? I am so excited about Mr Downing's book. We shall all feel so proud of it and then we shall know all about the Troubadours. When does it come out?'

'About Easter, all being well,' said Miss Pemberton.

'I know what you mean,' said Mrs Turner. 'Of course, one doesn't quite like to mention it in case it brought bad luck, as of course if there were Germans about I suppose there wouldn't be much time for reading, except of course that we might all be in prison, though even then I dare say the libraries wouldn't be working. It all seems very hard on people, doesn't it? Still we must look on the bright side and whatever is, is best, isn't it, Father Fewling?'

Father Fewling, thus appealed to, said with great presence of mind that it depended what it was, when the Misses Talbot descended on him and enveloped him from mortal sight. Willingly would he have escaped, but the bravest clergyman may be excused from showing fight when pushed into a corner by two middle-aged maiden ladies, both much taller than he is, though not really stronger.

'I said to Dolly as we came along,' said Miss Talbot, whose stitched beret stood up on one end in a very dashing way, 'that we might make our little confession to you, Father. We are quite prodigal daughters.'

'We have been wool-gathering,' said Miss Dolly, 'but we have come back to the fold.'

Poor Father Fewling, who deeply as he was attached to his own form of worship really did not mind in the least which brand of belief the Misses Talbot patronized and had very much enjoyed his brief immunity from their attentions, said Hislop over at Nutfield was an excellent fellow.

'You are so charitable,' said Miss Dolly. 'But when we heard what he does at Easter we felt we had indeed made a mistake in attending St Oregon's.'

'So we have come back to a decent Easter,' said Miss Talbot.

'That is if we get an Easter at all this year,' said Miss Dolly, 'for I could not possibly worship Odin.'

Miss Talbot said that even if anything happened, which she thought it better to prepare for calmly than to talk about as Dolly was doing, they could always hold Easter in their hearts, which frightened Father Fewling, who hated religious conversation in public, so dreadfully that in a moment he would have burst quite rudely away from them had not Colonel Passmore, seeing and realizing his plight, sent Captain Topham over to rescue him. This task, even with Betty's support, might have been beyond Captain Topham's powers but for an unexpected ally in the shape of Miss Hopgood's aunt, who with all the authority of the widow of a scientific man, bore down on the Misses Talbot and saying, 'Now, you girls have had Father Fewling to yourselves quite long enough,' routed them entirely, after which she and Captain Topham and Betty and Father Fewling had a good talk, partly about birds' nests, partly about looking at birds' nests from a great distance through a telescope to avoid disturbing the occupants.

Mrs and Miss Dunsford came up and paused for a few words.

'You see my velours is still quite well,' said Miss Dunsford, casting her eyes upwards to her hat.

Father Fewling, who had quite forgotten the episode of the mulberry velours hat on the church tower, smiled with a blank expression, which the Dunsfords did not observe.

'Yes,' said Mrs Dunsford, 'I was saying to my daughter only on Sunday that we must be very careful and make our clothes last for a long time because if anything happens we shan't be able to get at the shops. One could always write to London, but I suppose if the Germans were about it might be awkward. Still, it doesn't do to think of these things, does it? Come along, Barbara, we haven't said "How do you do" to Mrs Villars yet.'

The heat and noise were now terrific. All the guests were out-shouting each other and telling each other what they intended to do in the spring provided nothing happened. Mrs Villars, standing back from the party for a moment thought how peculiar it was, judging by almost forgotten pre-war standards, that what people called 'nothing happening' meant going on living in a state of darkness, discomfort, perpetual if unconscious anticipation of danger, or in less favoured places than Northbridge in actual and horrible danger. She remembered how before the war began the waiting had been so terrifying that the proclamation of a state of war was on the whole a relief, and wondered if with each trial ahead the waiting would be worse than the accomplished fact. One got used to each fresh set of unpleasant experiences with remarkable quickness, but just as one had settled down to them, something new and even more exasperating came surging up through the gloom, itself to be absorbed as a matter of daily routine before long. She thought of a dull and not very accurate comparison of her friends to oysters, avoiding careless talk and busy smothering their irritations and unease in coatings of habit; but rejected it, for the resulting pearls were not very obvious, unless trying to be well-behaved and obedient under perpetual pin-pricks and nettles in one's bed were a pearl; perhaps it was. Everyone she knew was jumbled up with strange companions on a raft, a tossing sea about them, and yet somehow not disheartened, not too unhappy. The great thing was not to think of the end, for that was as confusing as the thought of infinity or eternity, but to trust a good deal and see that all the guests at one's party had enough to drink and someone to talk to. Her husband, who had very meanly come in late to his own party, came and stood with her, observing his guests.

'Funny sight if you come to think of it, all in the middle of a totalitarian war,' he said.

'I really think,' said Mrs Villars, in whom the word 'jumbled' had evoked a new line of thought, 'that our heads are green and our hands are blue and we went to sea in a sieve.'

'Possibly,' said her husband, gravely considering the great work to which she alluded, 'but I would like to point out to you, Verena, that the effect of your party is that everyone says how happy they are as round in their sieve they spin. What is it, Jackson?'

'Sorry, sir,' said Corporal Jackson, 'but I thought you'd like to know that Major and Mrs Spender have just come.'

Having given this unwelcome news he retreated, lest the Rector should excommunicate him.

'I thought Major Spender had gone to meet his wife at Barchester and take her to friends for the night,' the Rector began, but at that moment the noise, insistent and roaring though it was, was partly drowned, partly heightened by the voice of Mrs Spender who, in a royal-blue three-piece costume with a royal-blue halo hat, came triumphantly in, carrying in her train her husband who looked thinner and more sensitive than ever.

'Here I am, quite unexpected-like, said she brightly,' were Mrs Spender's opening words. 'It is quite like coming home to be in the dear old Rectory again.'

'I am so glad you could come,' said Mrs Villars, trying to sound truthful. 'Your husband said you were only passing through Barchester or of course I'd have asked him to bring you.'

'That's so like Bobbie, dear old silly,' said Mrs Spender, putting her arm through her husband's to his intense misery. 'We are going to the Prestons near Nutfield, you'd love them; Jackie Preston is one of the best and her kids are just the age of mine but not so bright, though I says it as shouldn't. Her Joan is just two months older than my Clarissa, but the difference! When I tell you that Clarissa is top of her form at the Kindergarten and gets full marks for brushwork every week and Joan hasn't got further than a potato in plasticine, well I ask you! But here am I talking as usual, said she coming over all modest, and what was I going to say? Oh, yes, about Jackie Preston. Well, when I got out at Barchester there was Bobbie to meet me, the dear old goose, and he happened to mention you were throwing a party, so I said, "Well, well, they are the honeysuckle and I am the bee." Not that I meant anything by it, because though I like a drink when it's there, put me on a desert island and I'll be quite happy for *months*, but believe it or not, Mrs Villars, when I heard about your party I said to myself, "Here's your chance, my girl, to see the dear old Colonel and the Rectory folk," so I said to Bobbie, "Jackie won't notice if we're late," because, take it from me, that's what Jackie's like; she just takes life easily. So we popped into the car and came along, and here we are. And, lo and behold, who do I see but Mr Holden! This is quite like old times, isn't it? Is he still as devoted to you as ever, Mrs Villars? I'm funny that way, you know, I always see at once when there is a genuine feeling and I said to Bobbie the night we were here when we had the air-raid, "Anyone can see Mr Holden is quite devoted to Mrs Villars" didn't I, Bobbums?"

Major Spender looked as if he were going to cry. Mr Villars pressed mulled claret upon Mrs Spender, who drank two glasses, and expressing her regret that the Rector couldn't have one of his splendid services for them as it was Saturday night, for though she wasn't really religious she enjoyed a good service as much as anyone, she went like Alexander to spread her conquests further.

The Rector and his wife looked at each other.

'I can't tell you how sorry I am,' said Major Spender who had escaped from his wife, suddenly coming back. 'It is so awful and I don't know what you will think of us.'

Mr and Mrs Villars exhausted themselves in saying how pleased they were and what an excellent idea it had been to bring Mrs Spender to the party, but all in vain. He thanked them mournfully and buried himself in the crowd, obviously determined to commit suicide if he could find any poison.

'I didn't know Mr Holden was devoted to you,' said the Rector to his wife.

'Nor did I,' said Mrs Villars. 'At least he is a faint nuisance at times, so perhaps he is. But thank goodness not like Mr Lumford.'

'Was that the one who kept your handkerchief and found it was really Matron's?' said the Rector.

'Gregory!' said his wife reproachfully. 'Mr Lumford was only a science master! No, the handkerchief was Mr Longford, the one that married Porton Major's elder sister afterwards and went into Mr Porton's business.'

The Rector acknowledged his mistake and remarked to his wife that he was rather devoted to her himself, to which she replied that if there was one thing in the world she liked it was people called Gregory, especially, she added, if they went about being jealous of lieutenants.

'I should like to put my arm round your waist and say, "Buss me, my lass, and let bygones be bygones,"' said the Rector, 'but I don't suppose it would do.'

His wife said certainly not and they must look after their guests, so with a great deal of affection they separated.

I3

Taking Advice

Meanwhile Mrs Spender continued her tornado course round the room claiming old friends and disrupting groups that were happily chatting.

'Well, well! Mrs Turner!' she exclaimed, throwing herself like a wedge between that lady and Miss Pemberton who were talking quite amicably about the servant question. 'And Miss Pemberton! But you don't remember me.'

'Why not?' said Miss Pemberton, which simple riposte so winded Mrs Spender that we are able confidently to recommend it, for a more annoying statement than 'You don't remember me' hardly exists, putting one as it does in a false position whether one says one does or one doesn't. 'You said the German aeroplanes recited Lorraine Lorree. They don't.'

Mrs Turner, who had a softer heart than Miss Pemberton and would undoubtedly have used the offending expression herself without a qualm, said she hoped Mrs Spender hadn't been in any more air-raids.

'Air-raids? Believe it or not,' said Mrs Spender impressively, 'it is simply one mad *rush* of them. Almost continuous, if you know what I mean.'

Mrs Turner said they must be very noisy.

'We get no noise at all,' said Mrs Spender firmly. 'I suppose I'm funny about air-raids, but I *feel* aeroplanes. I'm a bit psychic, you know. As a matter of fact, we haven't had a bomb within twenty miles all this winter, but I KNOW they are about. I often say I feel things quite differently from other people if you know what I mean and of course being psychic one gives out a great deal. How is that nice little friend of yours who had written a book or something, Miss Pemberton? Mr Downing, that was his name. Oh, here he is. Talk of well-we-won't-say-who, you know. And how are you, Mr Downing? As devoted to Mrs Turner as ever?'

At this question Miss Pemberton went a dark, unbecoming brick colour, Mrs Turner produced that rare and charming thing a blush, while Mr Downing looked like a mouse cornered by a royal-blue cat.

'Mr Downing and I,' said Miss Pemberton with some dignity, 'are a great deal at Mrs Turner's. Her niece Betty and Mr Downing are great bird-lovers and go for long walks. Are you interested in birds, Mrs Spender?'

This gallant recovery quite took Mrs Spender aback for once and before she could fully explain that she simply adored birds if anyone knew what she meant, but did not know one from another whether anyone believed her or not, though she was funny in some ways and birds always seemed to KNOW that she liked them, and Billy her second boy was quite wizard with birds and had a thrush with a broken leg that died, Colonel Passmore, feeling that as the senior officer present and Mrs Villars's guest he ought to do something about it, mobilized his junior officers and descending upon Mrs Spender in full force kept her not unwillingly a prisoner till her husband, who had been biding in the office, could be found by Corporal Jackson and forced to take her away.

Meanwhile Mrs Turner, Miss Pemberton and Mr Downing were seized with such discomfort that by tacit accord they separated and drifted to other friends. Mrs Spender's well-meaning if arch remark had brought various underlying feelings nearer the light of day than was quite pleasant. Miss Pemberton was perhaps the least affected for she had thought as clearly about the matter as one can ever think of matters relating to oneself. Poverty and an ugliness that was only redeemed by the long working of brains and integrity were her portion and she knew it. Very few illusions about herself had clouded her mind. Her chief human need had been for something to look after and order about. Cats she could not abide and for the dependent slavishness of dogs she had no use at all, nor for the horrid noise they make. In mid-journey Mr Downing had crossed her path and become the object of her protection and tyranny. Only of late had it occurred to her that he might be tempted by an easier yoke and as we know she had fought this battle out with herself and indirectly given him permission to go. Now, at the back of her mind, was a faint, very faint contempt for her lodger because he had so far as she knew adventured nothing. Mrs Spender's silly question, far from making her jealous of Mrs Turner, had somehow strengthened the bond between woman and woman against the milk-and-water argle-bargle ways of men, or so Miss Pemberton put it to herself. If Mr Downing went on hanging about Mrs Turner and being devoted but doing nothing about it, and if Mrs Turner liked him as much as she seemed to, then Miss Pemberton thought poorly of Mr Downing and was prepared to push him out of the nest if he would not try his wings unpushed. So she went to talk to Mrs Paxon about an embroidery class for secondary school evacuee girls.

As for Mrs Turner her confusion was great. Mr Downing was a dear and probably didn't get enough to eat and certainly not enough to drink at Punshions and it was very nice for Betty to find a new bird friend, but it had gradually penetrated her mind that the bird-walks always ended in Mr Downing coming back to The Hollies for tea which merged into supper, when Betty, having had her bird-walk, shed Mr Downing for more congenial and younger company and, in fact, showed no interest in him at all. Mrs Turner had feared that he might be hurt, but he had seemed quite happy to chat to her (an expression which would have made Mr Downing shudder) and be a kind of intellectual tame cat, that bad girl Betty going so far as to call him Pussy behind his back. He had fitted in surprisingly well with the communal life of The Hollies, the young men respected him as a brainy old fellow who knew all about the troubadours, and he had gradually learnt to take part in such unintellectual sports as rummy and darts, and had even attempted to play on one of the evacuees' mouth-organs. But what he really liked, she well knew, was to have a cosy chat by lamplight when the young people were making their noise somewhere else. She could not call him devoted to her, for he never said anything of that sort, but he seemed very happy with her, and she honestly confessed that she felt very happy with him. He was certainly not like a pussy, he was more like a very sleek grey-headed bird, one whom one would like to stroke. And this thought led her to the remembrance of the late Mr Turner whom she had loved so very much during the unhappy year of their marriage and how his black hair grew from his forehead in a way like no one else's. And though she knew what harm he had done and that if he had lived she might have come to feel coldness and contempt for him, or even outraged hatred, she also knew that her heart was buried in his grave, an expression which represented the truth none the less for the intense literary and sentimental pleasure it gave her, though she glossed over in her own mind the fact that he was cremated. And the thought of her own secret loneliness and the thought of Mr Downing's hard life at Punshions, combined with Mrs Spender's words about devotion, made her feel so sad that Captain Topham passing by was quite struck by it.

'Hallo, Auntie,' he said, for as an aunt most of her nieces' young friends adopted her, half laughing, 'anything wrong?'

'Mrs Spender, I think,' said Mrs Turner, blowing her nose.

'Well,' said Captain Topham with the air of one making a handsome concession, 'she *is* an old bitch, not that I ought to say so with the Rector about. Come and have a drink.'

'That's just what I need, Topsy,' said Mrs Turner gratefully and they went over to the table where Foster was supplying fresh mulled claret and opening more bottles of sherry. Here Mrs Spender was carrying on a rather acrimonious argument with Captain Powell-Jones about the number of broadcasts in Welsh. If, she said, she wanted to listen to people talking nonsense there was always Hamburg or Bremen without having it at home.

'If you knew anything of Welsh,' said Captain Powell-Jones upon whose temper sherry and mulled claret mixed in large quantities were having a bad effect, 'you would know that it is the richest of all European languages and is gradually assimilating to itself the whole vocabulary of art, religion, poetry and culture.'

'Well,' retorted Mrs Spender with great spirit, 'I don't set up to be highbrow if you know what I mean, but you've only got to read the *Radio Times*. I'm funny I suppose that way, but I always notice what words are like in dialect and believe it or not I read the bits in the programme about Welsh every day.'

'Welsh isn't a dialect,' said Captain Powell-Jones indignantly and a little thickly.

'Whatever it is,' said Mrs Spender, 'you can't call it a language. Now here's a sporting offer. What's the Welsh for Radio?'

'Radio,' said Captain Powell-Jones rather sulkily.

'Well, I ask you!' said Mrs Spender triumphantly. 'If you call that a language I don't. Hallo, Bobbums, ought we to be moving?'

Major Spender who had been fetched almost by main force by Corporal Jackson from the office where he had taken refuge said he was afraid they ought to go at once. 'Good-bye all and mind you look after yourselves, said she coming over quite weepy-like,' said Mrs Spender. 'I don't know how it is, I seem to be funny about saying good-bye. I always say you never know in these times if you'll see anyone again if you know what I mean. Come along, Bobbie.'

'The three Evil Colours of Britain,' Captain Powell-Jones announced, looking fixedly at Mrs Spender.

'The colour of the peacock on a woman's head-gear,
The colour of the salmon on a woman's mouth,
The colour of the Saxon's blood on a woman's fingers.'

He then drank a whole tumbler of mulled claret.

Major Spender was so alarmed that he actually dragged his wife from the room. At the front door Corporal Jackson was waiting to light them to their car which was parked just by the back road to the kitchen yard. A figure moved away from the light of the torch.

'Good-bye, Corporal,' said Mrs Spender getting into the car. 'Are you still carrying on with Mrs Villars's cook? It's a funny thing but I always seem to notice that sort of thing.'

Corporal Jackson saluted and shut the door. As the noise of the car died away in the Rectory Lane the figure announced itself by loud sniffs and gulps to be Edie who was just coming back from the village where Mrs Chapman had sent her on an errand.

''Ere, Edie, what's up?' said Jackson. 'You didn't take no notice of what the old bluebottle said?'

But Edie, refusing all consolation, went sobbing and yelping towards the kitchen. Corporal Jackson whistled.

'Well, they say,' he remarked aloud to himself, 'that what's coming to you has your number on it. Seems to me that old bluebottle sent me one marked 3342571 Corporal Jackson, Arthur Fishguard. Hope the old girl won't see Edie coming in like that. Silly, girls are, that's what.'

And he returned to his duties.

In the drawing-room the party was thinning rapidly. Miss Crowder and Miss Hopgood seeing Mr Downing at liberty determined to take the rare opportunity of Miss Pemberton's eye being off him to discuss the literature of France and to that end ask him if he had read any Zola. Mr Downing said he had.

'He's a bit strong,' said Miss Crowder, 'but I always say the splendid thing about French is you can say anything in it without fear of being misunderstood. I mean a book like *La Faute de l'Abby Maury* would be quite impossible in England. No one would recognize the characters. But in France you simply see people like that every day.'

Mr Downing said he didn't know France very well, only parts of Provence.

'Ah well!' said Miss Crowder pityingly, 'of course you can't judge. At Menton one sees every kind of type. Miss Hopgood and I used to sit in the hall of the Pension Ramsden and watch the types. Really one could write a novel about them. Do you remember, chère amie, the Russian dancer that drank vodka at eleven in the morning and had a gold anklet? Such wonderful eyes.'

'Do you mean the one that went to stay with Lady Brown at Les Mouettes,' said Miss Hopgood, 'and she gave him bête noire to gamble for her at the Casino and he lost it all and his anklet too?'

Miss Crowder looked with loving pity at her friend and defiantly at Mr Downing, giving him to understand (or thinking she did) that if Miss Hopgood preferred not to use the expression carte blanche she doubtless had her reasons.

'You must miss France as much as we do, Mr Downing,' said Miss Crowder. 'Do you know the English tea-shop in the rue vingt-neuf-février at Menton where one can get Gauffrette Huntley et Palmer? I sometimes nearly cry when I think of it.'

'And the Eglise Protestant,' said Miss Hopgood, perhaps pronouncing this last word as in English in case Mr Downing, dazzled by excess of light, should not grasp the meaning in French, 'and dear Mr Honeyman. One gets nothing like that here. Not that we don't admire Mr Villars, but after all a church in England is *not* like a church in France.'

Mr Downing said he supposed not.

'Ah well, often do I wonder,' said Miss Crowder, 'how they are all getting on without us. Having the Germans there can't be a bit the same. Still, it doesn't do to dwell on these things and I feel sure chère amie and I shall yet go in the motor-bus along the Cornice,' said Miss Crowder, giving the impression that she and Miss Hopgood were in the habit of making excursions upon the ceiling like flies, 'and read the *Paris Daily Mail* with our morning tea.'

'And hear the school children singing their national songs like *Auprès de ma blawnd*,' said Miss Hopgood, her eyes gazing moistly into vacancy.

There was a pause during which Mr Downing wondered how he could best get away.

'Well, we must be off,' said Miss Crowder. 'Our pottofur will be burnt if we wait too long. You must come and have a real French meal some day, Mr Downing. Chère amie makes such good bouillabaisse with vegetable stock and whatever the fishmonger happens to have when it's not too expensive and a little cooking sherry that you would hardly know the difference. Not Mondays though for the fish is apt to be a bit off, if there is any at all. I shall read your book when it comes out. Vive la Repoobleek.'

And Miss Crowder took her friend away to make a dinner

plain not very hearty from the pot au feu, perhaps more accurately described by the little daily maid as that bit of Irish stew left over hotted up.

Colonel Passmore gallantly volunteered to drive Mrs Paxon home, who shook her finger at him and said she knew she oughtn't to be using the country's petrol but couldn't say no as hubby would be waiting for his supper.

'Lucky man,' said Colonel Passmore, at which Mrs Paxon gave a coquettish shriek and they went away. The remaining officers then returned to their quarters. Only The Hollies and Punshions remained.

'Come on, Auntie,' said Betty. 'Topsy's coming in after supper and we must get a move on. I say, Mr Downing, you look rotten. Come back with Auntie and me and have a drink and Miss Pemberton too.'

As Mr Downing had already drunk two glasses of sherry, which never suited him, he said he thought he had better be getting home, but Miss Pemberton, in an excess of self-discipline, gave her lodger a final push out of the nest, saying he might just as well go back to The Hollies as the fire was bound to have gone out at home and there was only cold supper. Before Mr Downing could remonstrate she had said good-bye and was stumping away home in the dark, so fortified and sustained by her sacrifice that she would have cried bitterly, had she not long ago forgotten how to cry.

So once more Mr Downing set his footsteps towards Armida's garden. Once more the familiar comfortable atmosphere of too much light, heat, food, drink, talk and noise enfolded him. Mrs Turner and her nieces went to get supper ready and as for once no other young people were about he was left in the drawing-room by the fire. Betty kindly thrust six illustrated magazines into his hands, but neither bathing belles in Hollywood nor gigantic close-ups of Bulgarian peasants with every pore on their faces showing seemed satisfactory at the moment. Poor Mr Downing had been really shocked by Mrs Spender's ill-bred remark and felt it quite as much for his old friend and his new friend as he did for himself: probably more, for in a gentle, foolish, scholarly way he was both chivalrous and humble. Ridiculous comparisons flitted through his head. There was Philibert le Matou who had managed to observe the strictest *amitié par amour* to two ladies at once for seventeen years and had been greatly praised in verse for his correct behaviour, but they all seemed to have plenty of money and nothing to do, and as the ladies both had husbands at the Crusades who had taken every recognized precaution before leaving, it was all very safe and comfortable. Then Macheath came into his mind saying: 'Here I stand like the Turk with my doxies around': but no one could call Ianthe a doxy, and though Mrs Turner was pretty enough to be one, that was not the way one thought of her. Then there was that depressing German Knight who went to the Crusades leaving his wife at home and came back with another who had saved his life, and they were all buried in one tomh; but here again money seemed to be no object. What a comfort the Crusades must have been. So he mused, till idly glancing at a literary magazine consisting entirely of extracts from other and equally worthless literary magazines, his eye fell on one of Adrian Coates's advertisements containing an advance puff of his new book which threw him into such a fever about a misprint (*miradéiou* for *miradéiéou*)

286

that he couldn't remember if he had forgotten to correct, that he quite forgot about love or friendship.

Meanwhile Mrs Turner's other niece, coming over to the gas stove to get the hot plates, was surprised and alarmed to find her aunt stirring something in a saucepan and having to stop every few seconds to wipe away her tears.

'What's the matter, Auntie?' she said anxiously.

Mrs Turner smiled moistly and said, 'Nothing.'

'Hi! Betty!' shouted the other niece. 'Come here. Something's happened!'

Betty, who was laying the dining-room table, came in with a glass-cloth and stood amazed.

'Here, you carry on with the saucepan,' she said to the other niece. 'What's the matter, Auntie? Burnt yourself? I'll get the picric.'

'It isn't that,' said Mrs Turner, now comfortably sobbing, 'it's that awful Mrs Spender.'

The other niece took the saucepan off the gas and both girls applied themselves to consoling their aunt and discovering what she was crying about. When among sniffs and gulps, but already a good deal cheered by sympathy, she reported what Mrs Spender had said, her nieces' indignation knew no bounds.

'Meddling old Judy!' said Betty indignantly. 'Of course Pussy is gone on you and you're a bit gone on him, but as for *devoted*! Don't you worry, Auntie. She's got it on the brain. I was talking to Topsy about him coming round after dinner and she barged in and said something about nice to see the young officers having nice girl friends. Topsy and I nearly died

287

of laughing. And she called me Miss Turner again, silly old fool. It's all right, Auntie. Pussy doesn't want to marry you if that's what's worrying you.'

'Are you sure?' said Mrs Turner cheering up.

'Anyway, if he did, Miss Pemberton wouldn't let him,' said Mrs Turner's other niece. 'Come on, Betty, if Topsy's coming in we must get on with supper.'

Much comforted by these practical comments, Mrs Turner put the saucepan back on the gas and in a very short time supper was ready. The meal was very cheerful, especially for Mrs Turner's nieces who, as they changed the plates, sang in strophe and antistrophe, 'I love little Pussy, his coat is so warm,' laying strong emphasis on the masculine pronoun, and making their aunt, who was still in an emotional condition, almost hysterical with laughing, so that her hair curled more wildly and her eyes shone more brightly and Mr Downing thought he had never seen anything more enchanting.

When they had finished, the nieces sent their aunt and Mr Downing into the drawing-room while they washed up, which they did with a great deal of shouting and laughter and the assistance of Captain Topham and several other young friends.

'I don't know what you must think of us,' said Mrs Turner to Mr Downing. 'The girls are too awful.'

'They are such nice girls,' said Mr Downing. 'I can't tell you how kind you have all been to me this winter. It really feels like a second home.'

'Well, I know we aren't brainy,' said Mrs Turner, looking gratified, 'but we do like having our friends. I always say one thing about a war is it brings people together, unless of course it separates them. We'd never have seen so much of you and Miss Pemberton if it hadn't been for the war. That reminds me I must get that bit of work done. I'm doing a kind of sampler for her embroidery class she's going to have for Mrs Paxon.'

She got a large bag, rummaged in it, and pulled out a piece of canvas on which she began to do stitches, looking up from time to time to smile at her guest.

'I know what you are,' said Mr Downing, after gazing with pleasure at her charming plumpness, her tendrilled hair and her friendly sparkling eyes, 'you are a Morland.'

'No, no relation really,' said Mrs Turner, stitching away. 'My husband was a very distant connection of Mr Morland's, but they both died years ago so it hardly counts. I do know Laura Morland a little. She's very brainy but she's awfully nice. Her youngest boy is still at Oxford, but he might be called up any time. Have you read her last book? I do like her books because they're all the same as each other so you know exactly what to expect.'

'I didn't realize you were a connection of hers,' said Mr Downing. 'I met her once at my publisher's, we have the same publisher you know, and found her very pleasant. I meant you are like a picture by George Morland, the English painter.'

'Oh I know, the one of pigs in a barn that Mrs Villars has a photo of,' said Mrs Turner. 'I didn't know he did portraits.'

Mr Downing gave it up, but found her none the less enchanting. The silence grew. Mr Downing, who had a Victorian devotion to Browning, felt he half believed it must get rid of what it knew, its bosom did so heave. To help it to this end he said:

'Mrs Turner,' and then stopped.

'Yes?' said Mrs Turner, not looking up from her work.

'I hardly know how to say what I am trying to say,' said Mr Downing, finding his voice a little out of control.

Mrs Turner looked up. Something passed across her face that Mr Downing did not understand. Great kindness and what looked like fear. It checked him for a second and then with a loud noise the washers-up poured in, and the two Derricks who had been to an evacuees' New Year Party at St Sycorax Church House came to show their presents and report that Little Derrick had a loose tooth and say good-night.

'We thought they would spell it D-E-R-E-K like Derek Hamilton, you know the one that he's a submarine lieutenant,' said Mrs Turner's other niece, 'but it's like the things at works and docks and things.'

Mr Greaves said he supposed their parents lived near a docks or something and got the idea.

'More likely they didn't know how to spell and everyone was afraid to tell them,' said Betty. 'I say, let's play the spelling game. I bet you're the worst, Topsy.'

With a great tumult the round table was pulled out and the box of letters found. Mr Downing suddenly felt he could not bear it and saying that Miss Pemberton was alone he took his leave.

'Come in to tea on Saturday,' said Mrs Turner, 'and bring Miss Pemberton. The girls will be at the Red Cross.'

'I think Miss Pemberton will be at Mrs Paxon's embroidery class,' said Mr Downing; 'but I would love to come. I want to ask you something,' he added.

Again the expression to which he had no clue passed over Mrs Turner's face: compassion and was it fear?

When he got outside his mind was so confused that instead of going straight home by the High Street he turned in the other direction, went down the Rectory lane and so round by the back lane past St Sycorax. On the piece of waste land he saw a line of light from the Wardens' Shelter and looked in. Father Fewling was there by himself, making cocoa on a stove.

'Come and have a cup, Downing,' he said. 'Mr Scatcherd is really on duty with me to-night, but he has a bit of a cough so I said I'd carry on. Cold, isn't it?'

'I believe you, my boy,' said Mr Downing, and sat down on one of the lower bunks, crouching forward so that his head would not hit the upper one.

'Don't burn yourself,' said Father Fewling, handing him a steaming cup.

Mr Downing burnt himself and put the cocoa down to cool.

'Nice party at the Rectory,' said Father Fewling. 'I'd have come on to The Hollies, but I'd promised Scatcherd to be here.'

Mr Downing said he had just come from there.

'You know, Fewling, I'm not much of a churchgoer,' he said. 'I've never felt the need of the church.'

'To be quite frank,' said Father Fewling good-humouredly, 'the church doesn't feel much need of you either, if that is your attitude.'

Mr Downing was slightly taken aback.

'She can afford to wait, you know,' said Father Fewling, 'on and off for days and days and days.'

'Like the frog footman,' said Mr Downing thoughtfully. 'Sorry, Fewling, I didn't mean to put it like that, but I am a good deal perplexed.'

'If I can help you, I will,' said Father Fewling, 'but don't get religion muddled up with getting things off your chest. When I was in the Navy the men used to come to me and to the padre with all sorts of troubles. He and I made a kind of working arrangement as to which kind of worries which of us would handle. I learnt a good bit of psychology that way. From what I know of you, Downing, spiritual perplexity isn't much in your line. You have too much intellectual pride. But if I can help as an ex-naval commander, here we are on neutral ground and no one is likely to disturb us.'

'The siren did go after supper,' said Mr Downing.

'Well, you know our siren,' said Father Fewling. 'Never yet has she let loose with any relation to anything that is happening. Carry on.'

Mr Downing took up his cocoa, spooned a thick layer of crinkly brown skin off the top and drank the refreshing draught.

'It is a little difficult,' he said.

'It won't be any easier for waiting,' said Father Fewling. 'But don't tell me if you don't want to.'

Thus goaded Mr Downing finished his cocoa and handed the cup back to his host.

'I really don't know how to begin,' he said miserably, 'I don't quite know what I ought to do, or what I really want to do.'

'Most of us don't,' said Father Fewling. 'I suppose it is something to do with The Hollies. Betty is a very nice girl.'

'Very nice,' said Mr Downing.

'Well, that disposes of *her*,' said Father Fewling.

There was silence.

'I do not wish to appear fatuous, Fewling,' said Mr Downing, 'but I feel as if two different people needed me and I don't know where my duty lies. On the one side I owe deep gratitude for more kindness than I can ever repay. On the other side I find a kind of affection I have never known before and a kind of life which though not what I am used to is extraordinarily restful. The persons to whom I allude are most generous in their different ways. All I want is to please them both and I do not see where my path leads at all plainly.'

'It sounds a bit awkward,' said Father Fewling reflectively. 'Of course I am only speaking in the dark, but it seems to me that you may be going to take a serious risk, for yourself and for the persons to whom you allude. To disturb a long and tried friendship is a serious thing. To embark on a form of living which is quite uncongenial to your normal self is also a serious thing for you and for the person with whom you might attempt to share it.'

'What am I to do?' said Mr Downing.

'I can't tell you,' said Father Fewling. 'The only advice I could give would be to consider what this new kind of life would be like without the person who makes it seem so pleasant. It will not be easy to alter your way of living at your age. If you can, well and good, and the older friendship may survive. If you can't you will have made both old friend and new very unhappy and be unhappy yourself. One has to consider these things, you know.'

Mr Downing said nothing.

'Have some more cocoa,' said Father Fewling. 'I find it very helpful.'

'No, thanks,' said Mr Downing, getting up. 'I am so grateful. It does one a lot of good to talk about oneself sometimes and you have borne with me very kindly.'

'Not at all,' said Father Fewling. 'I have talked quite as much as you have. Come in any time.'

The siren blew a blasting All Clear.

'That means we are bound to have planes over soon,' said Father Fewling. 'You'd better get back in case Miss Pemberton is anxious.'

'Thank you more than I can say for all your advice,' said Mr Downing. 'I don't suppose I'll take it, but it has been very good for me. I don't know if it would be any good asking you—'

He paused.

'Certainly not if you don't believe in it,' said Father Fewling. 'But I shall, in any case, for my own satisfaction.'

'How did you know what I was going to say?' asked Mr Downing.

'People always think they are different from everyone else and they are really exactly the same,' said Father Fewling blandly. 'To ask me to pray for you in your present condition is no better than superstition. However, I intend to pray for you whether you know what you want or not, and for everyone concerned. A little courage to examine your own mind and some common sense is what you need,' he added rather severely.

Mr Downing shook hands with Father Fewling and went on his way to Punshions in a very chastened frame of mind. Instead of standing like the Turk, he saw himself as a very wretched specimen of a spineless bookworm, capable neither of sustained gratitude nor genuine emotion. What Father Fewling had said about a life uncongenial to his normal self struck a chill to his heart, for his mind told him it was true. He thought of Miss Pemberton's chill austerities and her keen clever mind as a fevered man tossing under eiderdowns might think of the cool clear wind of a March day. As he put his key into the door of his home he determined not to go to The Hollies on Saturday and to spend the evening working at his article for the *Journal of Provençal Studies* which was somehow just weathering the storm owing to the enthusiastic secretary who had evacuated herself to her parents at Kendal and from there harassed the members without cease, admitting no excuses about subscriptions.

In the sitting-room Miss Pemberton was preparing canvas for her embroidery classes. She had been wrestling with herself not unsuccessfully, but the struggle had not improved her temper.

'Well, Harold, you are late,' she said. 'I hope you had a nice time with your Mrs Turner.'

As soon as she had said these words, she was sorry. But it was too late. All Mr Downing's good resolutions fell to pieces and the vision of Mrs Turner's good-natured Morland face rose in his mind.

'Very nice, Ianthe,' he said. 'And I am going to tea there on Saturday. Oh, and Mrs Turner asked me to bring you too, that is if you wish to come.'

Miss Pemberton threaded her needle carefully into her canvas, folded her work with great deliberation and put it away.

'As you well know, I shall be at Mrs Paxon's class on

Saturday,' she said. 'Good night, Harold. The boiler has gone out and there is no hot water, so you can't have a bath.'

She turned the lamp down and went heavily upstairs, leaving the sitting-room to darkness and Mr Downing.

14

Influenza

On the next day, being a Thursday, the influenza began. Mrs Chapman, who did not have it, attributed it entirely to Edie, who had come into the kitchen on the previous evening all be-blubbered with crying and refused to give any reason. She had then gone to the cinema where she cried all the time, partly with misery, partly with emotion over Glamora Tudor as Columbine in *Loves of a Court Painter*, a very unhistorical film in which everyone was killed in the French Revolution while Watteau painted their portraits. By next morning she had cried herself into a sick headache, which combined with the germ-infested atmosphere of the cinema made her an easy prey to what the *Barchester Chronicle* called the prevailing epidemic. The second housemaid, Colonel Passmore, Captain Topham, Captain Powell-Jones and Mr Holden all went down within the next day, and so did Hibberd, whose rage at having to leave to an underling the digging of old Mrs Trouncer's grave, on which he had set his heart ever since she attained her ninety-ninth birthday, considerably retarded his recovery.

'I said she wouldn't reach the hundred,' he said to his great-niece who was nursing him, 'and old Mrs Trouncer said to I, "Ah, I'll be a centiarian yet," she said, but I said to she, "I'll be digging your grave afore then, Mrs Trouncer, you mark my words," I said, and she said, she did, "I come of a long-lived family, Mr Hibberd, and my grandfather he was killed by the first railway engine that come through Barchester and the Oddfellows gave him a lovely funeral, they did, and he'd be a hundred and forty-three if he was alive now," and I said to Mrs Trouncer, I said, "When folks is dead there's no sense in saying how long they might have lived, and it'll be the same with you, Mrs Trouncer," I said, and old Mrs Trouncer she said to I, "Ah, you'll see I'll be a centiarian yet," she said, but I said to she—'

But at this point his great-niece, who was only a great-niece by marriage, always made him take his medicine or have his face washed, as she said she hadn't no patience with all uncle's rubbish. Luckily the old sexton was slightly delirious by then, or he would certainly have got out of bed and beaten young Bunce, aged sixty-three, over the head with a mattock for digging a grave in what he called his churchyard.

Mrs Paxon, her husband, both her husband's aunt and her evacuee had it badly, but the undaunted Mrs Paxon, wearing her siren suit night and day, struggled about, ministering to everyone. Miss Talbot, who had been a V.A.D. in the last war, hearing of their plight, came round and was a tower of strength, encouraging Mr Paxon to go and sleep upstairs in his own comfortable bed, though not until she had thoroughly aired it for him. And when Mrs Paxon finally collapsed, which she did not do till everyone else was convalescent, Miss Talbot actually carried her off to The Aloes where she nursed her, while Miss Dolly Talbot went down daily to shop and cook for the Paxon household. All this disarrangement of his life threw Professor Talbot into such a rage that he became reconciled by post with both his two brothers, and when Mrs Paxon got better she played chess with him and always lost.

At Glycerine Cottage poor Miss Hopgood had influenza very badly. Luckily Miss Crowder escaped, so she was able to nurse chère amie with rather incapable devotion, and bemoan to all inquirers the sad fate that kept them from the Côte d'Azur.

'Not one step inside, Mr Villars,' she said to the Rector, who called to inquire after his faithful parishioner. 'La grippe, you know, is most infectious and you must not run any risk. Chère amie is a little better. It is such a privilege to nurse her and we have our little jokes, she is la malade and I am la matrone. We feel we are almost back at the Pension Ramsden. To think that the mimosa will be coming out. Such a beautiful word in French, don't you think, mimosa. French names have such poetry in them compared with English ones. All the flowers and the scents. There is something so romantic about a perfume called Nweedermoor, when you compare it with eau-de-Cologne, such a *dull* word. Father Fewling has been so kind. He brought chère amie some French books, but she isn't quite up to them yet. One was called *Mon Oncle et mon Curay*. I suppose it would be all *right*, wouldn't it? I mean one knows Catholics are allowed to marry their uncles, but I hardly suppose even an *atheist* would say anything against a

Curay. Such good, hard-working men they are, not what you would expect priests to be in the least, rushing about Menton to death-beds. So different here. Not but what Father Fewling would go to any death-bed, I feel certain, but though we like him so much as a man, we would hardly care to have him at the Last Moment. Ritual somehow does not seem quite right at so solemn a time. The French have such a lovely word for death, they call it trespass; so if chère amie feels a little low I say to her, "Now, no trespassing," and it is quite a pleasure to see the smiles on her poor thin face. How is Mrs Villars?'

The Rector said she was very well, but had her hands full at the Rectory with two of the maids and four of the officers in bed, but Colonel Passmore only had it lightly and they hoped the others would be all right in a few days. As Miss Crowder would not allow him to come into the house and it was very cold on the doorstep he then took his leave and went on to The Hollies, where Mrs Turner's other niece was just up and Betty was still in bed.

Mrs Turner, who never caught anything, had been nursing her nieces single-handed and looked a little tired but still extremely charming, like a dark hyacinth that has been beaten to the earth by a storm and has a good deal of mud on its face, but is again raising its perfumed curls to the sun. Far from desiring to spare the Rector any risk of infection she pressed him to come into the little sitting-room and see her other niece as they were not using the drawing-room just now owing to Fitchett, who was the Coals as well as the grocer, having promised her five hundredweight on Tuesday but it hadn't come yet. As it was about tea-time, the Rector gladly accepted her offer.

'Hullo, Mr Villars,' said the other niece, who was curled up on a sofa with three library books, a bottle of tonic, a bottle of malt extract and a lot of khaki wool with which she was knitting at incredible speed, 'isn't this sickening? I was just going up to London to do V.A.D. in Tube Shelters for a fortnight and now Jean Scatcherd, who is an absolutely rotten V.A.D., has gone instead.'

The Rector said he was glad to find her up and she would be able to do her shelter fortnight later.

'That's all very well,' said the other niece mournfully, 'but Jean came down for a night's leave and she said the sanitary arrangements are getting awfully good and there's hardly any stink at all, at least not where she went. I *did* want to be in time.'

Much as the Rector admired this enthusiasm, he hardly knew what to say, but luckily Mrs Turner came in with a tea-tray, for it was the maid's afternoon out. So they settled down to a very comfortable little meal and gossip, and except for the other niece's rather revolting way of drinking her malt extract out of the bottle and getting a good deal of it on to one of the library books, the Rector enjoyed himself very much. When they had finished, Mrs Turner said she would just run up and get Betty's tray.

'You've done quite enough, Auntie,' said the other niece, heaving herself up with a great dispersal of books, wool and cushions. 'I'll go.'

'They *are* such good girls,' said Mrs Turner, as the door slammed. 'I shall be terribly sorry to lose them.'

'They aren't going abroad, are they?' asked the Rector, with visions of nursing overseas.

'Not yet,' said Mrs Turner, 'but of course one never knows. I hope myself they'll stay with me, at any rate till after the war and the boys can come home when they get leave.'

'Am I to congratulate them on being engaged then?' said the Rector.

'Not exactly,' said Mrs Turner, 'because no one has said anything yet, but of course it is quite obvious what's happening. I am very happy about it, but of course it will be a change.'

As Mrs Turner had vouchsafed him no direct information, the Rector felt a certain delicacy in inquiring, and was about to change the subject to the new jobbing gardener he had been employing while Hibberd was laid up, when the other niece opened the door and stood leaning against the doorway balancing a tray with one hand and one hip, while a cold draught came billowing into the room.

'Shut the door, dear,' said Mrs Turner.

'Can't, Auntie, or I'll drop the tray,' said Mrs Turner's other niece. 'I only just managed to open the door as it is. I say, Mr Villars, Betty says could you be most awfully kind and tell Topsy she'll be down tomorrow and to come and see her any time as it's too ghastly talking on the telephone with Corporal Jackson and everyone listening at the other end and to bring some records with him.'

'Topsy?' said the Rector.

'Well, Captain Topham, then,' said Mrs Turner's other niece. 'And would you be most awfully kind and tell Tommy I don't mind what it is. He'll know what I mean.'

'That's Mr Greaves,' said Mrs Turner.

The Rector said he would certainly give both messages, and

the tray-bearer hooked the door to by means of her foot with a resounding crash.

'I have no control over them at all,' said Mrs Turner proudly, 'but they are very good girls. And I must say,' she added with the voice of one who is being very fair, 'that they have very little control over me.'

'Do I gather, then, that Captain Topham and Mr Greaves—' the Rector began.

'I don't know,' said Mrs Turner, 'but I should say so.'

She heaved a deep sigh.

'Don't worry,' said the Rector sympathetically, 'I am sure both the girls are very sensible.'

'Oh, the *girls* are all right,' said Mrs Turner.

While the Rector was pondering this statement Mrs Turner's other niece suddenly appeared again, and standing as before in the doorway with a glass-cloth in one hand and three teaspoons in the other, said:

'Oh, Auntie, I forgot. Pussy rang up while you were at the shops after lunch, and said could he come to tea to-morrow as he couldn't come Tuesday last week because of us being in bed, so I said yes.'

'All right, dear,' said her aunt, and she shut the door with a crash.

'They will call Mr Downing Pussy,' said Mrs Turner with a pride in her nieces' bad manners that Mr Villars somehow found engaging. 'Mr Villars, do you think it's a good thing to talk over one's troubles?'

The Rector said that was a very large question, but he had found himself that on the whole one did better to keep them to oneself.

'Not that I wish to be unsympathetic,' he said kindly, 'but so often if one gives a confidence one says more than one means to say and repents it afterwards. Of course, I am very lucky because I have Verena to talk to.'

'You are very lucky,' said Mrs Turner with a sigh. 'Verena is the sort of person you could tell anything to, and I expect heaps of people do tell her things and she must be sick of it. Of course, I did have Cecil – that was my husband, you know – and except when he was drunk, which was mostly, and of course he died when we'd been married just a year, almost an anniversary, he was such a helpful person to talk things over with. One does miss it.'

'I didn't know about him,' said the Rector. 'I'm so sorry.'

'Oh, he died ages ago,' said Mrs Turner. 'If he had lived I wouldn't be worrying so much just at present. But we all have our troubles.'

She then fell into a muse, and the Rector, feeling something wrong which she was not going to disclose, and finding himself not much use, thought he had better go. Mrs Turner took him to the door with her usual kindness, but her manner was abstracted and he went away a good deal puzzled. His hostess then returned to the little sitting-room and remained there by the light of the gas-fire for some time, till a sudden noise and a blaze of light brought her out of her dream and she looked up to see her two nieces; Betty in a dressing-gown with a blanket round her, with her other niece in attendance.

'Betty!' she said.

'I know you said not to come down till to-morrow,' said Betty, 'but ackcherly I felt so bored and I'd finished all the libery books, so I thought I'd come down for a bit.'

'You've not been crying again, Auntie?' said the other niece accusingly.

'No,' said Mrs Turner, wiping her eyes. 'Get on the sofa, Betty, you know you oughtn't to be here.'

'I expect you felt a bit dull,' said Betty. 'Let's ring up Topsy. Oh no, bother, he's on duty to-night. I know, let's ring up Pussy.'

At this Mrs Turner showed such signs of distress that her nieces, who were very fond of her, felt something must be the matter and bent their powerful minds to solving the problem.

'I say, Auntie,' said the other niece, 'you're not worrying about Pussy, are you? He's coming to tea tomorrow and we'll leave you alone in the drawing-room, if the coal's come, that is.'

'Don't worry about us, Auntie,' said Betty. 'I mean ackcherly if you want to marry him we'll be frightfully pleased.'

'Of course we shall,' said the other niece. 'I know who won't, though, and that's Miss Pemberton.'

'Well, serve her right,' said Betty carelessly.

Mrs Turner had now stopped crying and told her nieces with affectionate severity that they were very silly girls and didn't know what they were talking about, and Betty must go back to bed at once as she was still an invalid. She and her other niece then made Betty's bed and prepared a light supper, some of which Mrs Turner took up to her on a tray, and no more was said about Mr Downing's visit. But when Mrs Turner was alone in bed she thought a great deal about the different kinds of ways people's hair grew, and must have come to some conclusion that calmed her mind, for about one in the morning she went to sleep and did not wake till eight o'clock.

As soon as the Rector got back he inquired for his wife and on hearing from Foster that she was with some of the gentlemen went up to look for her. She was not with Colonel Passmore, so he went in next door to Captain Topham and Mr Greaves who were making imaginary books on their faint hopes of a Grand National. His wife was not there, but the sight of the two officers reminded him to give them the messages from Mrs Turner's nieces, which appeared to give satisfaction. He then lost interest in wife-hunting and went back to his study to work before dinner.

When influenza had burst out, Mrs Villars had tried to get help, but the prevalent epidemic was late in reaching Northbridge and not a nurse was to be had. Luckily Private Champion in the office had been a male nurse in private life, and though his experience had lain chiefly among violent dipsomaniacs and epileptics, he knew enough of sick-rooms to make himself useful. Ruby Bunce, Miss Pemberton's Effie's sister, came to oblige while Edie was in bed, Father Fewling's landlady produced a niece as temporary second housemaid, and Mrs Villars, who was used to helping Matron in the school sanatorium, took over the lighter duties. Her husband bullied her into lying down half an hour longer every afternoon, and she managed pretty well.

Her patients varied in their attitude towards her sick-room appearances. Edie and the second housemaid were thrown into such wild confusion by her visits, manifesting a strong desire to get up and put on clean aprons to receive her, that she found it kinder, especially as they only had the epidemic lightly, to leave them to the care of Mrs Chapman and Foster, who treated them on the whole kindly, though never ceasing to tell them what a trouble they were and how hard it was on the feet running up and down stairs like that all day long. But as to lie in bed in an attic was Paradise to the second housemaid who had been brought up by an angry and semi-paralysed grandmother, and to Edie who had never known any home but an orphanage, both girls were quite content and got well again very soon.

As soon as Colonel Passmore's temperature began going down he took advantage of his enforced holiday to have great bundles of papers sent down from his office and drove his junior partner, who was medically unfit for the Army, nearly distracted by sending long letters of advice on cases that the junior partner was handling quite well by himself, so that the whole office prayed heartily that the Barsetshires might be sent to the Middle East. When Mrs Villars came to see him he was pleased by the attention and exerted himself to welcome her, but as his attention wandered and every chair in the room was collected by his bed and covered with papers which it would obviously pain him to disturb, she confined herself to a courtesy visit twice a day.

As for Captain Topham and Mr Greaves, who shared a room, she was happier with them than she had been since the last outbreak of measles before she and her husband left Coppin's School. Here, after one day of mild and intermittent rambling during which they had each, according to the other, given away every secret of a black past, joy was unconfined. Each had a portable wireless, and if Captain Topham chose to turn on a Balalaika orchestra while Mr Greaves tuned in to whatever was being given for the benefit of any half-witted members of the Forces, neither was in the least moved by the noise of the other, nor interested in his own. Mr Greaves had a portable gramophone and Captain Topham a quantity of records, cigarettes were unlimited and, as Captain Topham remarked, Ol' Man Influenza had to keep rolling along. The head housemaid when she came in to tidy up after breakfast was usually driven from the room in wild giggles induced by their light badinage, and even Private Champion compared them favourably with his late epileptic patient. Mrs Villars they hailed as the combination of the best kind of mother and matron, combined with an indulgent aunt. They confided to her their hopes and plans 'come the peace'; and as soon as Mr Greaves, who had it very lightly, was able to stagger out of bed, they won four shillings and threepence from her at cut-throat played on a large blotting-pad placed on Captain Topham's legs; they taught her the words of 'Roll Out the Barrel' and other well-known songs; entirely against doctor's orders they made cocktails in a tooth-glass from bottles blandly smuggled in by Corporal Jackson; they discussed with her all her Northbridge friends, being especially loud in their praises of The Hollies. But though Mrs Villars felt a mild curiosity about their feelings towards Mrs Turner's nieces, she could not discover that either gentleman had any particular leaning to either lady, treating them in a very communal spirit. So it was all great fun, and though Mrs Villars sometimes felt rather mangled by the end of the day, she also felt younger than she had done for some time.

Mr Holden did not behave so well. To be fair to him we must state that he had the severest attack and ran a temperature of 102 degrees for two days, but it would be

equally fair to say that he was a bad invalid and did not try
to behave in the least. Luckily Private Champion did not
expect good behaviour, finding it quite a change not to have
the patient throwing the tea-things at his head or rushing at
him with all his teeth outside like a hyena, but even he found
it difficult to deal satisfactorily with Mr Holden's petulance
about shaving, eating, drinking, washing and such matters of
routine, and told Mrs Chapman he would rather have a good
dipso than a patient like Mr Holden, to which Mrs Chapman
said, Pore gentleman, and she would thank Mr Champion to
use the back doormat next time he come in and the scraper
too if he could see it.

While lying on his sick-bed, Mr, Holden had ample
opportunity to reflect upon his feelings for Mrs Villars. Ever
since they first met he had been conscious that she was
different from other women, a quality, if he had stopped to
think, peculiar to every woman that has ever lived. Being a
publisher had not taken the bloom off the romantic side of
his nature, and having recognized a divinity in Mrs Villars,
he fed his passion so successfully upon his imagination that
he thought he was in love with her, though in a way that
could not possibly touch the Rector's honour. Having become
possessed by this idea it pleased his chivalry to look upon
Mrs Villars as a frail flower gallantly holding its own before
icy blasts, bowed but not broken, the icy blasts being her
really very comfortable and peaceful life at the Rectory. It
seemed to him suitable that so exquisite a flower, no longer
in the uninteresting blush of its first youth, should be for ever
languid, and as we have seen he hovered round his hostess
with suggestions that she was tired till he really made her

so. We hesitate to use so pretentious a word as sadism in connection with Mr Holden's highly respectable flame, but the fact remains that the more tired his idol looked the more did his passion grow. If he could have kept her in a state of syncope upon the drawing-room sofa he would have been satisfied. As it was, he had to content himself with a jealous watching of her face and a feeling of exaltation when he saw lines or shadows of fatigue. We do not attempt to explain this. As for any further expression of his devotion, or any particular recognition of it by Mrs Villars, his mind had not descended to such earthy details, and it is probable that his fastidious taste would have been offended by any such thing.

All this in any case would have made Mrs Villars's visits to his sick-bed rather trying for her, but when to his dark devotion were added a great deal of self-pity and a considerable amount of petulance, she found the result really tiring. But she was used to the fine selfishness of the nobler sex in bed, and though thirty-five is far more trying than eight to thirteen, she considered him more or less as a prefect who had suddenly grown beyond his strength and must be humoured.

On this particular day Mrs Villars had been at committees in the morning and also at tea-time, so she went in to see how Mr Holden was when she got back. As a rule she looked into the study first, but she knew that if she began to talk to her husband she would stay there, so she resolutely determined to do her duty first. Not but what she liked Mr Holden very much, but even her patience was wearing a little thin under the strain of his convalescence.

She found Mr Holden up, dressed, and writing in his little bed-sitting-room, surrounded by typescripts.

'Shall I come and pay you a call, or are you busy?' she said, pausing at the door.

Mr Holden rose hastily, and shutting the door behind her said he was not at all busy.

'It's only some novels Adrian Coates sent me to report on,' he said. 'Take this chair. No, not that one,' he added hastily, grabbing two socks, a vest, and a khaki handkerchief and stuffing them into a drawer. 'This one, near the fire. Your feet must be cold.'

Mrs Villars nearly said '*Che gelida manina*,' but not remembering the Italian for feet, she didn't.

'I like to see you sitting there,' said Mr Holden, wishing that the electric fire were a roaring wood fire on which he could throw yule logs till it roared and crackled again in his hostess's honour.

As this statement hardly called for comment, Mrs Villars asked if he had any amusing novels.

'There is one pretty good one,' said Mr Holden, becoming his natural publishing self, 'about a subaltern's wife in India who goes to a rajah's tent – though why a rajah was living in a tent I can't think – at night in pink chiffon pyjamas to get from him compromising letters that the Colonel's wife, who has always been rude to her, has written to him.'

'I suppose,' said Mrs Villars, much interested, 'that her very purity was her protection.'

'Not only that,' said Mr Holden, warming to his subject, 'but the rajah took no interest in married women, preferring droves of virgins, if you will excuse the word, so he had left the letters with his Prime Minister who was a Ptarn.'

'A what?' said Mrs Villars.

'Well, a Paythan, then,' said Mr Holden. 'It's one of those words I never say aloud. Anyway, he did not prefer virgins. But just as his lascivious hand – you will pardon these details in a literary man – was about to rip the thin covering from her rounded breast – that's another word I never say aloud – a shot rang out.'

'I know,' said Mrs Villars. 'It was her husband who thought she and the Prime Minister were in love.'

'My author,' said Mr Holden proudly, 'would say "were lovers". But you are wrong. It was the Colonel's wife who was a Mutiny grandbaby and had always vowed to bring the accursed family of whatever the Prime Minister's name was to ruin, because she thought they were the ones who had murdered her grandparents in the Mutiny. Am I making myself clear?'

'Perfectly,' said Mrs Villars, entranced.

'The shot,' Mr Holden continued with great relish, 'penetrated the P.M.'s heart and he fell without a groan. The Colonel's wife took off her own dressing-gown and wrapped it round the subaltern's wife—'

'Had the subaltern's wife come out without a dressing-gown, then?' asked Mrs Villars, rather shocked.

'Yes, the better to evade the rajah's sentries,' said Mr Holden, 'but we won't go into that bit. Anyway, hand in hand they walked back through the velvety Indian night to the cantonments or wherever it is soldiers live, only to find that the subaltern's wife's husband had been doped by Major Prendergast of the 175th to prevent him playing in a polo match that day. I have just got to the bit where the subaltern's wife is, I think, going to play in her husband's place, making every goal and winning by three chukkas, if that is right.'

'And not till a profusion of golden curls fall about her shoulders as she takes off her cap to the Viceroy who is presenting the cup—' said Mrs Villars eagerly.

'You are quite right,' said Mr Holden. 'No one recognized her except Maboob the sweeper, and he was silent for the honour of the house, and anyway he could say nothing but "Huzoor." I've just looked at the end and I believe the Colonel's wife recognizes in Major Prendergast the man who had Wronged her on a long scented voyage across tropical seas in her youth, and shoots him and then herself.'

'What a *lovely* book,' said Mrs Villars. 'Will you publish it?'

'I'm afraid not,' said Mr Holden. 'It isn't quite our style. But I wish we could. I'm all for a good bit of escapism. I'm sick of those clever novels by women writers all about everyday life. My trade is enough to sicken you of women altogether.'

'But isn't this novel by a woman?' asked Mrs Villars.

'No. A retired naval man,' said Mr Holden. His face then darkened as he added, 'When I said my trade sickened me of women, I said an unpardonable thing. Forgive me.'

'I never thought you meant me,' said Mrs Villars, quite truthfully.

'No, you wouldn't,' said Mr Holden, relapsing into his devoted mood. 'One can say anything to you without fear of misunderstanding, only one almost fears to take advantage of your kindness. You give and give to everyone. You have been giving ever since you came into this room, and now you are exhausted. I don't know what you can think of my selfishness. Men are not easy to live with.'

Again Mrs Villars felt the fatal secession of her upper and lower selves taking place. A voice that was not her own nearly said with quiet unselfish dignity, One does not think of Self, Mr Holden, when a fellow-creature needs one's help, but she caught it in time, put a cork into its mouth, laughed at herself inside, and said she knew one always felt horrid after 'flu, and now she must go and dress for dinner.

'Are you coming down to dinner, Mr Holden?' she asked.

'Yes. I mean, no,' said Mr Holden in a deeply expressive voice; though what he meant to express Mrs Villars did not gather, nor if the truth were to be told, did he quite know himself. So Mrs Villars went off to her room, leaving Mr Holden to go over in his mind his recent conversation with his divinity, making such imaginary improvements as his fancy suggested.

While Mrs Villars was doing her hair, her husband came in.

'A wire has just come over the telephone, Verena,' he said, 'to say that John is getting leave and hopes to be here to-morrow or the next day. It is lucky that our influenza patients are better.'

'How lovely,' said Mrs Villars. 'There's a meet at Pomfret Towers on Friday, and the beagles meet somewhere on Saturday, and there are some quite good films at Barchester, so I expect he will enjoy himself. And I know Mrs Crawley has those two charming young granddaughters of hers staying at the Deanery.'

The Rector looked admiringly at his wife. Not every woman, he proudly thought, would realize that the whole point of leave is to get out of one's home as much as possible. And he knew in his secret heart that it was for the best.

'Hurry up, Gregory,' said Mrs Villars, 'it's ten minutes to eight.'

'And another bit of news,' the Rector shouted a moment later from his dressing-room, 'Holden's captaincy has come through, Passmore tells me.'

'How nice,' his wife called back.

'And Passmore thinks he'll be sent to the fourth battalion at Sparrowhill Camp directly,' the Rector continued.

'I'm sorry he's going,' said Mrs Villars, 'but it will be a good thing to get his room turned out and then we might get the Birketts to stay for a few nights. I could put John in Mr Holden's room and give the boys' room with the two beds to Bill and Amy if they don't mind before term begins.'

So do the waters close over our heads. Captain Holden's journey had not begun, but already his memory was waning.

315

15

Rescue Party

On the following day Mrs Turner, having polished off the Communal Kitchen, was engaged in making marmalade with the help of her other niece, as the maid had gone out till tea-time. A dozen underfed and uninteresting little Seville oranges had been procured just before the influenza by the exercise of much tact (Mrs Turner), waiting for half an hour at the greengrocer's (Betty), and carrying them home in the basket on the front of her bicycle (the other niece). A store of sugar, towards which the girls' preference for sherry to tea combined with a general dislike for puddings had greatly helped, had gradually been accumulated over a period of months and the great winter ritual was now in progress.

'Of course we might as well have eaten the sugar and enjoyed it,' said Mrs Turner, sucking her left thumb which she had slightly wounded while slicing oranges. 'We only get a few pots of marmalade for all this self-sacrifice.'

'Never mind, Auntie,' said her other niece. 'We can always

give people some for a present. We'll use those little jam jars and then it'll look like more.'

Mrs Turner brightened at this philanthropic thought, and asked her other niece to go and get her a bit of sticking-plaster and see how Betty was. Her other niece brought back word that Betty was in the sitting-room on the sofa with a libery book and said she felt all right but a bit funny. Mrs Turner put the plaster on and got the preserving pan down from the top shelf in the larder.

'How long did we give it last time?' she said, but the other niece did not remember, so Mrs Turner opened her cookery-book. A bell rang.

'I expect it's Tommy; I'll go,' said the other niece, but it turned out to be Mr Holden who had come to announce that he was now a Captain and would be leaving Northbridge in a couple of days, and say goodbye.

At the news of his promotion Mrs Turner's kind heart was delighted, while with equal kindness she deplored his approaching departure.

'But I know what,' she said. 'It isn't to-morrow you go, is it?'

Mr Holden, as we shall continue to call him for the few pages that remain of this narrative, said it was the day after to-morrow.

'Well, then,' said Mrs Turner, 'I'll ask some people in to-morrow for sherry, and we'll have a jolly farewell party.'

'And ask a whole crowd of people,' said her other niece eagerly.

'And you must stay on to supper if you don't mind a scratch meal,' said Mrs Turner.

'And we'll make Topsy and Tommy stay and play rummy,' said the other niece.

317

Mr Holden said he would love to come to a sherry party but didn't know if he ought to stay to supper as it was his last night at the Rectory.

'I quite see what you mean,' said Mrs Turner, setting the preserving pan on the gas stove, 'but if you find you aren't wanted, there's always a welcome here. Oh dear, there's the bell again.'

'I daresay it's Tommy this time,' said Mrs Turner's other niece, and in a moment brought Mr Greaves in the kitchen, where that witty young gentleman gave a short demonstration of the goose-step and raised his hand, remarking 'Heil Holden!'

'Thank you,' said Mr Holden amiably.

'Congratulations and all that,' said Mr Greaves, becoming normal again. 'Powell-Jones told me the great news just now. He's as sick as anything at not being our only gallant Captain besides Topham. Marmalade! By jove, Auntie, you'll see me here for breakfast before long.'

'Shut up and don't be an ass, Tommy,' said Mrs Turner's other niece. 'I say, Auntie, suppose you and Mr Holden went to see Betty for a bit.'

'All right, dear,' said Mrs Turner, who was quite accustomed to her niece's simple methods. 'Only mind you don't let the marmalade burn.'

So saying, she led Mr Holden away to the sitting-room.

Mr Greaves, left alone with Mrs Turner's other niece, sat astride on a kitchen chair the wrong way round and looked over its back with great admiration at his companion as she stirred the marmalade.

'I say,' said Mr Greaves, 'they came this morning.'

'Hang on a moment while I wash my hands,' said she.

She laid the wooden spoon across the preserving pan, ran into the scullery and was back in a moment.

'The Rector said you said you didn't mind which,' said Mr Greaves, 'so I brought the lot along. I wrote to the fellow my mater always goes to and told him what was up and to send me along some. Sorry I didn't know the size of your finger, but we can always go up to town and get it altered.'

He pulled a cardboard box out of his tunic pocket and from it extracted a dozen or so sparkling rings which he put in a row on the red check tablecloth. They were all hideously ugly, being half-hoops of various precious stones set quite regardless of expense and even more regardless of taste, but to Mr Greaves they represented exactly what engagement rings should be, and to judge from his companion's long-drawn breath of satisfaction she felt exactly the same. By the greatest good luck a peculiarly hideous and very fat ring set with two diamonds and a sapphire entrenched in outsize claws was exactly the right size for the other niece's finger, and she turned and twisted her hand the better to admire it with infinite pleasure.

'I say, oughtn't I to put it on?' said Mr Greaves. 'Doesn't it bring bad luck or something if the fiancée puts it on herself?'

'Rot,' said the other niece. 'I say, am I really a fiancée? It sounds awfully funny. I hope the ring isn't too expensive. I'll choose another one if it is.'

'Let's have a look,' said Mr Greaves, taking an invoice from its envelope. 'Sixty-five pounds. It's a bit stiff, isn't it, but I dare say the old bank balance can stand it.'

'Well, thanks most awfully,' said the other niece. 'I suppose we'd better tell Auntie and Betty.'

'Bless your soul, my girl, they've seen it coming for weeks,' said the romantic swain. 'And it isn't as if we were getting married to-morrow. My mater'll have sixteen fits, but she always gives in.'

'Well, come the peace, we'll get married,' said Mrs Turner's other niece, giving the marmalade a stir. 'I couldn't very well leave Auntie and Betty to do the Communal Kitchen alone. Besides, one couldn't get any decent clothes now.'

'If you ask me, I should say Auntie and Betty could look after themselves,' said Mr Greaves as he packed the rejected rings away in their box. 'What price Pussy and Topsy?'

'Well, even if Auntie did marry Pussy,' said her other niece dispassionately, 'she'd need me and Betty. We love little Pussy, but he wouldn't be much use, just doing his writing all day long. Mrs Downing would sound awfully funny, wouldn't it?'

This brilliant thought amused the young couple so much that they laughed for nearly two minutes, after which they danced round the kitchen table to the portable gramophone till the maid came back. But to their great credit be it said that the marmalade did not suffer in the least, which shows what very good children they were.

Mrs Turner and Mr Holden found Betty, as the other niece had said, on the sitting-room sofa, with her library book, her tonic and her knitting, but not the Malt Extract because she said it made her sick. She too was delighted to hear of Mr Holden's promotion and on the strength of it prophesied an early end to the war. They talked very comfortably till the front-door bell rang.

'There's the bell, Auntie,' said Betty. 'If it's Topsy you and Mr Holden might go in the drawing-room. The fire's burning splendidly and the coal came just after lunch.'

'That bell always goes as soon as Doris is out,' said Mrs Turner, whose explanation of a common domestic phenomenon will be perfectly plain to all our readers.

'Let me,' said Mr Holden, and left the room, but it was Mr Downing that he brought back with him.

'Oh, hallo, I thought you were Topsy,' said Betty. 'He's coming this afternoon and I thought the bell was him. Do you know Mr Holden's a captain now, and he's going to Sparrowhill, or oughtn't I to have said that?'

Mr Downing expressed his congratulations and asked after the Villarses.

'They are very well,' said Mr Holden. 'At least,' he added, remembering himself, 'Mrs Villars looks very tired, she exhausts herself in thinking of other people.'

Everyone made sympathetic noises.

'I expect it's Mrs Chapman,' said Betty. 'Her niece, Effie Bunce, goes to my Girl Guides, and she says her aunt's a holy terror.'

'We all have difficulties,' said Mr Downing, thinking of his Egeria whom he had left typing her manuscript with a face of stone, and of the odious lunch of boiled fish, scraped carrots and a jam roll from the shop that she had almost thrown at his head. 'Living isn't easy now.'

'Ackcherly it's only partly living,' said Betty.

Mr Downing and Mr Holden looked at her in surprise, for much as they liked Betty it was the first time they had ever heard her formulate anything approaching to an idea.

'It was a play I got taken to before the war,' said Betty reflectively. 'I was going to the ballet with some people and when we got there it was a kind of cinema place and it was a play about Becket or someone getting murdered, so we thought as we'd gone all that way we might as well stay. It was a bit highbrow but ackcherly one girl had an awfully good line about living, or partly living. It sounds stupid, but it somehow got me,' said Betty, flushing very becomingly. 'I did try to read it afterwards because somebody gave it me at Christmas, but it didn't seem to make much sense, I mean if I hadn't seen it acted I wouldn't have understood it a bit, but I daresay that's what plays are for, I mean to be acted.'

Mr Downing said he quite understood and indeed rather sympathized with her feelings, and the front-door bell rang.

'Well, it won't be Topsy this time,' said Betty.

But Mr Holden went to the front door, and it was, so Mrs Turner, who knew better than to waste time over delicacies with her nieces, carried Mr Holden and Mr Downing into the drawing-room.

'I say, Topsy,' said Betty who liked to get to the bottom of things, an excavation that never took her very long, 'would you say Partly Living was a good description of this kind of life, I mean black-outs, rationing and air-raids and everything?'

'Partly living?' said Captain Topham. 'Not on your life, my girl. We're living all out and don't you worry. What's been biting you?'

''Flu, I suppose,' said Betty, her doubts now completely set at rest. 'I say, Pussy's come to tea with Auntie and now Mr Holden's there. Isn't it a shame?'

'Well, talking of getting married and all that,' said Captain Topham, 'you know that old uncle of mine that has the place in Norfolk where I do bird-watching. Well, he conked out last week, so I am the Squire.'

'Do you mean you can do bird-watching there whenever you like?' said Betty, sitting up.

'Well, only if I get leave,' said the practical Captain Topham, 'and anyway I'd rather spend my leave here. But come the peace I thought of doing something about it, and if you felt like giving a hand, I mean marry me and all that sort of thing, we might get the golden-crested mippet to breed in the copse. There's a decent little bit of rough shooting too, and a spot of sailing on Dewitt's Broad. It's really De Witt, after one of those old Dutchmen, but it's a nice bit of water.'

'You mean marry you after the war and live in Norfolk,' said Betty, who, as we know, liked to get everything clear.

'That's about it,' said Captain Topham, suddenly going bright red.

'That's all right, then,' said Betty, curling up on the sofa again. 'Of course we've got to see Auntie through the war, because even if she does marry Pussy he wouldn't be much help and we might have to keep Miss Pemberton off, because she'd be furious and might forbid the banns or poison the wedding cake.'

A short, sympathetic silence ensued.

'I'm awfully sorry,' said Captain Topham at length. 'I haven't done anything about a ring, but I had this little one that my mother used to wear, and it won't even go on my little finger. It's only a signet ring, but if you liked it I'm sure she'd have been awfully pleased.'

Betty held out her left hand and Captain Topham put the ring on the third finger.

'By jove, it's as if it were meant for you,' said Captain Topham. 'We'll get a real one when we go to London.'

'Ackcherly,' said Betty, 'I'd like to keep this. I mean being your mother's and all that.'

'Bless you,' said Captain Topham.

'It's so horrid and grey outside you might as well do the black-out now,' said Betty. 'And then you might read me about the giant condor. I've never seen one ackcherly.'

In the drawing-room all was snug, but not so was the heart of Mrs Turner and Mr Downing. Both had something to say, and it could not be said before Mr Holden, while this gentleman, although as a rule sensitive to the atmosphere, was thinking so hard of himself and his approaching departure that it never struck him how distracted his companions were. To add to the general discomfort, Mr Holden, wishing to make himself agreeable, talked at great length about Mr Downing's new book, a subject in which Mrs Turner, beyond a touching admiration for anyone who was highbrow, found it impossible to take an interest. Mr Downing, unable to resist the lure of talking about his work, hitched up his chair near Mr Holden, and they were immediately deep in Provençal origins, among which Mr Holden, considering that he knew nothing at all about them, acquitted himself remarkably well. Mrs Turner knitted industriously, and as the hands of the clock went round felt more and more despairing: for what she wanted to say had to be said. She would gladly have gone to the kitchen and begun to get tea ready, or written some letters in her little sitting-room, but her nieces had signified quite clearly their wish to be undisturbed, and Mrs Turner was not the woman to disturb them.

Just as she was thinking of beginning to cry the telephone rang, and by one of those coincidences which we can only explain by saying that in no other way could we have got rid of Mr Holden, Captain Powell-Jones announced himself and asked, in terms only slightly modified by knowing that a lady's drawing-room was at the other end of the line, whether it had occurred to Captain Holden that all those buff forms had to be got off before six o'clock, and as those young idiots Greaves and Topham were still nominally on the sick list, what about it?

'I am so sorry,' said Mr Holden, turning to his hostess. 'I'd quite forgotten a job of work. 'Flu madness, I suppose. All right, Jones,' he said down the telephone, 'I'll be along directly. Sorry.'

A volume of rather sarcastic language came rushing through the receiver.

'All right, I'll be along. Dim Sassenach,' said Mr Holden, with the pleasant object of annoying Captain Powell-Jones, and hung up.

His hostess did not press him to stay, but repeated her kind invitation to come to supper on the following night, and so he went away. Mrs Turner said she might as well do the black-out now and then they could be nice and cosy. Mr Downing, to whom it did not occur to help, so atrophied were the social graces in him by Miss Pemberton's determined and ungracious methods of spoon-feeding him, sat and watched her with approval as she shut the shutters and drew blinds and curtains. She made him think of Dickens and Christmas; the expression 'a neat ankle and a trim waist' rose involuntarily to his lips. In his mind's eye he saw her carrying the keys, dispensing plum-pudding, being kissed not unwillingly under the mistletoe, ladling punch from a smoking bowl. But in all the pictures that she suited so well, pictures of jollity, crowds, companionship, much food and drink, he did not see his own spare figure with its scholar's slight stoop. It was all very perplexing.

Mrs Turner, having finished the black-out, came back to the fire and settled herself comfortably.

'Do you mind,' she said, 'if we wait a bit for tea? Doris is out and I don't want to bother Tommy Greaves and my niece in the kitchen. When Doris comes in she will get tea. She can't be long now.'

Mr Downing hastened to answer her that he didn't mind a bit about tea, which was not quite true, for her teas he did dearly like, though his patroness's very nice China tea with a few decorated biscuits was not of a character to promote festivity.

Then there seemed to be nothing to say, so they did not speak. A deep afternoon silence lay on the room, only made more agreeable by the distant, muted sound of the portable gramophone in the kitchen. Mr Downing, looking into the comfortable red depths of the fire, felt his pale heart glowing with some of its heat. For several weeks he had been going his own way, while his benefactress behaved like the Spectre Bride, and the moment was rapidly approaching when he must make some decision. Dearly would he have liked to put off the moment, for like most men of an unassuming and scholarly disposition to have to make up his mind was sheer physical agony. He determined to speak when that piece of log fell, when that red cavern crumbled, when that little hissing gas-jet had burnt itself out; and still he did not speak. Mrs Turner, who would as soon have expected a domestic animal to do the housework as Mr Downing, got up and put another log on the fire.

With mad courage Mr Downing said: 'Mrs Turner.'

Mrs Turner went over to the round table and brought back the old photograph album with which she settled herself in a low chair close to Mr Downing.

'I thought,' she said in a voice always pleasant but less assured than usual, 'you might like to look at some of these snaps. We got interrupted when we were looking at them that day you read us about the Troubadours.'

Mr Downing did not in the least want to look at snaps, a word which in anyone else would have filled him with loathing, but to look at anything with Mrs Turner was pleasant.

'That's me just before I was married,' said Mrs Turner, pausing at a photograph of a very pretty, plump young woman with masses of hair done low, in whom he could just trace his friend's features. 'That's Pagham-on-Sea where we spent our honeymoon.' She turned the page. 'That's Cecil, my husband, you know. It's awfully like him.'

Mr Downing had to look. Undoubtedly a handsome young man, standing on a little rock on the sandy beach, tall, with a friendly smile; a too friendly smile he thought.

'Oh yes,' he said, trying not to hate the late Mr Turner, for ever since Betty's artless words about her uncle's death in a home for drunks, or a loony bin, words that had branded themselves on his mind, his imagination had painted for him very lively pictures of what Mrs Turner's brief married life might have been, pictures which sometimes wrung a groan of torment from him when he was alone; for to think of anyone being unkind to a creature so eminently charming and desirable as Mrs Turner was more than he could comfortably bear.

'He was frightfully good-looking,' said Mrs Turner with wistful pride. 'He wasn't perfect, but none of us are, and I daresay if he hadn't died I'd have learnt to be more patient with him. I was often impatient in those days and didn't make allowance for his temperament, because he was very artistic. I don't know if you have ever loved anyone very much, Mr Downing, but if you have you'll know how one can't forget them. Of course I cheered up to please my mother, and when she died I adopted the girls and they've been such a comfort to me, but I'd give it all to have Cecil back again. I know I could help him and understand him now.'

Mr Downing said nothing, and she turned the page.

'And that's Betty in her pram when she was two,' said Mrs Turner, 'and that—'

But she did not go on, for Mr Downing had bent his head into his hands and was perfectly still. He knew now quite well that Mrs Turner had spoken of her lost love to save him pain; but the remedy was very hard to endure. Mrs Turner laid the photograph album on the floor and looked at him. What she had said she had said deliberately, feeling sure that Mr Downing would understand as few others among her friends could have understood. Though she did not love him, she was very very fond of him and would most willingly have kept him on their pleasant, familiar terms. But this could not be. And now she had told him what she meant to tell and he would not need to offer his devotion and see it refused. Her heart was heavy for him and for her own cruel kindness. He sat quite still, his head bowed upon his hands. So at last she did what she had wished to do in earlier days, and very gently smoothed his grey hair. It felt just as she had known it would feel, like stroking a grey bird's head and shoulders. Then she got up and put the photograph album away.

Still Mr Downing made no sign and really concerned she came back and stood by the mantelpiece watching him, feeling very helpless.

'I think, perhaps,' said Mr Downing, sitting up and speaking with his usual precision, 'that I had better be getting back. I won't wait for tea if you don't mind. I hope you'll let me come again soon and bring Miss Pemberton.'

'Of course,' said Mrs Turner earnestly. 'Come whenever you like and do bring Miss Pemberton. Good-bye for the present, then.'

She held out her hand. Mr Downing took no notice of it, but coming to her side did at last what he had long before wished to do and put one arm round her waist.

'Poppy,' he said.

And the name, which was one he particularly disliked, sounded like an echo of lost happiness to him. To Mrs Turner, although she did not for a moment repent what she had just done, it sounded like the tolling of a bell for a dead friend, but one happily dead and at peace.

Mr Downing went back to his home, and Mrs Turner,

sitting down before the fire, had a very hearty but very comforting cry, in the middle of which Mr Greaves and her other niece came in and turned on all the lights.

'Auntie!' exclaimed her other niece. 'Here, Tommy, go and get Betty, quick.'

Thus summoned, Betty leapt from the sofa and neglecting the giant condor came flying into the room, followed by Captain Topham.

Together the girls did their best to console their aunt, while the gentlemen offered sympathy and were told to get out of the way.

'What is it, Auntie?' said Mrs Turner's other niece. 'And where's Mr Holden?'

'And where's Pussy?' said Betty.

But Mrs Turner was enjoying her cry so much that she couldn't answer, nor could she, without a great deal of spluttering, drink the glass of water that Captain Topham brought.

'Don't be an ass, Topsy,' said his newly affianced love with some asperity. 'Water's no good with people in hysterics. You slap their faces. I say, Auntie, do stop or we'll have to slap your face. What is it?'

Mrs Turner was heard amid sobs to mention the name of Mr Downing.

'Oh, Auntie! Did Pussy ask you to marry him?' said her other niece.

Mrs Turner wiped her eyes and shook her head.

'I know,' said Betty, 'you stopped him before he asked. Poor Auntie. Cheer up and we'll have tea. Doris has got the kettle on.'

'I told him,' said Mrs Turner, still crying, but more distinct,

330

'that I still loved your Uncle Cecil more than anyone, which is quite true, but it was a dreadful thing to have to say.' She began to cry again, but with far less abandon.

By this time the other niece had gone to the kitchen and told Doris to hurry up with the tea, and in a moment returned with a large cup of that grateful and comforting fluid.

'Get her an aspirin, Betty,' said the other niece. 'I left some on the sitting-room mantelpiece this morning, else she'll have a frightful headache.'

The rest of the tea equipage followed and Mrs Turner, ordered to sit by the fire, petted, fussed over and made much of by her nieces, gradually recovered her spirits and made a hearty meal. Just as they were finishing Doris announced Father Fewling, who was warmly welcomed.

'Bring some fresh tea, please, Doris,' said Betty, 'we've got loads, Tubby, so it's all right. Oh Lord!' she added.

'What?' said the other niece.

'I'd forgotten all about it till Tubby reminded me, because of him being a clergyman,' said Betty. 'I say, Auntie, can you stand a shock?'

Mrs Turner said she could if it wasn't anything horrid.

'Ackcherly,' said Betty, 'we got engaged. But we shan't get married till come the peace. Look at my ring, Auntie. It was Topsy's mother's and it's a real signet ring.'

'You'll have to pay a licence for armorial bearings for it, my girl,' said Captain Topham. 'I hope you won't mind, Auntie, but Betty and I thought we might get a golden-crested mippet to breed at my place in Norfolk if we get married.'

'And look at *my* ring, Auntie, it cost a frightful lot,' said the other niece, whose feelings though warm were not of the finer sort. 'And Tommy says his mother'll be furious but she always comes round.'

'I hope it's all right and all that,' said Mr Greaves, a little anxiously.

Mrs Turner could not have had a better antidote than this news and could hardly find enough words to express her delight. Father Fewling congratulated everyone. Doris, coming in to remove the tea-things, was told about the engagements and said she was sure she was very glad and everyone had been saying when was the happy event to occur, upon which both the prospective bridegrooms kissed her and she fled shrieking from the room with the cake-stand. As Captain Topham and Mr Greaves were supposed to be convalescent and in by seven, they joyfully accepted an invitation to stay to supper, at which meal everyone was very happy and Mrs Turner produced champagne.

After supper, while the girls and the officers were helping Doris to wash up in a very friendly, not to say riotous way, Mrs Turner, a little exhausted by so many emotions, sat by the fire with Father Fewling.

The aftermath of champagne was beginning to make itself felt in a mood of gentle though pleasant melancholy and a slight tendency to garrulousness.

'Tubby,' she said earnestly, 'do you believe in people marrying again?'

Father Fewling said it depended.

'Would you think it was silly for a person of my age to get married again?' said Mrs Turner.

Father Fewling said, very kindly, that he wouldn't think anything she did silly without very good cause.

'Well, I could if I wanted to,' said Mrs Turner, looking so pretty that Father Fewling saw no reason to doubt her sentiment, 'and I dare say you guess who it is.'

Father Fewling had indeed a remarkably shrewd guess, or rather a complete certainty, as to who the possibly favoured suitor was, but he merely looked at his hostess in a friendly way.

'So I think I'd better not tell you,' said Mrs Turner, 'except that with all the excitement of the girls getting engaged and everything and you hearing confessions at St Sycorax, which I suppose put it into my head, though I know one couldn't expect you to bring the office into the drawing-room, so to speak, it makes me almost want to tell. But I couldn't think of it, because you see, Tubby,' said Mrs Turner, her sparkling eyes becoming misty again for a moment, 'I really never stop thinking of Cecil. He was my husband, you know, that drank and died in a private nursing home a year after we were married, but I was very, very fond of him. It may sound silly what I'm going to say, because it has only this moment come into my head, and so often the things one thinks of are quite silly, but I have suddenly thought what I am. I am one of those women that can only Love One Man.

'A One-Man Woman,' she repeated. 'Do you think I'm very silly?'

'Heaven keep me from judging you or anyone else,' said Father Fewling, 'but I am quite sure that whatever you have done is right, because you are a very good, unselfish woman, and I don't think you have ever done an ungenerous thing or said an ungenerous word in your life.'

'Tubby!' said Mrs Turner in quite genuine surprise.

And then all the young people came surging in for the officers to say good-bye. Father Fewling left with them, and her nieces insisted on Mrs Turner going to bed with a nice cup of hot milk and another aspirin.

'Well, good night, Auntie,' said Mrs Turner's other niece when she was safely tucked up. 'And thanks most awfully for being so kind about it. Tommy is terribly pleased that you're glad.'

'We'll bring you breakfast,' said Betty, switching off the top-light at the door, so that only the reading-lamp by the bed remained alight. 'Good night, Auntie, and thanks most awfully. You've been marvellous to us always, ackcherly.'

The girls left her room, and Mrs Turner, tired by the emotions of the afternoon, lay comfortably back on her soft pillows. She tried to read a library book, but her attention wandered. She shut her book and put out the light.

'A One-Man Woman,' she said softly to herself; and there was no sadness in her voice, but the pride of the artist who had at last, painfully, achieved the *mot juste*.

As for Mr Downing, he walked down the High Street chewing the cud of sweet and bitter fancy. If we said that relief was his uppermost emotion, we should be doing him an injustice. He was for the moment almost exalted. The remembrance of Mrs Turner's comforting hand on his hair, the remembrance of the comfortable feeling of his arm round her waist, the melody of that revolting yet somehow exquisitely nostalgic name Poppy, murmured and echoed in his heart. From a region remote from his heart the voice of his brain remarked that he had now got everything he had wanted and had better apply his mind to his work. At Punshions, the voice informed him, although the fare was meagre and the temperature low, there was high and reasoned thinking. At Punshions, if he was a penniless scholar, he was an independent gentleman; at The Hollies he would have been lapped in warmth and comfort, but what would he have been himself save that highbrow husband of Mrs Turner's dispensing her drinks to her nieces' friends.

By the time he got to Punshions his exaltation was passing. When he had opened the front door, shut it carefully behind him and hung his coat and hat on their wooden peg, he felt not only depressed but frightened. Suppose Miss Pemberton, weary of his straying, had determined to give him notice. Where would he go? Where would he house his books and belongings? How would he ever manage his ration cards? Or, even more terrible, suppose she were to upbraid him fiercely before taking him back into some modified form of favour; or make him do some further dreadful penance of cold bath water, cold scanty meals and a miserly fire.

If there had been a pond he would have drowned himself, but there were no facilities in the little hall, so with the courage of despair he opened the sitting-room door and walked in. The curtains were drawn, the lamp lighted and a good fire was burning. Before the fire was the tea-table, and at the tea-table was sitting Miss Pemberton, munching hot margarined toast, drinking steaming tea, and reading the *Times Literary Supplement*. Mr Downing saw that there was another cup and saucer on the tray.

'Were you expecting me, Ianthe?' he said, sitting down.

'One never knows,' said Miss Pemberton oracularly. 'The toast is by the fire.'

335

Mr Downing got up, helped himself to a piece, and sat down again.

'Adrian Coates rang up from London just after you had gone out,' said Miss Pemberton.

'About my book?' said Mr Downing anxiously, for like many other authors he fondly imagined that his publisher and printer were the special target of hostile aircraft.

'No. It's all right, though,' said Miss Pemberton. 'He said you'll get an advance copy in a day or two.'

'Was it your book?' said Mr Downing.

'No,' said Miss Pemberton with what, with great respect to her years and plainness, one might call a contemptuous snort. 'When did Adrian Coates ring up on a trunk call about a cookery book? Here's your tea.'

She passed him a large cup full of hot, strong tea, such as he loved, and pushed the sugar-bowl in his direction.

'There's plenty,' she said. 'Coates rang up about the B.D.P. It seems he's found someone who might back it.'

Mr Downing was too much overcome to speak. These initials, so meaningless to our readers, stood for the *Biographical Dictionary of Provence*, that ill-fated work which, as our readers can hardly be expected to remember, had got so far as Falh-Féau when Fate cut thread and thrum. True, the compilers had already amassed material which would cover the ground as far as Félibre, but what with the war and no prospect of publication, the whole thing had tacitly been abandoned.

'An American, of course,' Miss Pemberton continued. 'Walden Concord Porter. He puts up the money and we go on with the B.D.P.'

'But why?' said Mr Downing, which was perhaps a reasonable question.

Miss Pemberton's austere countenance relaxed into what might almost be termed a grin.

'Professor Gawky,' she said.

'But she can't bear me,' said Mr Downing.

Miss Pemberton explained briefly that as far as she could make out from Adrian Coates, Mr Porter had flown over to London at the request of a very highly placed person, to see what a war was like and meet some intellectuals. At a party got together for that end he had met Professor Gawky, to whose personality and also to whose Communist view – for he employed seven thousand workmen – he had taken an immediate dislike, and on hearing from Adrian Coates that there was a far better authority on Provençal literature in the country had immediately written out an enormous cheque to enable the authority to continue his work and broadly speaking put Professor Gawky's nose out of joint. On the following morning he had called with his lawyer at Adrian Coates's office, had the whole thing put into legal form, and drove off to get the plane for Lisbon en route to the United States.

'So there we are,' said Miss Pemberton. 'Or rather, there you are, for you may prefer to go on with the work by yourself, Harold; or elsewhere. I couldn't do it alone, and know it. If you would like me to help, I will.'

Mr Downing felt as if a kaleidoscope had burst inside his head. The dream of his gentle life was within reach, the ideal helper at hand. His heart, a mild creature, had done its utmost and retired. His brain took over the command once more.

'If you don't help me, Ianthe, I can't carry it through,' he said. 'If you will, we may do some good work.'

'You are sure?' said Miss Pemberton. 'It isn't always as comfortable for you here as I could wish. If you need more comfort than we can afford, I expect you could find it. At The Hollies for example. Think.'

Miss Pemberton cut a slice of bread and began to toast it. She had thrown the die and much as she wished to know what number would turn up, she hadn't the courage to look.

'Ianthe,' said Mr Downing, addressing her uncompromising back. 'I came back to tea because I wasn't much wanted at The Hollies. Mrs Turner asked if you and I would go to tea there soon. We will go if you don't mind and then we will really get to work on the B.D.P. as we used. We'll show up the Gawky's false premises and her illiterate arguments! Women indeed!'

His thin face flushed as he gave a gentle bang on the table. Miss Pemberton, who was an excellent sort of fellow, took his remark about Women entirely as it was meant.

'Here's some hot toast, Harold,' she said, poking the toasting-fork towards him. 'And I've got more butter than I need this week. You have it.'

'Thank you, Ianthe,' said Mr Downing, with simple greed scraping out the butter in Miss Pemberton's private crock that stood by her plate.

Miss Pemberton hung the toasting-fork up and went back to her seat. As she passed Mr Downing she laid a hand on his shoulder. Even so had Mrs Turner given him a caress in which there was no love, but Mr Downing did not wish to encircle Miss Pemberton's practically non-existent waist. She then sat

338

gazing at the fire while Mr Downing ate his toast almost richly buttered for once. From time to time he cast a glance towards his patroness. Her strong, ugly face looked more lined than usual and he thought with a pang of remorse that it was his libertinage that had so aged his old friend. Mrs Turner's image faded. He would take Miss Pemberton to tea with her and always be glad to meet her, but as Mrs Turner, not as Armida, a Lorelei, or, as his mind swung round to his favourite subject, a Mélusine.

'I am extremely glad, Ianthe,' he said, 'this Mr Porter has made it possible to go on with the B.D.P. More glad than I can say. And I don't know what I'd do without you.'

Miss Pemberton was a gentlewoman. She did not answer what he had said, but her unprepossessing face showed unexpected tenderness as she remarked:

'The curious thing is that Mr Porter owns most of Porterville, and it was at the Observatory he endowed that Miss Hopgood's aunt used to live. It's a small world.'

'"Onc moult di lor passoun bielhiez,"' said Mr Downing softly; and we conclude that he and Miss Pemberton knew what he meant, for frankly we do not.

'And now,' said Miss Pemberton, suddenly becoming very businesslike, 'I'll clear away and you can get the notes out while I see to the supper. I got two ounces of cheese to-day and I'll make the onion soup you like with a slice of fried bread in it. The stock from that old hen that I steamed is very good indeed. And the coal did come to-day, so the water will be hot for your bath.'

She collected the tea-things on the tray and stumped into the kitchen. Mr Downing got out the notes for the B.D.P. and was soon plunged in work. He had escaped an enchanting shipwreck and his little bark was now in safe convoy. The scholar's hatred for ignorance and conceit burned brightly in him as he began the famous article on Félibrism which was to blast Professor Gawky for ever; and from the kitchen Miss Pemberton eyed him as she moved among her pots, well content.

16

Feeling Tired

Something told Mrs Villars on the following morning that it was not going to be an easy day, and Something, as it too often is, was right. Her husband had to go to Barchester on business and was asked to lunch at the Palace, an invitation which he could not refuse, and was in black despair, for the Bishop's lunches were in the true Barchester tradition and, as Mr Miller, the Vicar of Pomfret Madrigal, had said, were a mortification of the flesh.

Having heard all her husband had to say about his spiritual superior and said good-bye to him, Mrs Villars went as usual to the kitchen, where Mrs Chapman greeted her with such a thundercloud aspect that she would willingly have gone without lunch and tea sooner than face it. But her guests must be fed, so she tried not very successfully to pretend that all was well. To Mrs Chapman's gloomy joy the butcher had sent word that he was not opening that day as he had nothing to sell, the fishmonger's boy had brought a pound of what looked like bits of bad eel, described by him as cod steaks, while Mr Scatcherd when invoked on the telephone had said he had no cheese, biscuits, macaroni, soap-flakes or lard, but they could have some tinned jam if they liked.

'Well, madam,' said Mrs Chapman, 'this war was none of my making and if the Lord means us to starve, starve we will, and I would like to speak to you about Edie.'

Mrs Villars asked with no enthusiasm what was wrong.

'Well, I am sure I wouldn't like to say, madam,' said her cook.

'Well leave it for the present, then,' said Mrs Villars, but this was not at all what Mrs Chapman meant, so without wasting time she launched into a detailed account of Edie's crimes which seemed to Mrs Villars to consist chiefly of emptying her pail down the drain in the yard when Corporal Jackson was about.

'I daresay it's the other way round,' said Mrs Villars, 'and Corporal Jackson comes round when he sees her emptying the pail.'

'Well, of course you know best, madam,' said Mrs Chapman with icy incredulity, 'but talking about putting up the banns the way she did at tea yesterday, "You'll have a lot worse than banns to put up with from me, my girl" I said to her, "if you pass remarks like that. Mr Jackson has been to the Congregational Chapel the last four Sunday evenings," I said, "along with me, and take it from me," I said, just as I was standing here, "if there'd been any talk of banns I'd have heard of it, so now get on with your work."'

'Very sensible of you, Mrs Chapman,' said Mrs Villars, inwardly quaking as she thought of what her husband had told

342

her about the banns of marriage between Arthur Fishguard Jackson of Nutfield and Alice Edith Pover, spinster of this parish, which were to be read for the first time next Sunday, and got away from the kitchen as quickly as she could. As she wanted to go to her bedroom she decided to use the back stairs which went up from the back passage, which was very dark with the skylight blackened, and she nearly fell over a pail.

'Sorry, Edie,' she said, 'I didn't see you in the dark.'

'Please, m'm,' said Edie, wringing out her floorcloth and hanging it on the side of her pail, sitting back on her legs and wiping her hands on her apron, 'could I speak to you for a minute? Mrs Chapman said I wasn't to.'

Mrs Villars felt a faint surge of indignation against her cook and, much to her annoyance, a decided hope that Mrs Chapman would not come upon her unawares if she spoke to her kitchenmaid.

'What is it, Edie?' she said.

'Please, m'm, the Rector will read the banns all right, won't he?' said Edie, raising her vacant face to where her mistress stood on the bottom step. 'Mrs Chapman said they couldn't read banns not only in the Congregational Chapel.'

'Of course he will, Edie,' said Mrs Villars. 'The Rector is *much* more important than the Chapel.' With which comforting and highly questionable statement, she escaped upstairs, only to meet her head housemaid's ill-concealed joy on announcing that the wash had shrunk those curtains from Mr John's room so that they didn't cover the window, and what was she to do about the black-out? Mrs Villars was annoyed, but had the presence of mind to praise the

343

housemaid for telling her instead of putting them up and letting the police come and knock at the door. She then came down again, having forgotten what she came up for, and found her husband in the hall.

'I thought you had gone,' she said.

'So I have,' said her husband, 'technically speaking, but Jackson wanted to see me. He says Mrs Chapman seems to think she has a prior claim on his affections and is, I gather, a little frightened of her.'

'It's poor Edie who ought to be frightened,' said Mrs Villars. 'He doesn't want to break it off, does he?'

'Not now,' said the Rector, with the expression only too familiar to the sixth form at Coppin's when their Livy had been badly prepared. 'He is, I hope, a good deal more frightened of me than he is of Mrs Chapman now. I practically menaced him with bell, book and candle, and I rather gather that he is coming to church on Sunday morning to hear his banns read bringing half the regiment with him.'

'It would be nice for Edie if she could go too,' said Mrs Villars, 'but I really daren't ask Mrs Chapman to let her off on a Sunday morning. Hurry up, darling, or you'll miss the bus.'

'Good-bye, then,' said the Rector. 'Don't do too much, Verena. You look tired, and I will not have it.'

So the Rector hurried off and Mrs Villars did some telephoning, but not so much as she wanted to do because the exchange was aloof and several people were out and had left idiots in charge, or their line was engaged for ten minutes at a time. Exasperated, she gave up any further attempt and was just preparing to set out for Mrs Dunsford's sewing party when Mrs Paxon was announced.

'Well, here you see an early bird,' said Mrs Paxon, 'but I shan't keep you. It is just about those patterns for the evacuees' dressing-gowns. That stuff we used to get is four-and-six a yard now and I can't find anything cheaper. So I said to myself, I'll just run along on my bicycle and see what Mrs Villars thinks. We must have the stuff, because they have all grown out of their dressing-gowns, but the question is, can we run to it?'

Mrs Villars said if they must have it that was that, and if a small extra subscription would help—

'Thanks most awfully,' said Mrs Paxon. 'I feel quite ashamed, but it will be such a help. Then I'll get the stuff and cut it out at once. I suppose we shall go on dressing them for ever, so we may as well get used to the idea. Did you get any meat this morning?'

Mrs Villars said her cook had told her that the butcher was not opening at all.

'You go to Perry's, don't you?' said Mrs Paxon. 'That's quite right, he is shut, because I passed the shop on my bicycle and said to myself, "Hallo, Perry's is shut." But Walton's is even worse. He is open, but all he had in his window was two chickens and a bullock's heart and a brown china pig. Why chickens at a butcher's I don't know, but we have the Fewrer to thank for it. You are looking tired, Mrs Villars. I always say to myself, "Mrs Villars looks lovely," you will forgive me, won't you, but when I really feel a thing I say it, "but she does look tired." One doesn't like to interfere, but I really do think you ought to lie down after lunch.'

'I do,' said Mrs Villars, 'and really I'm not tired a bit. I had a slight domestic crisis this morning, that's all.'

'Then I mustn't keep you,' said Mrs Paxon, irrelevantly. 'I must fly in any case, as I have to see about my refugees' dinner. The twins are on bottles now and it is quite a business. The mother is far too mental to be trusted.'

She mounted her bicycle, leaving Mrs Villars deeply conscious of how little she did compared with Mrs Paxon and wishing that people wouldn't tell her she looked tired.

The rest of the morning brought her but little pleasure. Every member of Mrs Dunsford's working party had a sniffing cold and both her neighbours told her she looked tired and ought to rest. The book which one member was wont to read aloud to the others while they didn't listen was finished and suggestions were asked for a new one.

'We felt sure that you, Mrs Villars, would help us with some good names,' said Mrs Dunsford. 'Barbara and I thought perhaps *Two on a Tower*, by Thomas Hardy. Of course, some of his books are rather strong meat, but this I think is all about astronomy and seemed to me rather topical; I mean it would remind us of Miss Hopgood's aunt and Father Fewling who are such keen students of the stars.'

A lady whose name we do not know said that would be very nice.

'Or,' said Miss Dunsford, 'Mother and I thought perhaps *The Warden*, by Trollope. Quite an appropriate title with so many Air-Raid Wardens about.'

Someone's friend they had brought with them, this description being not ours but one of Mrs Villars's neighbour's, said she had heard that *Lady Chatterley's Lover* was a very nice book in spite of the title, at least in that new edition, a kind of *Empire* edition suitable for general reading.

Luckily half-past twelve struck and the party dispersed.

'Take care of yourself, Mrs Villars,' said Mrs Dunsford, 'we mustn't have our Rector's wife overtiring herself.'

'I always think,' said Miss Dunsford, 'how unselfish you were the day we went up the tower and my mulberry velours blew off. I have just had it reblocked and it looks as good as new. Now, do have a real rest after lunch.'

Mrs Villars said good-bye and escaped, hoping that she had concealed her irritation.

'The next person that tells me I look tired, I'll bite their head off,' she said aloud angrily as she turned into the Rectory lane, but these thoughts were diverted by the amount of noise coming from the kitchen quarters. Her curiosity made her go by the back way to the yard, where the French Revolution appeared to be in progress. Her whole staff, Corporal Jackson, several tradesmen's boys and an unknown young man in khaki were talking and laughing so loudly that they did not notice Mrs Villars till she was quite near.

'I just thought I'd come round this way,' said Mrs Villars to Mrs Chapman, conscious that she was in a very weak position. 'Has anything happened?'

'It's my Bert, madam, back on leave,' said Mrs Chapman, dragging forward the young man in khaki who was certainly his mother's son if no one else's. 'I was just saying to Mr Jackson, if Madam didn't mind, Bert could sleep in that other little room over the stables. I wouldn't have him in the house, not with them girls about,' said Mrs Chapman shuddering.

As everything seemed to be arranged, Mrs Villars said she thought it would be quite all right, weakly adding that of

347

course the Rector must be asked, which took no one in for a moment.

'And what do you think, madam,' said Mrs Chapman proudly, 'my Bert – here, Bert, you've not said How do you do to Madam.'

Bert put his cigarette behind his ear, extended a large unattractive hand and said: 'Pleased Tmeetcher.'

'I hope you will have a nice leave,' said Mrs Villars accepting his proffered handshake.

'Not *'ere*' said Bert, putting his cigarette back in his mouth. 'No life, Mrs Villars. Give me good old London every time. Nice place you 'ave 'ere, though.'

'That's enough, Bert,' said his loving mother. 'I was just saying, madam, who do you think I heard from today but Mr Chapman, my husband in all but name that is. Him and Bert came across each other quite accidental, being mess waiters in the same regiment, and Bert passed the remark to his dad it was time bygones was bygones, so he dropped me a line.'

'How nice,' said Mrs Villars, really not seeing what else she could say and heartily wishing that her cook would not brandish her past before so large an audience.

'But I shan't answer it,' said Mrs Chapman. 'Like his cheek. I'll just write a line to say what I think of him, which I could have done before if I'd a had his address. I'm a married woman in my own right, as you might say, and no need of Chapman coming after my money.'

'Quite right,' said her paralysed mistress.

'They say,' remarked Corporal Jackson who had been an interested spectator of the scene, 'that one wedding makes another and Edie and me will be the next. High time she got married with that young Bert of yours about, Mrs Chapman. The banns are to be read by the Rector next Sunday, eleven ack emma. I thought madam, you would like to know,' he added to Mrs Villars.

That lady was terrified out of her wits, expecting a general explosion, when to her great relief Mrs Chapman, evidently taking Corporal Jackson's innuendo as a tribute to her personal charm, gave a coquettish laugh and said one couldn't be young but the once and her young days were over.

'Tell you what, though, Edie,' she said to the fascinated kitchenmaid, 'you'd better go along to church on Sunday and hear your banns. They say it's unlucky but I don't hold with that, and anyway I don't hold with church weddings, being a member of the Congregational, but I'll come to yours, see. Now get on with that scrubbing and I'll see about letting you off on Sunday, that is if madam doesn't object.'

Mrs Villars said it would be very nice, and escaped, leaving the little crowd to discuss the news.

'I don't like that Bert, Mr Jackson,' said Edie to her betrothed. 'He looks at me.'

'He won't look at you twice, my girl,' said the gallant Corporal. 'Come on now and I'll give you a hand with that pail. Thanks for the good wishes, Ma.'

Before Mrs Chapman knew what had happened he had planted a resounding kiss on her large face.

'Go along now, all of you,' said Mrs Chapman, not displeased. 'You, Bert, come and give me a hand with the officers' dinner. That's one thing they'll have learned you in the army, though I don't know how they did it, all thumbs you are. And don't bring that cigarette in my kitchen.'

Bert unwillingly took his cigarette out of his mouth, laid it on a window-sill for future reference, and followed his mother into the kitchen. Corporal Jackson picked up Edie's pail and carried it into the back passage and the audience dispersed in great content.

And that, Mrs Villars thought, during a rather dull lunch with Colonel Passmore and Captain Powell-Jones, means a new kitchenmaid unless Edie will stay on. I must ask Jackson.

'Colonel Passmore,' she said aloud, 'do you think it will be all right for my kitchenmaid to marry Corporal Jackson?'

'Jackson?' said the Colonel. 'Good, steady man. Yes, quite all right, I should think. I don't know that he's married. He hasn't got a wife drawing an allowance, but you never know in the army. No,' he added, seeing his hostess look anxious, 'I was only joking. He's a fine chap and I wish them luck.'

'Do you think she'll stay on with me? It is so difficult to get kitchenmaids now,' said Mrs Villars.

Colonel Passmore said he would speak to Jackson about it, which comforted Mrs Villars very much, and if she would swear secrecy he thought he knew of some bacon and some cheese.

'The Three Wants of Britain,' said Captain Powell-Jones:

'A *dearth of hog's flesh in the stye,*
A *dearth of neats' cheeses in the press,*
A *dearth of scullions in the castle.'*

'And I'll tell you one, old man,' said Captain Topham, who had come in while his brother officer was speaking. 'Taffy was a Welshman, Taffy was a thief, Taffy came to my house and stole a piece of cheese. So sorry to interrupt, Mrs Villars, but Powell-Jones is wanted on the telephone. I've only just got in and took the message.'

Captain Powell-Jones left the room with a manner that boded ill to whoever it was that had rung him up.

'I suppose I oughtn't to have said that,' said Captain Topham repentantly, 'but he does ask for it. It's getting engaged, I expect. Goes to a fellow's head. Did you know, Mrs Villars, I'm engaged to Betty; I'm a frightfully lucky chap. We shan't get married till come the peace, but if the peace begins to grow whiskers we'll think again.'

Mrs Villars said indeed she didn't know and was perfectly delighted.

'I thought Auntie might have rung you up,' said Captain Topham, 'it's the sort of thing women do. Well, anyway, we are. And Tommy got engaged to the other girl, so it's a double event.'

'Entered for the Nursery Stakes, eh, Topham?' said Colonel Passmore, alluding to Captain Topham's sporting tastes, and then apologized to Mrs Villars, but so relieved was she about Edie that she thought it an excellent joke and would have discussed the delightful news at greater length had not Foster come in with the firm determination to clear away immediately.

Once more, and how very bored she was by the whole thing, Mrs Villars lay down on the drawing-room sofa with a hot bottle to have her rest. She dallied with *The Times* crossword, saw with annoyance that 'Astraea' had been used with different clues on two successive days, and gently slid into a light sleep. After an interval, the Something that had prophesied a trying day made her conscious that she was not alone, and opening her eyes she saw Mr Holden standing rather threateningly above her. She blinked, being a little unsure as to who or where she was.

'And now I have woken you,' said Mr Holden in a bass voice.

She then remembered all about herself, felt slightly annoyed with Mr Holden and hoped she didn't look very untidy.

'Do sit down,' she said. 'Will you stay to tea?'

Mr Holden said he had come to say good-bye.

'But I thought you weren't going till to-morrow,' said Mrs Villars. 'Did you get a wire?'

This matter-of-fact reception of his news made Mr Holden feel slighted, which he enjoyed.

'Officially I go to-morrow,' he said, 'but I wanted to see you alone, to thank you so much for all you have been to me,' and then wondered if he had gone too far.

'We loved having you,' said Mrs Villars truthfully, 'and I hope you'll come in before dinner and have a drink with Gregory. He's frightfully sorry you are going.'

This was not at all the turn Mr Holden wanted. Mr Villars was a charming person, but he had not come to Mrs Villars's drawing-room to talk about her husband. He tried again.

'I should have loved to,' he said, 'but I am going to Mrs Turner's. She is very kindly having a kind of farewell cocktail party for me. She was kind enough to ask me to stay to supper, but I didn't accept.'

He then wished he had not said one kindly and two kinds in two sentences.

'But do stay on to supper,' said Mrs Villars. 'It is so depressing to have to leave a sherry party just when it is getting amusing.'

'If you want me to, of course,' said Mr Holden, feeling that things were now going more as he wished.

'It's not exactly that,' said Mrs Villars, thinking in a way very unflattering to Mr Holden of assistant masters who used to take offence. 'I only meant it is such a bore to leave a party just when it is beginning to go; I mean beginning to be amusing, not going. Anyway, leave it. We shall be glad to see you if you come back, and if not we shall know you are enjoying yourself.'

'And *you* say that,' said Mr Holden.

Mrs Villars wished with all Mrs Gamp's fervour that Mr Holden was in Jonadge's belly. Quite fatally she recognized the well-known signs of a one-sided scene. With assistant masters she could always come the Headmaster's wife over them, a part it amused her to play, but over Mr Holden she had no such authority. Also to be lying on a sofa put one at a disadvantage. Mr Holden would tower over her so that she had to tilt her face uncomfortably. If she got up (a heroine, she admitted, would have risen), she would display her stockinged feet (for she had thrust her slippers under the sofa) and a very shabby hot bottle, while the couch her form had so lately pressed would look like an unmade bed.

'Why do you try to baffle me?' said Mr Holden. 'I only want to tell you how precious you are to me, one word before I go, and you laugh.'

Mrs Villars assured him that she had not laughed.

'Well, you mock,' said Mr Holden, now getting finely into his stride. 'Your mockery is adorable, but why not be yourself for a moment?'

Mrs Villars, disliking Mr Holden more every moment, as far as she could dislike a person whose company she had always found very pleasant, said as far as she knew she was herself and was so sorry they were losing him.

'And you lie there on the sofa and say that,' said Mr Holden, who really had not the faintest idea what he meant. 'We must have this out. Can't you for one moment speak the truth to me?'

Mrs Villars would have liked to say 'Yes, I can, and you are being a frightful bore and do go away, thank you very much,' but the Something told her that would not give satisfaction to her guest who was, she saw, by now in a state in which he would prefer to misunderstand anything that was said to him. In despair she shut her eyes.

'Don't shut your eyes,' said Mr Holden.

Mrs Villars opened her eyes again and made a movement to get up, but remembering the hot bottle and the slippers, cancelled it.

'And now,' said Mr Holden, 'I have made you tired.'

He then groaned.

'You haven't,' said Mrs Villars in a voice of controlled exasperation. 'Tea is just coming. You'll have some before you go, won't you?'

'You cannot hide your fatigue from me,' said Mr Holden. 'I know every shadow on your face. I have been a brute. Forgive me.'

Upon which to Mrs Villars's intense annoyance he knelt down, took her hand, kissed it and then pressed it to his burning forehead.

'That's all right,' said Mrs Villars, not sure if she would do better to withdraw her hand or leave Mr Holden to get tired of holding it. 'And now I really think I hear tea.'

'Your charity! Your long-suffering!' said Mr Holden, standing up, which was better, but still holding her hand in both of his and kneading it ferociously. 'No, I won't have tea.'

'And what about supper?' said Mrs Villars, in as ordinary a voice as she could assume and trying to pretend that she did not notice what Mr Holden was doing.

At this moment by great good luck the clanking of the tea-things was heard outside. Mr Holden released her hand and moved moodily to the hearth-rug, whence he said in a noble way:

'I think I had better stay supper at Mrs Turner's. You will understand.'

'Of course,' said Mrs Villars. 'Tea on the little table beside me, please, Foster. We shall both miss you so much, Mr Holden, and be sure to look us up when you are over this way. Gregory and I will see you to-morrow to say good-bye, of course.'

'Good-bye, Verena,' said Mr Holden, very meanly taking advantage of Foster having gone away to get the rest of the tea to use his hostess's christian name. 'I shall always be infinitely grateful – infinitely.'

'Oh, it was nothing. Gregory always loves having Old Boys or their relations,' said Mrs Villars. 'Give my love to Poppy and congratulations to the girls.'

Safely barricaded behind a table covered with tea-things, she sat up, slipped her feet into her shoes, and asked Foster who had just come back to take the hot bottle and the shawl away.

'Well, good-bye,' said Mr Holden.

A noise which had been drawing attention to itself in the hall for some time now became much louder and burst into the room. It consisted of Wing-Commander John Villars, covered with equipment till he was double his own size, and very red and healthy about the face.

'John, darling!' said his mother.

'Hallo, Mamma,' said John, unstrapping several articles of war and dropping them with a bang on the drawing-room floor. 'I did a record in hitch-hiking: did the whole thing in seven and half hours.'

'This is Captain Holden, darling,' said his mother, 'who has been billeted here. He is in the Barsetshires and going to-morrow, I'm sorry to say. His uncle was one of Daddy's staff.'

'Hallo,' said John, wrenching the guest's hand heartily. 'I remember old Holden. Merrylegs, we used to call him, I can't think why. He used to keep toffee in his desk and a boy called Finlay, you remember Finlay, Mamma, that had a squint, pinched some and got into a frightful row. Everything O.K. in the Barsetshires?'

Mr Holden thanked him and said it was and now he must be going.

'See you again,' said the Wing-Commander, undoing more of his equipment, by which means he looked less like the White Knight, and scattering it over the room.

'Good-bye,' said Mr Holden yet again. 'I know I have tired you.'

'Not a bit,' said his hostess and shook hands over the tea-things. With a glance of agony he left the room, and we will say at once that he enjoyed himself very much at Mrs Turner's party and didn't get back till after eleven.

'It *is* nice to see you, darling,' said Mrs Villars to her younger son. 'Have you had tea? And how long are you staying?'

'I've not had tea, Mamma, unless you count five pints on the way down,' said the Wing-Commander, 'and I'd love some. Not those little cups, though. Where's Foster?'

He opened the door.

'Foster!' he yelled, 'be an angel and bring me that big cup with roses on it, if you haven't broken it. About a week, but I daresay I'll go to town for two or three days. I want to see some chaps there and do a theatre and dance and see the damage. Or I might run down to Devonshire. Fairfax-Raven, the one I wrote to you about that hurt his foot parachuting, has a place down there, at least his people have, and he's awfully keen for me to go down and hunt. What's on at the Barchester Odeon?'

'I don't know, darling,' said his mother.

'I'll ring up and find out,' said John, taking the receiver off. 'Hullo, is that you, Norma? John Villars here. What's on at the Odeon? You don't know? Lord, Lord, what is the Telephone Exchange coming to? Oh, good, Foster, that's the cup I want. I say, what's on at the Odeon?'

'*Lion Cubs In the Air*, Mr John,' said Foster. 'It's ever so nice, all about our young flying heroes.'

'Oh, not that rot,' said John. 'I mean anything decent.'

357

'Well, there's *Virgin Flesh*, all about the love life of Florence Nightingale, with Glamora Tudor,' said Foster. 'It's lovely.'

'That's better,' said John. 'Hullo, Norma, don't go away. Look, I'm frightfully busy. Book me four seats at the Odeon for the last house, there's a good girl. And keep this line clear. I'll want it.' He put the receiver back, filled his cigarette case from the box on the mantelpiece and lit one for himself.

'Who is Norma?' said his mother, pouring out tea.

'Old Trowell's girl. One box of chocolates on each leave and she'll do anything I want. Oh, I brought you some rations.'

He pulled several packets, greasy or bursting out of their skins, from his pockets, and put them in the slop basin.

'Lord! It's nice to be back,' he said, emptying his cup at a draught and putting it down with a crash on the saucer which fell in half. 'Oh Lord! I've done it now. Never mind. How's Daddy?'

Before his mother could answer the telephone rang.

'Hullo,' said the Wing-Commander, 'who is it? Oh, you. Well, what about the Odeon to-night? There's a good girl. And bring two more along. I say, what time is the last house? Oh Lord! Well, I'll meet you there at six and we'll find a spot of food afterwards. I say, Mamma, could you lend me some money?'

Mrs Villars looked at her younger son with adoring disapproval.

'I'll give you the two pounds I was going to give you when you go back now,' she said. 'But you can't have it again when you go. Get me my bag. It's on the writing-table.'

The Wing-Commander tilted his chair backwards till with

his long arm he could reach the bag. One of the chair's back legs creaked and something snapped.

'Oh Lord! Now the chair's gone,' said John. 'Oh thanks awfully, Mamma. I say, Mamma, I've got some washing. Can someone wash it, because if I go to Devonshire I'll need it. It's here.'

He got up, and diving into a haversack as if it were a branpie, pulled out a loathsome assortment of underwear, handkerchiefs and socks, which he strewed on the floor.

'Sorry it's rather a lot,' he said, 'but I thought it would be cheaper to get them done at home. I say, Foster,' he said as the parlourmaid came in, 'can you wash all that, or someone? I want them pretty quickly.'

Foster said she would see, collected the washing, removed the tea-things and left the room.

The Wing-Commander stretched himself till he nearly touched the ceiling, and yawned.

'Don't anyone sit up for me,' he said. 'Can I have a key, Mamma?'

'What happened to the one you forgot to give me back after your last leave?' said his mother severely, as she took the latch-key out of her bag.

'I haven't the faintest idea,' said John. 'Thanks awfully, Mamma. What's wrong with the boyfriend?'

'If you mean Captain Holden, as I know you do, you are extremely vulgar,' said Mrs Villars. 'He thought I was the ideal woman, but I'm not.'

'Good for him,' said the Wing-Commander. 'I'll buy him a drink. Lord! It's five and I said I'd be at the Odeon at six. Is the bath water hot?'

Mrs Villars said it always was and not to take it all.

'You don't mind if I leave some of my things here, do you?' said John. 'I'll collect them when I come in tonight. Or I'll tell Foster to take them away. Oh Lord! That telephone again. Hullo! No, Norma, I'm not speaking to anyone to-night. I'm going out. Well, I can't help it. Tell her to ring me up to-morrow and not too early. Those girls,' he added as he hung up, '*will* ring one up.'

He lighted a cigarette and remained quiet for one moment before he took off on his next flight.

His mother surveyed him with her abstracted smile. Here was complete happiness. Her sitting-room littered with kit, a saucer cracked, a chair leg probably broken. Her extremely good-looking younger son would undoubtedly use the whole hot-water supply for his bath. He had already got two pounds and a latch-key simply by asking. He would evidently spend very little of his leave at home and what time he did give to the Rectory would be devoted to sleep and food at any hours convenient to himself and to endless telephoning. All this she felt with loving dislike to be quite perfect. But she had forgotten one thing. Her younger son, exhausted by his one minute's silence, threw his cigarette into the fire.

'Where's the wireless?' he said.

His mother said it was in the officers' room, but he could have her little portable from her bedroom.

'Thanks awfully, Mamma,' he said. 'I'll want it in my bath. Well, I must be getting along. Daddy not in? I'll see him when I came back.'

He went towards the door. When he was behind the sofa he turned and put a kiss on the top of his mother's head.

'For you, Mamma,' he said, and banging the door ran upstairs like an earthquake.

Mrs Villars surveyed her world with great satisfaction. As she began to clear up some of the mess she reflected that the rest of John's leave, or so much as he saw fit to bestow on his parents, would consist largely of clearing up after him, and she further reflected that, thank goodness, here was someone who would never notice if she was tired.

virago

To buy any of our books and to find out more
about Virago Press and Virago Modern Classics,
our authors and titles, as well as events and
book club forum, visit our websites

www.virago.co.uk
www.littlebrown.co.uk

and follow us on Twitter

@ViragoBooks

To order any Virago titles p & p free in the UK,
please contact our mail order supplier on:

+ 44 (0)1832 737525

Customers not based in the UK should contact
the same number for appropriate postage
and packing costs.